"Imaginative, dynamic, and highly entertaining."
—Clive Barker

"Nancy A. Collins has cast an undeniable shadow across the tradition of dark and fantastic fiction."
—William P. Simmons, *Cemetery Dance*

"Nancy A. Collins turned the vampire genre upside down and inside out ..."
—J.L. Comeau, *Creature Feature*

"Deftly weaves the literary and the metaphorical..."
—*Mystery Scene*

By the Same Author:

THE SONJA BLUE SERIES
Sunglasses After Dark
In the Blood
Paint It Black (new edition forthcoming)
A Dozen Black Roses
Darkest Heart
Dead Roses for a Blue Lady

OTHER TITLES
Angels on Fire

For all these titles and more, visit **www.twowolfpress.com**

DEAD MAN'S HAND

FIVE TALES OF THE WEIRD WEST

Two Wolf Press

A Division of White Wolf Publishing, Inc.

Atlanta, Georgia

ISBN: 1-56504-875-5
First Edition: October 2004
Printed in Canada

Two Wolf Press
1554 Litton Drive
Stone Mountain, GA 30083
www.white-wolf.com/fiction

FOREWORD

by Joe R. Lansdale
(his ownself)

Nancy Collins is a real writer, and that is the best thing to know. Anyone who knows the alphabet believes they are a writer... but Pilgrim, it ain't so.

Nancy, who I still think of as a young and new writer, has now been a published writer for some years. I can say with sincerity that she has learned her craft well.

She is established, but she's just as adventurous as when she was starting out. These stories will give you a taste of earlier work, and some of the more recent. The tales differ somewhat in tone, but all have a deep echo. Her more recent work has a more casual, richer texture to the prose, but that does not take away from the earlier tales, among which are some of my favorites.

Nancy is best known for Sonja Blue, her vampire "heroine," but her range exceeds this. Here are a variety of stories to prove it. They are, to my way of thinking, the best of her work.

Sonja Blue is neat, but she's just the tip of the iceberg. Though Nancy is best known as a writer of vampire stories, an author who created a hip modern interpretation of the vampire, she has written far more than that. Had she not, Sonja Blue alone might have been enough to cement her as an important writer in the field of horror.

Joe R. Lansdale

6

In fact, her influence is far greater than most are aware of. I see comics and films, books and stories, that show her influence all the time. Sometimes directly, sometimes subtly.

She has gradually been assimilated into pop culture.

Her best work is her short work, and it's the writing style—the attitude—that actually reveals the nature of her roots and interests: the rural South (her roots) and the West (her interests).

Nancy focuses on the dark aspects of these areas, and there are many. Darkness presents itself elsewhere as well. But when she writes these stories, I can't help but be involved, because she loves and knows of what she speaks. Yes, Virginia, you can love the darkness as a spectator sport, even if you are not a participant.

Of the newer works, "Hell Come Sundown" is a particular favorite of mine, but I must admit a strong partiality to the sweat and leather tale "The Tortuga Hill Gang's Last Ride." But there's also "Walking Wolf" and "Calaverada." They ain't plucked chickens, friends. All good. All memorable. All showing the aforementioned roots and interests.

Saddle up partners. Nancy is about to be your tour guide on some great, and often dark, adventures. You'll really enjoy them. I have no doubt.

When I read Nancy, I feel as if I'm reading a combination of Southern writers and Robert E. Howard, a touch here and there from a gaggle of Western writers. There's some of that old pulp meat in these tales; the best of the pulps; that part that pulls you along and throws you down and holds you tight, and says: "Listen. I have a tale to tale, and you must hear it."

Combine these sensibilities, and you have Nancy at her best, pulling it all together, creating her own story telling web, her own style, her personal accent.

I dislike selling stories. I admit it.

I like to sell the author.

I only sell products I believe in.

I believe in Nancy's work.

So don't take my word for it.

Open the book.

Have a taste.

The first taste costs you nothing more than the price of a book. Unless you borrowed it (don't steal) from the library, authors need their pennies to buy their shoes, so go out and buy a copy.

It will be money well spent.

And it will cause you to spend more of your hard-earned coins on this fine teller of tales in the future. Though she has been around a while, I believe her career is just beginning. Heating up.

Ladies and Gentlemen, and everyone in between those simple labels.

I present to you a great writer.

Nancy Collins.

Hell Come Sundown

Hiram McKinney glanced up from his Bible as the cherry-wood mantle clock chimed eight o'clock. The timepiece, with its hinged convex glass lens and elegantly embossed Arabic numerals, was one of the few luxuries that had survived the trip from Tennessee to Texas.

"It's time you got off to bed, young man," Hiram told his son, who was toiling over his *McGuffey's Reader* workbook.

"Please, Pa, can't I stay up a lit'l while longer?"

"You heard yore daddy, Jacob," Miriam McKinney countered, without looking up from the sock she was darning.

"Yes ma'am," Jake replied glumly, setting aside his schoolwork as he scooted his chair away from the table.

The seven-year-old walked over to where his parents sat before the fieldstone fireplace to bid them good night. His mother put aside her sewing and leaned forward, pecking her son the cheek.

"Night, Jake."

"Night, Maw. Night, Pa," the boy said, turning to his father.

Mr. McKinney glanced up from his reading. He gave his son a fond smile and a nod. While Jake would never be too old for his Maw to kiss, Hiram had recently decided that the boy was beyond such mollycoddling.

As Jake headed for his room, Mrs. McKinney called out after him one last time: "Pleasant dreams, sweetheart."

Neither saw the boy flinch.

The McKinneys came to Texas fifteen years before, setting down stakes on prime ranching land along the Nueces River, near Laredo. For the first five years they lived out of a one-room cabin. Then, as time moved on and they gradually became more prosperous, Hiram added a second room, so that he and Miriam no longer had to sleep where they ate. Three years later, Jake was born.

Jacob was not the McKinney's first child, but he was the only one to survive the cradle, his older brother and sister having succumbed to disease before they got their first tooth. For the first three years of his life he slept in the family bed. Then he was moved to a pallet in the corner. When Jake reached the age of five, it was decided that he was old enough to move to the lofted area above the communal room. For the next two years, Jake drifted off to sleep listening to his parents discuss their day's activities or plan what needed to be done to keep the homestead running smooth.

As the McKinney family's fortunes continued to rise, Hiram decided they could afford constructing a room for their son, placing it opposite their own, so that the layout of the house resembled a capital T.

Most boys Jake's age would have been thrilled to have their very own room. And, at first, Jake was very excited by the prospect. But all that changed after his first week of sleeping alone. The very first night, his screams woke up the house. His father charged into the room in his long johns, shotgun in hand, convinced that Comanches were dragging his son out the window. Once Hiram realized that was not the case, he cussed to beat the band.

When Jake told his parents about the thing that came out from under his bed, they listened for a moment then exchanged looks. Pa was more than a little put out by the whole thing, but when he saw how frightened Jake was, he made a show of getting down on his hands and knees to prove there wasn't a boogey man hiding under the bed.

Maw McKinney said it was only natural for a young boy to be frightened the first time he had to sleep on his own. All his life, Jake had slept within earshot of his family. Sleeping by himself in a separate part of the house would take some getting used to. His father had grudgingly agreed to that point—after all, he himself hadn't slept in a separate room until after he was married, and even then he'd never truly slept alone.

However, as Jake's night terrors continued, his father's tolerance rapidly eroded. Pa was of the opinion that Maw was mollycoddling the boy, where Maw felt that Pa was in too big a hurry to make a man out of a child.

This was not a new argument between the McKinneys, but it grew with each passing birthday. Since Jake loved his parents with all his heart, knowing he was the reason for them not getting along tore him up something fierce.

Jake wanted to be a man and make his daddy proud, really he did. But there was something going on that neither of his parents truly understood. The reason for his night terrors wasn't bad dreams or fear of being alone. The simple fact of the matter was that his bedroom was haunted. Jake wasn't real certain how that could be, as no one ever lived in it before. He had always been of the impression that it took someone dying in a place to make it haunted, but apparently that wasn't a hard-and-fast rule.

However, he had learned that whatever it was that lived under his bed did follow a pattern of behavior. Whatever it was didn't come out every night—just those that coincided with the dark of the moon. He also knew that the thing was scared away by screaming and light, even if it was the weakest candle flame. Just a hint of lamplight appearing under the crack of the door as his mother came to check on him was enough to cause the apparition to fold in upon itself like a lady's lace fan.

At first he thought that the thing that haunted the room could only harm him if he looked at it, so he slept curled up in a tight little ball, the covers pulled up over his head. At first this seemed to stymie the thing from under the bed, but it eventually figured out that it could force him to throw back the blankets by sitting atop his huddled form until its weight threatened to suffocate him. As terrible as the creature was to look upon, the very knowledge that the thing was sprawled across his bed was even more horrifying.

After the first couple of weeks, his father forbade his mother from checking on him whenever he cried out during the night. When it became clear his mother would no longer be coming to his aid, Jake realized that it was up to him, and him alone, to solve his problem.

He at first attempted to battle the monster by keeping the lamp burning beside his bed all night long. This worked at first—until his father began complaining about the amount of oil that was being wasted. The general store was in Cochina Lake, over ten miles away, and the McKinneys only went there once every six weeks. Because of the increase in consumption, they were close to being out of fuel, and with two weeks to go before the next trip.

Jake's nights were seldom restful, and his dreams rarely pleasant. Even on those nights he was not haunted by the thing from under the bed, he slept fitfully, waking every time a timber groaned or a branch scraped the side of the house. Still, as bad as things were, he could not bring himself to tell his parents the truth of his situation. For one, he knew they would not believe him, and another, he did not wish his father to see him as a frightened little boy. If being born and raised in Texas had taught him anything, it was self-reliance. This was his problem, by damn, and it was up to him to solve it, come what may.

⟹◆⟸

The light cast by Jake's lamp chased the shadows back into their respective corners as he entered the darkened room. The curtains his mother had fashioned from old flour sacks were pulled tightly shut against the moonless night. Aside from the bed, the only other furnishings in the room were a nightstand, a footstool and a double chifforobe, since the room had no closets. The walls were made from planks his Pa had cut at the local sawmill, and the chinks between the boards were caulked with river clay to keep the wind out. That the solitary window in the room boasted panes of glass instead of waxed cloth was a testament to the McKinney family's newfound prosperity in this unlikely promised land.

Jake carefully placed the lamp on the nightstand and began to undress, neatly folding his clothes over the foot of the bed as he did so. He removed his nightshirt from its place under his pillow and pulled it on over his head. Jake gave the room one last apprehensive look before blowing out the light and jumping under the covers. The interlaced ropes that supported the mattress groaned slightly as he tried to get comfortable under the pile of quilts that covered the bed.

Instead of burrowing down to the heart of the bed like a prairie dog—like he usually did—Jake lay on his back and stared at the ceiling, as rigid as the rafters above his head. His arms were stiffly extended along his sides atop the covers, his hands balled into tight fists as if prepared for a fight.

A finger as long and thin as a pitchfork tine emerged from the shadowy region under the bed. It was followed by its brothers, each as long and narrow as the first. The spidery, overlong digits were joined to a wide, flat palm, which was attached to a bony wrist. The fingers hooked themselves into claws, digging into the floorboards as the thing dragged itself clear of the bed. It stood up once it was free, unfolding itself like a pocketknife. Its knobby back made a clicking sound as it shrugged its shoulders, locking its spine into place.

It was pale as a frog's belly, with skin like that found on a pitcher of milk that's been left to sit too long. Its body was hairless, save for the tangle of lank, greasy curls that hung from its lopsided head like a nest of dead snakes. Its legs were as long and thin as tent poles, and bent backward at the knee so that it seemed to be both walking away from and toward its prey at the same time.

The face, if you could call it one, was toadlike in appearance, with wide, rubbery lips, a pair of slits in place of a nose, and two huge, blood red eyes that glowed like an angry cat's. When the thing smacked its lips, Jake could see the inside of its mouth was ringed with jagged teeth.

When the fiend stared down at Jake, the boy saw a brief glimmer of surprise in its hideous eyes. Clearly it had not expected its victim to be so exposed. Still, it knew better than to question its good fortune. The thing moved so that it loomed over the boy, bending low so that its hideous face was mere inches from Jake's own, its spiderlike talons poised to spear the terrified child's eyeballs.

Although the thing before him filled him with terror, Jake bit his tongue to keep from crying out. The time had come for him to face that which frightened him and become its master.

The horror that hovered before him blinked an inner eyelid, and the nasal slits that served as its nose dilated sharply, catching scent of the subtle change in the chemistry of fear. Emitting a low growl, the thing abruptly turned its head on its shoulders like an owl, so that it was staring over its shoulders at the chifforobe.

The moment the monster took its murderous gaze off him, Jake kicked back the bedclothes, causing the creature to swivel its head back in his direction. *"Now!"* the boy screamed at the top of his lungs. *"Do it now!"*

The doors to the chifforobe flew open with a bang, and out of its depths stepped a man dressed all in black, from his scuffed cowboy boots and floor-length duster to the hat on his head. He brandished a pistol in hands so pale it looked as if they had been dipped in whitewash. His face was equally pallid, save for his eyes, which burned like red-hot coals dropped in a snow bank. About the pale man's neck was cinched a bolo made from a polished stone the color of blood.

"Step back from the boy, critter," the pale man said in a voice that sounded as if it were coming from the bottom of a well.

The thing from under the bed flipped its head back around on its shoulders and snarled at the intruder, displaying a ring of razor-sharp teeth. A sane man would have fainted dead away or fled the scene, but the pale man opened fire instead. The thing clutched its midsection, a look of confusion and pain on its hideous face, before collapsing onto the floor.

"You did it!" Jake shouted gleefully, jumping up and down on the bed. "You killed him!"

"Don't get too excited there, son—you can't really kill these critters," the pale man replied, holstering his pistols.

There was a loud slam as the door to Jake's room flew open and Hiram McKinney entered the room, galluses dangling from his pants, shotgun ready.

"Who in hell are you, mister, and what are you doing in my boy's room?" he thundered.

The pale man raised his hands slow and easy, so as not to tense the rancher's trigger finger. "The name's Hell. Sam Hell. And I'm here at your son's request."

"That's right, Pa!" Jake said excitedly, jumping up and down on the bed. "This here's the Dark Ranger! He come here to get rid of the monster! See?!? It's real! It's really real! And it came out from under my bed, just like I tole ya!"

Hiram looked to where his son was pointing. "Sweet baby Jesus!" he gasped, his eyes started from their sockets. "What in Heaven's name is that?"

"Heaven has nothing to do with it, Mr. McKinney. May I put my hands down now?"

"Hiram, honey? What is going on in here—?" Mrs. McKinney poked her head around the doorjamb, a homespun shawl about her shoulders and her hair gathered into her nightcap. She gave out with a squeal of horror upon seeing the thing sprawled across the floor.

"Tell you the truth, Miriam—I have no earthly idea what's going on."

"I sent for him, Pa! I saw his advertisement in the back of this magazine, and I wrote him, telling him what was wrong, and he wrote back and said he could help and tole me what to do what to when he got here!"

"Excuse me, folks—but as I've been trying to explain to your boy here, this dance ain't over yet."

The man called Hell stepped over the body of the fiend on the floor, pushed back the sackcloth curtains and opened the window, which swung

Nancy A. Collins

14

inward on a hinge. A second later a woman dressed in the fringed riding chaps and beaded pectoral of an Indian warrior clambered over the sill.

"Comanche!" McKinney shouted, lifting his weapon.

Hell turned and grabbed the barrel of the shotgun in one milk white hand, forcing its muzzle to the floor. Hiram tried to yank the shotgun free from the pale stranger's grasp, but there was no budging it.

"Yes, Pretty Woman is a Comanche." Hell said matter-of-factly. "And I would kindly appreciate it if you did not point your gun at a lady—one who happens to be my business partner, at that."

The Comanche woman acted as if she did not see or hear what was going on about her as she knelt beside the creature on the floor. Muttering a chant under her breath, she removed a grass-rope lariat tied about her waist and hogtied the unconscious creature like a steer ready for branding. Just as she finished trussing it up, the thing made a wailing sound, like that of a wounded elk, and began to struggle.

Mrs. McKinney screamed and snatched her son off the bed, clutching him to her in an attempt to shield him from attack. Hiram McKinney attempted to pull his shotgun free of the stranger's grip in order to fire on the thing, but it was still held fast.

"There's no need to panic, folks," Hell said calmly. "Pretty's got it under control."

The Comanche medicine woman learned in close to the fiend's wildly gnashing mouth. She raised a clenched fist to her lips and blew a quick burst of air into it. A cloud of grayish white powder enveloped the creature's face. It abruptly ceased its howling, becoming as limp as wet laundry.

"Is it dead?" Mrs. McKinney asked, her curiosity having overcome her dread.

"Like I told the boy—there's no killing such critters," Hell said flatly, letting go of Hiram's shotgun. "You might as well try and murder a stone or stab the sea. Best you can do is make sure it can't do you more harm."

Pretty Woman removed a leather bag from her belt and emptied its contents, mostly dried herbs and other less identifiable artifacts, onto the floor. She glanced up her partner with eyes as dark and bright as a raven's, and he nodded in return.

"Come along, folks," Hell said, motioning for the others to leave the room. "We better leave Pretty to finish the breaking in peace. Something tells me y'all could do with a cup of coffee right about now."

Hiram McKinney sat in his favorite chair, his shotgun resting across his knees, while his wife busied herself with making coffee. He stared at the pale-skinned stranger who called himself Hell, who was now sitting opposite him in his wife's rocking chair. At first Hiram had thought the stranger was an albino, but now that he was able to get a closer look, he could see that Hell's complexion was more like that of the consumptives who had come out west for the Cure.

Uncertain of how to proceed in such an unusual situation, he finally decided there was no wrong way to go about it, so he opted to grab the bull by the horns. "Jake said something about him writing you—?"

"Yes, sir. That he did."

"Here, Pa—this is what I was talking about." Jake handed his father a copy of *Pickman's Illustrated Serials*, which was tightly rolled in order to fit in the boy's back pocket.

Hiram took the periodical and flattened it out as best he could across his knee. He frowned at the lurid illustration that adorned the front cover, which showed a band of outlaws shooting up a town, each of whom had swooning damsels and bags of loot clutched in the hands that did not hold smoking six-shooters. Floating over the desperadoes' heads was the title of the lead story, in ornately engraved script: *The Tortuga Hill Gang Rides Again.*

"You been wasting money on penny dreadfuls?" Hiram said sternly, glowering at his son in disapproval.

"Far be it from me to step in between a father and his son," Hell said. "But don't you reckon you're being a tad harsh on the boy, considering the situation?"

Hiram opened his mouth, as if to argue to point, then realized the foolishness of it. "I reckon you're right on that point, mister."

"Here, Pa—here's where I saw his advertisement." Jake pointed to a quarter-page ad, located just below an advertisement for Dr. Mirablis's Amazing Electric Truss. Unlike the other advertisements, it did not boast steel-engraved pictures or florid script, even though what it claimed to be selling was far more esoteric that the patent medicines and seed catalogs that surrounded it.

Troubled by Specters, Ghosts and Phantoms? Fear No More! There Is Help! Call For The Dark Ranger: Ghost Breaking A Specialty! No Spook Too Small, No Fiend Too Fierce! Write Care of: Box 1, Golgotha, Texas. Our Motto: 'One Wraith, One Ranger.'

"Dark Ranger?" Hiram rubbed his forehead, baffled by what he was reading. He glanced over at the man seated across from him with something akin to awe. "You a Texas Ranger, mister?"

A look of profound sorrow flickered across Hell's face and was quickly gone, like a cloud scudding across the moon. "I was. Back before the troubles."

Hiram raised an eyebrow. "Cortina?"

Hell took a deep breath and nodded, as if the very memory caused him pain. "Yep. I was at Rio Grande City. Now that the Rangers have been replaced with those carpetbaggin' State Police, I break ghosts and scare off things that go bump in the night."

"Any man who rode with Captain Ford and Robert E. Lee is more than welcome in my home," Hiram said, putting aside his shotgun. He stood and offered Hell his hand. "And I am eternally grateful for you helpin' out my boy here."

"You've got a very brave and resourceful son, Mr. McKinney," Hell said, accepting the rancher's handshake. The Ranger's grip was hard as horn, and as cool and dry as a snakeskin. "Not many boys his age would have had the gumption to do as he did."

"No, I reckon not," Hiram agreed, a hint of pride in his voice. "I'll be damned if I can figure out how you got into the house in the first place, though."

"I let him in, Pa!" Jake explained. "Miss Pretty Woman rode up this morning, while you was out tendin' the herd and Maw was out in the coop seein' to the chickens. She gave me this note that said Mr. Hell needed me to leave my bedroom window open so he could sneak in and hide before I went to bed. That way he could catch the haint unawares."

"Well, I'll be jiggered," Hiram said. "But, son—why didn't you tell your Maw and me what was goin' on?"

"I didn't think you'd believe me. Besides, I was afraid it might hurt y'all. I didn't want anything bad to happen to you and Maw on account of me."

Hiram looked into his son's face with a mixture of amazement, respect and love. "So you just kept goin' to bed, even though that thing was waitin' for you every night?"

"It weren't there every night. But, yes, sir, I did."

"Here you go, dear," Mrs. McKinney said, handing her husband a tin cup full of hot coffee. "How about you, Mr. Hell? Would could care for something to drink?"

"No thank you, ma'am," he replied, smiling without showing his teeth. "I don't drink—coffee."

Pretty Woman stepped out of Jake's room and coughed into her closed fist. Hell stood up, visibly relieved that he no longer had to make small talk.

"Ah! Pretty's finished with your unwanted guest. It's safe to go back in now."

"You sure?" Mrs. McKinney asked uneasily.

"Ma'am, there's not a lot of things in this world I'd bet good money on—but Pretty Woman's medicine is one of 'em."

As they entered the bedroom, the creature scuttled to the far corner, its head ducked low like that of a dog that's been kicked once too often. The speed of its movements made Mrs. McKinney cry out in alarm and clutch her husband's arm.

"No need to be fearful, ma'am," Hell said calmly. "The fight's been took out of it." He strode over to the creature and grabbed the grass-rope noose about its neck. "Come along, you," he snapped.

"What—what, exactly, is that thing?" Hiram asked, trying to keep the unease from his voice.

"I'm not rightly sure. I'll have to ask Pretty." Hell turned to the medicine woman and said something in Comanche.

Pretty Woman wrinkled her nose as she replied in her native tongue, pointing to the walls as she spoke. Hell nodded his understanding.

"According to Pretty, this here's a nature spirit of some sort. These critters attach themselves to things like rocks, trees, creeks and the like—I reckon you could say they live in them. Some are friendly towards folks, others ain't. Seems this one attached itself to the tree that the planks used to build this room were milled from. By using various incantations and spells, in combination with a specially prepared rope, Pretty has rendered this particular spirit harmless—as long as y'all keep the noose about its neck, and feed it nothing but salt."

"Beg pardon?"

"Salt weakens unnatural things," Hell explained. "That is why the signs of power used in calling down the things from between worlds are drawn in salt; it saps their strength and binds them to the will of the conjurer." Hell stepped forward and handed the loose end of the rope to Jake. "I reckon

he's yours, if he belongs to anyone. You'll find having your own private fiend has its advantages. For one thing, they chase off bad luck, as well as snakes. You feed this bogey a tablespoon of salt a day and he'll be yours until the oceans run dry and the mountains crumble. Provided you never take off the noose." "

"What happens if it's removed?" Hiram asked, eyeing the creature cautiously.

"Just see that you don't," Hell replied gravely. "I don't do refunds."

⟹◆⟸

After a few minutes of haggling, it was decided that five dollars cash money and a spool of ribbon was fair pay for a night of ghost-breaking. Though the McKinneys offered to let Sam Hell and Pretty Woman spend the rest of the night in the barn, the pair politely declined.

"It is most kindly of y'all to extend such an invitation," the Ranger said, touching the brim of his hat. "But the nature of our business demands that we be on our way long before sun-up."

As they rode off into the night, Hell turned to look one last time at the McKinney clan as they stood in the dooryard of their homestead. Hiram leaned on his shotgun as he waved goodbye, his free arm draped over his wife's shoulders. Miriam McKinney stood close to her husband, occasionally casting worried looks in the direction of her son, who was busy poking the captive fiend in the rump with a sharp stick.

⟹◆⟸

After they rounded a bend in the road and were no longer within line of sight of the McKinney ranch, Sam reached inside his duster and retrieved a long, thin cigar shaped like a twig.

"See? I told you advertising in the back of penny dreadfuls would pay off," he said, biting off the tip of the cigar with a set of very white, inhumanly sharp teeth.

"I'll grant you that," Pretty Woman replied in perfect English. "But I do not see how it will help you find the one you seek."

"Texas is a big place. I could wander forever and a day and never find him. But if something spooky is happening, odds are he might be near at hand. Kind of like high winds and hailstones mean a twister's nearby."

"There is something to your way of thinking," the medicine woman conceded. "But I still think it was a waste of perfectly good money."

"I wouldn't say that. After all—you got yourself a nice spool of ribbon out of the deal, didn't you?"

"That thing could have torn me apart like fresh bread! That's hardly worth a spool of ribbon."

"But it didn't, did it? And that ribbon should look real nice wrapped around your braids."

"Point taken," she replied with a smile. "Still, do you think it was wise telling them so much about yourself?"

"I didn't let on too much. There was plenty of Rangers that fought at Rio Grande City and Brownsville. Besides, they don't know my real name. And there's no Rangers headquarters left to contact anymore, even if they did decide to try and check up on me. As far as the state of Texas is concerned, Ranger Sam Yoakum is long dead."

⋙⋗◆⋖⋘

Sam Yoakum signed on with the Texas Rangers back in '58. Since then, he had fought more than his fair share of Comanche, Apache, Mexicans, cattle rustlers and outlaws, all for the grand sum of one dollar and twenty-five cents a day. Now that Texas had joined the Confederacy, Yoakum knew it was only a matter of time before the Governor would be forced to muster what was left of the Rangers into an army, despite very real concerns that Cortina and Juarez would use the war between the gringo states to their advantage and attempt to reclaim Brownsville and the surrounding territory in the name of Mexico.

But until the day he had to turn in his Ranger's star for a set of rebel grays, Yoakum's duty was to patrol his assigned territory and check on the various ranchers, settlers and townsfolk between Corpus Christi and the Rio Grande. One such town was Golgotha, Texas—population forty-six, give or take a chicken or mule.

Even from a distance, Yoakum could tell there was something not right about the town. Even the tiniest frontier settlement normally showed some sign of life, even if it was just a mangy dog wandering about or a horse tethered to a hitching post. As he rode into Golgotha, the only things roaming the streets were tumbleweeds and dust devils.

The town was still. Not in the sense of it being a sleepy little village where nothing much happened, but in the way a dead body is utterly motionless. As the wind shifted in his direction, Yoakum caught the odor of spilled blood. During the Cortina War, when the Mexican bandit lord had laid waste to the lower Rio Grande Valley, Yoakum had come to know the smell of death all too well to ever mistake it for anything else.

Yoakum reined his mount to a halt before Haygood Swanson's General Mercantile. In his five years ranging the frontier, he had come to know the various townsfolk under his general protection fairly well. Goody, as he was known, was an affable fellow, who could be counted on for a free chaw and a decent price on salt, biscuits and coffee.

"Goody? Goody, are you there? It's Sam Yoakum!" His boot heels struck hollow notes on the raised boardwalk that fronted the store. As he pushed open the front door, the bell that alerted the shopkeeper that someone had entered his store gave a deceptively merry jingle.

The interior of Swanson's General Mercantile looked as if a tornado had hit it. Bolts of cloth lay strewn about the countertops, and the barrels that held the flour, sugar and nails lay on their sides, their respective contents spilled across the plank floorboards. Glass cases had been smashed, cabinets overturned and the potbellied stove that dominated the central room had been pulled free of its ventilation pipe and knocked onto its side. As he moved toward the back of the store, something crunched under his boot, and Yoakum smelled a cross between paint thinner and fermented grain. He glanced down and saw that he was walking through broken bottles of redeye.

Yoakum pushed his hat back and scratched his forehead, clearly puzzled by what was before him. He didn't care how crazy they might be—Indians, outlaws and bandits never let whiskey—no matter how cheap—go to waste. If Cortina had raided the town, he would have taken every last barrel of flour he could have laid his hands on. After all, armies—even those comprised of bandits and outlaws—traveled on their stomachs.

As Yoakum turned to leave, something caught the corner of his eye. He bent over and picked up a shotgun from the tangle of unraveled cloth, broken glass and spilled sugar. The stock was marked with the initials H. S. and the barrel was bent back on itself. Yoakum dropped the useless weapon back where he found it and hastened out the door. Yoakum strode out into the middle of the empty street and cupped his hands to his mouth.

"*Hullo! Texas Rangers! Anybody here? Can anyone hear me?*" he shouted.

His only answer was the echo of his own voice.

Whatever had happened to the citizens of Golgotha, it was more than a one-man job. He'd have to ride on down to Brownsville, pick up a couple of men and come back to sort things out.

Just as he was about to saddle up his horse, the tolling of a bell broke the eerie silence. Yoakum turned and looked in the direction of the sound. It was coming from the church, which stood in the very middle of town, catty-corner from the general store. The frantic nature of the bell ringing was more like a call for help than a somber call to prayers. He cast his gaze about, but saw no signs of life from any of the surrounding buildings.

Yoakum approached the whitewashed wooden church with his gun drawn, not knowing exactly what to expect. As he drew closer, he could see several panes of stained glass had been busted out, as if by someone throwing rocks.

The front door of the church swung inward as he touched it with the muzzle of his gun. As he stepped inside, a beam of sunlight illuminated the dim interior, falling across the figure of a solitary man, who stood in the back of the church, pulling on the bell rope that lead to the steeple.

"Where is everyone, Reverend?" Yoakum called out.

The bell-ringer stopped and turned to look at Yoakum. His face was gaunt and pale, covered with several days worth of gray stubble. His hair was greasy and uncombed, and his eyes were red-rimmed and more than a little wild, like those of a man who has stood guard on the ramparts with far too little sleep for far too long.

"I ain't no preacher. And as for where everyone is—they're dead. Every last one of them. Ain't nothin' and no one left alive in Golgotha but me."

"And who would you be?"

"The name's Farley. I got me a place a couple miles east of town. I've been livin' in these parts since '52. You don't need to point a gun at me, Ranger," he said, nodding at Yoakum's pistol. "I ain't gonna give you no trouble."

"You say everyone's dead. Where are the bodies?"

"That's a long story," Farley said with a weary sigh.

"Humor me," Yoakum said, motioning for the other man to be seated in one of the nearby pews. As Farley sat down, Yoakum holstered his pistol but did not take his hand off its butt.

"It begun when Merle went and dug himself a new well. You see, he'd bought a parcel of land off this Meskin feller, name of Garcia. Merle already had him a place, but he wanted to build a little house on its own plot so he could bring his mama and the rest of his family down from back east.

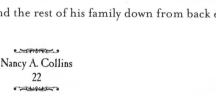

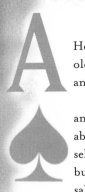He needed the new well, on account of the old one being too far away. Garcia's old grandpa gets all riled up when he hears what Merle's doin'. He rides out and tells Merle he can't dig where he's diggin'.

Merle tells him that he's bought the land off his kinfolk fair 'n' square, and if he wants to dig straight to hell, there ain't nothin' the old man can do about it. Then Old Man Garcia tells Merle that his grandson had no right to sell him the land without talkin' to him about it first. Merle says that's tough, but they've already signed papers on it and money has changed hands, so the sale is legal. Then Old Man Garcia offers to buy the land back from Merle—and at a good price, too. But Merle ain't havin' none of it. So Old Man Garcia, he goes home, packs up his family, and next thing you know they're gone—after bein' in these parts since the conquistadors.

"After a few days diggin', Merle's about eight feet deep, I reckon. He's far enough down that he's got to use a ladder to get in and out of the hole. And he's got a couple of good ol' boys from town, Billy McAfee and Hank Pierson, out there helpin' him haul the dirt and rocks up topside. Then his spade strikes something made of metal, but it's too dark for him to see what it is.

"Merle yells up to Billy to lower him down some light. So Billy sends down a lantern. Merle lights it and bends over to get a look-see. He finds what looks like the lid of a big iron box. There ain't much showin', but from what he can see it looks like it's the size of a steamer trunk. Merle and them get to talkin', and they decide that it must be buried treasure—maybe gold the Aztecs tried to hide from the Spanish, way back when. At first they mean to keep it to themselves, but as they get to uncoverin' the metal box, they realize it's too big and too heavy for just the three of them to pull it free of the hole.

"That's where I come in. I lived down the road a piece, and Merle knew I had me a string of mules. At first I didn't believe a word he said, but then he takes me over to where he's got the well started and tells me to climb down and take a look for myself.

"I have to admit that once they put the notion in my head, all I could think of was gold. I kept thinkin' that if that box was full of treasure, it would go a long ways to settlin' debts and makin' life easier for me an' mine. So I ran and fetched the mules and brought them back to the well. By this point, the boys had uncovered the whole damn thing. It was about four foot long, three foot high and three foot deep, with an old-fashioned hinged iron padlock.

"I hitched up the mules and wrapped the box in a set of chains I use to pull stumps. But when I laid my hand on the top of the box, I jumped back and hollered on account of it being so cold. My hand tingled and burned like I'd just stuck it in a bucket of ice water. Merle figgered it was cold like that because it had been buried so deep all them years. That didn't make much sense, but I was in too big a hurry to lay claim to my share of the treasure to give it much thought.

"I fastened the chains around the box and then climbed up top to fix them to the team. Usually my mules are pretty easy to work with, but that day they was givin' me fits, stompin' the ground and rollin' their eyes like they do when they smell somethin' fierce nearby, like a cougar or a bear. I really had to lay into them with the whip. Their rumps were runnin' red before they finally gave in and started to pull. But once they did, that ol' box was out of the bottom of Merle's well, just as easy as yankin' a rotten tooth. Still, it took all four of us to lift it up and put it in the back of Merle's buckboard.

"By the time we finally managed to get the chest over to Merle's place, it was gettin' on dark. Since the danged thing was so heavy, we decided to just pull the buckboard into the barn and open it out there, as opposed to tryin' to drag it into the house. Billy and Hank rassled the bastard off the back of the wagon and set it on the barn floor.

"While Merle was busy fetchin' his chisel and pry-bar, I took a few seconds to study the padlock on the chest. It was a big rascal—as large as a baby's head—and when I looked at it close, I could make out some kind of symbols through the rust and the dirt caked on it. The funniest thing about the lock, I noticed, was it didn't have no keyhole. Once that critter was locked, it was meant to stay shut.

"Merle came back with the tools he needed to open the box, along with a lantern so he could see what he was doin' now that the sun was set. Merle weren't a small man, and he sure as hell weren't a weak one, but it took him several good swings with the hammer before he knocked that lock open.

"When the padlock finally broke and dropped to the ground, we all stared at it for a couple of heartbeats, then looked up at one another. I don't know if it was the light from the lantern or somethin' else, but the other fellas seemed to be lit from inside with a terrible hunger that made their eyes burn like those of animals gathered around a campfire. I reckon I didn't look no different, though. Greed is a horrible thing.

"The lid of the chest was so heavy that Merle had to take the pry-bar and wedge it under the lip of the box. He levered it open enough so that Billy

and Hank could grab hold and throw it all the way open. We crowded around, lantern held high, eager to sink our arms up to our elbows in gold coins and precious gems. But there weren't no treasure buried in that chest. Not by a long shot.

"The only thing the iron box contained was the body of a man lying on his side, knees drawn up and arms folded across his chest. 'Cept for a thin covering of yellow gray dry skin and wisps of hair that were still stuck to the scalp, it was basically a mummified skeleton. Going by the rusty breastplate and helmet it still wore, the dead man had once been a conquistador. The only thing of any possible value was a silver medallion set with a highly polished stone hung about its neck.

"Merle reached in and yanked the necklace free, holding it up to the light. Merle was always one for lookin' on the sunny side of things, so he tried to put a good face on it, so we wouldn't be so disappointed.

"'At least it ain't a complete loss. This has to be worth at least fifty dollars...' That was the last thing I ever heard him say, at least that weren't screamin'.

"At that point we all had our backs turned to the box, as we was lookin' over Merle's shoulder at the necklace he took off the Spaniard's carcass. Suddenly there was this cracklin' sound comin' from behind us, like someone walkin' through a pile of dead leaves. So I turn around, and I see—sweet Lord Jesus—I see the dead thing in the box stand up.

"I know what you're gonna say, now. That I must be crazy. But if I'm crazy, it's on account of what I seen in that barn. The thing that got out of the box weren't nothin' but bones with dry skin the color and texture of old leather stretched over 'em. But it still had eyes—or something like eyes—burnin' deep inside its sockets. And when the thing saw us, God help me, it grinned—peeling back black, withered lips to reveal a mouthful of sharp, yellow teeth.

"We was so flabbergasted we was froze to the spot, just like a covey of chicks hypnotized by a snake. I was too scared to swaller, much less scream. The dead thing, it made this noise like a screech owl and jumped on poor Merle. It sank its fangs into Merle's throat like a wolf takin' down a lamb. It sure as hell was spry for somethin' that had to have been dead three hundred years.

"Billy grabbed the thing and tried to rassle if off Merle, but it was like tryin' to pull off a tick. Even though it weren't but a bag of bones, it swatted Billy aside like he was nothin'. Hank snatched up an axe handle and laid into

the thing, but just ended up splinterin' the handle on the iron breastplate it was wearin'. Still, he must have got its attention, cause it dropped Merle and turned on him instead.

"Things was happenin' and movin' too fast by this point for me to get a clear picture of what exactly was goin' on, but I remember that once the thing was finished with Merle, it didn't quite look the same. There seemed to be more meat on its bones, an' more juice in the meat. It was like the blood it had drained from Merle was fillin' its own veins.

"Billy starts screamin' 'It's got Hank! It's got Hank! We gotta save him!' He grabs up a pitchfork and charges th' thing, but it's too fast for him. It drops Hank and sidesteps Billy, snatchin' the pitchfork away like it was takin' a toy from a kid. Now Billy's screamin' for help, and—Lord, help me—instead of tryin' to save him, I ran away.

"I jumped on my horse and high-tailed it town, not lookin' back once for fear of what might be gainin' on me if I did. Billy McAfee's death screams were echoin' in my ears the whole way.

"I reached town and I went straight to Sheriff Winthrop's office. He was in th' middle of dinner, so you can imagine he weren't too happy to have me bustin' in goin' on about dead things with glowin' red eyes murderin' Merle and them. Instead of ridin' out to check on my story, he just locked me up and told me to sleep it off.

"Now, I admit that I have been known to bend my elbow, and that I have been known to disturb the peace when I do, but that was no reason for Winthrop to simply ignore what I had to say. True, me and the boys had enjoyed a few celebratory shots of whiskey before we set to openin' the box, but I weren't drunk. Just like I ain't drunk now. Leastwise, not so drunk I was seein' things that weren't there.

"Anyhow, when I woke up the next day, I was still holdin' to my story. As Sheriff Winthrop was unlockin' my cell, I stuck my hand in my pocket and pulled out the medallion. During the ruckus, I must have snatched it up off the barn floor when Merle dropped it. Up until I pulled it out of my pocket, I'd forgot I even had it on me. I showed it to Winthrop as proof that what I was tellin' him was God's honest truth.

"I could tell he still weren't gonna swaller some long-dead conquistador risin' up from the grave and killin' folks, but the sight of the medallion made him wonder if I was completely out of my head. He decided to ride out to Merle's place and find out what was goin' on for himself. As for me, he told me to stay put in town, in case there was any questions that needed answerin' when he got back.

"I told him there was no way in hell I was goin' back out to my spread. Not with that thing, whatever it was, wanderin' the countryside. If he wanted to find me when he got back I told him I'd be in the church. The sheriff looked at me funny when I said that, because I ain't much for settin' foot in the Lord's house on a Sunday, much less any other day of the week.

"So I left the jail and come straight over here. The church was shut up, on account of it being the middle of the week, so I had to go get Brother Stephens, the minister here, to unlock it for me. Brother Stephens, he was right surprised to see a sinner like me banging on his door. He asked me what I needed the church open for. I said I needed to do me some prayin'.

"He says, 'Well, that's mighty fine to hear, Farley. But you can pray to the Lord just as good at home.'

"But I tells him, 'Reverend, I got me some serious favors to be askin' of the Lord, and I figger its best I do my askin' on His ground, not mine.'

"Brother Stephens didn't rightly know what to make of my conversion, but I figger in the end he decided not to look it in the mouth. He went and unlocked the church and I set about praying as hard as I could, only lettin' up every so often to trot to the outhouse and back.

"Halfway into the afternoon, Sheriff Winthrop come back from Merle's spread. He tells Brother Stephens that he wants to talk to me some more, and would I come over to the sheriff's office. I tell Brother Stephens to tell the sheriff that if he's got any questions to ask of me, he better ask them to me in the church, because I ain't settin' foot outside it.

"So Winthrop comes in and sits down in the pew next to me. I can tell from his face that he's worried some.

"'Farley,' he says, 'I been out to Merle's.'

"'You seen the well he was diggin'?'

"'I seen the well.'

"'You seen the barn?'

"'I seen that—as well as the metal chest you told me about.'

"'You seen Merle and them?'

"'No. That's the one thing I didn't see out there. There were no bodies in that barn. Hell, there weren't nothin', livin' or dead, in that barn. Not Merle, not Billy, not Hank—not even horses, for that matter.'

"'What does that mean, Sheriff?'

"'Damned if I know, Farley. Maybe you and Merle and the others had a fallin' out over the treasure in the chest. Maybe that's what happened. But it don't make no sense for you to come runnin' into town with such a cock-and-bull story if you kilt them. And why in tarnation would you want to kill Merle and his livestock, right down to the very last chick and piglet? And even if you did, why in hell would you hide the carcasses? Maybe you ain't tellin' me th' truth about what went on out there, but maybe you ain't lyin' to me, either. In any case, I have to wonder about what could possibly chase you so far up under Brother Stephens skirts. So until I get a better feel of what's goin' on here, I ain't gonna lock you up. I just want you to stay in town, where I can keep an eye on you.'

"I told him he needn't worry about that. I wasn't settin' foot outside the church unless I absolutely had to, since Brother Stephens said I could sleep in the vestibule until it was safe for me to go back home. The sheriff nodded and went back to his office. Things stayed quiet in Golgotha until the sun went down. That's when Merle and the boys showed back up.

"The way I knowed they come back was the horse screamin' out in the street. I opened the door of the church and poked my head out and saw the three of 'em—Merle, Billy and Hank—swarming over the sheriff's horse, which was hitched outside his office. They was all over it like cougars. At first I thought they was just loco, y'know? I called out to them, more out of re-flex, I reckon.

"They looked up from what they was doin' and I saw how pale they was—like there weren't a drop of life left in 'em. There was blood drippin' from their chins, and their eyes was all lit up from within, with the same hellfire I seen in the eyes of the thing from the box.

"Just then Sheriff Winthrop comes out to see what's happenin' to his horse. He's already got his gun drawn, not that it did him no good. The three of them jumped 'im just like they did his horse. Winthrop emptied most of his pistol into Merle, but he might as well have been shootin' at a tree. They took him down right then and there. That's when I slammed the church door and started prayin' again, even faster and harder than before.

"Folks poured out of their houses to see what all the shootin' and screamin' was about—and found out all too quick. At least half the town was kilt that night by them things. Brother Stephens rallied the other half and told 'em to make for the church. I reckon he knew creatures of the devil when he seen 'em, and knew they wouldn't be able to enter holy ground. Or maybe he thought it would be easier to make a stand in the church. I don't know which, because he didn't make it. He stopped to try and drag Martha Tillberry free of one of them monsters, and got his throat ripped out for his trouble.

"Us folks in the church couldn't do nothin' but listen to the creatures outside as they roamed the streets, laughing and shrieking like the fiends from Hell they were. While they were able to enter other buildings freely, they wouldn't come closer than a stone's throw to the church. The reason I know this is because they were chuckin' rocks at us. They screamed and hissed like angry cats the whole time, too, like even lookin' in the direction of the church hurt 'em somehow. The rocks took out a couple of panes of glass, which is how we was able to keep an eye on them durin' that first night without openin' the door.

"It was horrible—there was bodies scattered all along the streets and boardwalks. Once or twice I caught sight of a tall figure moving between the buildings, the moonlight glinting off a metal vest and helmet.

"The next morning, when the sun finally came up, we looked back out the window and were surprised to see that the streets were completely empty. The bodies from the night before had vanished! It took a while, but we finally got the nerve to step outside and survey the damage. Except for the general store bein' turned ass over tea kettle and a few kicked-in doors and busted-out windows, there was little to show what had happened the night before—except for the lack of bodies. And it weren't just the townsfolk that was missin'. There weren't an animal carcass to be found—dog, cat, horse or pig. It was like everything that was livin' in Golgotha outside the protection of the church simply disappeared off the face of the earth.

"Those that survived the night were divided into two groups. There was them that wanted to get the hell out of town as fast as they could, and there was them that wanted to stay. Most of the folks that was for stayin' had loved ones missin'. I was one for stayin', but because I knew that without a horse, there was no way I could get far enough away before the sun went down. As bad as being holed up in the church might be, it was a damn sight better than bein' stuck out in the middle of nowhere with them things roamin' the countryside.

"The Wilhoyts and the Brubakers decided to pull up stakes and go. They took what provisions they could find from what was left of Goody's store and loaded them up in a wheelbarrow. They struck out north. That's the way you come in, weren't it? You didn't pass them on the road, did you? There was nine of 'em—two men, two women and five young'uns."

Yoakum shook his head no.

"That's what I was skeered of. If them hell-beasts didn't git 'em, then Comanches or bandits most likely did. Either way, they're dead. Anyways, once the Wilhoyts and 'em was gone, that just left fifteen of us. We scavenged what we could from the store and houses—lamp oil, water, food, guns and ammunition—and went back to the church to wait for the night.

"Soon as the sun was set, we could see things movin' outside. I watched as people—or what used to be people—wriggled their way out from under the boardwalks and dug themselves outta of shallow graves. I watched as they wandered the streets of Golgotha, kinda dazed like, as if they was all coming off the world's worst bender. They made this low, pitiful moanin' noise, like cattle lowing to be milked. They lifted their heads and started sniffing the air, like hounds casting for a scent. One by one they was drawn to the church, like iron filings to a magnet, but they couldn't get too close.

"It was horrible beyond any description. On the outside these were folks I'd worked alongside, broken bread with and called neighbor—folks like Goody Swanson, Tom Littlefield, Minnie Tillberry—yet, they weren't them at all. One of the dead'uns came forward. It was Lottie Gruenwald, and she had dirt in her hair and dried blood all over her dress.

"'Oscar—where are you Oscar? I'm frightened!'

"Ol' Oscar jumped like he'd been stuck with a pitchfork. 'That's my wife out there! She's in danger! She needs me!'

"I grabbed Oscar by the arm and tried to tell him that weren't his wife out there—leastwise, not anymore. But he wouldn't hear reason. He pushed me aside and ran right out the front door of the church, right into the arms of his lovin' wife—who put her cold, stiff arms around his neck and tore his throat out with her fangs. Funny thing is, he didn't scream or carry on, much less look scared. He kind of had this dreamy look on his face, even when she bit into him.

"Just as Lottie was startin' to drink Oscar's blood, there was a commotion among the others. Then this figure comes forward, partin' the crowd like Moses dividin' the Red Sea. It was him. The one from the box. The others started callin' his name, over and over, like children cryin' for their mama: 'Sangre, Sangre, Sangre.' I tell you, it was enough to put a bald man's hair on end.

"As he got closer, I could see this Sangre's a damn sight improved from the first time I laid eyes on him. Except for his eyes and the pale color of his skin, he don't look that much different from any other feller you might

meet on the street—'cept for the helmet and breastplate, of course. The moment Lottie saw him, she let Oscar drop to the ground, like a cat bringin' its owner a wounded mouse as a love-token.

"Now Oscar ain't dead yet, but he's gettin' there. He put one hand over his throat, the blood squirtin' between his fingers, and tried to drag himself back toward the church, but it was too late. Sangre bent over and sank his teeth into Oscar's neck, worrying him like a terrier does a rat. Whatever spell Oscar was under must have been broken then, 'cause that's when he started screamin'. The screams don't last long, though. Once Sangre's drunk his fill, he stepped back and the others closed in on the poor bastard, swarmin' him like ants on a lump of sugar.

"Despite what everyone saw happen to Oscar, the same damn thing happened again and again that night. Husbands called to their wives, children called to their mothers, mothers called to their sons, brothers called to their sisters....

"It didn't seem to matter that steppin' outside was certain death. There was no talkin' sense into them. Even when a bunch of us knocked 'em down and sat on 'em to keep 'em from leavin', they would still find a way of gettin' out the door. By the time the sun rose, there was only six of us left, and half of them had become gibbering idjits.

"Once the streets was clear, we were finally able to get some sleep. Later that afternoon, those of us that were still in our right minds left to replenish our supply of water and food. When we returned, we found the one we'd left behind hanging from the church rafters. There was nothing we could do but cut 'em down and place 'em outside, as it was too late in the day to try and bury 'em. That just left me, Cyrus Ledbetter and Joe Kelly.

"Once the sun went down, the dead'uns came back out from their hidey-holes and started fightin' with each other over the bodies we'd left outside. They got real violent about it, too—I seen what used to be Sheriff Winthrop rip the head off'n what used to be Hank. And Hank stayed dead that time. That tole me two things: that the pickin's had to be pretty slim, if they was scrappin' over corpse-blood, and that they could be killed—leastwise by one another.

"Their hunger made them more desperate, and they started movin' in closer on the church than they had before. It was plain to see that they was scared of comin' too close, but at the same time the pain in their bellies was making them bold. I guess starvin's the same, whether yore hankerin' for cornpone or human blood.

"Cyrus, Joe an' me decided to sleep in shifts. That ways one of us would be awake to raise the alarm in case the dead'uns got a hair up their ass and decided to storm the church. Cyrus was to take the first watch, Joe the second and me the third.

"I bedded down the best I could, tryin' to tune out the sound of the dead'uns outside, moanin' and wailin' like the damned souls they were. Next thing I know, I wake up to find Cyrus on top of me, his hands wrapped around my throat.

"'It's you or me, Farley,' he growled as he tightened his grip on my windpipe. 'I already kilt Joe and fed 'im to 'em. Now its yore turn.'

"Cyrus should have checked to see if I was as harmless as Joe before trying to serve me up to those damned bloodsuckers. I reached into my boot and pulled out my knife and drove it into his belly. Needless to say, it weren't my cold bones the dead'uns ended up scrappin' over.

"That was two days ago. I been holed up here alone ever since. Every night they come back out, gettin' closer and closer to the church, like they're huddling around it for warmth. Last night they started fightin' amongst themselves something fierce—rippin' off haids and breakin' off arms and th' like.

"When I heard you hollerin', at first I thought I was dreamin'. When I looked out the window and saw you standin' out there in the middle of the street, I knew my prayers had been answered."

Yoakum took a deep breath and let it out slow. "Well, now, Farley... that's a mighty unusual story. I can honestly say that in all my years rangering, I have yet to hear tell of anything like it before—and I fought against Ironjacket and Cortina."

"I know it sounds like complete and utter horse hockey. But you have to believe me when I tell you every word of it is true. You want proof?" Farley thrust his hand into his pocket and withdrew a necklace attached to a pendant. "This here's the medallion Merle took off the dead'un in the box," he said, shoving the piece of jewelry into Yoakum's hand. "This is proof I ain't talkin' crazy, ain't it? You can have it, far as I care. All it brung me is misery."

Yoakum frowned at the pendant, turning it over in his hands. He moved to the window and held it up by its chain so that he could get a better look at the stone. He had never seen anything quite like it before. Depending on its angle, it appeared black, while other times it seemed to glow red as a ruby. He was so preoccupied staring into the stone's depths, he did not realize

that Farley was behind him until the gun butt collided with the back of his head.

When Yoakum came to, it was to find himself alone. Late afternoon shadows filled the church. As he got to his feet, he grimaced and gingerly touched his skull. His fingers came away sticky with blood. He lurched out into the dying light of the setting sun. There was no sign of either his horse or Farley.

"Goddamn lyin' horse thief," Yoakum muttered under his breath. All that bastard had left him was a piece of junk jewelry, tucked inside the front breast pocket of his shirt, and the grandpappy of all headaches.

As he stood in the deserted street, Yoakum could not help but remember Farley's story about the living dead. It was pure poppycock, plain and simple—it had to be. But if Farley had been lying, then where had everybody gone?

As the Texas sun dropped its blood red eye, and the lengthening shadows drew the town into dusk, Yoakum heard what sounded like a dog pawing at a door. As he turned around, trying to pinpoint the source of the noise, he realized that the sound was coming from more than one place. The scratching was quickly replaced by a louder, more distinct noise—one that made every hair on the back of his neck stand on end. It was a chorus of human voices, united in an ululating wail of pain and despair. It was the cry of the dead'uns.

He saw the first one crawl out from under the shadows of the boardwalk, pulling itself along on its elbows like a Comanche brave sneaking up on a buffalo. The creature was covered from head to toe in a mixture of dirt, manure and mud, although there were enough clean spots for Yoakum to see that the flesh underneath was as pale as death. Its eyes locked onto Yoakum, shining with an unwholesome hunger. It took an active force of will for Yoakum to tear himself from the thing's gaze.

To his horror, there were dozens of similar creatures boiling out from under the boardwalks and crawlspaces of the surrounding buildings, like maggots escaping a corpse. He made a mental note to himself to amend his opinion of Farley. The man was definitely a horse thief, but he certainly wasn't a liar.

He turned to flee to the relative safety of the church, only to find his way blocked by more of the erstwhile citizens of Golgotha. They stood shoulder to shoulder, their bloodless faces fixed into masks of depraved longing.

He'd rescued men held captive by Indians until they where starved into scarecrows who didn't look that hungry. He fired his Colt .45 into the crowd that encircled him. Of the six dead'uns hit, only one dropped and stayed down—from a head wound that took off her sunbonnet along with the top of her skull.

With a collective shout of anticipation, the creatures surged forward, clawing at Yoakum with yellowed nails. They swarmed over him like rats attacking a wounded terrier, violently biting and clawing one another as they jockeyed for position. Yoakum kicked, punched, bit and gouged eyes as best he could, but they seemed immune to any punishment he meted out. In the end, there were simply too many of them. Within seconds of emptying his pistol, he was overwhelmed.

What had once been the town's blacksmith clamped cold, clammy fingers about Yoakum's throat. The Texas Ranger drove his fist into the undead thing's face with all his might. Though he could feel the creature's jaw break from the force of the blow, it continued to pull the struggling human inexorably toward its dripping fangs. As it opened its mouth, a graveyard stench rolled forth, causing Yoakum to gag. He didn't know what was worse—dying at the hands of fiends, or having to endure their stink while doing it.

Just as the blacksmith was about to sink his fangs into Yoakum's jugular, there was a shout that froze the entire undead congregation in their tracks.

"*¡La Parada!*"[1]

The undead things crowded about Yoakum abruptly withdrew. As the burly vampire let go of Yoakum's throat, the Ranger dropped to his knees, coughing raggedly as he fought to regain his breath. He looked up as he massaged his bruised and swollen neck, staring in mute amazement at the figure before him. Even if he had not heard Farley's story about the mummified conquistador, he still would have known that this was their leader, the one they called Sangre.

The Spaniard stood well over six feet tall, with long black hair that fell past his shoulders, and an equally dark beard and goatee that gave his face an appropriately saturnine appearance. Save for his pallid complexion and a set of overlong, yellowed fingernails, there was little to indicate to the casual observer that he was as cold as yesterday's mutton.

Sangre stared down at Yoakum with eyes that glittered like rubies held before a flame. Although he still wore rusty morion helmet and armored vest he had originally been buried in, the revived conquistador was now also

[1] "HALT!"

outfitted in a pair of denim trousers and cowboy boots, no doubt taken from one of his recent victims.

The others milled about him at a respectful distance. The way they kept their eyes riveted on him, while avoiding his gaze, reminded Yoakum of a pack of hounds anxiously awaiting their master's command. The others moved about nervously, murmuring their creator-lord's name over and over to themselves.

The undead conquistador pointed a talonlike finger at Yoakum and spoke in a booming voice. *"¡Primero sangres es mía!"*[2]

The dead'uns muttered to themselves. It was clear that they did not like what Sangre had to say, but were unwilling to argue the matter. The conquistador allowed himself a smile, displaying fangs the color of antique ivory.

"La paciencia, mis niños. Después que yo soy hecho, èl es suyo."[3]

"Like hell!" Yoakum growled, spitting a wad of bloody phlegm onto the vampire's boots. Like most Texans, he understood Spanish about as well as he did English. And he knew he didn't like what he was hearing, no matter what the language. "I ain't no side of beef to be parceled out among your kin!"

Sangre grabbed the Ranger by the front of his shirt as if he weighed no more than a child. As Yoakum looked directly into Sangre's burning red eyes, he heard a voice that was not his own murmuring inside his head, urging him to stop struggling and surrender.

Yoakum felt a sudden pressure on his throat, immediately followed by a piercing pain. Within seconds of being bitten, the wound went numb, as if a paralyzing toxin had been injected into his system. Yoakum felt as if he were somehow standing outside his own body, watching as he struggled to escape.

Summoning the last of his strength, he pulled himself away from the vampire. Sangre responded by tightening his grip. There was a tearing sound, and the pocket of Yoakum's shirt came away in the vampire's hand.

The medallion fell to the ground between the two men. Sangre yowled as if Yoakum was hot to the touch, and quickly distanced himself from the wounded Ranger.

"¡Recoja ese collar de diablo!"[4] Sangre snarled, pointing at the medallion at his feet as if it were a rattlesnake coiled to strike. The other vampires shuffled their feet and eyed the amulet cautiously. None moved forward to retrieve it.

---

[2] "First Blood is mine!"
[3] "Patience, my children. After I am finished with him, he is yours."
[4] "Pick up that accursed necklace!"

Yoakum did not know why the vampire lord should be so frightened by a piece of jewelry, but something told him it was his only chance of escaping in one piece. Clamping his hand over the spurting wound on his throat, he snatched up the fallen medallion and thrust it in Sangre's face. The vampire recoiled, shielding his eyes .

"¡Lo toma lejos!"[5]

Yoakum swung the medallion in a wide arc, turning to face the others as they crowded in. The undead moved back, parting before him like the Red Sea. Yoakum could either go back into the church, or he could strike out on foot. Either way, he'd be dead before dawn. Better that he die under the open sky than holed up somewhere with his back to the wall, like a baited bear.

Yoakum half expected the creatures to dog-pile him the moment his back was turned, but they simply stood by and allowed him to walk away. It was clear from the hungry looks they gave him they wanted nothing more than to tear into him like a Sunday dinner, but something was holding them back—and that something was the mysterious pendant he held aloft.

Within minutes he was outside the city limits of Golgotha. He had never been so happy to put a town behind him in his life. The relief he felt upon escaping, however, was quickly replaced with concern. As usual, he was out of the frying pan and into the fire. He was a white man wandering alone, wounded and unarmed in the most hostile territory in Texas. He had no food or water, and nothing more than the clothes on his back to protect him against the elements. It was dark, and he had nothing to light his way but the rising moon and the evening stars.

Once he was convinced that Sangre and his followers were not coming after him, he slipped the amulet around his neck and turned his attention to the bite on his throat. Though it was not particularly deep, it continued to bleed long after it should have normally clotted. He was able to temporarily staunch the wound by wrapping it with his bandana, but it was not long before the cloth was saturated. He was weary from walking and becoming increasingly lightheaded, but he knew better than to stop and rest. Even if Sangre's whey-faced spawn weren't after him, odds were the smell of his blood would attract any number of predators. The last thing he needed in such a weakened condition was to find himself face to face with a mountain lion or a pack of coyotes. Hell, the way he was feeling, he wouldn't be able to lick a prairie dog.

[5] "Take it away!"

As he continued walking, he became dimly aware that he was no longer traveling alone. There was a figure keeping pace with him, one that he could only see from the corner of his eye. The figure was that of a man, dressed in overalls and heavy boots, and he carried a chopping hoe in his left hand, which he used as a walking staff. Though Yoakum could not immediately place the stranger, there was something familiar about him. Then the man turned his head and smiled at him, and, with a start, Yoakum realized he was looking into the face of his father.

"Daddy?"

"Best be careful, son," Silas Yoakum said. He extended his right hand, in the palm of which was the severed head of a rattlesnake. "They can still bite after they're dead."

The elder Yoakum smiled and quickly closed his fist about the viper. As he did, his features began to rapidly swell and turn purple, the eyes bulging from their sockets, until he looked like he did the last time his son had seen him, twenty years ago.

Sam had been working the fields, chopping cotton, when he heard his father cry out in pain and anger. As he hurried to his father's side, he saw Silas Yoakum's arms rise and fall numerous times, swinging the hoe he carried down onto something near his feet. By the time Sam reached him, Silas had chopped the rattlesnake into ribbons. The older man waved his ten-year-old son away. 'Go fetch your Maw,' he rasped. Those were the last words Silas Yoakum ever spoke.

Suddenly he was back at the house, sitting in the kitchen at his place at the table. The stove must have been on, because the room was hot. Yoakum heard the door open, and he turned to see his mother enter the house, holding out her apron, which was full of blue bonnets from the pasture.

"Aren't they lovely, Sam?" she asked. "They're dead but they still look like they're alive. Mercy, it's so hot in this kitchen! They'll need to drink if they are going to keep looking lively. They're dead, but they can still be thirsty. Be a good boy and draw me some water."

"Yes, ma'am," he replied, dutifully walking across the kitchen to the sink. He had to give the kitchen pump handle a couple of good pushes before the water spurted forth. As he watched the cold, clear spring water splash into the waiting catch basin, he was suddenly aware of just how hot and thirsty he was.

He leaned forward and placed his lips against the spout, eager to drink his fill. To his surprise, the water was not cool and refreshing, but warm and slightly salty. He drew back and saw that it was not well-water spurting forth, but blood. Even as he retched, something in the back of his mind urged him to drink deeply from the gushing gore. Though he knew he should resist the urge, he was helpless to fight it. It was as if his body were being devoured from the inside out by a ferocious heat, which could only be slaked by the blood of others.

As Yoakum fought against the dark fire burning inside him, he became dimly aware of what felt like a soothing, feminine hand on his fevered brow, accompanied by a slowly expanding numbness. The numbness overwhelmed the hellfire within his veins, dampening it to a tolerable level, if not exactly extinguishing it altogether. As the lack of sensation spread throughout his body, he wondered if he was dying. The idea did not bother him overmuch. Better to die a man than to live as a monster.

The next thing he was aware of was the smell of wood smoke and the sound of a woman's voice, chanting in a language he recognized as belonging to the Comanche.

It took him a moment to realize he did not need to open his eyes because they were already open, staring at what looked to be the backside of a horse blanket. He reached up and pulled it away, and found himself gazing up at the night sky.

As he sat up, he saw the source of both the smoke and chanting. An Indian woman dressed in buckskin riding trousers hunkered before a small campfire, her back to him. Her hair was long and wild and hung down her back like the mane of a wild pony. Upon hearing him move, she turned her head to look at him, and he could see she was naked from the waist up, save for a beaded pectoral and the paint on her face.

"Who are you?" he rasped, his voice drier than ginned cotton. When the woman did not respond, he asked the question haltingly in her own language.

"I will speak in your own tongue," she replied. "Your Comanche hurts my ears. I am called Pretty Woman."

"How long have I been asleep?"

"You have been dead three days."

"You mean unconscious."

She gave him a look that would wither an apple on the branch. "I know dead when I see it."

"How can I be dead if I am talking to you?"

"How can a rattlesnake bite after it is no longer alive?"

Yoakum blinked. "I had a dream where someone said that to me. But how—?"

Pretty Woman shrugged her shoulders and went back to poking at the fire with a stick. "Dreams tell us many things. My dream told me where to find you, and to protect you from the sun."

"I don't understand."

"I don't, either. For now it is enough that I saw you in my dream and found you before you burned with the rising sun."

"And you sat with me this whole time? Three days?"

"Yes."

"Why?"

"I am a shaman. As was my grandfather and his mother before him. My medicine is strong, but I am still young. I am—unseasoned," she spoke in a way that told Yoakum she was quoting someone else's words. "So I was sent out into the wilderness to seek a vision, and make its medicine my own.

"For four days and four nights I wandered without food or drink, or sleep. Then, on the fifth night, I looked up and saw the moon weeping blood. The bloody teardrops fell upon the land, and from them sprang forth a man with eyes of fire and the heart of a devil. I saw the devil-man go forth and bring pestilence and death to the Whites and the Mexicans, and to my people as well. I saw towns and villages laid to waste, filled with the dead who are not dead. I saw the fire that burned in the devil-man's eyes glowing in the eyes of all those he tainted—including my own kin. The vision frightened me beyond any fear I have ever known. I looked back to the moon for guidance, but it was no longer there. In its place was a man whose face was whiter than a cloud, and whose eyes blazed red, but not with the same fire that burns within the devil-man. That face was yours."

"The devil-man you saw in your vision—he is real. His name is Sangre." He put his hand to his throat, a baffled look on his face. "But if I am, indeed, dead—how is it I still have my wits about me? I've seen what happens to those he bites. They're little more than animals, driven by the need for blood. "

"The charm you wear protects you," Pretty Woman said, pointing at the medallion still looped about his neck. "I do not know the medicine that worked it, but it is very old and very strong."

He looked down at the pendant hanging against his chest, taking the stone in the palm of his hand. His flesh tingled and burned for a few seconds, as if reacting to the silver, before the pain was replaced by a familiar numbness. Where the stone had previously appeared red laced with skeins of black, now it resembled a glass filled with red and black ink that had swirled together, yet never mingled.

"All I know about this necklace is that Sangre had it on him when he was found, and he didn't come back to life until it was removed. And I know that he, and the others like him, are scared of it."

"Ah!" Pretty Woman said, nodding her head as if it all suddenly made sense. "It is a containment charm. Its medicine holds and binds evil spirits that dwell within the flesh of the walking dead. It has placed the demon inside you under a spell, so it can not control your flesh."

"What would happen if I took it off?"

"The evil spirits would be free to do as they like."

"I have to go back to the place where this all began. It's my job to ride the range and deal with those situations the local law can't handle. I've got to go back and see to it that Sangre doesn't do to the rest of Texas what he did to Golgotha. That son of a bitch started shit on my watch, in my territory—I'll be damned if I ain't the one who's gonna stop it."

"Do you think that's wise? You don't even know if you have the power to stop this Sangre."

"I've always done my duty by going where I was needed, no matter what the circumstances, whether it was riding down rustlers, hunting banditos or fighting redskins—no offense, ma'am. I don't see why I should stop now."

"I know the place of which you speak. It is a half-day's ride from here— if we had horses. Besides, you can not travel during the daylight hours."

"Who said anything about *we*? I'm the one who has to go, not you. Besides, it will be far more dangerous after dark for you than it will be for me."

"I have ways of protecting myself against such creatures," Pretty Woman replied. "Besides, this is part of my quest. I not only saw you in my vision, but the one you call Sangre as well. That means our destinies are inter-twined."

He dropped his shoulders in resignation. He could tell there was no talking her out of it. And, truth to tell, part of him did not want to strike out alone.

They walked for the rest of that night, before holing up in an outcropping of rock that provided enough shade to wait out the daylight. Upon the setting of the sun, they resumed their march. It was close to midnight by the time they reached the outskirts of the town.

Sam frowned and paused, tilting his head. "He's gone," he said flatly.

"How do you know?"

"I'm not sure. It's like the hairs going up on the back of your neck when you know you're close to something dangerous. You just feel it—or, in this case, I *don't* feel him."

It had been just over three days since Yoakum had last been in Golgotha, but the town was almost unrecognizable. Save for the church and the general store, every building had been burned to the ground. Among the still-smoldering timbers were a number of bodies covered in soot and ash, their limbs contorted and scorched.

"What happened here?" Pretty Woman asked in a hushed voice as they surveyed the carnage.

"I'm not sure," Yoakum replied. He scanned what was left of the town, trying to apply his lawman's knowledge to an outlaw beyond human experience. "Lord knows I've seen more than my fair share of massacres, but nothing like this! Whatever happened, it looks as if they did this to themselves. It's as if they were winnowing themselves out.

"And if Sangre isn't here—where is he? I know for a fact that there wasn't a living pack animal for twenty miles in any direction. If he did leave on foot, how could he do so without the risk of exposing himself to sunlight?"

He fell silent as his gaze fell on the town cemetery, located behind the church. Cursing under his breath, he motioned for Pretty Woman to follow him. As they drew closer, Sam could see that a number of the graves had been desecrated, the bodies pulled from their final resting places and tossed about like so many macabre dolls.

"There are thirteen open graves and thirteen missing caskets," the Ranger said. "That means, of the forty-plus souls that lived in Golgotha, only twelve are left, plus Sangre. Judging by these tracks, they all left on foot, taking their coffins with them. That way they can travel by night and are guaranteed a place to hide from the sun during the day. These drag marks show them heading in every direction of the compass. And there's no way for me to know which track belongs to Sangre."

As he stared out into the vast emptiness of the Texas wilderness, a sense of hopelessness rose within him. During his life he had never known such feelings, even after his father died. He had been faced with ruthless enemies and impossible odds before, but back then he had been part of a larger organization. If he could not handle a situation on his own, he knew there were other Rangers he could call on to back him up. But that was all gone now, sucked into the same void that had claimed his life.

"Merciful God, it's like a ship running aground and all the rats in the hold swarm out of the ship before anyone realizes that everyone on board is dead of the plague. How can I possibly stop this from spreading across the country? I'm just one man."

There was a touch on his shoulder as light as a butterfly's. He turned to find Pretty Woman standing beside him. As she brushed back the hair from her face, he realized for the first time how true her name was.

"You are wrong about two things, Sam. You are no longer a man. And you are not alone."

<hr />

The sun was down. Yoakum knew this because he was able to move once more. Over the last eight years, he had developed a means of surviving as a creature of the night in a land of relentless sunshine.

Every morning, just before the dawn, he would crawl into the custom-made shroud of canvas, secured on the inside by leather laces set in metal gussets. Then Pretty Woman would sling the shroud—with him inside—over the back of his horse, so that they could continue to travel. Upon growing tired, she would find an appropriate spot to make camp. Once dusk had settled, he would awake and once more resume his semblance of life.

One of the first things Yoakum had learned upon becoming one of the undead was that despite his superhuman strength and relative immunity to physical harm, it was difficult for a vampire to survive in the world of the living without the help of humans. He knew for a fact that he would never have survived to see his first night as a vampire, much less his first year, if not for Pretty Woman's intervention. After all, it was she who guarded his shroud while he slept. She was the one who handled buying feed for their horses, dealing with tradesmen and other such mundane business situations that required someone able to travel about in the daylight.

Indeed, three of the original twelve Golgotha vampires had perished within their first week. The first had made the mistake of attempting to ford a river, unaware that running water renders the undead immobile. The current quickly separated the vampire from the coffin he was carrying, sending both spinning downriver, where the casket was dashed to bits on the rocks while the creature was snared by the branches of a partially submerged tree. The vampire remained trapped, helpless to free himself, until the sun rose. Sam and Pretty Woman found what was left of him the next evening, still entangled in the deadfall's scorched embrace.

The second vampire had managed to find a small cave in the foothills, where he hid in his coffin during the day. However, while he was asleep, a pack of coyotes that usually made the cave their home dragged his carcass out of the casket and devoured it. Hell found a pup busily gnawing away at the creature's skull as if it were a ball.

The third vampire had more sense when it came to finding a place to hide her casket, choosing the hayloft in an old barn. However, her fatal mistake was that she lost track of time while out hunting. As the sun began to rise, her long, unbound hair caught fire. As she fled back to the safety of her coffin, her hair trailing behind her like a blazing bridal veil, she ignited the surrounding bales of hay, burning the entire structure to the ground, herself along with it.

However, the rest of undead spawned of the Golgotha massacre proved themselves far better at survival than those three. Over the last seven years, with Pretty Woman's help, of course, he had succeeded in tracking down and exterminating the remaining nine, as well as their own unholy spawn.

While Yoakum had put his skills as a tracker to good use in hunting each of them down, what he relied on the most was a kind of sixth sense he acquired after being bitten. Whenever there was anything supernatural within a certain radius, he could feel it drawing him forward, like a magnet attracts a piece of iron. The closer he was to something of the supernatural world, the more intense the pull became. In the years he had spent hunting monsters, it had yet to let him down.

And now, he was feeling the persistent tug of the paranormal yet again. It was as if he were an angler, and something gently nibbled on his line.

"There's something out there," he said. "I can feel it."

Pretty grunted and tossed what was left of the coffee onto the campfire. "Can you tell what it is?"

"Not yet," he said with a shake of his head. "Might be a ghost. Could be something more tangible. Hard to tell. I need to get closer before I can draw a bead on it."

"What direction?"

"Thataway," he said, pointing west.

<hr>

The McKinney's ranch and the gently rolling rangelands of the Lower Rio Grande Valley had long since given way to the less forgiving landscape of western Texas. Upon crossing the Pecos River, the flatlands were replaced by the mountains that marked the boundary between the Great Plains and the

Cordillera. They were now in the high desert, where the lowlands and highlands were equally bare of trees, and where only the highest mountain peaks supported stunted forest growth.

They had been following the pull for the better part of a week when they finally made the crest of a rise, and Hell found himself looking down at surprisingly familiar surroundings.

"I know this place. At least I used to, back during my Ranger days," he said as he stared down at a large, two-story house surrounded by several smaller outbuildings. "It's called Tucker's Station. It's a trading post that doubles as a way station for the San Antonio–San Diego stage route. Fella name of Jimbo Tucker runs this place, along with his wife, Dottie. Decent folks, if memory serves."

"Do they know you?"

"I only met them once or twice, and that was before the war. Odds are they wouldn't recognize me. Besides, there's always the chance they've moved on and someone else is running things now."

"Do you want to risk it?"

"We'll have to. Whatever I've got a line on has been here recently. I can feel it."

As they approached the trading post, Hell pulled the reins in on his horse, bringing it to a sudden halt.

"You hear that?" he whispered.

"I don't hear anything."

"That's just it. It's too quiet. The Tuckers had themselves a big ol' coonhound that would howl like the dickens the moment anyone rode in. And even at this time of night, we should be able to hear the livestock making some kind of noise. I've only been one other place that was as quiet as this place is right now—Golgotha."

Hell dismounted, signaling for Pretty Woman to do the same. They approached the main building from opposing sides, moving fast and low, weapons drawn. Pretty Woman circled around back while Hell approached the front.

No lamplight came from any of the windows facing the dooryard. None of the curtains so much as twitched. As Hell approached the front door, he caught a stench so foul it made him stagger.

"Hold it right there!" a voice called out from the deep shadow cast by the wooden overhang suspended above the door. "One step closer and I'll blow you to Kingdom Come!"

"I mean no harm, friend," Hell replied, holstering his gun.

The owner of the voice stepped forward, revealing himself to be a man in his late fifties, with unkempt gray hair and whiskers. The old-timer had the wiry build and sunburned skin of a veteran fence-rider, dressed in a denim work shirt and well-worn dungarees. He was also armed with a shotgun, which was pointed level with Sam's chest. As the older man moved closer, favoring his left leg, the stink moved along with him.

"Who are you, stranger?"

"The name's Hell. Sam Hell," he said, coughing into a clenched fist. "What is that stink?"

The muzzle of the shotgun wavered slightly. "That's me," the old-timer said, gesturing to his pants, which were soaked from the knees down. "Now what do you want, mister?"

"I want you to put down your shotgun."

"I'm afraid that just ain't gonna happen."

"Want to put money on that, old man?" Pretty Woman asked as she reached around the old-timer's shoulder and placed the blade of her knife against his grizzled throat.

"Let's not do anything rash," the old man said, dropping the shotgun and putting his hands on the top of his head.

"You have nothing to fear from us. As I said, my name is Sam Hell, and this is my traveling companion, Pretty Woman."

The old-timer raised an eyebrow and let out with a low whistle. "My my! Ain't you as fine as cream gravy, even if you is a squaw."

"I could have slit your throat from ear to ear, old man," Pretty Woman growled in reply as she returned her knife to its sheath. "Don't make me regret that."

"A feisty one, eh?" the old-timer said with a grin, displaying missing teeth.

Pretty Woman rolled her eyes and did her best to ignore him. "I checked the back way. No sign of life. Even the pigs in the sty are gone."

Hell fixed the old man with a hard stare. "Okay, mister—?"

"Johnson. But most folks call me Cuss."

"All right, Cuss—where is everybody?"

"They're gone. Carried off by fiends."

"Come again?"

"You wouldn't believe my story, even if I told you."

"You'd be surprised by what I'll believe," Hell replied, pulling a handkerchief from his back pocket and placing it over his nose. "But would it be too much of a bother for you to change out of those clothes before you start telling it?"

In deference to Sam and Pretty Woman's olfactory senses, Cuss lead them to his living quarters, a small shed near the livery stable that served as his living quarters. The interior was spartan, but surprisingly tidy, with the only furniture being a rope bed fitted with a horsehair mattress, a chair and small washstand with an accompanying basin.

"Normally, I'm a modest man," the ranch hand said as he reached under his bed and dragged out a pasteboard suitcase. "I don't change my drawers in front of them who ain't kin, or at least I haven't rode with. But modesty be damned! I can't stand myself any longer!"

Cuss removed a folded pair of dungarees from the suitcase and snapped them open with a practiced flick of his wrists. He kicked off his boots and unbuttoned the fly of his soiled jeans, peeled them off and tossed them into the corner of the room. Dressed in nothing but his union suit, he sat down in the solitary chair and began to pull on his clean pants.

"Aren't you gonna change your long johns, too?" Hell asked.

"Ain't got but the pair," Cuss grunted as he threaded a belt through the loops of his pants. "Besides, they been through worse without needin' a wash."

"Maybe you could borrow a pair from the Tucker's inventory? I'm sure they wouldn't mind."

"I already checked the trading post," Cuss sighed, picking up one of his boots, wiping at the muck with an old rag. "Them thievin' marauders took everything that weren't nailed down. Pots, pans, blankets, bolts of trade cloth... you name it, they hauled it off."

"You want to tell us what happened?" Hell asked, folding his arms across his chest.

The ranch hand stared at the boot he held in his hands for a long moment, then carefully set it aside and picked up its mate and began cleaning it as well. "I been workin' for the Tuckers for the last five years. Ever since I got throwed by that bronco over at the Lazy J. It busted up my leg something awful. Doc said I was lucky they didn't take it off at the knee. It's good for walkin' and such, but it keeps me from ridin' herd. Jimbo, he took me on after that. Mostly I see to the horses, while Jimbo and Dottie tend to the folks that come through.

"The pay ain't much, but I got a clean, dry place to bunk, and I'm allowed to take my meals in the house. For an ornery ol' hoot-owl like myself, I have to say it's a sweet deal.

"We don't get much in the way of trouble out here. The stage comes and goes twice a week, and that's about it in terms of excitement. The Tuckers have made a point of bein' fair in their dealings, and it helped keep them in good stead with the Injuns and Meskins hereabouts. The worst we've ever had to worry about was a horse thief or two. But that was before today.

"I knowed there wasn't something right with them folks the moment I clapped eyes on 'em. There was ten of 'em: eight men and two women. They was drivin' three covered wagons. Claimed they was homesteaders headed out west. They said they'd been on the road for the better part of a month and were low on necessities and were hankering to spend a night under a solid roof.

"But they didn't seem like homesteaders to me. For one thing, the men seemed a touch hard for farmers, if you get my drift. The womenfolk didn't strike me as proper ladies, neither. And there weren't a young'un to be seen, which struck me as funny. Not funny ha-ha, but funny strange. Besides, I don't trust folks that smile when they ain't got no damn reason to, and these folks were showin' way too much teeth for my liking.

"I ain't the most sociable of fellers, but Jimbo, he's a natural-born host. Always happy to see folks, eager listen to their stories and do whatever it takes to sell 'em whatever they need before sendin' them on their way. Jimbo told me to go make sure their horses were properly stabled.

"So I go to unhitch their horses and put them up in the barn, so they can get watered and fed, and one of 'em comes runnin' up and says he'll tend to it himself. It weren't no skin off my nose, but it struck me as peculiar. I couldn't help but feel like maybe there was something in them wagons they didn't want me to see about. But all I saw in the first wagon was a long wooden box.

"I told Jimbo I thought maybe the newcomers might be gunrunners looking to deal with the Apache, but he said I was too suspicious for my own good. Suspicious, hell!" Cuss said with a bitter laugh as he spat on the boot he was cleaning. "I'm just cautious is all. Anyways, just before dusk, the El Paso stage pulls up, more or less on time. Besides the driver, Clem Jones,

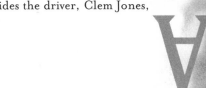

and his assistant Elmer, there was an older married couple name of Crocker and some flannel-mouthed salesman out of St. Louis, which meant that the station would be packed to the rafters come suppertime.

"Like I said, normally I take my meals at the Tucker's table, but the idea of breaking bread with those homesteaders didn't sit right with me. So when Jimbo told me that there weren't no room for me, I weren't sore about it. Dottie fixed me up a plate of fried chicken and cat-head biscuits, smothered in white-eye gravy, and had her youngest, Loretta, run it out to me, along with a jar of sassafras tea.

"After I was finished with my feed, I fetched my pipe and tobacco so's to have my evening smoke before turnin' in. The sun had only been down about five minutes when I heard screams. I look out my door and see lit'l Loretta run out of the house, two of the homesteaders hot on her heels. Seeing how she's a wee thing, and they was big, strong men, it didn't take much for them to tackle her and drag her back indoors. I grabbed my shot-gun, snuck up and looked in the window to see what was going on.

"Them phony homesteaders had Jimbo and the others lying on the floor, trussed up like turkeys ready for a shoot. In walked this tall drink of water I ain't seen before. He was dressed in a fancy embroidered silk vest with smoked glass cheaters, like a high-card gambler. By the way the others kowtowed to him, I could see he was the boss of the outfit.

"At first I figgered he must have just rode in from wherever it was he'd been hiding during the day, but there weren't a spot of dust on him. I wondered where this feller had been keeping himself, if he'd been here all along without me seein' him. Then he smiled, and I seen his teeth, and I remembered the wooden box in the back of the wagon.

"I ain't an educated man, but I ain't no fool. I don't normally hold with superstition. But I been around the barn more than once, and I seen things in my day there weren't no way of explainin'. And what I saw through that window was the Devil made flesh, and there's no way anyone can tell me different.

"The boss-devil, he snatched up Jimbo off the floor and tossed him onto the table like he was a Sunday ham. He buried his fangs into Jimbo's throat and drank his blood like a hound lapping up buttermilk. When I saw that, I couldn't help but call out to Jesus. The boss-devil, he yanked his head up and stared right at where I was hiding and pointed a finger in my direction. The nails on his hands were as long and yellow as the claws on a buzzard.

"I knew there was no way I could outrun 'em with my bum leg, even with a head start. I had to hide, and hide quick. The closest place at hand was the outhouse. I pulled the door shut just as the boss-devil's posse poured out of the house, runnin' here and there, checkin' the barn, sheds and other buildings. I could tell they weren't gone stop lookin' until they found me.

"What I did next was the only thing I *could* do if I wanted to live—I lifted up the privy box and crawled down the hole. Lucky for me, it was a relatively new crapper—Jimbo and me had dug it just a couple months before—so I was only standing in muck up to my knees, not my chin. As bad as I smell now, it ain't nothin' compared to the stench down there!

"I'd just pulled the box back into place, when I heard the outhouse door open. I dropped back into the pit, fearful they might have seen me. The smell in the pit was enough to gag a maggot. I had to put a hand over my mouth to keep from retching, for fear the noise would give me away. And if that weren't insult enough to my pride, he dropped his pants and relieved himself right on top of me! I still had my shotgun, and believe you me, I was sorely tempted to haul off and blow that bastard's bowels out the top of his skull!

"Although I couldn't see a damn thing, I could hear them laughing and shouting as they rustled the livestock and loaded up their wagons. I made out Loretta and Dottie's voices amid the ruckus. Dottie was calling out to Jesus for help, while Loretta was crying for her daddy. Listening to that little girl wailing her heart out nearly made my own break in two. I wanted to go and save them, but I was so damned scared, all I could do was stand there up to my knees in shit."

"There's nothing you could have done that would have helped the Tuckers," Hell said.

"I might be a graybeard now, but there was a day when I could look a curly wolf in the eye and make him blink. Hell, a man don't get to be my age in this part of the country and not know how to take care of himself. It's a sad state of affairs when a man like myself hides in a shit-hole. I tell you what, though—it was a far sight easier to crawl down than it was to crawl up. I hadn't been free but a few minutes when I saw you sneakin' through the dooryard."

"How long do you reckon it's been since they lit out?"

"Judging from where the moon is now, I'd say it's been at least two hours."

"I saw wagon tracks leading west, Sam," Pretty Woman said, confirming what Cuss has told them. "Judging from their depth, they're heavily loaded, and they're running a string of at least ten horses, besides the ones hitched to the wagons."

"Good—then there's a chance we might be able to catch him before day-light breaks. Thank you for your help, Mr. Johnson," Hell said, touching the brim of his hat. "C'mon, Pretty—time to ride!"

"Now hold it there, you two!" Cuss snarled, hurling the boot he'd been cleaning to the floor. "What about me?"

"You should be safe. Sangre and his men won't come back."

"Fuck Sangre and the horse he rode in on! You ain't leavin' me behind like some useless piece of ol' junk! I'm goin' with you!"

"Too dangerous."

"Dangerous? What part of my life's been safe, son? I figure I'll be end-ing up in the bone orchard a lot sooner than later, no matter what happens. But how is that any different from what becomes of any man born of woman? It's what you do between comin' into this life and goin' out that marks you as a man. The Tuckers took me in when I was lower than a snake's dick. They're the closet thing I've ever come to havin' a family. And a man don't stand by and do squat when his family's in trouble.

"I figger Jimbo for a goner, but I got to trust in the Lord that it's not too late for Dottie, Loretta and the other two kids. This is my chance to do right by them."

"I can appreciate how you feel about this. But I said no, and I meant it!" Hell said sternly. "Sangre on his own is deadly enough, not to mention the gang of hardened killers he's got doing his dirty work for him. I don't need to have a crippled up civilian in the way when things get hairy, even if he does have his heart in the right place. Now, if you don't mind, Mr. Johnson, Pretty and I have some riding to do if we're going to catch up with them before its too late." With that Hell and his companion turned back in the direction of their horses.

Cuss jumped out of his chair and limped to the door of the shack, grasp-ing the frame with both hands in order to steady himself. "I know where they're going!" he shouted after the retreating figures. "I overheard a couple of them jawin' while I was hiding in the biffy!"

Hell turned and glowered at the ranch hand. "Where are they headed?"

"No, sir!" Cuss said with a vigorous shake of his head. "I ain't gonna tell you nothin' unless you agree to take me with you!"

"I could *make* you tell me, old man."

"I don't doubt that. But something tells me you ain't that kind of man, partner."

"There are only two horses."

" I figger I can ride double with one of y'all."

Hell heaved a sigh and cast his eyes in Pretty Woman's direction. "Your medicine got anything to say about this?"

Pretty reached into one of the pouches tied to her belt and withdrew a handful of small, polished bones and tossed them onto the ground. She squatted on her haunches and squinted at the pattern they made in the dirt at her feet. She quickly snatched the bones back up, returning them to their pouch.

"Bring him," she said, with a weary sigh. "But if you think I am going to allow that stinking old coot to ride double with me, you got another think coming."

>◆<

"When are you going to tell me where Sangre's gang is headed?" Hell asked over his shoulder.

"When we're far enough away that I know you can't just ditch me and ride on ahead," Cuss replied. "What about you? What's this Sangre feller to you?"

"Let's just say he and I have some unfinished business and leave it at that."

"You been huntin' this Sangre varmint long?"

"More years than I'd care to remember. This is the closest we've gotten to him since we started. This is big country, and it's real easy to lose yourself in it, even for someone like Sangre. Especially if you don't want to be found."

"This 'unfinished business'—does it have something to do with you be-ing dead?"

"Beg pardon?" Hell said, turning around in his saddle to scowl at his passenger.

"I might not be book-learned, but I ain't dumb. You've got the same pale cast to your skin as that devil in the fancy vest. And then there's the fact

your eyes tend to shine like a coyote's around a campfire, not to mention that I've been riding nuts to butt with you for the better part of an hour and I've yet to feel a heartbeat. Your skin is as cold as a rattler in January, by the way."

"You ain't scared?" Hell asked, surprised by the old-timer's nonchalance.

"Son, I'm so scared I could shit peach pits! But I ain't scared of *you*. I like to think I can get a bead on a feller pretty good. Something tells me that no matter what, at your deep-down core you're someone who can be counted on to do what's right. That's mighty hard to find in folks that are still alive, much less dead. Uh—you don't drink human blood, do you? Just askin', mind ya."

"Nope. Mostly I feed on rabbits and the like. It works out fairly well—I drain 'em, and Pretty eats 'em. Now, are you going to tell me where they are or not?"

"They're headed for Diablo Wells."

"Doesn't ring a bell."

"No reason why it should. It ain't a real settlement. Not anymore, anyways. It's located just east of the Salt Flats on the Diablo Plateau. It started out as a Spanish village, a long time ago. It even has a church—or what used to be one. Then there was a smallpox outbreak about thirty years ago. Those that didn't die packed up and left everything behind. The whole place ain't nothing but ruins, and it's got a reputation for being haunted. The wells are still there, though. The only visitors it gets anymore are occasional cowpokes lookin' to water their herds and outlaws aimin' to avoid the law."

"Sounds like the ideal place for Sangre and his gang to hole up."

They rode on in relative silence, following the wagon tracks through the hard, dry soil of the Trans-Pecos Basin, until Hell's attention was attracted by something glittering on the ground. He reined his mount to a halt, signaling for Pretty Woman to follow suit.

"Huh—? What?" Cuss snorted, startled from a light doze. "What's wrong?"

"It's getting closer to dawn. They're lightening their load." Hell said, swinging down from his saddle in order to pick up a discarded copper pan. He walked a few more steps, kicking aside the collection of cookware littering the ground. "Seems they tossed whatever was handy out the back of the wagons."

"What's that?" Cuss asked, pointing at what looked to be a couple sacks of grain lying beneath a stunted yucca alongside the trail.

Pretty Woman trotted her pony forward to investigate. As Hell moved to join her, she gave her partner a short, sad shake of her head.

Although the body was sprawled belly-down on the desert floor, they could still see its face. Something had turned the dead man's head completely around on his neck just as easy as winding a watch stem.

"What in blue blazes is going on?" Cuss dismounted and was leading the horse over to where they stood over the body. "What's so special about a few bags of oats tossed off the back of a—"

His voice trailed off as he stared at the corpse. Cuss wiped his mouth with a clenched fist. "That's Jimbo," he said, his voice tight as a drumhead.

"I'm sorry, Cuss," Hell said, squeezing the old man's shoulder.

Cuss took a deep breath and turned his gaze skyward, as if searching it for respite from pain. "Why would someone do that? Ain't it enough they kilt him?"

"It prevents the victims of vampires from coming back as one of the undead," Hell explained. "It keeps down on the competition."

"We've got to bury him."

"That'll take too long."

"I don't care. I ain't gonna let the buzzards and coyotes scatter his bones from here to San Antonio. I owe this man that much."

"I find your loyalty admirable. But he's beyond caring now, Cuss."

"Yes, but I ain't."

Hell sighed and dropped his shoulders. "There's no time to dig a grave. You'll have to be satisfied with piling rocks on top of him."

"Thank you, Mister Hell."

"Call me Sam."

"Very well. Thank you, Sam."

Pretty Woman folded her arms and favored her partner with a half-smile. "For someone without a heart beat, you sure are a soft touch."

"Bite your tongue. Come on, let's lend a hand. The sooner we get finished, the sooner we can leave."

After twenty minutes, the three had succeeded in building a cairn over the body of the late Jimbo Tucker. As Cuss placed the last rock atop the pile, he dusted his hands on his thighs and turned to face the others.

"I guess this is as good a time as any to confess that I haven't been honest with y'all."

"How so?" Hell asked, raising an eyebrow.

"What I said about Jimbo helpin' me when I was down and out was true enough. But I lied to you about how I got my leg busted up. I weren't a hand on the Lazy J. I was a gunrunner. I sold mostly to the Apache, or anyone else who could meet my price. Then, three yeas ago, I made the mistake of taking on a real hard case for a partner. He decided he could make out a hell of lot better without having to split his share of the profits with me. So he snuck up on me while I was sleeping one night and broke my leg with an axe handle, then left me out in the desert to die. It was Jimbo Tucker who found me, more dead than alive, and brought me home.

"He and his wife nursed me back to health, even after I told them the truth about myself. I was a sinner, yet they forgave me my trespasses and offered me a chance to live an honest life. I didn't have no family to speak of as a young'un, so I pretty much made my own way since I was a boy. The world ain't shown me much kindness over the years. But the Tuckers..." Cuss stopped and cleared his throat. "The Tuckers did good by me. And I figure to do good by them. I'm gonna do my damnedest to see to it that Dottie, Katie, young Jimmy and Loretta make it out of this alive, even if it means I gotta die tryin'."

<hr>

All that was left of Diablo Wells was a collection of single-story adobes gathered at the foot of a small hill, on top of which sat a church, whose badly cracked whitewashed stucco facade revealed the red mud bricks underneath. The wells that gave the village its name and reason for existence were still in evidence, located in the center of what had once been the town square.

At the edge of the ghost town were two corrals constructed of the same red mud bricks as the rest of the village. One contained the horses stolen from Tucker's Station. The other housed the passengers from the stage and what remained of the Tucker family.

From his vantage behind an outcropping of rock and cactus, Hell could see that the women were doing their best to console the frightened youngsters, who ranged in age from seven to fifteen years of age. While the women and children were free to move about, the men had their hands tied behind their backs and ropes looped about their necks, like a string of prize bulls

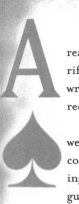

ready for market. One of Sangre's followers sat on the corral wall, a cocked rifle in his hands, watching the prisoners with the detached air of a bored wrangler. Every so often, he would cast a look over his shoulder in the direction of his fellow bandits, who were whooping it up back in the village.

The two female thieves, one a strawberry blonde, the other a brunette, were outfitted in new dresses taken from the trading post, while their male counterparts eagerly downed bottles of trade whisky. The brunette was dancing with one of the men in the group, while one of their comrades played a guitar. As Hell watched, the strawberry blonde hiked her skirts up over her hips and took one of her partners in crime, a large man with a scarred face, between her legs. The others clapped their hands and whistled loudly, urging on their companion's rut with rude comments and raucous laughter.

There was an abrupt hush as the bandits halted their revelry in mid-debauchery. Hell looked in the direction their heads were turned and saw Sangre standing framed in the doorway of one of the adobes.

The vampire snapped his fingers and pointed to the corrals. The scar-faced man fucking the strawberry blonde nodded and stood up, leaving the others to resume their carousing. His place atop the woman was quickly taken by one of his fellows, who resumed where he had left off.

Sangre strode purposefully toward the pen where the humans were being held, his hands clasped in the small of his back. Upon reaching the corral, the scar-faced man retrieved a four-foot-long catchpole. After properly adjusting the noose of rope at the pole's far end, he stood by and waited for his master to make his pick.

Sangre methodically stroked his chin as he studied the assembled prisoners before pointing to the little girl. The scar-faced man nodded and hopped over the wall as if he were setting out to rope a calf for branding.

"No!" Dottie Tucker screamed at the approaching outlaw. "Don't you dare touch her!"

Dottie grabbed Loretta, trying to put herself between her daughter and the monster who had killed her husband of sixteen years. But Loretta was so frightened she wriggled free of her mother's grip and dashed across the corral. Even though she was small and fast, she never stood a chance. The scar-faced man was on her like duck on a June bug.

"Mamaaa!" Loretta screamed as the catchpole's noose dropped about her neck. Her screams for help were choked off as the scar-faced wrangler pulled on the slack end of the rope. Her legs folded under her as her fingers clawed at the rope cinched tight about her throat.

"Let her go, you son of a bitch!" Cuss bellowed as he broke cover, standing up to fire upon the scar-faced bandit, catching him between the eyes.

"Goddamn it, Cuss! I told you to hold your fire until I gave the signal!" Hell shouted in exasperation. Now that their cover was blown, he had no choice but to follow the old gunrunner's lead. What he had intended no longer mattered. They were committed to action now, and extreme action at that.

Hell, Cuss and Pretty Woman charged the corral. Pretty Woman put a bullet into the armed guard, knocking him off the wall. Cuss fired at the vampire, striking him in the chest, but Sangre didn't so much as blink. Sangre bared his fangs and moved forward, sneering his disdain for his attackers.

"Don't waste your ammo on him!" Hell yelled. "Let me handle Sangre." He fired his pistol, catching the vampire in the right shoulder. Where the previous bullet seemed to have no effect, this time Sangre shrieked like a cat and clutched his left arm. There was anger in the vampire's scarlet eyes, but also fear. Never before had he been wounded by a conventional weapon.

Hell raised his pistol higher for a headshot but was distracted by the volley of gunfire from the direction of the village. Sangre's followers had tossed aside their liquor in favor of their guns and were rushing to their master's aid.

Pretty Woman threw open the gate to the horse pen and fired her pistol over her head. The frightened animals bolted forth, charging right for the onrushing bandits. The strawberry blonde screamed as she disappeared under the hooves of the stampeding livestock.

Upon seeing the chaos before him, Sangre tossed back his head and gave voice to a cry so high-pitched it was more felt than heard.

"What in the hell is he doing?" The stage driver asked as Hell freed his hands.

"Calling for reinforcements," Hell replied, as pale, gaunt-faced figures emerged from the shadows of the ruined buildings, their eyes gleaming in the dark. "We have to get to the church—*fast!*"

Sangre's unholy offspring were an odd mix of gamblers, Indian braves, dancehall girls, cowboys, sodbusters, horse thieves, outlaws and school marms, most of whom were still dressed in the clothes they had died in. Hell gave up counting their numbers when he reached thirty.

"Get to the church! All of you!" he shouted.

"What about you, Sam?" Cuss asked.

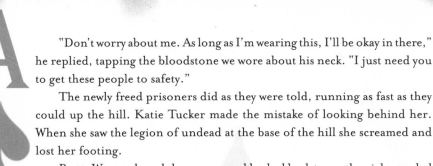

"Don't worry about me. As long as I'm wearing this, I'll be okay in there," he replied, tapping the bloodstone we wore about his neck. "I just need you to get these people to safety."

The newly freed prisoners did as they were told, running as fast as they could up the hill. Katie Tucker made the mistake of looking behind her. When she saw the legion of undead at the base of the hill she screamed and lost her footing.

Pretty Woman heard the scream and looked back to see the girl sprawled on the ground, too paralyzed by fear to move as Sangre's undead spawn swarmed up the hill in their direction. Cursing under her breath, the medicine woman reversed her course.

"Damn it, child! If you want to live, get up!" Pretty Woman barked, grabbing the girl's upper arm.

"I—can't. I'm too scared!" Kate sobbed.

"Don't look at them! Look at *me*!" Pretty Woman shouted, jerking Katie to her feet. "Now run, and don't look back! *Run!*"

Katie lurched up the hillside, alternately sobbing and gasping. Even though her heart was beating so fast it felt like she had a hummingbird stuck between her ribs, she did as the medicine woman told her. She did not look back until she reached the door of the church, where her mother and younger brother were waiting for her. Only then did she turn around, just in time to see Pretty Woman disappear under a mass of pale, dead flesh.

⟹◆⟸

The interior of the church was empty save for some wooden pews, an altar located in the nave and a full-sized wooden cross hanging from the wall above it. The stained glass windows had long since been destroyed by the ravages of time, leaving the floor covered with rainbow-colored shards of glass.

"Is everyone here and accounted for?" Hell asked, a concerned look on his face. "Where's Pretty Woman?"

"I fell down and she came back to get me and—and—" Katie burst into tears, burying her face in her hands. "They were all over her!"

Though the news hit Hell like a kidney punch, he tried his best not to let it show in his outward demeanor. He was surrounded by frightened, confused people way out of their depth, and they were all looking to him to

get them out of the situation they were in. He had to keep a strong facade, or the others would come unraveled like so much bad knitting.

"We've got to barricade ourselves the best we can. I need you, Clem, and you, Elmer," he pointed to the stage driver and his assistant, "to move these pews in front of the doors. And I want you two to try and do the same with the windows," he said, pointing to Mr. Crocker and the salesman.

"Why bother? We're doomed, no matter what!" The salesman spat, kicking at the shards of colored glass that littered the floor. "This being a holy place might keep the hell-beasts at bay, but it won't slow down the others."

"That's no way to be talkin' in front of the women and kids!" Cuss snapped. "Now you do as Sam says, or I'll toss you outside myself! You savvy me, slick?"

The salesman opened his mouth to argue, but there was something in the old-timer's eyes that made him decide better. Grumbling under his breath, he set about his task.

Cuss took Hell's elbow and pulled him away from the others. "Remember I told you I was a gunrunner? That's the reason I know about Diablo Wells in the first place. Last time I was here was just before my lowdown snake of a partner tried to turn my leg into firewood. I had a feeling he was up to something, so I hid a cache of guns here, just in case he tried to run off with the goods."

"Lot of good that does us stuck here, " Hell sighed.

"Son, when I said I hid them *here*, that's exactly what I meant." Cuss grinned, pointing at the altar. "The inside's hollow. Help me move the lid. It comes off, but its damned heavy."

Mrs. Crocker, who had been doing her best to comfort the weeping Katie, frowned her disapproval as the two men laid hands on the altar. "Here now! What are you two doing? That's the Lord's table!"

"And the Lord helps those who help themselves, my good lady," Cuss said, touching the battered brim of his hat before returning to his task.

"I'll get it," Hell said, lifting the heavy oaken altar top as if it were made from balsa wood.

Cuss peered into the interior of the altar and let loose with a whoop. Inside were a box of rifles and two cases of ammunition.

"*Hallelujah!* We might not exactly be shittin' in high cotton, my friend," the former gunrunner said with a grin. "But at least they can't see us from the road!"

As Cuss distributed the guns among the men, Hell climbed onto an upended pew to look out one of the windows, and what he saw was enough to make his heart skip, if it weren't already as cold and unbeating as a stone.

The church was ringed by Sangre's spawn, who kept about six feet of distance as if held back by an invisible barrier. They muttered and moaned among themselves, staring at the church with an awful hunger in their crimson eyes. Sam had first thought Sangre's men had stolen the horses and the rest of the livestock from the trading post for their own uses, but now he realized it was to feed their vampire counterparts.

"*¡Salga de mi manera, los tontos!*"[6]

The pallid hungry faces parted, allowing Sangre to stride forward. His left arm was in a makeshift sling fashioned from a bandana. The vampire was accompanied by two of his human servants, who held between them the limp body of Pretty Woman. Her head had dropped forward, so her hair obscured her face. The toes of her moccasins dragged the ground behind her.

"*Ranger!*" Sangre shouted. "Ranger, do you hear me?"

"Yeah, I hear you!" Hell shouted back.

"As you can see, I have *su puta india*[7]. It was all I could do to keep my followers from eating or raping her—if not both. As for myself—I do not think I will make her one of my brides. She is too headstrong, and willful women never make good wives." Sangre grabbed Pretty Woman's hair, pulling her head back so that her bruised and swollen face could be seen. "However, I do think her skin would make an excellent leather vest—do you not agree?"

"Damn you! What do you want?"

"The same thing you want from me, Ranger—to look you eye-to-eye as I kill you! But I am willing to make you an offer, *mi amigo*. I will spare *la india* if you are willing to come forward, and meet me, *mano a mano*."

"Why should I believe you?"

"What choice do you have? You do as I say, or the squaw dies now." Sangre motioned to one of the bandits, who pulled a machete from his belt and positioned the blade against Pretty Woman's exposed jugular. "Either way, it is your decision."

"Very well! I'm coming out!" Hell replied, jumping down from his perch.

Cuss and the other men were gathered by the front door. "What are you doing, Sam? It's a trap!"

---

[6] "GET OUT OF MY WAY, YOU FOOLS!"
[7] "YOUR INDIAN WHORE."

"I know. But I have no choice. You told me you had to do right by the Tuckers—well, it's the same for Pretty Woman. I've got to try and get her back. Just shut the door as fast as you can and make sure that barricade stays in place. If it's a trap, don't hesitate to open fire. Don't worry about shooting the vampires, just focus on the humans Sangre's got helping him, otherwise you're just wasting ammo. I'm counting on you to hold the fort until dawn. That shouldn't be more than a couple of hours from now. If you can make it to sunrise, then everything else will seem like a cakewalk."

"I got you, Sam. Good luck out there, partner."

"Same here."

The doors to the old church opened just wide enough to allow Hell to step out. The sound of the barricade being quickly put back in place behind him was as final as Judgment Day.

As Hell strode to where Sangre stood waiting for him, the other vampires drew back, quivering like whipped dogs. One of the human bandits stepped forward and aimed his pistol at Hell's head. He froze, shooting an angry look in the direction of the Spaniard.

"I though you said this was to be *mano a mano.*"

"It shall be, *mi amigo,*" Sangre said with a crooked smile. "But first, please be so kind as to hand over your gun belt. I do not know what sorcery you have used to charm the bullets in your gun, and I do not intend to suffer any further such wounding at your hand."

Hell glowered as he unfastened his holsters and gun belt and handed them over to the bandit pointing the gun at his head.

"You have proven yourself a worthy adversary, Ranger," Sangre said with a crooked smile. "Ah! I see you are surprised that I know of you. How could I not, when each time you destroy one of my disciples, I, too, feel the wound, one step removed? As one of the undead, you know that all I create are bound to me by blood.

"I made a gross mistake when I did not hunt you down and destroy you the night you escaped Golgotha. Like the living, the undead are made in their maker's image, yet not all of my spawn are created equal. Most are weak-minded, sheeplike creatures, good for little more than cannon fodder. Feeding may spread the seed of our kind, but such promiscuity dilutes the breed. That's why I reserve the right to feed on humans to myself, and myself alone. The others must make do with horses and other livestock.

"Those humans of strong character and powerful will are rarely good choices for resurrection, because they are the ones who weary of servitude and eventually challenge their maker for control. Those prone to virtue also make very poor undead. Take that dreary little man from the trading post, for example. I drained him as needed, but I denied him rebirth in my image. You combine both qualities, *mi amigo*. And that is dangerous for one such as myself.

"I knew you were too strong-willed, too 'good' to be gifted with eternal life. But I was still giddy with freedom after spending centuries folded in on myself like an empty suit of clothes.

"I came to this accursed new world with Cortes, our hearts burning for gold and glory. But where he was proclaimed a god, I was declared a devil. Not that I did not give them good cause. It was the Indian slaves who first gave me the name 'Sangre.'

"I heard stories of a tribe of wizard-priests dedicated to Xipe Totec, god of the Aztec goldsmiths, said to be guardians of a great treasure. I took my men and went in search of their temple. It took me several weeks, and I lost many of men to fever and jaguars, but in the end I found them. They claimed to be the result of the mating of human women and gods. Perhaps that is true, for they all possessed six fingers and toes. But if they possessed divine blood, it did not save them.

"I roasted each and every one of them alive, turning them on spits above a pit of coals just like suckling pigs, but they refused to tell me where they had hidden their gold. Their high priest cursed me, saying that he would turn the invaders' own sword upon them, then spat in my eye just before he died.

"When I returned to Cortes empty-handed and told him what I had done, he had me clapped in irons. Not long after I was placed in the stockade, I fell ill from a fever and died. But I did not stay dead. Three days after I was buried, I clawed my way free of my grave. It did not take long before Cortes and his followers realized there was a demon in the midst.

"My plan was to remake the entire Aztec Empire in my image and name myself their demon-king. Once I secured my hold on the New World, I would then set my sights on the Old. All this was within my reach, if not for Cortes's concubine, that wretched whore Malinche.

"She was the one who coerced the old Aztec wizard into helping her lover. At first the sorcerer saw no reason to do anything to benefit the invaders. But when she claimed that Huitzilopochtli, the sun god, would punish the Aztec for turning their face from his shining countenance in favor of eternal darkness, he relented and cast the spell that created the bloodstone.

"Malinche knew that since I had lusted after her in life, I would eventually come for her in death. She pretended to lay sleeping as I slipped into her hut. As I leaned forward to take her blood, she sat up and placed the charmed amulet about my neck. I was instantly rendered powerless and fell onto the floor as if dead. Although I was still in possession of all my senses and knew everything that transpired about me, I was unable to move or speak.

"Cortes and the others did not know how to destroy me. After all, how do you kill something that is already dead? So they elected to lock me away and hide me in a place where I would never be found. I was placed in an iron box, the protection of which was assigned to Cortes's most trusted servant, Garcia. He was given a wagon, provisions, horses, a couple of Indian slaves, as well as a saddlebag full of gold, and was told to go as far away as humanly possible and never return.

"And so I spent three hundred years trapped in eternal darkness, unable to move or speak, immobile yet aware. I felt my skin wither and the flesh rot from my bones as I was tormented by a dreadful thirst that burned in my belly like the coals over which I had roasted that accursed six-fingered priest! I would have probably stayed buried down there until the sun dwindled to a cinder, if not for those fools searching for water.

"I am far older and wiser now. I shall have my empire, but I know now to take my time building it. The mistake I made before was thinking in terms of human spans of time. Because of that, I exposed myself to the human cattle on which I preyed and gave sworn enemies a chance to unify against a greater threat. What are years, even decades, to one who measures his existence in centuries?"

Hell spat into the dirt at his feet in disgust. "So, are we gonna get on with this, or are you gonna keep jawing?"

"I had hoped you, of all my spawn, might be able to appreciate what I had to say. But I see you are as thick-witted as the rest of the natives of this wretched continent! But before we continue, you must rid yourself of that horrid bauble you wear about your neck."

Hell looked over at Pretty Woman. The left side of her face was so swollen it looked as if someone had managed to shove a small rubber ball under her eyelid. She turned her head slightly, so that she could see him with her good eye, and mouthed the word *no*.

Hell's fingers closed about the medallion, pulling it free from around his neck with a single yank, and let it drop to the ground.

Nancy A. Collins
62

As the bloodstone fell from his gasp, he was overcome by a rage so intense and all encompassing it tinged everything red, as if someone had dipped everyone and everything around him in blood.

It was as if he had been standing on the beach and a great wave had suddenly come up from nowhere and crashed down on him, dragging him out to sea. He could not see, hear or breathe, and he could not regain his footing as he fought against the tide. But instead of water, he was surrounded by a fearsome darkness, and the harder he struggled, the more he drowned.

His belly burned as if packed with hot sand, and his tongue felt as if it was made of jerked beef. The agony was so intense he cried out, burying his face in his hands. He knew he would do whatever it might take to quench the thirst raging within him, even if it meant crawling on his belly through barbed wire and broken glass. Suddenly a voice broke through the screeching white noise that filled his head. When it spoke the words were like a cool hand on a feverish brow.

You need not suffer so. All that is needed to end the pain is a little blood. Drink from the woman. Her blood is yours. Take it, my son.

Hell lifted his face from his hands and stared at the woman before him. A part of him found her familiar, but he could not push aside the fire in his gut long enough to think of where he knew her from.

Her blood will be sweeter than any wine. It will slake your thirst and make you strong. Drink deep, my son, and bind yourself to my service for all eternity.

Hell slowly approached the trembling woman. Although she struggled mightily to escape, she was unable to free herself from the two strong men pinning her arms behind her back. Her one good eye was wide with terror, and the fear coursing through her body made her carotid artery pulse even faster. If he concentrated, he could hear her blood rushing through her veins, pumping through her racing heart. It was as if it were calling out to him, begging to be set free.

He leaned forward, brushing his cheek against the side of her head. She involuntarily gasped and held her breath. Her perfume was a heady mixture of fear, sweat and blood. Something buried deep inside Sam Hell stirred, twisting about like a snake trapped in a jar.

"Sam," the woman whispered, a solitary tear trickling from her good eye.

Hell grabbed her hair, jerking back her head so that she could see his face as he grinned, exposing his teeth. He opened his mouth wide, arching his neck like a cobra preparing to spit its venom—and sank his fangs deep into the neck of the man holding Pretty Woman's right arm.

The bandit screamed and let go of his captive in a desperate attempt to pull himself free. With a savage sidewise shaking of his head, Hell tore open the bandit's jugular vein. The blood that spurted into his mouth tasted sweet, quenching the fire in his guts. Part of him wanted to keep drinking until his skin was as full and tight as a tick's, but he forced himself to stop for fear of losing himself in a feeding frenzy. The mortally wounded bandit fell to the ground, one hand clamped over the pumping gash in his throat, blood squirting between his fingers like water from a hose.

The smell of spilled blood was making the assembled vampires increasingly agitated, since they had yet to feed for the night. An undead dancehall girl leapt onto the wounded bandit before he even had a chance to scream, and within seconds he was buried under a writhing carpet of pale, dead flesh. The vampires snarled and snapped at one another like a pack of jackals as they fought to feed.

The bandit holding Pretty Woman's left arm recoiled from the sight of his comrade being ripped to shreds. *"Madre de Dios!"*

The second her remaining captor loosened his grip, Pretty Woman turned on him, slamming the heel of her palm into his nasal bridge while bringing her knee into his groin. He went down hard, cupping his hands over his shattered nose. He had time to scream only once before he, too, was swarmed.

"Run for it, Pretty!" Hell shouted before he disappeared under a sea of grasping hands and flailing limbs. *"Run!"*

The shaman sprinted toward the church with two of Sangre's human followers on her heels. Suddenly there was a hail of gunfire from the church, dropping one of the bandits dead in his tracks and causing the second to dive for cover.

The door to the church opened, and Pretty Woman darted inside. Cuss and Clem continued to lay down fire from the windows while the rest of the men hurriedly replaced the barricade.

Once Pretty Woman was safely inside and the doorway was blocked once again, Cuss handed his rifle over to Elmer and dropped down from his sniper's perch.

"Good to have you back, missy."

"It's good to be back, Cuss. But this is far from over. Sam's still out there, and in greater danger than any of us could possibly imagine. I've got to help him." She went over to where the Tucker children were busily loading the spare rifles with ammunition. "Girl!" she said, pointing at Katie. "You must answer the question I am about to ask truthfully. Have you ever been with a man?"

Katie Tucker's cheeks turned bright pink and she lowered her eyes.

"What kind of question is that for a squaw to ask a god-fearin' white girl?" Mrs. Tucker said indignantly.

"Stay out of this!" Pretty Woman snapped. "It is for the girl to answer!"

"It's okay, mama," Katie said. "I owe her my life. I can answer her question. I've never been with a man. Not the way you mean, anyway."

"Good," Pretty Woman replied, taking the girl's hand and slashing it across the palm with her knife. "Then we stand a chance. But we'll still need a distraction."

<hr/>

"¡*Bastante!*"[8] Sangre shouted, kicking the seething mass of undead flesh before him. "Stop it, you mindless fools! Stop it before I destroy you all!"

The vampires quickly retreated, trembling before their creator's rage like cowed dogs fearful of their master's lash.

"Get him on his feet!" Sangre snarled, pointing to Hell's prone body.

Two vampires grabbed the former Ranger and jerked him upright.

"We undead are a hardy breed," Sangre said, retrieving the knife tucked into his boot. "We break a leg and it knits within hours. Pluck out our eyes, and they grow back in a fortnight. While we cannot regenerate severed limbs, or survive a fire, for all practical purposes we are immortal. That can be both a blessing and a curse.

"I shall have you drawn and quartered, so that you can never again raise a hand to me or run away from me. Then I shall have your eyes gouged out, your ears cut off and your nose sliced off." Sangre mimed the actions with short, sharp jabs of his knife. "I will keep you in your own little box, like I was kept for so long. And whenever your eyes, ears and nose start to grow back, I will have them removed yet again. And again. And again!" Sangre pressed the flat of the blade against Hell's cheek, angling the tip so that it was directly under his right eye. "Perhaps then you will learn your lesson, eh?"

[8] "ENOUGH!"

"Lord Sangre!" one of the bandits blurted. "Something's happening!"

The vampire turned to see the double doors swing wide open. Cuss Johnson come barreling out of the church, bellowing at the top of his lungs, a huge wooden cross clutched in his hands like a battle standard.

Sangre's spawn, made bold by their feeding frenzy, surged forward, shrieking in delight at the prospect of another meal. The first vampire that came within striking distance of the cross burst into flame as if made of dry kindling.

"Come on, you sorry sons of bitches!" Cuss yelled as he swung the cross like a giant baseball bat. "Come and get it!"

The vampires drew back, their hunger overridden by their sense of self-preservation. Since the enemy was refusing to attack, the former gunrunner waded in among them, swatting them like so many flies.

"Hold on, Sam!" he shouted as he set an undead Apache brave ablaze with a backhand swing.

Sangre cursed and motioned for his remaining human servants, who were gawking at the sight before them with open mouths, to close ranks around him. "What are you fools waiting for?" he shouted. "Shoot him!"

The bandits opened fire and Cuss went down in a hail of bullets, the cross falling from his hands before he hit the ground. Hell used the distraction to break free and run to where his friend lay dying on the hard earth and, without a moment's hesitation, snatched up the fallen cross.

Though he was wearing leather gloves, he could feel his hands grow hot the moment he touched the icon. Screaming in anger, grief and pain, he charged toward Sangre, who stood behind his wall of human killers. Hell could feel bullets enter his chest and belly, but they meant nothing to him and hurt even less. Smoke curled from his palms as he brought the cross down onto a bandit's skull, and he put the searing pain from his mind.

As he flailed away, all he could see in his mind's eye was his father, desperately chopping at the rattlesnake that had bitten him before it had a chance to slither away and kill someone else.

The bandits protecting Sangre fell away, their heads crushed and necks fractured, until there was nothing separating him from Sangre. Hell swung the cross high above his head, but as he was about to bring it down with all his might, his leather gloves dissolved in a burst of flame, setting his hands afire. Though he tried to maintain his hold on the cross, the agony was too great. He dropped it to the ground, where it continued to burn.

Gasping in pain, Hell fell to his knees, holding his charred hands before him in a grotesque parody of prayer. The skin was blackened, like that of roasted meat, with deep fissures that exposed the bones underneath.

Sangre stepped forward, clearly amused by the turn of events. "You continue to amaze me, Ranger. You are damned, yet you seek to walk in the light. You battle against your own kind in the name of a deity who has turned his countenance from you. It is utter folly to deny what you are, to fight against the dictates of your nature—and yet you continue to do so, even when you know it is hopeless. You are either a deluded fool or the bravest man to have walked this planet. Either way, you are far too dangerous for me to allow you to continue to exist, even as a pet torso."

Sangre retrieved Hell's gun belt from the fallen bandit who had taken it from him earlier. He removed the revolver from its holster, holding it so that the barrel pointed to the sky like a steel finger.

"If your bullets have enough magic in them to wound the immortal, then they must also be able to kill them."

Sangre pointed the barrel directly at Hell's forehead. Hell wanted to pray, but he knew that the words would burn in his mouth, so he closed his eyes instead.

Sangre paused, a confused look on his face. He tilted his head to one side, then another, sniffing the air as if trying to identify an odor.

"Do you smell that?"

"Smell what, my lord?" replied a vampire with a United States Marshal's star pinned to his vest.

"Brine."

A flash of lightning abruptly tore across the night sky, immediately followed by a crash of thunder. Thinking he'd been shot, Hell opened his eyes and looked around, surprised that his brains were still in his head A strong wind had come from nowhere, kicking up dust devils that danced among the undead assembly, tugging on their clothes and hair like unruly children.

Fat raindrops struck the dusty ground hard enough to be heard. Instinctively, Sangre lifted his head to stare up at the clouds overhead. As a raindrop struck his cheek, the skin began to bubble and sizzle. The Spaniard screamed and clutched his face. His shriek was quickly picked up and echoed by his spawn, who began to claw at their flesh like things possessed.

A raindrop struck the back of Hell's neck, burning the exposed skin as if it were a drop of hydrochloric acid. As he leapt to his feet, yowling in pain, he could see Pretty Woman running toward him, a bundle under one arm. Upon reaching him, she threw a man's jacket over his head.

"Mr. Crocker was nice enough to loan you this. Don't take it off, if you want to keep your skull in one piece," she warned.

"The bloodstone—I can't go back inside the church without it," Hell gasped.

"I already have it." The medicine woman held up the amulet and quickly looped it around his neck. "I snatched it up without any of them noticing when I escaped."

"*Bruja!* You are the one responsible for this!" Sangre shrieked as great beads of liquid fat rolled from his face like tallow from a candle. He raised his good hand to point an accusing finger at Pretty Woman, the flesh dripped off its tip as if he had just dipped it in honey. "This is no natural storm! *¡Mátelos todo!*"[9] Sangre screamed as his face sloughed away, revealing the skull underneath.

If Sangre's army of the night heard him, they gave no sign of it as they darted about frantically, the flesh running from their bones. Those who had lost their eyes to the downpour stumbled into the fellows, causing them to trip and fall into pools of rainwater mixed with viscera.

Elmer and Mr. Crocker stood in the open doorway, watching the destruction of Sangre and his unholy legion with a mixture of disgust and fascination.

"My God," Mr. Crocker said. "It's like when my wife pours salt on the slugs in our garden."

Pretty Woman hurried her charge past the two men and into the safety of the waiting church. As Hell tossed aside the jacket that had protected him from the murderous downpour, the others closed in about him.

"Cuss told us what Sangre did to you," Jimmy Tucker said, fixing Hell with a curious eye. "He said that you were like those things outside, but different. Is that true?"

"Yes, son. It's true," Hell said with a slight smile that showed his teeth.

"Well, I don't care if you *are* one of them things or not, you saved my life, mister—and I want to shake your hand!" The salesman said, thrusting his hand forward. He froze when he saw the blackened ruins jutting out of the end of Hell's shirt cuffs.

"Dear Lord!" Mrs. Crocker gasped.

"Don't worry, ma'am, " Hell said with a weak smile. "I'll be good as new in just a few hours."

[9] "KILL THEM ALL!"

Loretta Tucker jumped up and pointed in the direction of the door. "Mama! Look! It's Cuss!"

Hell turned and saw the old gunrunner standing in the door of the church, rainwater and blood pouring down the front of his clothes. Elmer and Clem ran to help him into the building, where he was laid out in one of the pews, a folded petticoat under his head. Dottie Tucker was seated beside him, holding his hand while the Tucker children stood by and watched.

"Cuss?"

"Hey, Sam," the dying man said with a weak mile. "Glad to see you got back safe."

"Good Lord, Cuss—why did you risk such a damn fool stunt just to save me?"

"Seemed like the thing to do at the time," the old man rasped, attempting a shrug. "But before I go—I just want you to know, Sam, that you're a better man dead than most folks livin'."

"Back at you, partner," Hell said as he closed his friend's eyes.

<hr />

When Hell next awoke, he found himself lying flat on his back, staring up at the underside of a church pew. He crawled out from under his makeshift shelter and stretched his stiff muscles. The interior of the church was deserted save for Pretty Woman, who was seated crossed-legged atop the altar.

"Where is everybody?"

"They returned to Tucker's Station after burying Cuss this morning," Pretty Woman explained. "They took the bandits' wagons and horses. I told Mrs. Tucker where we buried her husband along the trail."

"Good. I'm glad they made it out of this okay. How are you feeling, by the way?"

"Like I was kicked in the head by a buffalo." Pretty Woman unfolded her legs and hopped onto the ground. "So—do you want to see what's left of him?"

"Might as well get it over with," he sighed.

Hell gave out with a low whistle as he surveyed the hillside outside the church. The ground was littered with dozens of skeletons, their bleached white bones gleaming silver in the West Texas moonlight.

"Which one is his?"

"This one," she said, pointing to a skeleton dressed in a fancy embroidered vest with one arm still fixed in a sling and Hell's pistol clutched in its bony hand.

"I'll take that back, if you don't mind," Hell said, retrieving his weapon and gun belt. He stared at Sangre's peeled skull for a moment before bringing his boot heel down, reducing it to powder.

"Mind telling me how you managed to pull off that little rain dance of yours?" he asked, as he fastened his gun belt back on.

"I remembered Cuss saying something about the Salt Flats being to the west of here. All I needed was the blood of a virgin and the right words to appease the spirits. Once that was done, it was relatively easy to create a strong enough wind to mix a cloud of salt dust with a rain cloud."

"You never cease to amaze me, Pretty, even after all these years!" Hell chuckled, shaking his head in admiration.

"Now that you've finally hunted down and killed Sangre, what are you going to do now, Sam?"

"Keep doing what I've been doing, I guess. From what Sangre said, these weren't the only spawn he created since Golgotha. I bet he's done what he did there a hundred times over since then—create an angry mob of undead, then force them to fight it out among themselves until they winnowed themselves down to the meanest of the lot, then sent them out into the world to spread his contagion even further. Sangre may be dead, but the evil he created is still out there. I can feel it." Hell turned to look at Pretty Woman. "But what about you? You said your destiny was tied to those of Sangre and myself. Now that he's gone, you're free to go back to your people."

"Yes, that's true."

"Well, are you? Going to go back, that is?"

"My people have their own path to walk, just as I have mine. For the time being, my path is the same as yours."

"I'm glad to hear that," Hell said with a smile. "Because I've gotten used to having you around." He reached up and touched the bolo cinched just above his breast bone. "After all, you're one of my two lucky charms."

"You don't really need that thing, you know," she said. "When you removed it you were able to reclaim your mind and free yourself from the bloodlust. The reason the bloodstone rendered Sangre powerless was because he was evil even before he was one of the undead. When the evil within him was made dormant, he was unable to so much as move. The fact that you are talking to me now proves that what evil exists inside you is far outweighed by the good."

"I know," Hell nodded. "I guess I always have. Still, I think I'll keep it just the same. Lord knows I can use all the help I can get, even if it is from some Aztec god whose name I can't pronounce."

"Are you afraid of being tempted?"

"Of course I'm afraid. After all, I'm only human. Besides, if I get rid of it, what am I going to use to cinch my string tie? Now, if you don't mind, I've got a twitch in my foot that tells me there's a poltergeist due north of here."

Pretty Woman groaned, rolling her eyes. "Not another one! The last time we broke one of those things, I got a chamber pot, a sauce pan and a spinning wheel hurled at me from across the room!"

"Sorry, it's too late to back out now," Hell said with a crooked grin, exposing his fangs. "The Dark Ranger rides again!"

A
♣

Lynch

CHAPTER ONE

He woke up drunk and reckoned he'd go ahead and stay that way.

It took Johnny Pearl a second to remember where he was. For one brief, sweet moment, he imagined he was dozing on the summer porch, listening to the clatter of buckboards on the cobblestones as they headed for market. But then he opened his eyes and found himself in the shabby backroom of a frontier bar.

Charleston was far away and long ago, replaced by yet another starved-dog town, this one clinging to the edge of the Wyoming territory like a tick. He wasn't sure if it had a name, or even needed one. But at least it had a saloon.

He'd ridden into town two days back, covered in trail dust so thick that from a distance it looked like he was still wearing his old uniform. The first thing he did upon setting foot between the swinging doors of the saloon was call for a bottle of rotgut and a hot bath, which he got toot-sweet.

Pearl wasn't sure if the yokels recognized him. The likeness on the wanted posters wasn't a good one, that much was certain. But they didn't have to know his name to see he was trouble. The way he wore his guns was giveaway enough. And once Pearl knocked off the dust, the color of his clothes left no doubt in even the thickest cowhand's mind that this was a dangerous man.

Johnny Pearl stepped out of the spare room, pausing only long enough to take a deep breath and slick his hair back. The interior of the saloon was close to threadbare, with the bar little more than planks atop sawhorses. A beefy man with a ruddy face sat behind a battered upright piano, diligently hammering away at what might have been "Clementine." Upon catching sight of him, the pianist got to his feet.

"Afternoon, sir. How you feeling today?"

"Like I need a drink."

The piano player nodded his head and hurried behind the bar. Or at least what passed for one in this godforsaken wilderness. At least they had a mirror behind it.

"One whiskey coming right up."

As he turned to pick up the shot glass, Pearl caught sight of himself in the mirror's silvery finish. He was only thirty-one, but you couldn't tell it by looking at him. His dark hair was already graying at the temples, and his eyes resembled coals dropped in a snow bank. The lines about his mouth were hard and sharp, as if they'd been cut into his face with a knife. But then, three years fighting Billy Yank and four years fighting everything else could do that to a man.

Still, thirty-one was a dangerous age for someone like Pearl. The territories were full of half-crazy man-boys with nothing to lose but their lives. When you're seventeen, eighteen years old, you're full of piss and gunpowder, fearless as only those who've never seen death firsthand can be. You're quick to take offense and just as quick to give it.

But once you get into your late twenties—once you've spilled more blood than beer, seen a grown man lie in the mud and wail like a baby while trying to stuff his guts back inside him after he's taken shrapnel, known fear so well you wake up tasting it—that's when things start getting truly dangerous. That's when you're more likely than not to get yourself killed. Not because you're green and shooting before you think, but because you're more apt to think before you shoot.

And, inevitably, with each passing birthday, the reflexes slow a tad more, the joints ache a little sharper. Pearl knew he had a few more years left before rheumatism or the shakes got the better of him, assuming he didn't let his guard down before then. After all, mercy and a conscience have no place in a gunman's heart. Still, traveling alone as he did, he constantly had to

watch his back. Not that he was famous back east like Wild Bill, or Kit Carson or Jesse James, but he had his reputation...

"Johnny Pearl!"

He paused, the shot glass halfway to his mouth and glanced in the mirror at the reflection of the farmhand standing behind him. The yokel stood just behind him and to the left, a few feet in from the swinging batwings. The gun strapped to the farmhand's hip was, like the rest of what he wore, too big for him and looked like a hand-me-down. The boy 's face was sunburned and spotty, with bright yellow hair that stuck out like straw and made him look even more like a scarecrow.

"I'm a-callin' you out!" the yokel said in a loud voice that cracked halfway through his sentence.

Pearl gave a small sigh and turned from the bar to regard the would-be gunslinger. "Kid, why don't you do us both a favor and go back home and help your daddy get his crops in?" he said, his voice weary but not unkind. Having said his piece, he turned back to his drink. While he sipped at the liquor, he kept his eyes fixed on the mirror.

The kid's face quickly developed hectic blotches of angry red. "Yer yeller, Pearl!" the boy yelled, his voice breaking yet again. "Scart yeller I'll git ya!"

Pearl smiled then. "I'm scared all right, kid. But you only got it half right."

"Yellerbelly!"

The kid pulled his gun and fired at where Pearl was standing at the bar, but the gunman was already moving, throwing himself forward and low. The kid's first shot went wild and shattered the bottle of redeye that had been at Pearl's elbow, sending a shower of glass and brownish liquid across the bar. Pearl had his gun out before he hit the sawdust, automatically returning fire. The kid's feet went out from under him like he'd slipped on dog shit, landing hard on his back, the gun flying from his rawboned hand.

Pearl lay on his belly, his smoking gun clutched tight in his hand. His heart beat fast and the smell of cordite burned his nostrils. It was a full thirty seconds before he was satisfied he hadn't taken a hit.

"Mister? You all right?" The bartender was leaning over him.

As he got to his feet, Pearl could see a couple of townies peering in through the door.

"Don't you worry none, sir," the bartender said in a low, reassuring voice. "I'll swear to the magistrate when he comes 'round you didn't have no choice in the matter. The boy drew on you, plain and simple."

Pearl stepped forward, looking down at the dead kid sprawled at his feet. Funny, it was only now that the boy was dead that he could see how young he truly was. Still, part of him was surprised, and secretly pleased, that he'd managed to nail the kid right between the eyes.

Pearl motioned to the dead boy. "Do you know who he is—was?

The bartender nodded. "Looks to be Ezra Sutter's boy, Caleb."

Pearl wiped at his mouth with the back of his hand, which was still gripping the smoking pistol. Try as he might, he couldn't take his eyes off the hole in the kid's forehead.

"How old is he?"

"He ain't more than thirteen, I reckon..."

Pearl reached inside his waistcoat pocket and pulled out a gold piece, tossing it onto the bar. "I want two bottles of whiskey brought to my room. What's left over is to be put toward burying the boy."

"Y-yes, sir. Anything else?"

"Just see that that I ain't bothered," Pearl said quietly as he stared at Caleb Sutter's blood and brains seeping into the sawdust on the barroom floor. "All I want is to be left to myself."

Chapter Two

The gun was calling to him again.

Pearl hated when it did that. The gun usually waited until he was drunk or tired or simply sick of it all. It was tricky that way.

Although he had two revolvers, it was always the same one that called out for him: the one with the pearl handle. He'd had the grip custom-made down in New Orleans years ago, back when he had more fire in his belly than whiskey. He could have easily had both pieces fitted that way, but he chose just the one. The one he used. His killing iron. A bit of theatrics is what it was. Something for the penny dreadfuls.

But sometimes he wondered if by acknowledging its importance—its unique function—he had not imparted to the weapon a dreadful vitality. After all, it's the sick oyster that has the pearl. It rode heavier on his hip with each passing year, as if fattened by the souls of those it had escorted into the Great Beyond. Or so it seemed in his mind.

Johnny Pearl wasn't sure if he believed in ghosts. But he certainly believed in Evil. Lord knows, he'd done enough of it to recognize it when he heard its voice. And the voice of the gun was Evil indeed.

Like all things made of sin, the gun called to him only when he was weak. As a young man, the possibility of vulnerability had been unimaginable. Perhaps such frailty was the inevitable state of Man. But it all seemed so unfair to him that the Lord should demand perfection, yet leave His children to dwell in perpetual temptation.

Pearl sat on the sole chair in his rented room, drinking by himself, as these thoughts came to him. Not that there was much else for him to do *but* drink. The one window in the room looked out onto the rear of the stables, permitting a view of churned muck and a couple of bored pigs the blacksmith kept in his backyard.

He had started off drinking out of a glass, but after an hour he'd given up on such niceties and drank the rotgut straight from the bottle. He stared at the unpainted plank walls as if they held the pattern of the world within their knotholes and whorls.

Pearl had come a far piece from his boyhood in the Carolinas—but he was neither proud nor amazed by this. He had been born the scion of a well-respected family. And when the war drums rolled, he had been among the first to enlist. He'd been full of romance and chivalry and other damn fool ideas back then.

He'd fought hard and suffered more physical and emotional wounds than a callow youth eager to teach Billy Yank his place could ever imagine. He'd lost friends beyond number, bearing witness to their death throes in the muck and the mud. He had watched them die every way a man could: bravely, cruelly, fearfully, foolishly... uselessly.

And when it was all over, he'd made his way back to the place of his birth to find his home burned, his family dead of the fever that had tagged along after the invading troops like a hungry dog. He'd gone a little crazy then, like a lot of young men who'd fought for Dixie and seen it come to naught. Some folks would say he was still a little crazy. Even him.

Seeing how there was nothing for him, and that the world he had once known was never to return again, he set out to make a new life for himself. However, he didn't have the temperament to become a settler. Nor did he have the wherewithal to set himself up in business. Without family or friends to temper his anger, anchor his feet or salve his soul—the way of the gun seemed as good as any for a man of his background. Perhaps better than most. And since there wasn't much that Johnny Pearl knew how to do except kill his fellow man, that's what he did.

For the first few years, it wasn't a half-bad life. There was excitement and thrills, like those he'd known during the war. And although there was a great deal danger in the life he led, there was also freedom. But as the killings started to add up, the excitement began to be replaced by weariness, the wildness became more and more like madness, and the freedom a trap.

And, to make matters worse, the gun started talking to him.

When he first started hearing the call of the gun, its voice was far weaker than it was now. But as his resolve lessened, the gun's voice grew stronger, more distinct. At first he could not quite identify its voice. But now he recognized it not to be just one voice, but many, woven together like the braid of a rope. The voice of the gun was comprised of the voices of all those he had killed, all those he had wronged, all who were lost to him.

Its voice cajoled and chided and ridiculed and argued, the myriad voices losing their individuality, merging and melding until it became a wordless, plaintive wail, like that of the siren of legend who lured ancient sailors to their deaths.

The gun only wanted one thing. The same thing Pearl wanted, really. Peace. But there was only one way it could ever know *true* peace. And that was if he used the gun one last time...

"*Don't!*"

There was a girl standing in the door of his room, her eyes showing more white than a billiard ball. She was young, dressed in a gingham skirt, with long dark hair pulled back in a single braid that fell almost to her waist. She carried a fresh slop jar in one hand, a skeleton key in the other.

Johnny Pearl wondered why she looked so frightened, then he realized he had the muzzle of the gun pressed against his temple.

"Pardon me, ma'am," he said thickly, lowering the weapon. "Didn't mean to scare you none."

The girl hesitated for a moment, as if trying to decide whether to flee the room.

"You're not going to kill yourself, are you?" she asked.

Pearl shrugged, but did not reholster the gun. "Who would it matter to if I did?"

"It would matter to me," she replied quietly.

Pearl squinted at the girl, struggling to bring her into focus through the haze of rotgut. "You Injun?"

Her cheeks colored slightly. "Half. My mama was Cheyenne."

"No shame in that," Pearl smiled gently. "My grandma was Cherokee."

He was suddenly aware of just how wretched he must look, with his unshaven jaw and filthy hair. He returned the gun to its holster, its voice strangely silent for the first time in years.

"What's your name, gal?" he rasped.

"Katie. Katie Small Dove."

"That's a right pretty name." He cocked his head to one side. "You ain't scared of me, are you?"

"No, sir. I ain't."

"Why is that? You know who I am—what I done?"

"Yes, sir, I know all them things. But I still ain't scared of you. I seen bad men before—more than my share. I know what they're like, and you ain't like them. I seen how you tried to keep from havin' to kill that boy. A bad man—a *real* bad man—wouldn't have bothered with that. He'd have shot that boy soon as look at him. So's that's why I ain't scared. Leastwise not for myself. I'm more scared *for* you than *of* you."

Pearl smiled and got up from the chair, motioning for her to take his place. "Come sit and visit with me a while, Katie. Its been a long time since I talked to anyone with horse sense."

She glanced over her shoulder. "I got work I need to do...."

"Pretty please? With sugar on top?"

Katie giggled. It was a sweet, natural sound, like birdsong in the trees. "I guess I can talk for a lit'l while, mister," she said, stepping into the room.

"Call me Johnny," he said.

"All right—Johnny," she replied, beaming him a smile that could raise the dead.

CHAPTER THREE

It was autumn, and even though the days were still warm, it didn't take a trained eye to spot winter approaching. The last couple of mornings Pearl had awoken to find a thin skin of ice covering the rain barrel outside the cabin door, and frost in the shadow of the rocks.

It had been over a year since Johnny Pearl did something he had never thought possible—traded in the black garb of the gunslinger for the buckskins and homespun of a settler. And he had yet to regret one minute of a single day since then, despite the long hours and hard work.

He could take no credit for his rebirth; it was all Katie's doing. She was the one who had given him the strength and incentive to turn his feet from the destructive path he had walked so long. Her love had raised him up from the shadows, just as Jesus brought Lazarus back from the Land of the Dead. Pearl had given himself up for lost, but she still managed to guide him back to the land of the living, the land of hope. She was a miracle worker, that woman.

Although there was no proper preacher to be had, Johnny Pearl considered Katie joined to him as surely as Eve had been to Adam. Since there was no preacher to be had, they had ridden into the foothills one day, and, when their horses had climbed as high as they could go, Pearl took her hand in his and shouted up at the sky:

"Lord! This here's Johnny Pearl! I'm taking Katie Small Dove for my wife!"

He figured that was probably as official as they could get, given the circumstances.

Now that Katie was carrying their first child, Pearl felt as if he had been blessed by God Himself. For the first time since the war had come into his life, he could look to the future and see something besides smoke and ashes. As a symbol of his rebirth, he took his old clothes and the pearl-handled pistol and buried them underneath the cabin's flagstones.

When Katie asked him why he didn't just burn the clothes and throw the gun in the river, he shook his head. "I'm not proud of what I used to be, but there's no denying it, either. I need to be reminded of what I was once was so I won't turn back into it again."

He and Katie made their home in a cabin abandoned by a faint-hearted settler, and their closest neighbor was ten miles away, the nearest town nearly a hundred. All of which was fine and dandy, as far as Pearl was concerned. Their existence was humble but adequate; Katie tended a small garden near the cabin—mostly corn and squash—while he ranged for antelope, short-horn and rabbit. For those few items they couldn't make themselves, Pearl took bear, coyote and panther skins with him on his rare trips into town.

However, just because their nearest white neighbor was a two-hour ride away, that didn't mean they were total recluses. They received occasional visits from some of Katie's Indian relatives, one of her favorites being her elder cousin, Ohkom Kakit, known to the whites as Little Wolf.

Little Wolf was a respected war chief among the Cheyenne, which guaranteed the Pearls a certain amount of protection—at least from the natives.

It wasn't an easy life, but it was a free one, and for that Johnny Pearl was thankful. He had never thought he would settle down the way he had, but damned if every evening he couldn't be found sitting on the modest porch of his cabin, enjoying a quiet smoke as he contemplated the land as the sun went down.

He had the river running at his door, the rolling expanse of the plains on one hand, the mountains stretched out like sleeping giants on the other, and a sky like a great blue bowl turned upside down overhead. How could he not look out on all that and not think that this was indeed the best of all worlds, these the finest of all days, and that it would never end?

He was wrong, of course.

They appeared without warning—a neat trick, given the terrain—while Pearl was busy chopping wood. One minute he was by himself, the next he was surrounded by snorting, stamping ponies. Normally a settler on the high plains would be alarmed by the sight of several armed Cheyenne warriors, but Johnny Pearl merely smiled in recognition.

"Greetings, cousin," he said, setting aside his ax so none of the braves accompanying his wife's kinsman might get the wrong idea.

"Greetings, Johnny Pearl," Little Wolf responded.

There was something in the old chief's voice that gave him pause. Pearl glanced at the assembled Cheyenne. Even though their skin was darker and their uniforms different, he still knew soldiers when he saw them.

Katie emerged from the cabin, wiping cornmeal from her hands. "To what do we owe the honor of this visit, Ohkom Kakit?" she asked.

Little Wolf shook his head. "This is no visit, Small Dove. I come to warn you." Johnny frowned and put his arm about his wife's shoulder. "Warn us? About what?"

Little Wolf glanced at his men, then took a deep breath. "Three moons past there was a great battle between the white man and the red man along the Greasy Grass."

"You mean Custer," Johnny Pearl said grimly. "I heard tell of it last time I was in town."

"Yes. The yellow-hair," Little Wolf nodded. "It was a great victory for the Cheyenne and the Sioux. We counted great coup against the pony soldiers."

"You were there?" Pearl asked, genuinely surprised.

Little Wolf nodded and smiled crookedly, trying to keep his pride from showing too much. "It was a great fight. But now the whites are angry and seek to hunt us down and punish us for this thing."

"The U.S. Army don't take kindly to gettin' whupped," Pearl sighed. "I can tell you that firsthand."

"The pony soldiers are rounding up all Cheyenne, all Sioux—warriors, women, children, grandfathers—all of us! They seek to lock us away from our hunting grounds and our sacred places as punishment for daring to fight. They will try and take Katie away from you, Johnny Pearl."

"Why would they do that? She ain't full-blooded. Besides, she's my wife. "

"Perhaps you are right, Johnny Pearl," Little Wolf conceded. "You know the mind of your people better than I. But you would be wise to leave this place and come with us. We are headed for Dull Knife's village. There we stand a better chance against the pony soldiers when they come."

"We appreciate the concern, Little Wolf," Pearl said. "But we're staying put. Besides, Katie is in no condition to travel." He smiled and patted his wife's swollen belly.

Little Wolf frowned. "All the more reason to leave."

Katie glanced anxiously at her husband but said nothing. Seeing the fear in his kinswoman's eyes, the Cheyenne chief's grim demeanor softened as he leaned down from his pony to kiss the top of her head.

"Do not be frightened, little cousin. Your husband is a good man and a fine warrior. Farewell, blood-of-my-blood. And many blessings on your child."

"I thank you, Ohkom Kakit, " Katie replied, blinking back a tear. "You're welcome to stay here as long as you like."

Little Wolf shook his head and pointed to the clear, cloudless sky on the horizon. "We must go. There is a storm coming."

⟞⬩⟝

Two days after Little Wolf and his followers left, the storm arrived.

It wasn't a storm that brought with it thunder and high winds and hail-stones. No, the storm that bore down of Johnny and Katie Pearl was a mor-tal one—the kind that rains fire and hot lead.

Pearl had just finished milking the nanny goat and was bringing the pail into the house when the thunder rose through this boots. It had been a long time since he last felt anything like that—but it wasn't something a man could forget. Many men on horseback were coming their way—riding hard.

Katie was in the front yard, throwing feed to the chickens. When she saw the look in her husband's eyes, she let her apron drop and ran into the cabin, re-emerging seconds later with the carbine.

"Git in th' house and stay there!" Pearl ordered as he loaded the Win-chester.

Katie hesitated, placing a hand on her husband's arm. "Perhaps its only my cousin...."

Pearl shook his head, his mouth set in a grim line. "Whoever they are, they ain't Injuns!" Katie gave his arm one last squeeze and disappeared in-side the cabin just as a horse cleared the rise.

Most whites in the Wyoming and Dakota territories heaved a sigh of relief when they saw the U.S. Cavalry. Johnny Pearl wasn't one of them.

He'd spent too many years shooting at blue uniforms—and being shot at by them—to find their presence comforting.

He watched uneasily as the squadron of troopers, roughly thirty in all, made its way toward his cabin. As the soldiers drew closer, Pearl stepped off the porch into the dooryard but did not lower his weapon.

The squadron's scout trotted his mount forward to where Pearl was standing, lifting his empty hand in greeting. There was something about him Pearl didn't trust. He fidgeted in his saddle too much, like he had a ferret down his pants.

"Howdy," the scout said, looking about. "Where's John Myerling?"

"He pulled up stakes and went back to St. Paul. I took over his cabin," Johnny replied.

"That a fact?" The scout glanced in the direction of the soldiers, but Pearl could make out who he was looking at. "Have you seen any Injuns?"

"Sure, I seen Injuns. See 'em all the time. Now get off my land."

The scout twitched in his saddle again, his eyes narrowing. "You sure got a smart mouth for a sodbuster."

"I *said* get off my land," Pearl replied, his voice hard as an iron bar.

The scout's eyes narrowed a split second before he reached for his holster, which was all the warning Pearl needed to step forward and jam his rifle directly into the other man's crotch. The scout yanked his hand back like his gun had turned into a red-hot poker.

"Y-you're bluffing, honyocker," the scout sneered.

"I *never* bluff."

There was something in his voice that that made the scout decide not to push his luck. He licked his lips nervously and fidgeted even more in his saddle.

"What the hell is going on here?" boomed an angry voice. An officer dressed in the uniform of a Cavalry captain rode forward. He was a big man, the way trees are big and rocks are big. His shoulders were as wide as an ax handle and his hands could easily hide Bibles. However, the captain's most intimidating feature was not his sheer physical size, but the wavy mass of red hair that fell below his shoulders, and the matching beard and mustaches he wore combed out over his chest, which made him look like a lion. His stern face was burned by the sun, and his pale eyes were startling in contrast to the darker blue of his uniform and the vibrancy of his hair.

"Put that weapon down, farmer!" the captain barked. It was clear he was used to being obeyed, be it by soldiers or civilians.

"Like hell I will!" Johnny snapped in reply. "And who might you be?"

"Captain Antioch Drake, United States Cavalry. Now do as I say, sodbuster, or I'll forget I'm talking to a white man and have my men open fire!"

Pearl glanced at Drake, then stepped back, lowering his gun. What he'd seen looking at him through Drake's eyes was all too familiar. He'd known men like Drake during the war: bloody-minded and scarlet-handed, incapable of separating friend from foe, soldier from civilian. Quantrill had been one such monster. If the war had taught Pearl one thing, it was that a bastard's a bastard, whether suited up in blue or gray. And what he saw before him was a bastard in a blue suit.

"That's better," Drake said. "Now—are you going to answer the question my scout put to you or not? Did you see Injuns pass this way a day or two ago?"

"What makes you think there's been Injuns through here recently?" Johnny asked, trying his best to sidestep the question.

"We've been following their trail—and it lead us to you," Drake responded. "Now—did you or did you not see Injuns passing through?"

"What do you want them for?"

"They were amongst those murderin' redskins responsible for the massacre of the 7th Cavalry under Lieutenant Colonel George Custer at Little Big Horn," Drake replied, his tone growing extremely reverent.

"Do tell," Pearl said, spitting in the dirt.

Drake seemed surprised by Pearl's blatant indifference. "You *do* know about what happened at Little Big Horn, don't you?"

Pearl shrugged. "Yeah. I know. But that still don't explain why *y'all* are on *my* property, askin' *me* questions about Injuns."

Drake's scowl deepened. "That's some accent you've got there. You're not from around here, are you?"

"Funny. I was gonna say th' same about y'all," Pearl grunted.

Drake leaned back in his saddle, his pale irises seeming to disappear against the whites of his eye. "You wouldn't be lyin' to me about them Injuns just to make up for Stonewall Jackson, would you, Reb?"

Johnny Pearl's cheeks burned, but he would be damned if he let this Union-suited son of a bitch get his goat. Still, he could not keep a waver of anger from entering his voice when he spoke.

"How can I lie if I ain't tole y'all nothin'! Now, get off my land! I got better things to do than to spend my day jawin' with Yankees!"

Nancy A. Collins
86

One minute the cavalry officer's hand was empty, the next the muzzle of his Colt was pressed against Pearl's temple. There was no way Pearl could bring the carbine up in time to squeeze off a shot without Drake putting his brains on the ground, and both men knew it.

"Who's in the cabin?" Drake growled.

Johnny struggled to speak around what felt like a rock wedged in his throat.

"J-just my wife."

Drake's eyes narrowed into ice-blue slits. "I thought you said you was alone, Reb."

"I didn't say *nothin'* about bein' alone!" Johnny protested. "Y'all are just twistin' everything I say!"

"We'll just see about that," Drake replied. He motioned with his free hand for a couple of his men to come forward. "Take his weapon, and see that he stays out from underfoot."

With Drake's service revolver cocked and aimed just above his right ear, Pearl was helpless to prevent the troopers from confiscating his rifle then roughly binding his hands behind his back. Satisfied Pearl was no longer a hindrance, Drake reholstered his weapon and turned to speak to his junior officer.

"Lieutenant Barnes! I want that cabin searched!"

"Yes, sir!" Barnes barked, saluting Drake. He promptly dismounted and motioned several troopers to do the same. Guns drawn, they advanced on the cabin.

Johnny Pearl was no stranger to terror. Sometimes it seemed he was born knowing it. But before now, the fear he had experienced on the battle-field and in shootouts had always been for his own life. None of what he had undergone before had come close to preparing him for the sick dread that overcame him when he heard his wife scream.

"*Katie!*" Pearl shouted, struggling to break free of the troopers holding him. He wanted to scream, explode, turn himself inside out if need be—anything but let the bastards see his fear. "Don't you *dare* touch her, you stinkin' Yankee bastards!"

"Mind your mouth, Reb!" snarled one of the troopers as he smashed Pearl in the face with his gun butt. Through the stars exploding behind his eyes, Pearl saw his wife being dragged out of the cabin.

"Here y'go, Captain," the scout said. "Weren't no one but her in the house."

Drake took in Katie's long dark braid, high cheekbones, dusky skin and almond-shaped eyes, then turned to glower at his captive disapprovingly.

"I thought you said there were no Injuns around here."

"I ain't said no such thing!" Pearl snarled, spitting out a mouthful of blood. "Besides, Katie ain't full Cheyenne."

"Even a *drop* of heathen blood is enough to mark her as theirs!" Drake sniffed. "She'll have go on the reservation—the brat, too."

"No! She's my *wife*, damn it! That's my baby she's carryin'!"

Drake fixed him with a look of utter contempt. "Which makes you a squaw man—and as such, no better than a dog!"

Pearl lunged forward, his teeth bared in pure, murder-hot rage. If the troopers had not been holding him back, he would have leapt onto Drake and taken him off his saddle like a mountain cat bringing down an antelope. Instead, all he got for his trouble was his own rifle butt slammed across the back of his head, dropping him to the ground.

As he lay writhing in the dirt, clutching his skull, he heard a shriek of pain and surprise from the scout; "*Jesus H. Christ!* That Injun bitch damn near bit off my finger!"

Pearl raised his head in time to see Katie running as fast as she could away from the soldiers, but her belly was getting in her way. Within seconds the mounted troopers had surrounded her. They were laughing and making whooping noises, waving their hats at her as if she were no more than an errant cow they were trying to return to the herd. Katie dashed frantically to and fro, clutching her belly as if trying to protect the child within it. She tried to find an opening in the tightening ring of champing horses.

It all happened so fast, so horribly, horribly fast. One moment Katie was calling out her husband's name amid the chaos and the churning dust—the next she was under the horses' hooves. Pearl wasn't aware he was screaming until Lieutenant Barnes put a fist in his gut to shut him up.

Barnes massaged his knuckles as he watched Pearl gasp and choke for air. "What do we do with him, Captain?"

Drake's eyes were as cold and unyielding as sapphires. "Make him an example for all those who would pollute the white race. Lynch him. Burn the cabin, while you're at it."

"Yes, sir!" Barnes responded, saluting sharply .

As his captors dragged him toward the nearest tree, Pearl felt as hollow as a dry gourd. It was as if they had reached down his gullet and yanked his soul out by the roots. Death, no matter how violent or unjust, was prefer-able to life in a world without his Katie.

The last thing Johnny Pearl saw before they chased the horse out from under him was the sight of his world in ruins: his house ablaze, his wife's body sprawled in the bloody dust, and the scout bending over her, knife in hand.

CHAPTER FOUR

As the covered wagon made its way across the high plains, each jounce of its wheels made the utensils hanging in the back rattle like cowbells. If the old man perched on the driver's box noticed the incessant clatter, he did not show it. Instead, his eye was fixed on the plume of smoke on the horizon. On the side of the canvas canopy was painted in bold, somewhat faded script: DR. MIRABLIS WONDROUS ELIXIR RE-VITAE $1 (50 CENTS TO VETERANS & WIDOWS).

"Pompey!" Dr. Mirablis croaked. "Come front!"

The head of a middle-aged Negro, the hair liberally laced with gray, popped out from behind the canvas flap separating the driver's seat from the interior of the wagon.

"Take the reins on Alastor," Mirablis wheezed. "We're getting close. I must check on the elixir."

Pompey nodded his understanding and moved aside, holding back the canvas so the old man could climb back into the wagon's bed. He then seated himself on the driver's box and took up the coal black horse's reins. The beast flared its nostrils and rolled its eyes. It could smell death mixed with the smoke wafted their way by the wind. As could they all.

Pompey flicked the reins across the horse's flanks, forcing it to move faster.

⟫◆⟪

"Would you look at that," Dr. Mirablis sighed, shaking his head in amazement as he viewed what was left of the homestead. "They even shot the nanny goat."

Twenty-four hours ago, this had been a place where people lived, worked and planned for the future. Now it was a scene of carnage. The cabin still smoldered. Although the roof had fallen in, the stone chimney still stood, but little else remained. The modest garden had been trampled into the dirt, and the livestock slaughtered and left to rot. Such barbarity was nothing new to a man who had survived the chaos of the Napoleonic Wars, but it still grieved him all the same.

Pompey grunted as he helped the old man down off the driver's box. Mirablis was bent with age and walked with a cane. His hair was white and thin as cobwebs. His scalp was dappled with the same spots that covered his wrinkled hands. Despite his advanced years, there was an intensity in his eyes—the kind found only in those of fierce intellect and even fiercer determination.

"Bloodthirsty savages," Mirablis muttered under his breath as he shuffled through a litter of trampled chickens.

The old man paused and pointed with his cane at something lying in the dirt nearby.

"What's that?"

As they drew closer, Mirablis's eyes widened and he began hobbling faster, despite Pompey's attempts to keep him balanced. With a snarl of impatience, the old man yanked his arm free of his servant's grasp and knelt beside the body of Katie Pearl. He grimaced in disgust and clucked his tongue.

"This one is of no use to me—her skull has been smashed, as you can plainly see—since some barbarian saw fit to take the poor thing's scalp! Such a waste! And in the later stages of pregnancy as well...."

Mirablis's eyes dimmed, as if the fire held within them was turned inward. A moment later he gestured for Pompey to help him back on his feet.

"Still, if there was a mother," he said. "There had to be a father...."

His companion gently touched Mirablis's shoulder and pointed to a flock of carrion crows circling a copse of trees that lined the nearby river.

"Ah, trusty Pompey!" Mirablis smiled, flashing his wooden and ivory dentures. "Ever my eyes and ears, old friend! Come, let us hurry! I can only pray those damnable birds haven't had their way with our new friend!"

———◆———

They found the body of Johnny Pearl hanging from the stout limb of a cottonwood tree. The tree was within sight of the homestead's front yard. Though the dead man was not visible from the cabin, the lynched man's final view from his unenviable vantage had been of his home ablaze and his wife's mutilated carcass.

However, what made Mirablis cry out in outrage was the sight of a large crow perched atop the hanged man's head, its inky claws buried deep in his scalp.

"Pompey! Get that wretched thing *off* him!"

Producing a slingshot from his back pocket, the mute quickly snatched up a small rock from the ground and sent the missile flying at the bird. The crow abandoned its grisly perch with an angry caw. Mirablis positioned himself directly under the hanged man's feet, peering up into his distorted face.

"We're in luck, Pompey! The scavengers didn't get too much of a head start. It's a good thing winter's on its way—the flies should be mostly inactive by now, so there shouldn't be much in the way of infestation to worry about."

The old man laughed and held up a shaking hand.

"Look at me, Pompey! I'm trembling like a school girl!"

Mirablis's giddy smile was quickly replaced by a more grim manner. "Go fetch Sasquatch! We'll need him to transport our new friend here into the pouch. I'll stay here and play scarecrow until your return."

Pompey nodded and hurried back to the wagon. He rapped his knuckles loudly on its wooden side. After a moment, the tailgate dropped open and the canvas flaps that covered the rear were thrown back, and something that once was a man emerged into the cold light of a September afternoon on the high plains.

The thing was tall and not exactly put together the way a human is supposed to look. Its left arm was shorter than the right—or was it that the right arm was longer than the left? The legs seemed to be equally mismatched, with one foot severely pigeon-toed while the other pointed straight. Scars of various lengths and widths crisscrossed the creature's exposed flesh, giving it the appearance of a walking crazy quilt.

Though it was naked save for a leather loincloth, and was lean as a winter wolf, the creature did not seem to notice the chill wind blowing from the

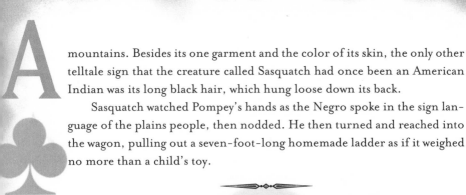

mountains. Besides its one garment and the color of its skin, the only other telltale sign that the creature called Sasquatch had once been an American Indian was its long black hair, which hung loose down its back.

Sasquatch watched Pompey's hands as the Negro spoke in the sign language of the plains people, then nodded. He then turned and reached into the wagon, pulling out a seven-foot-long homemade ladder as if it weighed no more than a child's toy.

Mirablis rubbed his hands together anxiously as he paced back and forth beneath the swaying body of the hanged man. He brightened immediately upon spotting Pompey approaching with the ladder. A few steps behind the mute was the shambling figure of Sasquatch, the leather pouch folded under the shorter left arm, the cask of elixir under the longer right arm.

"We must hurry!" Mirablis said breathily. Though the weather was somewhat brisk, he mopped his brow with a silk handkerchief. "We were exceptionally fortunate this time, as I believe our friend here has been inconvenienced less than twelve hours. But time is still of the essence!"

Pompey placed the ladder against the cottonwood and began to climb, while Mirablis supervised Sasquatch as he unrolled the pouch. It was made of oiled cloth and resembled nothing so much as a wineskin, except that it was six feet long and three feet wide. At one end was a huge stopper fashioned from wood wrapped in treated leather.

Pompey made a grunting noise, signaling the others that he was ready. Sasquatch moved to position himself directly under the swaying feet of the hanged man. After a few slices from Pompey's buck knife, the body dropped from the tree like strange fruit, directly into Sasquatch's waiting arms. With surprising grace and gentleness for a creature of such ungainly appearance, Sasquatch laid the corpse on the ground at Mirablis's feet and proceeded to undress it.

The old man studied the body with a critical eye, then nodded his head and smiled.

"This is even better than I hoped!" he said, pointing to the corpse's livid but otherwise unmarked flesh. "From all outward appearances, our friend here was in exemplary physical condition before he was so rudely inconvenienced." Mirablis waved his cane in warning as Pompey began to pry off the noose cinched into the dead man's neck. "Leave that for later! Its too deeply embedded in the flesh to be removed on the scene."

Having finished his inspection, Mirablis stepped back and motioned for his servants to proceed with their duties. While Pompey held the neck of the giant flask upright, Sasquatch slid the body through the man-sized opening as easily as a mother might put a sleepy child to bed.

Once the body was fully inside the pouch, the plug was put in place, then driven home by Sasquatch with one swift rap from a cooper's mallet. At the top of the plug was a hole the width of a man's finger, down which Pompey ran one end of a length of tubing. The other end was attached to a spigot at the bottom of the cask of elixir. With a turn of the spigot, the elixir flowed through the tubing and into the watertight container.

While they waited for the pouch to fill, Sasquatch moved the wagon closer to the scene and made a fire, over which he warmed a small bucket of tar. When the pouch was filled enough that it sloshed upon Mirablis nudging it with his cane, the tubing was removed and the hole sealed with the hot tar.

As Pompey disconnected the tubing from the spigot, a small amount of viscous greenish yellow fluid spurted forth onto the ground.

"Careful, fool!" Mirablis snapped, bringing his cane down on the mute's shoulder with surprising force. Pompey did not even flinch. "My elixir is far too valuable to waste on worms!"

Mirablis looked around, frowning. "Where in the name of Perdition did Sasquatch get off to?"

Pompey pointed in the direction of the ruined cabin. The patchwork creature was kneeling beside the dead woman, making passes with his mismatched hands over the body. Part of Sasquatch had been a shaman, but just how much Mirablis wasn't sure. As a man of science, Mirablis tended to dismiss such silliness. But he had to admit he found some aspects of the medicine man within his servant useful on occasion, so he allowed him his delusions. After all, revived from the dead or not, he was still a red savage.

"Sasquatch! It's time to go!" Mirablis shouted "Our new friend needs to get situated!"

Muttering under his breath about heathen superstitions, the old man returned to where Pompey was standing guard over the pouch. A few seconds later, Sasquatch reappeared and lifted the pouch and placed it in the back of the wagon as easily as a farmer hefting a ten-pound sack of seed. After making sure the pouch and its occupant were firmly secured, Sasquatch crawled back into rear of the wagon, closing the tailgate behind him.

Mirablis paused to glance up at the sky as Pompey helped him back onto the driver's box. "It'll be dark soon. We better get out while the getting's good, my friends," he observed. "The less time spent at the scene of a crime, the better—whether it's of our making or not. Still, not a bad day's work, if I don't say so myself."

CHAPTER FIVE

The covered wagon traveled for three days and nights without pause. On the morning of the fourth day, Mirablis and his peculiar entourage arrived at their destination, hidden within the forbidding wilderness of the Grand Tetons; from a distance, it looked like nothing more than a cabin pressed close against the side of a foothill. But what appeared to be an isolated shack was actually camouflage for the entrance to a large cavern.

The cabin's furnishings were exceptionally modest. Indeed, the only evidence that someone other than a mountain man lived there was the walnut and glass bookcase in the corner crammed full of medical texts and other, more arcane volumes, written in German, Latin and Greek.

The door set in the back wall of the cabin opened onto the cave. The cave extended far into the hillside and had natural ventilation, a floor that was relatively level and access to an underground spring. Mirablis was not the first to have found it advantageous, judging from the flint arrow heads and broken bowls they'd found scattered among the stalagmites.

When Mirablis accidentally stumbled across the cave years ago, he realized it would be the perfect location for his experiments. He had grown weary of spending so much of his time and energy looking over his shoulder. He could no longer count how many times he had been on the verge of a major breakthrough, only to abandon his laboratory because of some snooping neighbor or meddling constable.

He had learned from poor Viktor's hapless example never to arouse the scrutiny of outsiders—and to always erase his mistakes before they could call attention to themselves. Now, for the first time in fifty years, Mirablis was free to continue his work without fear of discovery and censure—and what progress he had made!

It was here, hidden from the prying eyes of a distrustful and ignorant public, that Mirablis worked to free mankind from the inconvenience of mortality. There was no doubt in his mind that in the centuries to come, this wretched hovel would be made into a shrine greater than those in Rome, Bethlehem or Mecca. A shrine dedicated to the genius that struggled so mightily in order that mankind might know Life Without End.

But those days were yet to come, and he still had much to do before they would arrive.

While he had far surpassed his notorious colleague, Mirablis had yet to produce a suitable enough subject that would allow him to unveil his discovery to the world at large. With something as profoundly earthshaking as the death of Death, one had to be absolutely perfect, or it was all for naught. Viktor had proven that, if nothing else.

While Pompey unharnessed the wagon and Sasquatch unloaded their new friend, Mirablis busied himself by starting a fire in the cabin's potbellied stove. While neither Pompey nor Sasquatch seemed to notice the cold, the same could not be said for their master.

"Wait, you heathen fool!" Mirablis shouted irritably as Sasquatch lurched toward the cave entrance with his precious burden. "You might be able to see in the dark, but I require light!"

Sasquatch came to a halt and glanced over his crooked shoulder at Mirablis. In the dim light, the whites of the Indian's eyes glowed with a pale greenish yellow luminescence. The patched-together Indian waited patiently as his creator fumbled with an oil lantern and a box of brimstones.

Pompey stepped unhesitatingly into the stygian darkness of the cavern, the lantern held in one hand while he lead his elderly master with the other. The floor of the cavern sloped gently beneath their feet for a few steps, then leveled out again. As Pompey lifted his arm higher, the light from the lantern struck the glass walls of the tank.

At first glance, it resembled nothing so much as an oversized aquarium. It stood on long, ornate copper legs, the feet of which resembled the claws of lions, and had a burnished copper lid held in place by tension screws. It was four feet wide, ten feet deep and seven feet long, with side panels made from a greenish-colored glass several inches thick. Through this glass could be glimpsed gallons of the good doctor's special elixir. Along one side of the tank was a raised wooden platform, on top of which was situated what passed for Mirablis's operating theater.

While Pompey hurried about lighting crude pitch torches in order to provide more light, Sasquatch stumped its graceless way up the thirteen stairs that lead to the gallowslike platform, then carefully placed his burden onto the operating table. He then loosened the tension screws holding the lid in place and lifted it using a block and tackle.

Once the lid was removed, an elaborate cat's cradle of leather straps was visible just below the surface of the viscous fluid. Pompey then removed the plug with a chisel and, with a practiced movement, Sasquatch expertly decanted the contents of the pouch into the tank.

The body of the hanged man landed in the cradle of leather strips with all the grace of a dead mackerel striking the dock. For a man several days dead, his color was surprisingly good, and his flesh was pliant. Using a winch attached to the side of tank, Pompey cranked the cradle closer to the surface. Upon putting on a pair of canvas gloves, the mute arranged the corpse's tangled limbs so they were in a rough semblance of natural rest.

"Don't touch that!" Mirablis snapped as his servant tested the cinch on the noose. "I don't need you accidentally damaging the poor bastard's voice box anymore than it has been already!"

Mirablis looked over the edge of the tank from his perch atop his step-ladder. He had abandoned the lantern in favor of a miner's headlamp, its wavering candlelight reflected and intensified by the mirror directly behind it. After slipping on a pair of gloves, the doctor gently palpitated the dead man's throat, then smiled.

"Good! Our friend is merely inconvenienced by a broken neck, not a shattered larynx or crushed windpipe. Whoever handled the lynching knew what they were doing, that much is for certain."

Mirablis produced a scalpel from his pocket and quickly sliced through the rope. With a disgusted snort, he tossed the severed noose onto the floor of the platform, where it lay like a perverse umbilical cord.

"Now... lets see about that eye...." Mirablis muttered, turning the damaged portion of the corpse's face toward the light.

The head lolled like a rag doll's on its snapped neck. Mirablis frowned at the punctured eyeball and exposed optic muscles and clucked his tongue in mock reproof.

"I'm afraid it will have to go, my friend! But I believe I have a suitable replacement in stock—although I'm not certain as to its color. Still—beggars cannot be choosers, eh?"

Chuckling to himself over that particular witticism, Mirablis stepped down from his ladder and motioned for his servants to reseal the tank.

"There is much to be done before we can revive our new friend. But first, I must avail myself of a nap and a hot meal! Would it not have been better for God to have slept before Creation, rather than after, Pompey?" Mirablis yawned, massaging his lower back. "Think of all the trouble that would have been avoided!"

Pompey merely grunted as he helped his aged master down the stairs of the platform. If there was anything to be read in the silent Negro's eyes, their phosphorescent glow obscured it.

Chapter Six

Mirablis prepared for the revivification of his newest subject as he always did: by going over his notes and journals—and those of his dear colleague, destroyed so long ago by the forces he sought to control. There was a great deal of inspiration to be found in Viktor's writings. But Mirablis learned as much—if not more—from his friend's failures than he did his successes.

Poor Viktor. He had indeed been brilliant—his mind shining like a star in the wilderness. In the decades since his death, Mirablis had yet to find another man with which he could discourse as an equal. However, Viktor's one failing was his tendency to fixate simply on achieving a goal. He was never good at making contingency plans in case things did not quite work out as he had hoped. And in the end, his myopic optimism cost him dearly.

Of course, Mirablis was far more forgiving of Viktor's faults now that he was dead. During his life, these differences eventually lead to their falling out. But that was all so long ago, so far away. What were such petty jealousies and disagreements now?

Viktor may have realized his goal first, but it was Mirablis who had refined it—and repeated it—and one day soon he would be able to restore his old friend's reputation to the honor it once knew.

Of course, the accounts of his late friend's experiments and his subsequent bad end were grossly inaccurate, if not actually fashioned out of whole cloth, in an attempt to feed the overheated imaginations of shopkeepers' daughters. It galled him to think that all his friend and mentor's hard work had come to was a slander on his family's name and fodder for the thrill-mongering, ill-born wife of a decadent poet.

But enough of that foolishness. He had more weighty duties to attend to. Mirablis pushed himself away from the table and shuffled over to the sea chest he kept under his bed. He groaned aloud as he bent on arthritic knees and opened the lid, revealing an array of sealed jars of varying sizes and shapes. After a quick inventory, he chose a smallish jar containing a pair of eyes, then closed the lid.

Mirablis moved far more spryly now that he was home. Traveling took a serious toll on his aged system, affecting everything from his sleep to his digestion. Unfortunately, there was no way he could continue his work without leaving the security and familiarity of his sanctum. He certainly couldn't send Pompey and Sasquatch out into the world unsupervised. The very thought was enough to give him the shivers.

Mirablis opened the second door of the cabin and crossed the threshold into his subterranean kingdom. The interior of the cavern was now illuminated by strategically placed torches and lanterns, revealing a series of ropes stretched between the outcroppings of rock that served as guideposts in case of blackouts.

From where he stood, Mirablis could see Pompey and Sasquatch preparing the operating platform for surgery. The tank had been unsealed, its lid dangling from the block and tackle rigged from a gibbetlike support.

Upon noticing Mirablis's approach, Pompey put aside the straight razor he had been using to shave the body's head and hurried down the steps to escort his aged master onto the platform. As he was helped into his surgical gown, Mirablis scanned the body laid out before him on the operating table with a discerning eye.

Despite being dead for nearly a week, the cadaver was in wondrous shape, thanks largely to the elixir re-vitae. The limbs were supple, the muscles pliant, yet not softened by decay. If not for the grotesquely unnatural angle of his head, the hanged man could easily be mistaken for asleep.

Mirablis clucked his tongue upon seeing a darkish fluid seeping from the body's mouth and nose. He made a mental note as he pulled on his gloves to drain the bowels in order to prevent the subject from inhaling his own filth upon revival.

He squeezed and flexed the corpse's arms and legs to make sure there was no muscular decay or contraction in the limbs, then moved the arms so that they hung over the ends of the table, allowing the blood to drain into the vessels and expand them as much as possible. He then took a small wooden headrest and placed it under the back of the subject's skull so that the head was elevated above the chest, to avoid discoloration in the head and neck tissues.

Pompey stepped forward and presented a silver tray on which operating tools were arranged. Mirablis picked up one of the surgical knives and, without hesitation, began to cut away the skin over the left common carotid. Once it was exposed, he skillfully severed it and lifted a portion of the artery out of the body and quickly inserted a metal cannula into the opening. He quickly sealed the hollow tube and moved to repeat the operation on the right carotid. After that, he made a drain incision in the right internal jugular.

Pompey set aside the instrument tray and signed for Sasquatch to bring forward a five-gallon jug of the elixir. The mute then filled two oversized syringes with the greenish yellow fluid and affixed them to the carotid tubes. Then, with Pompey on the left, Sasquatch on the right, the plungers on the syringes were slowly but firmly pushed home, forcing nearly a gallon of elixir re-vitae into the subject's veins.

There was a burst of black, oxygen-depleted blood from the dead man's jugular as it was displaced by the invading liquid. The smell that accompanied the expulsion was a familiar one for Mirablis, but unpleasant none the less. He coughed thickly and daubed his upper lip with a mixture of lanolin and rose oil in order to better tolerate the stench. He then methodically repeated his drainage procedures on the femoral arteries, draining blood from the right leg while forcing elixir into the left. The old blood collected in the gutters gouged into the table's surface and flowed sluggishly into pails positioned under drains in the table.

Mirablis walked back to the head of the table, lifting the cadaver's hands to make sure gravity had done its job properly. He paused to marvel over how refined the subject's hands were. Not the sort one would imagine to find on the wrists of a farmer. But there was no point in dwelling on who or what this man had been. He would be able to tell Mirablis all these things himself soon enough—providing he survived the revivification process with his wits and language center intact.

Mirablis whistled tunelessly to himself as he exposed the axillary arteries in both the left and right arms. While he was waiting for the last of the blood to drain into metal catch basins, he busied himself with replacing the crow-pecked eye with a new one. Luckily for their new friend, one of the elixir's properties was its ability to prevent tissue rejection. And when it came to organ transplants—he could not be in better hands, aged though they were. Even though Mirablis was no longer as young as he once was, he was still capable enough to splice optic nerves.

However, he did not feel nearly as confident in regard to the subject's broken neck. From his experiments and observations, Mirablis had learned that while the revivification process returned the dead to life and imparted them with a vitality that bordered on the immortal, it had its limit. And damage to the spinal cord and brain after revival seemed to be it. But that decision would have to wait after he'd finished purging the body.

Mirablis moved back and forth, checking and double-checking the limbs, massaging them vigorously to ensure the elixir was spread evenly throughout the emptied veins. It was exceptionally important that the hands and the face were thoroughly saturated; any discoloration in the subject's body and legs could be easily disguised, but the hands and the face were necessary in order for him to pass as normal. Bandages and masks invariably called attention to themselves, and gloves interfered with dexterity.

Besides, physical appearance had everything to do with how the subject would be received by the public. Something as grotesque as Sasquatch was good enough for testing out theories and techniques, but it would be of little use in winning the hearts and minds of the hoi polloi.

Mirablis motioned for Pompey to roll the corpse over to one side so he could inject dosages of the elixir re-vitae directly into its buttocks. Without natural circulation to speed the fluid on its way through the body, Mirablis had discovered it was better to be safe than sorry.

Mirablis eyed the corpse's slightly distended belly then thumped it experimentally with his thumb and forefinger before selecting a long, slender trocar and inserting it through the navel. There was a sound similar to that of air escaping from a child's balloon, immediately followed by a strong, foul odor that forced Mirablis to turn away from the work at hand. Once he had recomposed himself, he pumped an infusion of elixir into the abdomen via a large hypodermic.

Satisfied with his handiwork, Mirablis stepped away from the body. Pompey silently moved in and, taking up the needle and thread from the instrument tray, began to suture the veins together again then return them to their rightful places with the exact same care he gave to darning his master's socks.

Mirablis stripped off his gloves and pulled a handkerchief from his pocket to mop his brow as he sat down on a nearby chair. Though he was tired, his energy was still high. He was very excited about the prospects for this subject. In many ways, this was the ideal specimen.

Mirablis desperately needed this one to succeed; he knew that this was very likely his last chance. He was close to a century in age. He'd outlived virtually everyone he'd ever known, with the exception of Pompey—and Pompey didn't count, really, since he technically died nearly forty years ago.

To bring back a walking, talking, reasoning white man from beyond the grave was all he needed to finally be able to announce to the world: "This is my gift to you, and it is good!"

He could only hope that the new subject did not share the same unfortunate side effects of revivification as Pompey and Sasquatch. And, if he did return to the land of the living, that he could use the tongue in his head to do more than scream. The last three revivals all had to be dismantled because of their unfortunate tendency to do nothing more than shriek and claw at their own flesh—and anything else that moved.

Pompey tapped his master on the shoulder, awaking the old man from a doze.

"Ah! Finished already, are we?" Mirablis said, peering at the sutures that ran along the dead man's neck, thighs and inner arms. "Excellent work, Pompey! Excellent! I'll make a surgeon of you yet! You may return him to the tank."

Pompey glanced at the unnatural position of the body's neck then back at Mirablis.

"No, I did not forget, Pompey!" Mirablis said with a dry laugh. "I am not that old a fool! I've decided not to repair the neck surgically and run the risk that the scalpel might slip and damage the spinal cord after the elixir has started its work. I have elected to use a less... intrusive... means of correcting our friend's neck problem. But all that will have to wait."

As Sasquatch placed the body within its cradle, Pompey stepped forward and fitted a metal skullcap onto its shaven head. An umbilicus of braided copper wire as thick as a man's finger ran from the top of the skullcap and passed through a hole drilled in the lid of the tank, where it lay on the cavern floor in a great coil, like a serpent from ancient myth. At the other end of the umbilicus was a huge lightning rod.

"You know what to do," Mirablis said to Sasquatch.

The Indian silently strapped the lightning rod across his back and hefted the heavy coil of copper wiring onto his shoulder. Then, with barely a grunt, the patchwork shaman began his climb from the bowels of the earth to the vault of heaven.

CHAPTER SEVEN

One of the primary reasons Mirablis had chosen this particular cavern to set up shop was that it possessed a natural chimney that permitted the circulation of fresh air from the outer world. As it so happened, the flue that served as the ventilation shaft was wide enough to accommodate a solitary climber. A normal, healthy adult male could make his way to the surface in three hours. Sasquatch, on the other hand, usually reached the top in just under forty-five minutes.

Sasquatch enjoyed climbing the chimney, as it was one of the few times where he was free of the old man. Without Mirablis's stream-of-consciousness monologues filling his mind, Sasquatch's thoughts were finally able to emerge. However, his thoughts were no more his own than were those given by Mirablis.

Once, long ago, Sasquatch had been a shaman. A warrior. A maker of shields. A buffalo hunter. But not as one man. Before the pony soldiers came, his name had not been Sasquatch, but Iron Crow. And Small Eagle. And Lean Bear. And Yellow Elk. There were others living within him as well—but these four were the loudest inside his head.

Sasquatch often sat in the darkness of the cave and traced the scars that covered his body, listening to the voices inside himself as they counted and cataloged what part belonged to whom.

Lean Bear would always start it off by saying: "The right arm is mine."

Then Small Eagle would chime in with: "The left arm belongs to me!"

"The right leg was once my own," Yellow Elk would reply.

Often the voices got into arguments as to whose body part was the most useful or strongest. Sometimes the discussions would get quite heated. Just when Sasquatch thought that the three would come to blows, Iron Crow would intone in his wisest voice: "But *mine* is his head and *mine* is his heart." This always made the others fall silent, much to Sasquatch's relief.

But try as he might, not even the part of Sasquatch that was Iron Crow could understand Mirablis's drive to conquer Death. A world without Death was a world out of balance—the very essence of madness. Yet, if there was one thing Sasquatch had learned, it was that most white men were crazy.

Over the years Sasquatch had watched Mirablis try time and time again to bring white men back from the spirit world. Those that emerged from the tank had all been worse than crazy, even in the eyes of the whites. They shook and foamed at the mouth like rabid animals while screaming and trying to bite and claw everything around them. Sasquatch believed they came back from the spirit world that way because most white men are a part of nothing but themselves, even when they are made of pieces of other white men. They were simply not used to living together, fighting together and dying together, as his people were.

Or perhaps the reason for their madness was because the white men Mirablis had tried to bring back were men whose bodies were unmourned and buried in paupers' graves. Maybe what they had seen while they were in the spirit world was what made them scream so horribly.

However, Sasquatch had a feeling the hanged man might be different. It was said among his people that the life of a man could be read in the manner of his death. In that case, the hanged man had died trying to protect something that was and yet was not of himself. Sasquatch knew what it was like to die that way.

The giant's train of thought was broken by a strong blast of cold air whistling down the flue. He shrugged the lightning rod off his crooked back and shoved it and what remained of the coil of copper wiring through the crevice that opened onto the surface. He then wriggled out through the narrow opening.

Sasquatch straightened himself as well as his crooked back allowed, blinking the dirt from his eyes. Glancing over the edge of the cliff, he could glimpse the roof of the cabin a hundred feet below. Looking out on the surrounding foothills and the imposing mountains that rose just beyond them, Sasquatch smiled as a feeling of peace came over him. He muttered a small prayer to the ancestors of his people.

Unlike Pompey, Sasquatch was not truly mute, but the effort it took for him to speak aloud effectively rendered him speechless under normal circumstances. Having finished his prayer, Sasquatch picked up the heavy lightning rod and jammed its sharpened point into the ground, then crouched low on his haunches and opened the leather pouch he wore on his breechcloth. He removed from his medicine pouch a pair of thunderstones, marked with the signs known only to shamans and the spirits who served them. As Sasquatch rattled the bones of the ancient beast-gods in his cupped hands, he began to chant in a voice twisted by disuse.

Even though it was the wrong time of year, and the conditions not right for such weather, storm clouds began to mass in the sky above. Sasquatch's distorted chant grew louder, more like the cry of an animal than a voice lifted in prayer. The clouds became heavier and darker, their bellies sporadically lit from within by brief flashes of purple white light. Sasquatch's chant grew faster and louder, until he was shouting over the howling wind that shook the stunted trees and scrub that surrounded him. Then, with a final, agonized cry that sent bloody spittle flying from his lips, a burning finger stabbed forth from the storm clouds and struck the lightning rod, followed by an explosion than shook the entire hillside.

Immediately following the thunderclap came a sudden clattering noise, as if a horde of giant warriors were banging their shields with their spears. Hailstones the size of quail eggs began to pour from the sky. Even though the chunks of ice struck with the force of stones from a sling, the nearly naked Sasquatch did not flinch as he knelt to embrace the storm, his jet black hair crackling like the pelt of a well-groomed cat.

Chapter Eight

Johnny Pearl never really had a good picture in his mind of what Heaven might look like. To tell the truth, he never really saw much point in worrying over it, since he was pretty sure he wasn't ever going to be let in.

Back when Johnny was a boy growing up in North Carolina, the preacher always seemed a lot more interested in warning the congregation about what was waiting for them in Hell than what they had to look forward to in Heaven. Still, Johnny had been under the general impression that Paradise was full of folks dressed in long white gowns with little wings sticking out their backs and halos over their heads, plucking harps and the like.

Johnny Pearl wasn't exactly sure where he was, but one thing was certain—it wasn't any Heaven he had heard tell of. But it wasn't any Hell he was familiar with neither. There weren't any mansions in the sky, or angels sitting on clouds, but there sure weren't any fellows with horns and pointy tails poking him in the butt with pitchforks.

As far as he could make out, he was at a big barn dance of some sort, with lots of other folk milling around, though he couldn't remember arriving or how he got there. Some of the people who were laughing and talking and dancing looked sort of familiar, though. He could have sworn he saw

Abraham Lincoln walk by, strolling alongside Stonewall Jackson. The two sipped cider and chatted like old school chums.

Pearl frowned and turned to study the other guests at the barn dance. Some of the people seemed on their own, while others walked arm in arm or in the company of entire families. Some looked happy, others looked frightened, but the vast majority wore expressions not too different from that of Johnny Pearl's—polite bafflement.

As he continued to scan the crowd, Pearl spotted a face in the string band he seemed to know but couldn't place. Then, with a jolt, he recognized the young mandolin player as having been a member of his regiment— one he had personally watch die of a shrapnel wound to the belly. The dead soldier paused long enough to nod hello to his war buddy, then resumed playing his mandolin.

"Johnny!" Someone was calling his name. Someone whose voice he'd thought was stilled forever. "Johnny! Over here!"

Katie waved at him from halfway across the barn, hopping up and down to get his attention. Pearl ran to his wife and snatched her up in his arms, twirling her about so fiercely Katie's feet left the ground.

"I missed you *so* much, Katie!" he said, though he could not remember how long it had been since he last laid eyes on his wife. Had it been weeks? Months? Seconds?

"I missed you too, Johnny." She smiled in return, her gaze fixed on a point just beyond his shoulder. "We *all* did."

Pearl turned to follow the direction of her gaze. Behind him stood his parents and younger brother. They looked exactly as he remembered last seeing them, the day he marched off to join his regiment.

Pearl opened his mouth to say how glad he was to see them, how much he had missed them, how sorry he was for not being there when they needed him most, but all that came out was a whispered, "Mama?"

Mrs. Pearl held out her hands to her eldest child, her eyes shining with tears of joy. "Oh, Johnny—I *knew* you'd make it."

Pearl made a soft sobbing noise as he took his mother's hands in his, covering the palms with kisses.

"It's good that you could make it, son," Mr. Pearl said, squeezing his son's shoulder. "We're proud of you, Johnny." Mr. Pearl stepped forward and pulled his son into his arms, kissing his cheek as he had wanted to do the day Johnny went off to war, but never did. "Always *have* been, always *will* be." Pearl was relieved to discover his father still smelled of his favorite pipe tobacco and penny licorice.

"Hey, Johnny!"

Pearl looked down at his younger brother, forever frozen at ten years old. "Hey, Tommy," he smiled, his hand dropping onto the boy's curly head.

Tommy frowned and cocked his head to one side. "How come you look different, Johnny?"

"It's been a long time since you last saw me, Tommy," Pearl explained gently.

"That's okay," Tommy replied, beaming up at his older brother. "Even though you look different, I still knew it was you."

"Come, Johnny," Katie said, holding out her arms to her husband. "Come dance with me."

Pearl smiled. He remembered how they used to dance to keep warm during the long, cold winter nights, their only music Katie's sweet voice lifted in song and the howling of the wind in the eaves.

As his arm closed about Katie's waist, Pearl felt something grab hold of his suspenders and yank. He frowned and glanced over his shoulder, but there was no one hovering behind him, trying to cut in. He shrugged and turned back to face his wife, pulling Katie close. There was a second, stronger yank on his suspenders—but this time it pulled him backward several feet, wrenching him free of his wife's embrace.

"Johnny!"

Pearl threw himself forward, doing his best to fight against whatever it was that was pulling him. Katie grabbed his outstretched hand and tried to keep him from slipping away any further, but it was no use. It felt as if someone was pulling him by the hair at the back of his head. Even though his feet were motionless, he continued to slide backward, like a iron filing dragged by a magnet.

As the other guests turned to stare in amazement, the barn doors flew open with a loud crash, revealing a white void beyond their threshold. There was a sound like a great wind roaring. With one final, mighty tug, Pearl was yanked off his feet and sent flying into the emptiness.

The last thing he saw as he was sucked into the maelstrom at the heart of nothing was Katie leaning out over the threshold, her hand still outstretched in a vain attempt to stop what was happening.

"I'll wait for you, Johnny—!" she called after him. "No matter what—I'll be waiting!"

And then the barn doors slammed shut.

Everything was blurry, and his left eye ached as if it had been yanked out of his head and stuck back in again. He coughed fitfully, expelling a lungful of thick, foul-tasting liquid.

Though his eyes rolled in their sockets like greased marbles, he was somehow aware of others standing over him. He tried to follow the ill-defined blobs that bobbed in and out of his impaired field of vision, but it was difficult to move his head. All he could make out was that one of the persons leaning over him was male and seemed to be very old. Suddenly the sound cut in, loud enough to make him wince.

"—neck brace. I repeat—don't try to move your head just yet. Do you understand what I'm saying?" Mirablis froze as the subject opened its mouth to reply. He glanced anxiously at Pompey, who showed him the revolver was ready, just in case.

But instead of screaming and clawing at his own flesh, the hanged man whispered one word—*"Why?"*—then lapsed once again into unconsciousness.

Mirablis grinned and shook his fists in the face of God. *"Yes!"* he shouted. "At long last—I've beaten you at your own game, Jehovah!" Still giddy with triumph, he motioned for his servant to put away the revolver. "I must enter all this into my journals while its still fresh in my mind! See that our new friend is made as comfortable as possible, and alert me the moment he begins to show signs of emerging from dormancy!" As Mirablis headed down the platform steps, he paused halfway, tapping his lower lip thoughtfully. "It occurs to me that it is time I picked a name for our new friend. He needs to be called *something*, doesn't he? And its only fitting that *I* name my creation, don't you agree?" Mirablis's wrinkled brow creased even further, then a mischievous light dawned in the old man's eyes. "Ah! Now I have it! I'll call him—Lynch!"

CHAPTER NINE

The darkness flowed over him, pouring in through the openings in his skull to flood his being from the inside out, like ink in a bottle. Then, in the very heart of the darkness there emerged a light—at first dim, then gradually growing in intensity, until it made his eyes swim with tears.

"Excellent!" said a voice from somewhere behind the light.

As the candle was moved away, an old man's wrinkled face emerged from the half-world of shadows.

"I was afraid the tear duct might have been damaged during the replacement, but that appears not to be the case," the old man said as he returned the candle to the miner's lamp he wore strapped to his head.

A Negro male with salt and pepper hair loomed suddenly into view. There was something peculiar about the black man's appearance, though he couldn't quite place it at first. Then he realized what it was: The whites of his eyes were glowing.

"Wh-where—?" he whispered hoarsely. His throat ached as if it had been cleaned with a curry comb.

"You needn't worry, Mr. Lynch. You're amongst friends now."

He frowned. "Lynch?"

"Yes. That's your name."

Though his mind was a jumble of pictures, voices and places, none of them in order, what the old man claimed didn't sound right to him. But he said nothing. It was easier simply to accept what he was being told than question it. If the old man said his name was Lynch, then that was who he was.

Lynch tried to turn his head to get a better look at his surroundings but met with resistance. Confused, he reached for his collarbone and encountered metal and leather.

The old man read the consternation on Lynch's face and patted his hand. "Don't worry, it's merely for... cosmetic purposes," he said gently.

"What—what happened?"

The old man's eyes narrowed. "Do you not remember?"

"N-no."

"You've been away for awhile, my dear boy, but now you're back."

"I want to sit up," Lynch said, his tone urgent.

"Very well. Pompey—help Mr. Lynch up." The old man moved aside, watching Lynch's movements with the same appraising stare a horse breeder gives a new born colt.

From what he could see, they were in a cave that had been retrofitted for human habitation. Mixed in with the more mundane pieces of furniture, such as a table and chairs, were items of such an arcane nature it was hard to tell if they were medical instruments or art objects. After taking in his surroundings, Lynch turned his body slightly toward the old man.

"Who are you?"

"I am Doctor Anton Mirablis, late of the Academy of Sciences, former physician to His Excellency, Napoleon I, and graduate of the University of Vienna—"

"You a sawbones?"

Mirablis winced slightly. "In so many words—yes."

"What's wrong with my neck, Doc?"

In way of a reply, Mirablis picked up a silver-chased hand mirror from the nearby table and held it so that it reflected Lynch's body from the torso on up.

The face that looked back at him was his own, yet not his. His head and face were as hairless as those of a newborn babe. There was new scarring about his bright blue left eye—which stood in extreme contrast to the brown eye on his right. The brace that supported his upper neck extended from just below his chin to his shoulders and looked like a cross between a medieval torture device and a corset. After a moment, Lynch met Mirablis's gaze.

"You said I've been away. Where was that?"

"Where no one need ever go again."

<hr />

It really wasn't that difficult for Lynch to accept the fact that he had died and been brought back to life by this kindly old man with the long white hair and slight European accent. It did bother him, however, that he could not remember much about the life he had lead before his death, even though Dr. Mirablis had assured him that such memory loss—he called it amnesia— was not uncommon in connection with electrical shocks.

It had been three days since he had been delivered from the artificial womb of the tank, and Lynch was now able to move about without Pompey being there to make sure he didn't fall. It had taken him a while to grow accustomed to the neck brace—especially how it necessitated that he turn his entire body if he wished to look to either side—but it soon became second nature to him. Mirablis had been pleased by how quickly he had adapted to the situation.

Lynch sat in a chair as Mirablis poked and prodded him and hit his knee with a little toy tomahawk-looking hammer. Every so often he would mutter to himself and scribble something down in a big leather-bound book on the table.

"How am I doin', Doc?" he asked.

"Your progress is most exceptional, my dear boy!" Mirablis replied. "Your recovery following revivification is much swifter than those of either Pompey or Sasquatch."

Noticing how Lynch shifted uneasily upon the mention of the patch-work creature's name, Mirablis simply laughed and shook his head. "You should not be afraid of poor Sasquatch!" he chided. "He cannot help being as I have made him. And, in a way, you owe him a debt of gratitude."

"What do you mean?"

"Though I devised the method that brought you back—it was Sasquatch who provided the energy to rekindle your spark of life."

"How can that be?" Lynch frowned, even more baffled than before.

"I, myself, have seen Sasquatch summon the lightning the way a country gentleman might whistle up his hounds. It has proven most advantageous for my work to be able to summon the celestial fire at my whim, rather than waiting for an opportune thunderstorm. It is amazing that such a creature composed of illiterate savages, little removed from their prehistoric ances- tors, should hold such awesome power, is it not? But then again—is it any more amazing that the dead rise from their graves? But enough about Sasquatch!"

Mirablis produced a small, smooth rock from the pocket of his waistcoat, holding it between his thumb and forefinger. "Do you see this stone, Lynch? In a moment, I'm going to let it drop. I want you to grab it before it strikes the ground while looking straight ahead. Do you understand?"

"Yes, sir," Lynch replied, his gaze automatically fixing on the older man's eyes.

"Very good." To the old man's surprise, no sooner had his fingers loosened their grip on the stone then Lynch's hand snatched it away. Indeed, the movement was so quick, a casual viewer might have thought the younger man had simply grabbed the stone out of Mirablis's hand.

"Amazing! Truly amazing!" Mirablis said, mopping his wrinkled brow with a handkerchief. "Such reflexes—!"

"It wasn't just reflexes," Lynch said matter-of-factly. "I knew when you were going to drop it."

Mirablis lifted an eyebrow. "How so?"

"I looked at your eyes. A split second before you let go, I saw the corner of your eyes tighten and your pupil contract. That's when I knew to make my move."

Mirablis stopped daubing his brow and stared at Lynch. "Most extraordinary. How did you *know* to look for these signs, dear boy?"

Lynch shrugged as best he could while wearing a neck brace. "I dunno. I just did. Do you think it's something I learned back when I was alive the first time, Doc?"

"It's possible," Mirablis said absently. The old man took Lynch's hands and opened them, staring at the palms as if they held some mystery within them. "But I did not expect such an instinctual response from a man of your background...."

"Background?"

"You were a settler... a farmer," Mirablis said cautiously. "You were killed by Indians. Do you remember?"

There was a faraway look in Lynch's brown eye, while the blue remained disturbingly clear. "I remember a cabin. And something about Injuns. But everything else is foggy."

"You memory might come back, or it might not come back at all. But in case you do not reclaim your lost memories—do not dwell overmuch on it, my friend. In many ways, the life that was once yours is no more an integral part of your new existence than a cocoon is to the butterfly.

"You are of a new breed—*Homo Mirablis*. I hope you don't think me too forward for naming your species after myself. You are stronger now, possessed of a stamina beyond that of mortal men. You can withstand incredible physical stress and trauma without registering a moment's pain. You need little more than a hour's sleep a day.

You need to eat only once or twice a month. Your eyesight is as sharp as that of a cat. No matter if it is the dead of winter or the height of summer, weather means nothing to your physical comfort. Disease, old age, infirmity… these things no longer hold meaning for you. You are free to pursue all your dreams, all your ambitions without fear or distraction."

"That all sounds mighty nice, Doc. But what are the drawbacks?"

"Drawbacks?" Mirablis blinked, genuinely baffled by the question. "What do you mean?"

"Well—everything's got two sides, Doc."

Mirablis's cheeks flamed red. "You are speaking nonsense! There is no drawback to immortality! I am very tired now and need to rest." Mirablis turned and hurried back to his aboveground quarters with the jerky movements of a man trying to contain his anger.

Lynch could not understand what he did to upset Doctor Mirablis. He certainly had not intended to do such a thing. So far the old gentleman had shown him nothing but kindness. It made him feel bad to think he had done something to agitate the doctor in such a way.

Lynch returned to the narrow army-issue cot that served as his bed and sat down on its far edge, staring at the stalagmites. He felt as he had when his father used to punish him for whispering in church. Except he could not remember, exactly, what his father's face looked like.

The sound of a foot scraping the ground nearby startled him from his reverie. He glanced up and saw Sasquatch hovering in the shadows, the whites of his eyes glowing eerily. Lynch suppressed his natural urge to scream and instead met the creature's lambent gaze.

"What do you want?"

The crooked giant took a tentative step forward, eyes burning like twin suns. "She says she still waits for you."

Lynch was not sure what surprised him more: that the creature's voice was like that of rocks being ground together, or that Sasquatch had spoken Cheyenne—and he had understood him perfectly.

CHAPTER TEN

When Mirablis next came to see Lynch, the old man wore a contrite expression on his face. "I have been thinking about what you said the other day. You are right. It is only fair that you understand—truly understand—the reasons for what I do and what I have done. It is important to me that you comprehend the scope of my experiments and discoveries, so that you may help me in my work, in your own unique way, as Pompey and Sasquatch do in theirs.

"In order to do this, my dear Lynch, I must tell you my story. It begins in a different world, indeed, a different century, than the one we inhabit now. Do you know that I was not brought into this world as Anton Mirablis? My true name is of no importance, really. I cast aside my old identity when I fled Europe for this wondrous country of yours. A new life is deserving of a new name, don't you agree?

"Still, for all of America's raw-boned lawlessness, it is nothing compared to the chaos and madness of the Terror and the wars that followed. This was the world of my youth. I was a gifted child, showing a natural aptitude for the physical sciences early in life. My parents were among those who benefited from the fall of the ancient regime and therefore could afford to indulge my precocious nature.

"I was little more than a boy when I was shipped off to the university in Vienna to study medicine. It was there I gained the attention of a brilliant anatomist of the name Viktor von Frankenstein... perhaps you have heard of him?"

Lynch frowned and squinted. "The name sounds familiar—but I can't remember nothin' about it except that its from a made-up story."

"Oh, Viktor was real enough, I assure you! Just as Kit Carson and Wild Bill Hickock and Buffalo Bill are real. And, like them, the story told about my old friend and colleague was just as far removed from the truth.

"I soon learned that Viktor and I shared similar interests—mainly a desire to break Death's grip on the mind of man. He needed someone to help him with his research, but he did not want a mere assistant—he required someone as intelligent and as dedicated as himself. He needed someone who could be trusted to understand the problems such unorthodox experiments faced, someone willing to brave the dangers they held, both physically and socially. And, to his credit, he was capable of recognizing those qualities in me despite my tender years.

"Ours was a close and, by default, secretive relationship. The intensity of our shared obsession, at times, bound us more tightly than lovers. We worked side by side, in an atmosphere of such emotional intensity that it was bound to happen that we should have a serious falling out.

"What caused our disagreement was a divergence between us on how best to realize our goal. Viktor was convinced that a body stitched together from the undamaged pieces of cadavers could be given life through applying electrical current to the nervous system. However, I was concerned with the question of decay, which lead to my creation of the elixir re-vitae as a means of restoring and preserving soft tissues.

"Essentially, our difference lay in our own very personal interpretations of the act of Creation. For Viktor, it was all very Promethean and Old Testament, with lightning and fire from Heaven and the like. He would fashion himself a man of clay and breathe the fire of Life into it and that was that.

"I, on the other hand, looked not to mythology, but man himself—or should I say, woman?—for my inspiration. Dissecting the cadavers of pregnant women revealed to me that we are creatures of the sea, and that within every female there lies a secret ocean, in which the evolution of our species is re-enacted, from briny shrimp to naked ape.

"In the end, though Viktor was my elder, it was he who suffered the problem most associated with youth—impatience. He wanted results. My method was far too slow to suit his tastes. In any case, there was a serious falling out between us, which resulted in us going our separate ways.

"I made the best of my situation by attaching myself to Napoleon's personal entourage, eventually becoming one of the physicians in charge of the battlefield hospitals. This gave me unprecedented—and unsupervised—access to all the amputated limbs I could ever want.

"However, when I traveled with him to Egypt, my interest was piqued by rumors of certain recipes and formulae concerning the preservation and resurrection of the dead found in a scroll believed to be written by the lord high embalmer to the pharaohs. However, not long after my return to Europe from the mysterious Orient, I received a package containing the journals and notes of my former friend and colleague. Along with these was a letter from Viktor, informing me that he had been forced to abandon his experiments.

"He conceded my method of reviving the dead was superior to his own—though he warned me of dire consequences should I pursue my interests. As I read his journals, I learned that Viktor did, indeed, build a man from the bodies of the dead. He succeed in bringing it back to life using the harnessed power of a thunderstorm. That much of the story is true. However, the creature who rose from that slab was no more capable of narrating its own plight than it could fly to the moon.

"The thing was... damaged in the brain. And, to make matters worse, not long after its was revived, it began to rot. To spend so many years and so much energy on research, and to have nothing to show for it but a wretched, stinking imbecile! It was all too much for Viktor, I'm afraid.

"He took the creature out onto the glacier and left it there without food or shelter, thinking it would surely die. Then he returned home and, in a moment of utter despair, wrote what would prove to be his final letter. Unfortunately for poor Viktor, he had no way of knowing at the time that the story was far from over.

"Instead of freezing to death on the glacier, Viktor's creature made its way down the mountain and proceeded to ravage the countryside, devouring sheep and sheepherders alike. Although incapable of speech or higher brain functions, it was somehow possessed of a perverse homing instinct, and it eventually made its way back to Viktor. It attacked and killed my friend and his young wife in the most barbaric manner imaginable, devouring them both.

"Not long thereafter, the walking cadaver was found in a hut in the nearby woods. It was surprised by a local hunter while it dined on the intestines of the hapless blind man that called the hovel his home, and was finally dispatched by a musket ball to the head.

"However, when the rumors concerning Viktor's connection to the creature that had slain not only him, but at least six other people, began to circulate, I deemed it wise to remove myself from the Continent.

"That is when I came to this country. I first arrived in Philadelphia, where I quickly established myself under my new name... that of Dr. Anton Mirablis. For several years, I was able to pursue my experiments in relative secret, with able assistance from Pompey, who I purchased from the master who abused him so cruelly.

"It was during these years that I attempted to refine the elixir re-vitae, combining it with the ancient Egyptian formulae and rituals. It was very difficult to locate the necessary elements needed for the mixture, and the slightest variation in temperature during the distilling could have proven disastrous.

"It was a long process of trial and error, but eventually I succeeded in keeping amputated limbs and other organs from not only rotting, but continuing their original functions as well. Yet, try as I might, I was unable to generate the necessary spark of life that Viktor had managed to infuse in his creation, hapless as it may have been.

"I eventually came to the decision that what was needed for me to succeed was to combine my technique with that of Viktor's. So I set about creating a giant womb, if you will, and filling it with elixir, whose special properties would be activated by passing massive electric currents through both it and the subject.

"Are you ready for some fresh air—?"

"Sure," Lynch said, taken aback by the suddenness of Mirablis's suggestion.

"Very good. I'll use the occasion to introduce you to the subject of my first successful revival."

⊷◆⊶

After the darkness of the cavern, the pale light of a winter day was enough to make Lynch's eyes water. He stood for a moment in front of the cabin and stared at his surroundings, hoping to summon forth a memory that might tell him who he was.

"So—where's this fella you brought back from the dead, Doc?" he said, glancing over at Mirablis, who was bundled in a buffalo-skin coat and a hat made from a rabbit.

"He's over here, my boy," he said, gesturing toward a small barnlike structure built alongside the cabin.

The interior of the stable was dark and close, with most of the space occupied by Mirablis's medicine wagon. Standing in the solitary stall was a coal black stallion, nosing a mound of straw. In the dim light, it looked as if the beast's eye sockets were filled with smoldering fire.

Lynch turned to fix Mirablis with a stare of utter disbelief. *"A horse—?!?"*

The old man shrugged. "It was a matter of convenience. I needed to test my technique on something large—and it was far easier to get my hands on a livery animal than a baboon or gorilla. I suppose I *could* have used a pig, but their flesh spoils so quickly...."

Mirablis shuffled forward, smiling indulgently at the beast as it pawed the ground. "Do you know anything about mythology?"

"I can't rightly say," Lynch said, shrugging his shoulders. "I remember something about a guy with thunderbolts—and something about a fella with wings on his feet and a pie plate on his head."

"It doesn't really matter if you do," Mirablis replied. "Viktor used to joke about how he was Prometheus while I was Pluto. Ironic, don't you think, considering where I have ended up—and how he ended? Still, that is why I chose to name this fine animal after the horse that pulled the chariot of the Lord of the Underworld.

"In any case, as of June 27th, 1840, Alastor became the first successful subject of my revivification process, and he has served me most ably ever since." Mirablis's hand dipped into his coat pocket and produced what looked like gobbets of raw meat. To Lynch's surprise, the horse eagerly gobbled them down as it they were lumps of sugar.

"That's a good boy," Mirablis smiled, stroking the beast's neck.

"Y-you just fed that animal meat!"

Mirablis's smile disappeared instantly. "It is cold out here. Let's go back inside. I felt the need for some hot tea."

——⊰◆⊱——

Pompey hurried forward and helped Mirablis out of his burdensome coat and hat as they entered the cabin. The old man hobbled to the table, where a white porcelain tea pot sat, along with a solitary matching cup. Mirablis motioned for Lynch to take the seat opposite him at the table.

"You asked me the other day about the... side effects that accompany revivification. I will admit that I was... unprepared for such a question, and I responded most rudely. But you are right—if anyone deserves straight answers as to what to expect, it is you.

"When I killed Alastor the first time he was a three-year-old stallion at the height of his stamina. In the decades that have passed since, he has not aged a day, nor has he ever been ill. He can ride for days on end without rest or food and still remain as strong as a dozen horses.

"Yet there have been—changes in his nature. Such as the one you saw. Alastor is no longer a harmless herbivore, like others of his kind. He now has a taste for flesh. Raw flesh, to be exact. However, Alastor only needs to be fed once every six weeks... not unlike certain large snakes."

"But he's just a *horse*," Lynch said anxiously. "That doesn't mean those changes will occur in a *human*—right?"

Mirablis sighed as he lifted his tea cup. "There is much even *I* don't understand about the revivification process, I'm afraid. *Why* is there heightened strength? *Why* is there a reduction in the need for sleep and a suppression of appetite? And, most important of all, *why* can't the subjects digest anything but raw meat?"

"You mean I'm some kinda *ghoul*?" Lynch shouted, his voice cracking as he jumped to his feet.

Pompey stepped forward and pointed a pistol directly at Lynch's head.

"Pompey! Put that away!" Mirablis snapped. "There's no need for it! Our friend is merely upset—and justifiably so! Please, Lynch—sit back down. You're making Pompey nervous."

Lynch sat down slowly while keeping an eye on the mute. Pompey, for his part, did not lower the gun until Lynch was once again seated.

Mirablis clucked his tongue in reproof. "You're agitating yourself for no reason, my boy! As I said, feeding occurs only once every six weeks, and is easily controlled, if you prepare for it properly. A couple of bighorn sheep is usually enough to keep Pompey and Sasquatch satisfied. Just because you *must* eat raw flesh in order to survive does not make you a monster!

"Besides, your diet is the least of your problems. One major drawback to your new life is that you must pay a great deal of attention to your physical integrity. Since your pain threshold is so incredibly high, it tends to block signals regarding "minor" injuries. What this means is you are in constant danger of accidentally losing a body part without being aware of it. Fingers and toes are the most vulnerable, as well as the ears. However, its nothing a little needle and thread can't fix.

"You will need to undergo periodic checks for signs of corruption… since its likely not all portions of your body were infused with equal amounts of the elixir re-vitae. Those areas that may have been missed will gradually begin to rot, if not caught in time. I'll show you the proper means of administering injections to yourself later on. Should access to the elixir re-vitae prove difficult, soaking your body in cold water is a suitable stopgap."

"That's all well and good, Doc—but you still haven't told me how you ended up living in a cave with Pompey and Sasquatch for company."

Mirablis blinked. "No, I haven't, have I? I'm afraid I'm easily distracted nowadays. Thank you for reminding, my dear boy. Now, where was I—? Well, you can imagine how pleased I was by how Alastor turned out. Then, less than a week later, I was presented with a chance to try my process on a *human* subject!

"I was holding a dinner party for some of my fellows at the Academy. While I despise such charades, I've long accepted the necessity of maintaining the proper respectability, especially in a city such as Philadelphia.

"However, much to my chagrin, Pompey suffered a massive heart attack and died while in the middle of serving the poached trout! Of course, it was simply 'not done' to cancel a dinner party because a servant—a slave, at that—had keeled over dead during the main course.

"Imagine, if you can, my consternation as I was forced to endure several more hours of meaningless chit-chat with those empty-headed boobies, all the while knowing that Pompey's body was succumbing to decomposition! After the evening sherry and cigars were done with, I lost no time in hurrying my tiresome 'fellow intellectuals' out of the house.

"I took hours for me to prepare Pompey's body for revivification, using a variation on the voltaic cell developed by John Daniell to force a sufficient electrical charge through Pompey's body, thereby activating the elixir and reviving him. I was delighted to have my faithful assistant returned to me, but I was frustrated by Pompey's inability to express his experiences and physical symptoms to me, except in dumb show. And since he had never learned how to read and write—after all, teaching slaves such things was sorely frowned on in those days—I was at something of a loss.

"Then there was the question of how to explain Pompey's return after he had died very publicly, in front of my so-called peers, without alerting them to what I was doing?

"Since I did not feel my work was ready for such scrutiny, I decided to leave Philadelphia and pursue my research elsewhere. For several years I wandered the country, keeping households everywhere from New Orleans to Minneapolis—all the while attempting to replicate my success with Pompey, but with disappointing results.

"I discovered there was still much to learn—as Pompey and Alastor soon showed me. Little over a month after his revivification, Alastor went berserk in New Orleans and kicked down his stall—assaulting and devouring his stable mate.

"Not long after that happened, Pompey ate three servants in my employ. Luckily, they were slaves, so their disappearance did not raise any alarms. Believe me, Pompey was most contrite about what happened. And except for occasional lapses into frenzy—not unlike those of a woman enslaved to the cycle of the moon—he has remained as sober as a judge. Once I began to understand the nature of his attacks, I was able to prepare in advance, thus making sure Pompey received nourishment without killing anything more sentient than a steer.

"When the war between the states erupted, I knew neither North nor South would be safe for me—so I opted to head West. I assumed the guise of a medicine-show drummer, which allowed me to continue my experiments—and for a nickel, Pompey would bite the head off any animal the audience cared to provide, which helped cut down on expenses, as you might expect.

"I used the medicine show to test various weakened and recombined formulas of the elixir re-vitae designed specifically for oral consumption, and discovered that while it could not cure the croup or the Regrets of Venus, it *did* seem to have an effect on cancer. Then, eight years ago, I came across the remains of an Indian camp.

"There had been a recent massacre of unspeakable barbarity. Not only the braves, but the women and children—even the elders of the tribe—had been systematically butchered. I was lucky in that the massacre sight was relatively fresh and had yet to be scavenged by crows and coyotes. I harvested the least damaged body parts and proceeded to make myself a composite human, just as Viktor had once done.

"I will admit that my motives were a combination of scientific curiosity and pride. I was determined to stitch together a human that would be an improvement over Viktor's infamous monster. The result was Sasquatch.

"There is no doubt in my mind that he is superior to Viktor's poor mad, rotting creature. However, Sasquatch was basted together from bodies that were far from... fresh, which may account for the difficulty he has with speaking. Another problem is that compared to Pompey, Sasquatch is noticeably... awkward, though astonishingly strong. Still, aesthetically speaking, he is far from pleasing. That is where you come in, my handsome lad."

"Handsome—?" Lynch snorted derisively. "You're calling *me* handsome?"

"In comparison to that which has gone before, you are Michelangelo's David!" Mirablis said with a flourish of his hand. "Granted, the neck brace is far from fashionable, and your eyes don't match—but you are otherwise presentable. Most importantly, my boy, you are *white*. What good would it do me to show the Academy a redskin I've brought back from the dead—? After all, they're doing their damnedest to wipe them off the face of the planet!

"More importantly—I need you to serve as a heir to my work. You have demonstrated the intelligence and dexterity necessary to be trained in the techniques of reviving the dead. With my knowledge and your innate skill, mankind need never be inconvenienced by mortality ever again! Think of it, Lynch—just *think*!"

"Yeah—I'm thinkin'," Lynch muttered. "Look, Doc—I realize you did all this to help folks out, just like that fella that invented laudanum or Mr. Fulton and his steam engine. But did it ever occur to you even *once* while you was doin' all this—that mebbe there's better things than simply being alive... and worse things than being dead?"

Mirablis frowned and cocked his head to one side. "Interesting. I wonder if you were as prone to philosophy before your death. Pompey, return our new friend to the cave."

The mute stepped forward and motioned with the muzzle of his gun for Lynch to rise.

Chapter Eleven

That night she came to him, emerging from the shadows as if she had always dwelt within them. She was lit from within by a pale fire that burned like a swarm of fireflies trapped in a jar.

"Hey, Johnny."

Even though Lynch did not know his first name, upon hearing it on her lips, he knew it to be his. "Hello," he replied.

"Do you remember me?" she asked.

"Yes, I remember you, Katie," he said, his voice shaking.

"I still wait," she whispered. And, having said that, she disappeared like a candle flame snuffed between wetted fingers.

Lynch lowered his head into his hands and stared at his feet. He remembered it all now: his family, the war, his life as an outlaw... and Katie. And he remembered how all those things had been lost to him, and then found—only to be torn away from him a second, horrible time.

He opened his eyes to find the twisted visage of Sasquatch peering down at him. To his surprise, the patchwork creature no longer frightened him.

"How can you serve him?" Lynch asked the giant, speaking in his native tongue.

Sasquatch shrugged his uneven shoulders. "Mirablis repaired me the best way he knew how. And now my tribe, though dead, lives within me still. In my own fashion, I am content, my brother."

"Why did you show her to me? It *was* you who did that, wasn't it?"

"I did it so that you would not forget. You were a man of honor, Johnny Pearl—and that sense of honor lives within you still."

"How did you know that was my name—?"

"There are no secrets for those who speak with the dead," Sasquatch said. "I saw it as my duty to awake your memories, since Mirablis was unwilling to do so. The old man is afraid you will insist on hunting down those who killed you."

"Then he was right to be afraid—because that's *exactly* what I intend to do!"

Sasquatch nodded his head sagely. "I will show you how to escape this place, if that is what you want."

"Escape—? You mean I'm being held prisoner?"

The giant fixed him with a dubious look. "Do *you* feel you are free to leave this place?"

"Good point," Lynch grunted. "So—what do you propose? Wait until the old man's asleep and then sneak out the door?"

Sasquatch shook his head. "Mirablis is no real concern—the problem is Pompey. He is loyal to his master without question. And he does not sleep. He stands guard over the old man while he slumbers, effectively blocking the way through the cabin."

"So what are you telling me—that I'll have to kill Pompey to get out of here?"

Sasquatch shook his head. "No, there is another way out—one that not even Mirablis knows of."

The giant stood up and motioned for Lynch to follow, leading him into one of the smaller tunnels that branched off from the main cavern. The tunnel quickly narrowed so that they had to turn sideways in order to squeeze through. Suddenly the passage widened again, ending in a cul-de-sac. Sasquatch shot Lynch a conspiratorial smile over his shoulder as he reached out and moved a chunk of the wall.

There was a sudden gust of chill air and a spill of dim light that—in comparison to the gloom of the cave—seemed like the heart of the sun. Along with the burst of cold air and sunlight came the odor of manure and straw.

Alastor did not seem at all surprised to see Sasquatch and Lynch emerge from the wall. The stallion snorted and tossed its head, pawing the floor of its makeshift stall. Sasquatch smiled with his crooked mouth and stroked the beast's raven black neck.

"This animal has a great heart. He will take you where you must go without complaint or fear."

Lynch opened the barn door and glanced outside. The wind was blowing a mixture of sleet and snow down from the mountains. "There's a storm coming."

"That is why you must hurry. If you wait much longer, it will be impossible to leave before the spring."

"I can't leave now! I'm not dressed for it! I don't have any provisions—"

"Have you eaten since you emerged from the tank?"

Lynch paused. "No," he said slowly.

"Are you hungry?"

"Now that you mention it—no."

"Then what need have you for provisions? And as for your clothes—" Sasquatch gestured to the buckskins and woolen shirt Lynch was wearing. "You will find you are dressed warmly enough."

"Are you *mad*—? My blood will freeze in my veins!"

Sasquatch smiled crookedly. "*Blood?* You have no blood." Sasquatch held up his left hand and sliced open the palm with the knife that hung from his belt.

A greenish yellow fluid welled from the wound, like sap from a sugar maple. "The cold is nothing to our kind, little brother." He reached behind a bale of hay and produced a laden saddlebag, which he tossed to Lynch. "All you need is in that bag: flasks of elixir re-vitae, a syringe, and some needle and thread. Use it wisely."

Alastor fixed Lynch with a curious stare but did not resist the bit placed between his teeth or the saddle cinched about his belly. There was a self-awareness to the beast, born from living decades beyond its natural span, that Lynch found almost human.

As he swung himself into the saddle, he found himself eye to eye with the patchwork giant. Lynch felt a flush of shame as he remembered how he had first reacted to the Indian's appearance.

"I cannot thank you enough for what you have done for me, Sasquatch—"

"The part of me who helped you is called Iron Crow."

"Then I thank that which is Iron Crow," Lynch replied . "But still—I don't understand. Why do you stay here, if is so easy for you to leave? Why do you serve Mirablis as you do?"

"I attend the white man out of respect for his wisdom, for he is indeed wise. But he is also mad. He made me, and in his way he is both my father and my mother—as such, I owe him my life and my loyalty.

"And I know, for as much as he desires to free mankind from Death, he fears the process he has created. When he dies—his knowledge dies with him. So I stay with him—to make sure it does." The giant suddenly shook his head, as if trying to dislodge something from his ear. "Enough talk! Iron Crow says you must leave now or not at all! Go—! And good hunting to you, Lynch-who-once-was-Johnny-Pearl."

Lynch put his heels to Alastor's flanks. The horse took flight, nimbly making its way down the twisting path that lead to the cabin. As they made their way down the side of the mountain, Lynch looked back, but there was nothing to see except a jumble of scrub and rock.

CHAPTER TWELVE

The winds howled down out of the mountains and across the high plains like damned souls loosed from the coldest regions of Hell, tearing at the flesh and clothes of the solitary rider making his away across the forbidding steppes. Yet, despite a naked scalp covered by a gleaming skullcap of frost and buckskins so stiff with ice they creaked, the lone horseman showed no sign of discomfort. Nor did his mount slow its relentless pace as it made its way through the stinging sleet and snow, even when it was forced to shoulder its way through drifts as tall as a man.

———◆———

All that was left was the chimney.

Once, not that long ago, Johnny Pearl and Katie Small Dove had danced before its fire, made love before its warmth. Now it jutted from the jumble of charred timber like a skeletal finger, pointing at the bleak winter sky. If it had not remained standing, Lynch would have ridden past without realizing it, since what few landmarks that existed were otherwise shrouded in snow and ice.

Once he spotted the chimney, he used it to triangulate the location of the stand of cottonwood trees. When he found the one they had used to hang him, he stood for a moment, staring up at the six-inch length of frayed rope still flapping from the branch.

It took him somewhat longer to find what was left of Katie's body under the snow. As he swept the snow away from her, he was struck by how perfectly preserved she appeared to be—like one of those snow princesses in the fairy tales his mama used to read to him as a child.

She was laying on her side, much like the last time he remembered seeing her before he died. The scavengers hadn't done much to the carcass, possibly because she froze to the ground quickly, which made the mutilations even more bestial.

It took Lynch two days to build the cairn using the natural stone from the chimney. He used a rusty shovel he found amid the ruins of the shed and, summoning the fearsome strength that was his new birthright, single-handedly demolished the fireplace. He worked day and night without respite, oblivious to the damage he was doing to himself. When the blisters burst, a yellowish green ichor streamed forth across his palms instead of blood.

Once he had built the cairn over his wife's body, Lynch turned his attention to the flagstone that ringed the hearth. When the shovel's blade shattered, he tossed it aside and continued digging at the frozen ground with his bare hands until he succeeded in finally unearthing a package wrapped in oil cloth, inside of which was a bundle of neatly folded black clothes and a pearl-handled revolver.

Lynch lifted the killing piece and pressed the length of its cold muzzle against his cheek, stroking his face with it as if it were made of the finest silk.

"I knew you would not forsake me," whispered the gun.

Lynch closed his eyes and said nothing.

———◦◦◦———

The dying man crawled on his hands and knees, dragging a piece of gut in his wake. The dying man's name was Polk and, up until a hour ago, he'd been out on a toot with a couple of his desperado friends.

Polk knew O'Donoghue and Wagner from when he used to scout for Drake. But, unlike them, Polk did not consider himself an outlaw. And since someone had been making a point of going after men from Drake's regiment the last few months, he was quick to remind folks that he was just a scout who kept colorful company, nothing more.

It was Wagner's idea that they hit the saloon as a team, just to be on the safe side. O'Donoghue was of the opinion the killings were done by vigilantes who'd gotten brave now that Drake was officially declared a renegade back east. It wasn't surprising, given the red-headed bastard's proclivities.

Wagner and O'Donoghue had deserted a while back, but whoever was gunning for Drake probably wasn't one for splitting hairs. Wagner had said there was safety in numbers, and this way they could drink, gamble and whore while watching one another's backs, which had made sense to Polk at the time.

But that was before the man in black showed up.

Polk had figured the stranger for trouble when he first entered the saloon. He was tall, dressed in a tattered black duster that had blotches of graveyard mold on the sleeves. He wore a pearl-handled revolver low on his hip. The stranger walked real stiff, like that steam-operated mechanical man Polk saw at the circus once. But the strangest thing about the man in black was his eyes—they didn't match.

The stranger had walked right up to their table and opened fire without so much as a "howdy doo." Wagner and O'Donoghue were dead before they could put down their cards—and Polk would have met the exact same fate if that fancy pearl-handled gun hadn't misfired.

Polk didn't know what the stranger's quarrel was with Wagner and O'Donoghue, and he wasn't about to waste time asking. He jumped to his feet and fired point-blank into the other man's chest. The man in black staggered but did not go down.

As Polk tried to flee past the man he'd just shot, the stranger lashed out with a knife, catching him across the gut. Polk had been so frightened that he was on his horse and a mile out of town before he realized the seriousness of his wound.

Yeah, there was nothing like looking down and seeing your lower intestine hanging out of your belly, that much was for sure. Once the adrenaline wore off, the pain took over. Polk fell off the horse not long after that.

Still, even though he was in more pain than he'd ever know again—Polk continued to crawl. Some long-buried sixth sense told him that he had not escaped the man who had tried to kill him. Indeed, it was as if the stranger's mismatched eyes were staring down at him from a great height, watching as he dragged his guts behind him like the losing cur in a dog fight.

It wasn't until he heard the stranger's horse whinny that Polk realized he was lying on his back like a tipped turtle, staring up at a dark figure framed against the hard blue sky.

Lynch carefully dismounted and knelt beside Polk without actually look-ing down. As he leaned across the dying man to relieve him of his weapons, Polk glimpsed a metal and leather neck brace underneath the long woolen muffler wrapped around the stranger's throat.

"Where the hell do you think you're runnin' to, you damn fool idjit—?" Lynch snarled. "You think Drake can protect you?"

"Fuck Drake!" Polk spat. ""Mister—I don't know what you're talkin' about or why you come after me like you did—I ain't never done nothin' to you—!"

"Like fuck you're innocent!" Lynch growled. "I know you got it on you—that drinkin' buddy of yours in Caspar said so. So where is it?"

"Where's what—?!?" Polk moaned, licking his lips. He was so thirsty he could almost forget the pain in his belly. "Please, Mister... I'll be more than happy to tell you whatever it is you want to hear, if you just gimme a drink of water.... I need a drink real bad...."

Lynch snorted in disgust and began to search the dying man's pockets. As his fingers closed on what lay coiled in Polk's breast pocket, he gave voice to a groan as pained as Polk's own. He lurched stiffly to his feet, pulling the braid from its hiding place like a conjurer producing a scarf.

Lynch ran Katie's hair between his fingers, marveling over how little it had changed. The months since her death had done nothing to diminish its luster or texture. Lynch closed his eyes as he stroked the braid against his cheek. It even smelled of her. The only thing different from when it was still on her head was that Polk had bound the end that had attached to the scalp with a piece of rawhide, so it would not unravel.

"Mister..." Polk rasped. "Please... I gotta have some water."

Lynch pocketed the length of hair and turned to remove the canteen from his saddle horn. Alastor pawed the ground, tossing its ebony mane.

"I don't like how your hoss is lookin' at me," Polk said.

"What you gonna do about it?" Lynch said, throwing the canteen on the ground.

"You know—drinkin' with a belly wound will kill you," Lynch commented laconically as he watched Polk eagerly slurp down the water he'd given him.

"What do I care—I'm dyin' anyway, ain't I?" rasped Polk, wiping his lips with a trembling hand.

"Reckon so," Lynch replied, studying the length of intestine hanging out of Polk. It oozed blood and less identifiable matter, and had little pieces of gravel stuck in it. It looked bad and smelled worse.

"Tell me one thing before I die, mister," Polk whispered. "Why'd you come gunnin' for me? It weren't just for some squaw braid, was it?"

"You don't recognize me," Lynch sighed. "I don't blame you for that, really. I reckon you never expected to see me again—so why bother commitin' th' face to memory?"

Polk squinted at his killer's face with rapidly failing eyesight. "Hold on... *now* I remember you... You're that squaw man that was squattin' on Myerling's old homestead. But—I saw you *hang*."

"Lynched, to be exact."

"That ain't possible!" Polk shook his head, trying to fight the swell of fear rising within him. Dying was one thing, but talking to a dead man was another. "You *can't* be him!"

"But I am. Or at least I *was*. I ain't exactly the man I used t'be—but then, who amongst us is? You're rememberin' correctly. You *did* see me hang. Just as *I* saw you desecrate my wife's body. I made a promise over her grave that I would hunt you down, you son of a bitch, and take back what you took from her. I've got her braid—now I want to know what you did with the baby."

"B-baby?" The fear in Polk's eyes was replaced by bafflement. "W-what baby?"

"Don't play dumb!" Lynch growled through gritted teeth. "Tell me what you did with the child she was carryin'!"

"I swear as I'm dyin', mister—I took your woman's scalp, but I didn't touch nothin' else on her! What kind of man do you take me for—?!?"

Lynch stared down at the dying man and shook his head. Without saying anything else, he turned his back on Polk and removed the bit from Alastor's mouth. He patted the beast's velvety black neck, then motioned to where the mortally wounded Polk lay sprawled on the ground. Alastor tossed its mane in excitement, eagerly licking its teeth with its tongue.

Polk struggled to lift his head, squinting up at the dark blur looming over him. "Mister—is that you?"

Chapter Thirteen

Antioch Drake was the master of all he surveyed.

Which meant at that particular moment he was the lord and master of twelve houses, a general store, a livery barn, a church, a saloon, nineteen men, twenty-three women and nineteen children—not counting the ones lying dead in the street.

It was the third day of Drake's reign over what once had been the frontier settlement of Newtonville. Now, after seventy-two hours of near-continuous rapine, it bore a closer resemblance to Hell than any other place on Earth.

During the fifteen years he'd spent dealing with Indians, Drake had become an expert on overcoming small communities of civilians. The techniques he had used to place Newtonville under his control were no different from those he once utilized against the Cheyenne and Sioux: He came in fast and early, striking while his opponents were still in their beds.

While Drake no longer had a battalion at his command, those who had remained loyal and followed him into the wilderness were more than a match for sleepy-eyed settlers in their long johns. His first order was the systematic slaughter of all males young enough and healthy enough to prove troublesome. Their bodies now lay side by side in the street as both a warning and reminder to the others as to what to expect should they step out of line.

His second order was the culling of those women who could pass muster as whores. The third order was to lock up all those who remained in the town church—mostly older men, grannies, and young'uns—until he was ready to give his fourth and final order. And when that order came—it would be heard as far away as Washington.

He had been betrayed by his government—and now he was going to make his former employer pay by taking out his revenge on the people it held so dear. For fifteen years, Washington had turned a blind eye to how he handled the "Indian problem." Hell, he had even been given medals and commendations for treating Cheyenne camps the exact same way he was handling Newtonville! Drake knew what his role was in the Manifest Destiny of his country—exterminator.

It was Drake's job to see that all the pesky, potentially dangerous vermin that infested the plains would not interfere with the settlement of the Wyoming and Montana territories or the conversion of the buffalo hunting grounds into cattle ranches. And he had been very good at his job. Very good indeed.

But now his rank, his medals, his career had been stripped away from him, just as vultures tear at the flesh of a fallen lion. And for what? All because some whey-faced city slicker back east decided he didn't like how Drake was handling the relocation of Injuns to the reservations—as if what had happened at Little Big Horn wasn't proof enough that the red-skinned devils were dangerous savages.

So what if he burned down a few farmhouses and lynched some settlers along the way? This was a war! There could be no middle ground for those who were sympathetic to the enemy—or refused to take sides. And no matter how they might deny it, there was no trusting half-breeds, either—their red blood would always turn against the white. It was a scientific fact. Better to eradicate them entirely than to suffer the indignity of betrayal later on.

When the dispatch came, ordering his return to Washington to answer questions concerning his actions, Drake knew what he had to do. That night he called on those who were loyal to follow him—and rode off with close to twenty men at his side. Thus began the legend of Drake's Devils.

That was nearly six months ago. He had less than half that number still riding with him. Some had deserted, some had died in action, others he'd killed himself. Still, as brigand gangs go, his had proven extremely successful in eluding capture.

For all their bluster about being ready to apply for statehood, the Wyoming territory was an isolated, thinly populated place. It was easy for even a larger number of men to evade the authorities—especially if they were lead by someone who knew all their pursuers' tactics by heart. Unless the territorial governor was willing to bring in Texas Rangers to deal with the problem, Drake and his Devils were free to plunder the countryside with impunity.

Drake glanced out of the window of his new house. A week ago, the house had belonged to the mayor of Newtonville. But Drake had commandeered it solely because he wanted an unobstructed view of the church across the street. He wanted to make sure the guards didn't slack off and let any of the captives escape.

Ferguson and Powell were seated on the wooden steps leading to the doors of the church, smoking hand-rolled cigarettes. Each man had a loaded shotgun resting across his knees. The moment the front door of Drake's house opened, they snapped to attention. Drake stalked past them without so much as a sidelong look.

He would make Washington pay for turning against him. It was not in his nature to forgive a slight, no matter how minor. He had been raised on the Bible and a leather strap, with an emphasis on the angry God of the Old Testament—the one who demanded eyes for eyes and ordered that all who bowed to the golden calf were to be put to the sword.

His country had made him a renegade—and, by damn, he was determined to be the biggest, nastiest thorn in its side. He would fight his country as relentlessly as he had fought *for* it—and with the same mercy he had shown the Injuns he had so diligently exterminated at their command.

Drake paused for a moment to study the dead men lined up at the foot of the boardwalk. After three days they were beginning to stink and draw flies. He glanced up at the lowering sun and made his decision.

Come the dawn he would order his men to kill the women, then nail the doors to the church shut and torch it. Drake chuckled as he imagined the look on the president's face.

⟹◆⟸

The woman wouldn't stop screaming. Even after Dawson climbed off her, the woman still kept shrieking. It was getting on Drake's nerves.

"Shut her up!" he barked. "I've listened to enough caterwauling tonight!"

"Yes, sir!" Barnes saluted. He drew his service revolver from his holster and stepped up to the poker table where the naked woman lay huddled, screaming into her hands.

The other Drake's Devils fell silent, their debauchery momentarily forgotten, upon hearing the revolver's report. The only other sound was that of the player piano hammering away mindlessly at "My Darling Clementine."

"What are you men staring at?" Barnes bellowed as everyone silently stared at the woman's body. "Ain't you never seen a bitch put out of her misery before?"

"You mean you put her out of *our* misery, lieutenant!" Lewes laughed, toasting Barnes with an upraised bottle of rotgut. "Ain't that right, boys?"

A ragged chorus of laughs rose from the men. The women's laughter was noticeable for its absence; then again, they hadn't done anything except scream, cry, moan in pain and beg for mercy the whole time.

When the men weren't fucking them on top of the gaming tables, the captive women stayed huddled together like baby rabbits trying to keep warm. Whenever one of Drake's men felt the need, he would stagger up and drag off one of the women.

A few of their number were professional whores, but the rest were the mothers, daughters and sweethearts of the men lying dead in the street. The working girls tried hard to put themselves between the outlaws and the other women, but there was simply not enough of them to do much good.

Drake watched the women weep and shiver in fear, scowling in disgust. As loathsome and primitive as they might be, he had more respect for squaws than he did white women. At least a proper squaw would kill herself before allowing herself to be raped.

As Drake's Devils once again resumed their monstrous revelry in full force, another scream rang out. But this time it came neither from inside the saloon nor from a woman. Seconds later, Ferguson's body came flying through the batwing doors and landed in the sawdust of the barroom floor, right at Lewes's feet.

Lewes stared at the halo of blood forming underneath Ferguson's head, his face drained of color. "Where's his ears?" he croaked, nervously wiping his upper lip with the sleeve of his shirt.

Drake leapt from his chair and grabbed one of the women, a young girl who would have been pretty if not for the bruises on her face. The girl sobbed in fear and pain as he dragged her to the door of the saloon by her hair.

Drake positioned himself in the threshold, using the girl as a shield, and pressed his pistol against her temple.

"I don't know who you are out there—!" he shouted at the darkness. "And I don't care!" Drake wrapped another length of the girl's hair around his fist, pressing her tear-stained cheek even closer to the muzzle of his gun. "Pull another trick like that, and I'll have my men open fire on the whole lot! You hear me?"

There was a long silence, then a lone voice spoke from somewhere in the darkness. "I hear you, Drake."

Drake backed away from the open door then roughly cast the sobbing girl aside. Though on the outside he appeared in command of the situation, inside Drake's head was a chaotic swirl as he frantically rethought his strategies.

Whoever killed Ferguson must have taken out Powell as well, which meant that Drake no longer had the church. That left him with only the women in the saloon as bargaining chips.

"Captain—did you recognize the voice?" Barnes whispered.

Drake shook his head, preoccupied.

"Do you think it's the Army?"

Drake snorted and pointed at what remained of Ferguson. "Whoever did that ain't reg'lar Army. I'm bettin' on vigilantes."

"Vigilantes?" Barnes frowned. "How would they know to look for us here?"

Before Drake could answer, there came the sound of horse's hooves hammering against a boardwalk at full speed. Drake grabbed his gun and spun to face the door just in time to see the Devil himself come crashing through the front window.

The Devil rode a coal black horse with eyes that burned like coals snatched from the inferno's hottest forge. In his right hand, he held a pearl-handle revolver, in his left a shotgun, and between his teeth he clutched the reigns of his mount.

The Devil's horse landed on one of the flimsy tables nearest the door, sending empty whiskey bottles and poker chips flying, but the roughness of the landing did nothing to shake its master's aim. Within seconds Lewes, Childers and Dawson were dead, bullets lodged in their brains, hearts and lungs.

Realizing they were under attack, the remaining outlaws dove for cover and began immediately laying down fire. The women, forgotten in the confusion, ran in the direction of the backdoor of the saloon.

Lynch glanced up at the wagon wheel that served as the barroom's chandelier. He counted six kerosene lamps fixed to the spokes. Ignoring the hot lead whistling past him like angry mosquitoes, he raised his gun and fired at the pulley mechanism. The wagon wheel crashed to the floor, killing the outlaw standing under it instantly. The lamps shattered on impact, sending burning kerosene flying in all direction. Within seconds, the saloon was on fire.

"You murderin' son of a bitch! I'll get for what you done!" Detweiler screamed as he lunged from cover, burying the blade of his knife in the other man's right leg.

But to Detweiler's amazement, his victim did not so much as flinch. The horse he was riding, however, closed its white, strong teeth firmly on Detweiler's Adam's apple, shaking him back and forth as a terrier would a rat.

<hr />

Drake saw the Devil staring at him through the smoke and fire he'd brought with him from Hell. Drake knew the man dressed in the black duster with the scarf thrown round his neck was the Devil because he had mismatched eyes—and the face of a dead man.

The Devil saw the look of horror and fear on Drake's face and grinned. Drake was frozen, unable to look away from the pale specter as he made his slow, stately way toward him from across the burning barroom, the fire reflecting in his mismatched eyes until they glowed like live coals.

Suddenly Barnes was there, shouting in Drake's ear, tugging on his arm. "Captain! We've got to get you out of here before the whole building comes down on our heads! Grunwald! Obermeyer! Help me get him out!"

Drake looked into his second-in-command's face, his piercing blue eyes clouded by confusion. "He's here to take me back."

"Take you back where—? To Washington?"

"To Hell."

Suddenly there was a loud groan and a burning timber came crashing down from the ceiling, blocking the Devil's path. Someone screamed, and Drake turned and saw the flames swallow Grunwald.

Barnes grabbed Drake by the collar and dragged him through the shimmering curtain of fire toward the door that the women had used to make their escape. A second later they were outside, coughing smoke out of their lungs and swatting at the burning cinders clinging to their clothes and hair.

Upon sucking in a lung-full of fresh air, Drake seemed restored to his usual vigor.

"That son of a bitch double-crossed me!" he roared. "He sent one of his monsters after me!"

"Sir?" Barnes gasped, blinking in confusion. "I don't understand—"

"Its not your place to understand, Barnes—only obey!" Drake shot back. "How many men are left?"

"Just Obermeyer and myself, sir."

"Then that will just have to do. We're saddling up and leaving right now."

"Where are we going, sir?"

"To settle the butcher's bill, lieutenant."

<hr />

It took Lynch a few hours to dig his way out from under the rubble of what had once been the saloon. When he saw the ceiling coming down, he dived under the bar, which saved him from getting his back broken or his skull smashed by falling rafters.

He looked down at his hands—the skin covering them was reddened and blistered from the intense heat but otherwise whole. He touched his face, making sure that everything was still in its proper place. A large flap of skin hung from the side of his face like a piece of wet tissue paper, but outside of that he seemed to be intact.

As he stumbled out of the jumble of charred timber and burned bodies, he heard a shocked gasp. He looked up and saw a knot of townspeople standing on the nearby boardwalk, staring at him in horror.

Lynch dusted the ash off his clothes as best he could, then smiled and tipped his hat. "Don't mind me, folks," he said, smoke curling from his mouth as he spoke. "I'm just passing through."

Chapter Fourteen

After Lynch dug himself free, he spent some time tracking down Alastor, who at least had the horse sense not to stay inside a burning building. Once he had finished sewing the various bullet and knife wounds in his body shut and given himself an injection of the good doctor's marvelous elixir re-vitae, there was the question of provisions for the journey ahead.

He waited until it was dark to sneak back into Newtonville and drag Powell's body from under the stairs of the church. When he first arrived, he'd been tempted to steal one of the corpses Drake had left lying in the street, but he was afraid of drawing the outlaws' attention to his presence before he was ready. Besides, they were a little too ripe for his tastes.

Once Lynch had finished butchering Powell into easily carried choice cuts, Drake had a three day start on him. But that didn't mean much to a man who didn't sleep and never got tired. Besides, it wasn't like the ren-egade was going out of his way to hide his tracks. Either Drake thought he was dead, or he didn't give a good goddamn that he was being followed.

At first he wondered where Drake thought he was going. But as he fol-lowed his prey's trail across the plains, toward the towering peaks of the Grand Tetons, he realized that, for some reason, he was being lead back to Mirablis.

The cabin was in shambles. The bookshelf had been knocked over, spilling its cache of rare volumes and medical texts across the floor. The table was upended, its chairs reduced to kindling. The door that lead to Mirablis's secret cave stood wide open, sagging on broken hinges.

Lynch hurried into the darkness on the other side of the threshold without hesitation. To his eyes, at least, the cave's shadows held no secrets, its darkness no mystery.

"Doc! Where are you?"

The only response to his call was his own voice echoing back to him. As he continued his search for Mirablis, he stumbled and nearly fell across a body sprawled on the cave floor.

Lynch recognized the dead man as Barnes, Drake's second-in-command. He was the one who had knotted the rope that snapped Johnny Pearl's neck so neatly. Barnes's face was staring up at Lynch, even though the dead man was lying belly down.

Pompey lay a few feet away from the outlaw's body. The mute had been riddled with bullets, but what had snuffed out the second life of Mirablis's faithful servant was the shot that parted his sinus cavity down the middle. And if Pompey was dead... what had become of Mirablis?

Lynch got his answer when he reached the tank. The artificial womb's glass panels were smashed, and a huge puddle of elixir re-vitae had pooled underneath the structure. Mirablis's body lay face down in the greenish yellow fluid, blood seeping from his bullet wounds.

Despite himself, Lynch cried out in alarm upon seeing the old man. He hurried forward and awkwardly knelt beside his creator. Lynch rolled Mirablis over, hoping against hope that the old man might still be alive, but his prayers were in vain. Though his wounds were still fresh, Mirablis's flesh was already taking on the chill of death.

Lynch sobbed as he cradled the dead scientist in his arms, rocking back and forth as the grief rose within him. As much as he had resented Mirablis's interference with his life—and afterlife—he had never wished the old man any harm. He clutched Mirablis's body to his breast, mourning him as Johnny Pearl had never been allowed to mourn his own father, all those years ago.

"No—not like this—I didn't mean for it to be like this—" he moaned. "I never meant for anyone but Drake and his men to die!"

There came the sound of a boot heel scraping against rock, and Lynch found himself looking at the muzzle of Drake's gun. Though he knew he was moments removed from his second and final death, all Lynch could think of was how shabby Drake looked.

The renegade officer still wore his cavalry uniform, but the company insignia and his officer's stripes were stripped from the shoulders and sleeves. His handsomely coifed red mane and beard was tangled and liberally shot with gray, the whiskers about his mouth permanently stained by tobacco juice and whiskey. Drake's eyes still shone as brightly as the first time they met, but now they burned with true madness.

"That's right. You were too late to save your master," Drake snarled, blood smeared across his lower lip and chin whiskers. "Still, the old bastard put up a hell of a fight—more than Barnes and Obermeyer were expecting, that's for sure. Or should I say his pet monsters put up the fight?" Drake waved a bloody hand in the direction of what was left of Obermeyer, scattered about the cave floor.

"Where's Sasquatch?"

"You mean the Injun? When it realized the old man was dead, it hollered like a stuck hog and ran off into the cave. Its dead, too. Or will be soon. God knows I emptied enough lead into it."

"I don't understand—how did you know to come here?"

Drake laughed and spat a wad of bloody phlegm on the floor of the cave. "Don't play innocent! He didn't have no more use for me, once I was drummed out, so he sent you out after me! Ungrateful sack of shit! Who was he to think he could treat me that way after all I'd done for him over the years!"

"What do you mean all you'd done for him'?"

"Who do you suppose it was who allowed that medicine wagon to travel unmolested by Injuns—or dissatisfied customers, for that matter!" Drake snorted. "Hell, I even provided him with bodies-to-order for those damn fool experiments of his!"

"Y-you mean you and Mirablis—you were working together?"

"Let's just say we had us a business arrangement. The old geezer paid me in order to get first crack at the spoils of war, as it were." Drake gave a short laugh that sounded like a bark of pain. "You ain't shittin' me, are you? You really don't know about me and th' old man. I guess Mirablis was right when he said this was all a big misunderstanding."

"Oh. There's no misunderstanding, Drake," Lynch said as he lay Mirablis's body gently on the ground, his voice strangely calm. "I *am* gonna kill you, you murderin' Yankee bastard."

"You can try, you broke-neck freak," Drake snarled. "But better men than you have died tryin'."

Lynch smiled, his eyes glowing like stars as he slowly got to his feet. "Be that as it may, Drake. But then again—I'm already dead."

The bullet struck the neck brace, knocking Lynch on to his back. Drake moved forward and pointed the gun point-blank at Lynch's head and pulled the trigger again and again, only to have the hammer come down on an empty chamber each time.

"Damn you!" Drake screamed in rage, hurling the useless gun aside. He turned and fled as fast as he could, stumbling through the darkness toward the light that marked the cabin's open doorway.

Lynch took his time getting to his feet. There was no point in hurrying after Drake. After all, where could his prey possibly go that he could not follow? Drake was a dead man and knew it. Lynch could afford to stalk him at his leisure—after all, he had all the time in the world.

Chapter Fifteen

Drake ran through the cabin's single room, bursting through the door and into the open air. He was bruised and cut from slamming into rock formations in the dark, and he was nursing a cracked rib from where the Injun freak had hit him, but he was alive—which was more than could be said for Barnes and Obermeyer right now.

He had to get some space between him and that broken-necked son of a bitch. Once he had space, he could figure out a battle plan. But right now he had to grab his horse and ride.

Drake hurried toward the barn, but came to a sudden halt when he saw the doors standing wide open. The horses that he and the others had arrived on were lying on their sides. Standing in the middle of the fallen animals was a black horse, tearing at their flesh as if grazing in a field of clover. The black beast raised its head and made an angry snorting noise as it pawed the ground. Drake was too shocked by what he had seen to do more than make a choking sound.

The outlaw turned and fled on foot, following the narrow winding path that lead toward the top of the mountain. As he neared the first bend, he looked over his shoulder and saw the hanged man standing in front of the cabin, watching him.

Lynch watched Drake run until he was out of sight, then fished out his pocket watch and Katie's braid. He sat down on a nearby rock and stroked his dead wife's hair, the time piece resting beside him with its case open. When five minutes had passed, Lynch snapped the case closed and returned the watch to his waistcoat pocket. He began walking in the direction his prey had gone.

By the time he was halfway up the mountain, Lynch noticed that the wind had grown stronger. He paused to tilt his head back as best he could and stare up at the sky. There were clouds gathering overhead—growing larger and darker with every minute.

Lynch grunted to himself and returned Katie's braid to his breast pocket.

A few minutes later, the foot path disappeared, and Lynch found himself alternately hiking and scaling his way up the side of the mountain. Though there were plenty of natural handholds in the form of rocks and stunted shrubs, the rigid neck brace made it difficult for him to maintain his balance while climbing.

He was within feet of the pinnacle when something wet and cold splashed against his cheek. As Lynch paused to wipe the raindrop from his face, a large rock struck him in the shoulder, sending him sliding ten feet down the side of the mountain. As Lynch struggled to regain his footing, a second, even bigger stone struck him squarely on the spine.

In the months since his rebirth in Mirablis's tank, Lynch had forgotten what true pain actually felt like. He routinely suffered shootings, stabbings and being burned alive much as anyone else would endure a scraped knee or bruised elbow. However, the pain exploding along his spine was so intense it was all he could do to keep from screaming. As he lay there, groveling in agony, Lynch could make out Drake's silhouette on the ledge above. The outlaw looked like a wild-haired caveman about to bash out the brains of his enemy.

"I'm gonna kill you, dead man!" Drake shouted as he lifted what looked to be small boulder over his head. "And this time you're gonna stay dead!"

As if to punctuate his statement, the storm clouds swallowed the sun. The winds howled like wolves scenting blood. Lynch stared up at his killer, awaiting the final blow that would return him to his wife.

A crooked shadow rose up from behind Drake, and a pair of mismatched arms encircled his barrel chest, lifting him off the ground as if he were a child. Startled, Drake dropped the boulder, which bounced harmlessly past Lynch, then sailed off the side of the mountain into the valley below.

"Put me down!" Drake screamed. *"Put me down, you red-skinned freak, or I'll yank your guts out your ass and feed them to you!"*

If Sasquatch heard Drake's threat, he showed no sign of it. The crazy-quilt Indian had his eyes shut and his head thrown back. Lynch could just make out the sound of ritual chanting over the rumbling of the thunder. Suddenly Sasquatch's eyes flew open, and his gaze fell on Lynch's and held it. The giant smiled as best he could and mouthed the words "forgive me" in English. Then there was flash of blue white light so intense that it transcended sight, followed by a noise so loud it sounded as if the mountain were cracking open.

When Lynch regained the ability to see and hear, the first thing he noticed was that his eyebrows were singed off. The second thing he noticed was that he was alone. He lurched to his feet, trying not to overbalance and slide even further down the side of the mountain.

He scoured the top of the mountain for signs of his friend, but all he found was a blasted patch of rock located roughly where Sasquatch had been standing. Lynch called his friend's name over and over, but there was no answer except the distant rumble of the passing storm.

EPILOGUE

Lynch searched through the books scattered about the floor of the cabin until he found Mirablis's private journals and the Frankenstein notebooks. The pages were yellowed and filled with cramped handwriting, most of it in a language he did not recognize, along with involved chemical and mathematical formulae. How was he supposed to decipher this in time to figure out how to make more elixir re-vitae before his already dwindling supply ran out?

If the notebooks had proven somewhat disappointing, the chest tucked under the old man's bed made up for it. Inside he discovered a variety of glass jars, in which various human body parts were suspended in elixir re-vitae. Lynch lost no time in tossing out the collection of hands, livers, hearts and genitalia, then decanting the precious elixir into containers more suitable to transport.

The last jar was also the largest, roughly the size of a five-gallon jug. As Lynch lifted the container out of the trunk, the contents seemed to move of their own accord. To his surprise, he saw an unborn child floating in the murky yellow green fluid. A child with Katie's cheekbones and his chin.

Lynch stared at the rubble that was all that remained of the entrance to Mirablis's underground laboratory. It was amazing what a little gunpowder could do.

He was still trying to make sense of everything, and he was fairly sure he was most of the way to understanding it all. For one, he was pretty sure Drake was the one responsible for the slaughter of Sasquatch's tribe.

For someone with a body so horribly twisted, the giant had proven himself a master manipulator. Sasquatch knew he could not travel on his own, so he had to bide his time until Mirablis succeeded in resurrecting a subject capable of realizing his scheme for him. And when it looked like amnesia might prove a problem, Sasquatch had used his shaman's tricks to summon forth Katie's shade to jumpstart his memory and set his feet on the path of vengeance.

Whether Lynch succeeded in killing Drake on his own or caused him to seek out Mirablis, thereby placing him within convenient striking distance of the resurrected shaman didn't really matter. Either way, Sasquatch would have revenge against the man who slaughtered his tribe.

Lynch knew he should be angry about how he had been used and betrayed, first by Mirablis, then by Sasquatch, but he could not bring himself to hate them.

What was done was done. There was no way of changing the past, only learning from it.

As for himself, he had a new mission in life—one that demanded far more of him than killing. He had lived the life of the destroyer before and found it empty. It was up to him learn how to defeat the dark hunger that threatened to make him a monster. And possibly, in time, he might be able to find someone who could decipher the old man's journals and help him change his nightmares back into dreams.

After all, he had his son to think about.

Walking Wolf

PROLOGUE

Every kid plays at Cowboys and Indians, sometime or another, no matter what their sex, race, background or temperament. I was no different—except I wasn't playing. It was how I lived.

My name is William Skillet. That's my white name. My Indian name—some would say it was my *real* name—is Walking Wolf. I was raised by the Comanche as one of their own on the open plains of what are now the states of New Mexico, Oklahoma and Texas.

Now I know what you're thinking. I can't be more than fifty years old, by the looks of me. And the last time the Comanche lived free of the reservations was before the turn of the twentieth century, which would make me either quite well preserved or a damn liar.

Well, I have been known to lie on occasion, but this time I'm giving you the straight skinny. To the best of my knowledge, I'm one hundred and fifty, give or take a year. The reason I'm vague as to my exact age is that I don't really know when I was born. Eight Clouds Rising—my adopted father—could tell me only that he found me during the season the buffalo cows dropped their calves, the year after the smallpox went through the tribe, claiming the life of his only natural son. Which probably means I was born sometime in 1844.

But I *can* tell you the reason for me being so youthful-looking for a man a century and a half old. I'm not exactly what you'd call human. Hell, I'm not human at all. The closest thing you might be able to relate me to is what's known as a "werewolf," but not the kind you see in the picture shows that sprout hair and teeth every time there's a full moon. The truth of my kind is a lot more complicated—and frightening—than that.

What you're about to read is the story of my life—leastwise, the early part of it. I wrote it more for my sake than anything else. As I've gotten older, the past has a tendency to be both fuzzy and painfully distinct. Sometimes when I get up in the morning, I'm surprised to find myself in a house, not a tipi. And when I look out the picture window, I almost expect to see a herd of buffalo grazing in the valley below. Other times, I find myself grasping for the name of a loved one like it was a bubble in a stream. I do not want to forget that time, to lose the truth under the weight of a new century's memories.

Now I don't want anyone reading this to think I'm bragging about having led an interesting life. Life ain't nothing more than the things that happen to you on your way to dying. Some folks just have more things happen to 'em—and in an entertaining fashion.

I guess I've said all that needs to be said in the way of an explanation, except that anyone attempting to find a moral will be gut-shot.

CHAPTER ONE

I don't remember my real family. And although I've had all kinds of names in my lifetime, both Indian and white—I don't know the name my flesh-and-blood folks gave me when I was born.

All I know about my ma is that she was human, probably from the Old Country. My pa was a *vargr* (that's what werewolves call themselves) who went by the name of Howler. And for some reason, in the early 1840s they moved out into the wilderness surrounding what would eventually become Dallas, Texas.

My story begins with a Comanche brave named Eight Clouds Rising coming home after a successful attempt at stealing Apache ponies. Eight Clouds belonged to the Penateka band, who were famed for their lightning-fast raids, hence their nickname of "Wasp Riders." As he made his way back to his camp, he caught sight of a thin spume of smoke on the horizon. Then he spied the buzzards. Eight Clouds, being inquisitive by nature, decided to check it out.

The cabin was still smoldering when he arrived. To hear him tell it, he'd been surprised to see a white homestead so close to Comanche territory. Whites preferred being within a half-day's ride of one another, yet the nearest white settlement had to be a good three days' journey from there. As he drew closer, the ponies rolled their eyes and whinnied at the stink of death hanging thick in the air.

There was a body sprawled before the collapsed ruin of the two-room cabin. The corpse was that of a boy of nine or ten—the same age as his own son, Little Eagle, who'd died last spring. The boy was dressed in a rough-woven flaxen shirt and crude canvas overalls, his feet bare and tough as leather. He'd been shot in the chest and his throat slit from ear to ear. His scalped skull was black with clotted blood.

My ma's body lay between the barn and the cabin, carrion birds picking at her eyes. She lay on her back, her skirts hiked above her hips. Her killer had cut out her sex and removed her left breast. Eight Clouds was so disgusted he spat in the dirt. He'd claimed his fair share of trophies, but there was no honor in making a trophy of a woman's breasts or adorning a war spear with the scalp of a young boy. But then, this wasn't the work of Comanches, or Apaches either for that matter. The horses that left their tracks at the massacre sight had been wearing shoes. This was a white man's crime.

My pa was lying near my ma. He'd been skinned alive, judging by how his limbs were twisted and contorted. As Eight Clouds knelt to examine the butchered remains, he noticed the peeled, snarling muzzle of a wolf jutting from my pa's face.

If Eight Clouds had ever needed proof that the whites were bad-crazy, this was certainly it. While he had never seen one himself, Eight Clouds knew the Comanche legends that told how Coyote—the first and greatest of the skinwalkers—had helped human beings by giving them fire, teaching them language and interceding with the Great Spirit on their behalf. And damned if the whites hadn't gone and skinned him alive!

As Eight Clouds stood pondering the immensity of the whites' folly, he heard what sounded like a baby crying. He looked around and noticed a smokehouse next to the barn, and it was there the crying seemed to be coming from. Like I said, Eight Clouds was inquisitive by nature, so he decided to take a look inside.

My folk's smokehouse wasn't any different from any other smokehouse you'd find at that time—except that there were a couple of human carcasses hanging up with the dressed-out antelopes and jack rabbits. There were also a couple of barrels set behind the door, and it was in one of these that Eight Clouds found a baby wrapped in a blanket, crying to beat the band. That squalling infant was none other than me.

According to Eight Clouds, I instantly stopped crying when he picked me up—a good luck sign according to the Comanches. I looked him straight in the eye and smiled. He could tell by the color of my eyes—yellow—that I weren't no human baby. Eight Clouds couldn't believe his luck! Here he'd been worrying about his squaw, Thunder Buffalo Woman, being so sad on account of their son's death, and now he finds a baby skinwalker!

Eight Clouds wasted no time in making a papoose cradle out of some antelope hide and a couple of barrel staves. Pretty soon I was accompanying him on his way back to camp, dangling off the horn of the saddle he'd taken from a Mexican *ranchero* he'd killed the season before.

When Eight Clouds got home, he showed me to Thunder Buffalo Woman. The prospect of having a young'un around the tipi cheered her up to no end. She suggested to Eight Clouds that they take their new son to old Medicine Dog, the tribe's shaman, so I could get myself properly named.

Medicine Dog was a wise man and was quite old, even when I was coming up. He was the one who tended to the tribe when folks fell ill, the one who could look at buffalo afterbirth and tell whether the next season was going to be cold, the one who could see the future in the tossing of the bones. He was also in charge of naming the babies born to the tribe—at least the boys.

Medicine Dog was sitting outside his tipi, smoking his pipe, looking like he'd been expecting Eight Clouds and Thunder Buffalo Woman the whole time.

"Good day, Medicine Dog."

"Yes, it is a good day, Eight Clouds. What is Thunder Buffalo Woman is carrying? Have you a new son?"

"I found this child in what was left of a white homestead. I would make him my son." Eight Clouds motioned for Thunder Buffalo Woman to show me to Medicine Dog.

Medicine Dog squinted at me with his left eye—he'd lost the right to an Apache arrowhead years before—and puffed on his pipe. "Your new son is a skinwalker, Eight Clouds. You have brought good luck to the Penateka." Getting to his feet, he motioned for Thunder Buffalo Woman to hand me over. He stood there for a long moment, staring down at me as I played with his medicine necklace, then entered his tipi.

Several long minutes passed before he returned, handing me back to my new mother. He nodded to himself, as if pleased by what had transpired. "I offered smoke to the sky and earth and to the four corners of the world

Walking Wolf
157

and to the Great Spirit. In the smoke I saw the name of your son. It is Little Wolf."

And so that's how I got my first name and became an official member of the Comanche.

When I was younger, folks used to always ask me all kinds of questions: What was it like being raised by Injuns? Were the Comanches really murdering red devils? Were they really cannibals?

Well, the Comanche was a warrior society, no two ways about it. They were born horsemen, and proud of their skill in combat. They thought farming and settling down was for weak and cowardly types. They valued bravery and courage above all else, even to the point where a warrior preferred to die young in battle than to grow too old to wage war. Needless to say, they were always fighting someone or other.

Before the whites came, the Comanche had running feuds with the Pawnee, Cheyenne, Arapaho, Dakota, Kiowa, Apache, Osages and the Tonkawas. Later, when the Europeans started trying to settle Texas, they switched over to fighting first the Spanish, then the Anglos full-time. But just so you won't think they were completely inhospitable, they were on decent terms with the Wichitas, Wacos and Tawakonies. Most of the time.

As for them being murdering devils—I'll grant you they could be downright merciless to those they decided were enemies. I've seen Comanche braves bury Apache warriors up to their ears in hot sand and coat their heads with honey so the ants would pick their skulls clean while they were still alive. Then again, I've known a Comanche brave to give water to a white he found dying of gangrene on the open prairie, wrap him in a blanket and sit up with him just so he wouldn't die on his lonesome out in the middle of nowhere. The Comanche could be funny that way.

Like I said, they were a proud people. And fearless. They were the lords of the southern plains and they damn well knew it! The Mexican *rancheros* who first settled the area lived in fear of them. Comanche braves were often in the habit of riding into San Antonio, thronging the streets and public squares, swaggering around like they owned the place. Hell, they even made the townspeople hold the reins of their ponies as they went about raiding the shops and houses! Leastwise, that's what Medicine Dog told me. By the time I was coming up, things were already changing for the Comanche in Texas, and not for the better.

And as for them being cannibals—well, that story got started on account of this band of Comanche called the Tamina, also known as the Liver-Eaters. There weren't very many of them and they felt inferior to the bigger, more powerful tribes like the Wasp Riders and the Antelope People. So they came up with this story about eating the livers of their enemies. Now, the Comanche have this big taboo concerning cannibalism, and no Comanche in his right mind would even think about eating another human being, but it sure did make them sound fierce, didn't it? Unfortunately, most settlers tended to take things at face value and believed they really were cannibals. Needless to day, the Tamina got exterminated mighty quick.

Thanks to Eight Clouds Rising and Thunder Buffalo Woman, I grew up a happy, healthy child. And, personally, I couldn't have asked for a better childhood. The Comanche cherished their children, seeing how they tended not to produce that many in the first place, and a baby's chance of getting to be a full-grown adult was pretty dicey.

Now one thing you've got to remember about the Comanche: They were a pragmatic people. While they believed in the Great Spirit and the Spirit World beyond this one, they didn't spend much of their spare time fretting over it, unlike other folks both red and white. They didn't hold with coaxing children toward good behavior by promising them all kinds of sweets after they die, or frightening them away from evil by threatening eternal damnation. Instead, the children were shown by word and example that the respect of their fellow tribesmen was to be desired for itself, and the condemnation and contempt of the tribe was to be dreaded like the plague. Men who were brave and generous were applauded and respected as role models. And since it was practically impossible to live a secluded life in a Comanche encampment, everyone was aware of the conduct of everyone else. It was a remarkably effective way of keeping kids in line, let me tell you.

I learned to ride as soon as I could walk. The Comanche didn't cut you any slack in that area. If you weren't handy with a horse, then what good were you? Every Comanche child, boy and girl alike, was expected to know how to handle a full-grown horse all on their own by the age of five. When I was three years old, Eight Clouds lashed me to one of his ponies with a rawhide lariat while he held the pony by a tether, and he circled that pony around and around until I literally *became* a part of that animal.

As a child, I had plenty of friends. It didn't make a difference to them that I was white—even less that I was marked as Medicine Dog's understudy as the tribe's shaman. Kids is kids. Like I said, I had plenty of playmates, but my favorites were Small Bear, Flood Moon, Lean Fox and Quanah, who would later become better known in the world outside the *Comancheria* as

Quanah Parker. Quanah and I also had something in common, since he was half-white, the son of a captive woman and the great war chief, Peta Nocona.

Many a summer day was spent running around the plains, naked as jay-birds, whooping it up in grand old style, playing games like "Grizzly Bear" and hunting hummingbirds and bull-bats with our toy bows and arrows. Sometimes we'd play "camp," and each of the boys would team up with a girl, so they could pretend to be man and wife. The girls would set up wind-breaks on the banks of a stream, while us "men" would go out and hunt squirrels, so they could have something to cook for us when we came back to camp. I always made it a point to snag Flood Moon as my "wife" every time.

Sometimes we'd get into mischief—like the time Quanah, Small Bear and I got one of Eight Clouds's ponies and backed into the tipi where the elders of the tribe who were too old to wage war spent their time smoking the pipe and chewing the fat about the good old days. Lord, did that thing buck! The old men came pouring out of the smoke lodge like angry bees, shouting and carrying on. Quanah got away, but the old men latched onto me and Small Bear and started making noises about punishing us for our lack of respect. Just then, old Medicine Dog came up and motioned for the elders to be quiet.

"Now, you old fellows, you were once boys like Little Wolf and Small Bear! Don't you remember what devils you were? Forgive them their ac-tions—for will boys not be boys?"

The old men looked at one another, laughed and let the matter drop. After all, they were old men—peaceable after all the years spent on the war-path, not young warriors jealous of their dignity. All in all, they were fine old gents.

Every year, near winter, the various bands of Comanche would gather together. It was a time when news was swapped, friends and family see one another, marriages and liaisons between different bands become formal-ized, and the braves take a breather from the hunting and raiding that filled the rest of their year.

There were several different branches of Comanche back then, some of which were more powerful than others. Like I said before, I was a member of the Penateka, or the Wasp Band. Others included the Yamparika (the Yap-Eaters), the Kweharena (the Antelope People), the Kutsuaka (the Buf-falo-Eaters), the Pahuraix (the Water Horses), and the Wa'ai (the Wormy Penis), to name just a few. But even collected together in all their glory, there couldn't have been more than ten thousand Comanche. So you can

imagine the damage that was done when smallpox broke out in 1850. I couldn't have been more than six or seven at the time, but I remember it being worse than any nightmare I'd ever had—or ever will again.

It was then that my adopted mother, Thunder Buffalo Woman, died. It broke poor Eight Clouds's heart, and he was never quite the same after that, even though he ended up taking her younger sister, Little Dove, to wife a year or two later.

I was twelve years old by the time I finally got to go on my first real buffalo hunt. I was riding with Eight Clouds and several other braves from our band, including one who went by the name Grass Rope. Grass Rope's specialty was lying low in the grass and sneaking up on the buffalo while they were grazing. He wore a coyote skin draped over his shoulders to mask his scent. Since coyotes were always haunting the fringes of the herds, looking to scavenge afterbirth during the calving season, the buffalo didn't pay much mind, since coyotes were too small to bring down even the youngest calf.

When we spied the herd, Grass Rope got off his pony and motioned for me to follow him. Holding his bow at the ready, he got down on his hands and knees and started creeping through the prairie grass in the direction of the herd. I followed him, doing my best to keep upwind of the grazing buffalo. I was very proud that a skilled stalker such as Grass Rope had chosen me to accompany him, and I was determined to cover myself with glory the best I could. But as we crept closer and closer to the herd, something strange began to happen.

My sense of smell had always been acute, but for some reason it was incredibly keen that day. I could smell the grass as the sun dried the dew from its stems, the pungent odor of buffalo wool, the reek of their flops—but, more importantly, I could smell the coyote pelt Grass Rope was wearing. I caught its scent, and for the briefest moment I knew everything there was to know about the beast it had once belonged to: its sex, age, health and social standing in its pack. The surge of recognition was so powerful, I had to lower my head and whine.

Grass Rope gave me a hard look. Hunting was serious business, and it was no time for foolish pranks. "Be quiet, Little Wolf!" he whispered.

I tried to keep silent, but I was suddenly gripped by a strange fire that burned deep inside me like a banked coal. I bit my tongue to keep from crying out, causing blood to flow. The fire in my belly was growing, and my skin felt as if it were covered with biting ants. My bones seemed to be inflating inside my flesh, and for a fleeting second I was afraid I'd been bitten by a rattlesnake without knowing it.

Grass Rope grew very angry with my whimpering and twitching. He turned to give me the sharp side of his tongue, but what he saw made him forget about scolding me. Even though I was in great pain, I knew something must be very wrong, because his face suddenly went pale under his paint. Next thing I know, the buffalo start to bellow and stampede, running away from us.

Without thinking, I leapt to my feet and started chasing after the fleeing buffalo, running like a band of Apache was at my heels. I vaguely remember seeing some of the other braves from the hunting party sitting astride their ponies, pointing in my direction, their lances and arrows forgotten. I spotted a young buffalo calf that had lost its mother and panicked, placing itself on the fringes of the herd. I closed the distance between us, separating it from its fellows, snapping at its trembling flanks. The frightened youngster bellowed for its mother, but it was too late. She was already miles away, trapped within the nucleus of the herd, helpless to defend her errant child.

Without realizing what I was doing, I leapt onto the calf's wooly back, sinking my talons and teeth into its neck. The calf shrieked and, overbalanced, fell on top of me. (And seventy-plus pounds of buffalo calf is nothing to sneeze at, believe me.) Although I had the wind knocked out of me, I refused to let go. The dying calf jerked and kicked, but to no avail. I tore out its throat with my bare teeth.

I stared down as the calf bled its life onto the prairie grass. I threw back my head and howled in triumph. And it was only then, as I licked the fresh blood off my snout, that I realized I was covered in fur and that my hands boasted cruel, curved talons in place of fingernails.

Eight Clouds rode up, reining his pony at a safe distance. The pony rolled its eyes and stamped the ground nervously, uncertain whether to stay or flee. Eight Clouds looked the same way.

"My son—are you still inside?"

"Yes, father. I am still here." My voice was strangely distorted and gravelly, like an animal given the power of human speech.

Eight Clouds nodded, relieved. "You have hunted well. You bring honor to our lodge."

Grass Rope rode up, looking positively thunderstruck. "What manner of thing is this?" he demanded, pointing at me.

Eight Clouds smiled, proud enough to bust. "It is not a thing. It is my son, Little Wolf."

Grass Rope shook his head in amazement. "He is a walking wolf! Never have I seen such a thing!" And that's how I got my adult name—and how I shapeshifted for the first time in my life.

I didn't realize it then, but my boyhood days were gone forever.

Chapter Two

After my first experience with shapeshifting, my life amongst the tribe became very different. The first, and most radical, change came with my apprenticeship to Medicine Dog. The old shaman had always taken a grandfatherly interest in me, but now I was expected to move my meager belongings from my father's tipi into his.

Medicine Dog was a wise man, full of knowledge acquired during a long and eventful life. I remember I once asked him if he hated the Apache for blinding him in the right eye, and he laughed.

"My life was good in the old days. But it was the life of a fool. I was a mighty warrior back then. I was very proud. Too proud. My vanity made me weak. When the Apache took away my eye, I may have lost the ability to see things in this world, but I gained the ability to see into the Spirit World. Should I hate the Apache for giving me such a wonderful gift, Walking Wolf?"

Like I said, Medicine Dog was a wise man, but I, like other boys, was young and still aching to prove myself as a brave, so I tended to ignore a lot of what he told me. I genuinely liked the old fellow, but it chafed me that I had to tend his fire and fetch his water, just like a woman, while my old playmates Quanah and Small Bear were off hunting buffalo or out on pony raids. It pains me to look back and realize just how big a fool I was back then.

But Medicine Dog didn't seem to mind it—I guess he expected a certain amount of thick-headedness on my part.

Still, I did learn things, in spite of myself. Medicine Dog schooled me as to the prayers necessary to ensure successful raids and hunts, the prayers that correctly guide the dead to the Spirit World, and the prayers that confuse evil spirits so they can't tell which tipi is the one they're looking for at night. He also taught me breathing and meditation exercises that helped me control my shapeshifting, so I could summon what he called my "true" skin at will and with minimum discomfort. He also warned me to never tell a white that I was a skinwalker.

"Whites are jealous of things they don't understand. Of things they cannot have. That is why the human beings—we who lived on this land before they came—have had so much trouble with them. If you tell a white that you have more than one skin, they will try and take it away from you. Just like they did your natural father. Be very careful who you show your true skin to, Walking Wolf, if you want to keep it on your bones."

Medicine Dog also told me stories of Coyote, the trickster god from whom all skinwalkers are descended. I reckon it was on account of their most popular folk hero having the head of a coyote that the Plains Indians I knew back then rarely got upset by me sprouting hair, claws and fangs. Instead of seeing a monster, they saw a god. After all, according to their folklore, Coyote was responsible in part for human beings coming into existence in the first place, and he gave them fire and corn and the buffalo to make their life on earth easier. While the whites' reaction to my condition was far more reasonable, it did nothing to prepare me for what I would run up against in their world, although I did get a taste of rejection early on.

<hr />

I've already mentioned Flood Moon. As I said earlier, I'd known her all my life. She was a pretty thing by Comanche standards, with long, straight black hair woven into two thick braids. She had this shy way of smiling that was enough to melt my heart every time she looked at me.

I'd known from the time I was seven years old that Flood Moon was going to be mine, and once, when we were still very young, I even got her to promise to be my wife when we grew up. But that was back when I was Little Wolf. Things became very different once I became Walking Wolf and, like the young fool I was, I refused to admit it.

As I said, most of the Comanche took my being not exactly human as a matter of course. Occasionally I'd get asked by an exasperated older sister to threaten to eat a misbehaving youngster, but that was quite rare, and the children usually knew better. Flood Moon, however, was one of the few who had genuine trouble with my condition.

Before I'd learned how to shift, she'd been all smiles and flirts, but when we rode back from the hunt that day—me still wearing my true skin—she grew ashen-faced and hurried into her family's tipi and wouldn't come out.

Despite Flood Moon's sudden coolness towards me, I was still sweet on her. Whenever I could manage it, I would sneak away from Medicine Dog's tipi and loiter near the creek, waiting for her to pass by on her way to gather firewood or water.

One thing you've got to understand about the Comanche way of courting is that it was all very proper. Boys and girls, after a certain age, weren't allowed to be in one another's company unchaperoned. And there's nothing more bashful than a love-struck brave. So young lovers had to sneak what time they could together during daylight.

I spent agonizing hours waiting for just a glimpse of Flood Moon. And when I finally did get a few minutes alone with her, I was so tongue-tied I never said much. She would tolerate my presence well enough if I was wearing my human skin, but if I was wearing my true skin she'd be as nervous as a pony staked out to trap a mountain cat, hurrying through her chores as fast as she could, often slopping half the water she'd drawn from the creek on her way back to camp.

Although I was nowhere near as bold as some of my friends, who would lie outside their chosen one's tipi at night and whisper promises of love and marriage through the seams in the tent-skins, I was determined to make Flood Moon mine and set about saving up ponies to give her family as marriage tribute. But first I had to make sure her father and brothers would not turn down my offer.

I talked one of the older, more respected women in the tribe into approaching Flood Moon's father, Calling Owl, and putting my case to him. Calling Owl was very pleased that his daughter had caught the fancy of the tribe's resident skinwalker, as it meant good luck for his family. But when Flood Moon heard that I'd sent the old woman over, she begged her father to ask for thirty horses. Although Calling Owl saw having a skinwalker son-in-law as a good thing, he loved his daughter enough to agree to her wishes—at least for the moment.

When the old woman told me how much Calling Owl wanted for Flood Moon, I was dismayed. Thirty ponies! I was thirteen years old and only had one pony to my name—and that was one Eight Clouds had given me! How was I to get thirty ponies? Well, the same way any Comanche got ponies—it was up to me to steal some.

Now, let me digress a bit and explain horse-stealing, Comanche-style. The Comanche set a great deal of stock in horseflesh—and if there was ever a people born to ride, it was them. Compared to, say, the Cheyenne, the Comanche were a short, squat race. On the ground, they were far from graceful—but on the back of a horse, they were poetry in motion. Since their society revolved around the horse, the Comanche used them as a rate of exchange. And the mark of a rich man was to have more ponies than he ever possibly ride. A truly powerful chief would have dozens, if not hundreds, of ponies, most of them taken in raids from either other tribes or settlers. And while whites considered horse-stealing the lowest thing next to snatching an infant nursing at its mother's breast and dashing its brains out against a wall—if not lower—Indians saw it as a truly worthwhile skill. In fact, when they weren't out hunting buffalo, the Plains tribes seemed to spend the vast majority of their spare time stealing horses from one another. Still, it wasn't without its hazards.

Although I was apprenticed to Medicine Dog, he did not forbid me riding with the others on raids. After all, how else was I going to make myself a respected member of the band if I didn't distinguish myself on the warpath? Medicine Dog might have had one eye in the Spirit World, but he was a practical man. So I began joining the raiding parties, doing my best to help steal as many ponies as possible, so I could benefit when the spoils were divided at the end of a successful raid. Still, it was slow going for a brave as young as myself, since the elder warriors got preferential treatment.

A year passed, and ten horses were and all I had to show for it. I still ached for Flood Moon, and the waiting was driving me to distraction. Medicine Dog cautioned me and suggested I had much to learn about patience. Many Comanche braves waited until they were well into their twenties and were solidly established with many ponies and buffalo robes to their name before taking a wife. But my blood burned, and I was convinced that the only way I was ever to know happiness was if I took Flood Moon into my tipi as my wife.

One night, the Apaches raided our herd when most of the braves were away hunting, and all of my ponies were stolen. At first I was devastated. It had taken me so long to acquire those ten ponies, only to have them stolen! Then my grief turned to anger, and I became determined to go after the Apaches and reclaim my horses, plus as many more as I possibly could!

I set off after the Apache raiders on Medicine Dog's pony that very night, armed with nothing but a bow, some arrows and a knife. They had stolen close to a hundred horses; their trail wasn't hard to find. Still, they had a head start, and I knew once they made it to the hill country I wouldn't stand a chance.

I caught up with the raiders near dawn, several miles west of the camp. They had decided that they had gotten away scot-free and had stopped for a brief meal along the banks of a dry riverbed. As I watched them from a distance, I could tell the six braves responsible for the raid were very young—some no older than myself—and overconfident. A couple of them had rifles, which added to their cockiness. It occurred to me that my decision to leave ahead of my fellow braves had been foolhardy. Here I was alone, armed with nothing but a bow and a knife, while my enemies carried guns. There was no way I could reclaim the horses without exposing myself to attack… Unless I took a lesson from the trickster himself.

<hr>

The Apache brave keeping watch was surprised to see me. Then again, he probably hadn't seen many upright wolves dressed in breechclouts and buckskin leggings before.

"Greetings, Brother Human Being," I smiled, licking my snout and speaking passable Apache. "I am Coyote."

The Apache was so thunderstruck his knees began to wobble like a new-born colt's. He called out to his fellow braves, who hurried to see what was the matter. Naturally, they were equally amazed to see the trickster god of legend standing before them.

"I hope I am not bothering you fine warriors this beautiful morning," I said, gesturing to the rising sun. "But I was passing by on my way to visit the Great Spirit, to ask him certain favors for those who are my friends, and could not help but notice what a beautiful herd of horses you have."

"Th-thank you, Father Coyote," stammered the raiding party's leader. "You are going to see the Great Spirit?"

"Yes! Those blessed to Coyote receive good hunting and coup against their enemies. Did I mention before how fine your horses are?"

The Apache braves looked amongst themselves then glanced back at the herd.

"Yes, the Great Spirit shows great respect for those who prove their generosity to others," I continued, lying through my fangs. "Why, just the other day, the Wasp Band of the Comanche gave me ten horses..."

"Ten! Is that all?" snorted the Apache leader. "I would not call that generous!"

"Perhaps so," I said. "But in any case, I must be on my way. Have a good journey, friend human beings."

As I made to leave, the lead Apache called after me. "Father Coyote! We cannot let you leave without giving you a gift!"

"A gift, you say? What of?"

"Ponies."

"How many?"

I could tell he was trying to figure out how many ponies would be enough—he surely didn't want to offend a god important enough to put his case to the Great Spirit.

"Twenty—?"

I had him dangling but good. "Twenty? What a coincidence! Why, the Kiowa gave me a string of twenty ponies just last week...."

"Forty!" the Apache blurted.

I made a great show of scratching my chin in deliberation. I was actually enjoying the part of sly trickster, but I knew I was running the risk of irate braves unwilling to part with their share of the night's raid calling my bluff.

"Forty? Friend human being, you are truly a generous and great man! I shall be certain to mention your name first when I speak with the Great Spirit!"

You can imagine how surprised my tribe was when I rode back into camp, leading a string of forty ponies. When I told Medicine Dog how I succeeded in tricking the Apaches into returning my original ten horses, plus thirty more, the old coot came close to busting a gut laughing.

"Walking Wolf, you are indeed touched by the hand of Coyote! Only he could have wrested forty ponies from Apache braves without resorting to violence!"

                        ═══◆═══

I showed up the next afternoon in front of Calling Owl's tipi with the thirty horses needed to buy his daughter from him. Calling Owl was very pleased. Flood Moon, on the other hand, looked less than thrilled. She stood there, staring at her feet, as her father talked about how he was look-ing forward to grandchildren. After Calling Owl and I had sealed the transaction with a smoke from his pipe, Flood Moon went into her family's tipi for the last time and removed her sleeping roll, her feeding bowl and a few other belongings. Walking behind me with her head still bowed, she followed me to my tipi. Suddenly I was married. Like I said, the Comanche were practical people who didn't go in much for ceremony.

"How do you like your new home, Flood Moon? Isn't this better than the lean-to I built when we were children and played camp together?"

Flood Moon grunted and started to unroll her sleeping blankets. She didn't seem too impressed by her new home, but I tried not to let her lack of enthusiasm bother me. I reached out to embrace her, only to have her go rigid in my arms.

"Flood Moon, what is the matter?" I lifted her chin with my thumb and forefinger, but she looked away.

"I am frightened, Walking Wolf. I have never been with a man before."

"But I am your husband! You need not fear me!"

She looked at me from the corner of her eyes, smiling shyly. "Go outside and smoke your pipe. When you finish, I will be waiting for you inside my sleeping robes, ready to be your wife."

I was ready for her to be my wife right *then*, but I knew better than to hurry her. Comanche women could be shy, but once you got under them under the sleeping robes they were randier than a she-bear in heat. So I went outside, had me a smoke and watched the sun go down.

When I'd finished my pipe, I got up and stood by the tent flap. I called softly to my wife. "Flood Moon? Are you ready? I'm coming in now..."

The moment I set foot in the tipi, something crashed into the back of my head, knocking me to the ground, where I stayed—unconscious—until the next morning. When I came to, I discovered Flood Moon and her belongings were gone. The only thing she'd left behind was the grinding stone she'd used to coldcock me. Judging from the amount of blood on the grinding stone, it looked like she'd been meaning to crack my braincase open for the whole world to see what a witless fool I was.

I staggered out of my tipi to find Medicine Dog waiting on me, puffing on his pipe. "So. You aren't dead," he said, by way of greeting.

"Where's Flood Moon? Where is my wife?"

"She is gone."

"Gone? Where did she go?"

Medicine Dog shrugged. "I do not know. She and Small Bear were very scared. They thought they had killed you."

"Small Bear? Flood Moon is with Small Bear?" I could feel the anger swell inside me. My head still ached and I did not want to hear what Medicine Dog was telling me.

"They left together last night."

My best friend. The woman I loved. Both had betrayed me. And worse, they had robbed me of my pride. I had been made to look a fool in the eyes of the tribe. Such a crime against my honor could not go unpunished. My distress was quite obvious. Medicine Dog put aside his pipe and tried to calm me.

"My son, do not let your anger drive you to do something worse than foolish."

My head throbbed like a war drum and I doubled over, pushing at the sides of my skull to keep them from exploding outward. My anger was fueling the pain inside my head, forcing my body into its true-form. Medicine Dog stepped away from me. I had the bloodlust on me and he knew words would be useless. Snarling like a beast, I fled the camp. I had the scent of Flood Moon and Small Bear, and I was determined to hunt them down and make them pay for their treachery.

⟫◆⟪

It did not take me long to catch up with them. Like most *vargr*, I am a tireless runner. The rage burning deep inside me kept me from growing weary. Although they had a whole night and day's head start on horseback, I found them not long after dark.

I saw their fire long before I saw them. They were alone except for each other and their horses, huddled against the coming night. Careful to keep upwind of their mounts, least they catch my scent and alarm Small Bear, I circled their camp, listening to them as they talked.

I could tell from their words and actions that they had been lovers for some time. Small Bear sat with his rifle at the ready, Flood Moon pressed close to him. The sight of my best friend sharing an intimacy with my wife that I myself had never known stoked my anger even higher, until everything I saw was covered by a blood red scrim.

One of the ponies whickered nervously. Small Bear tightened his grip on his gun, peering into the dark beyond the fire as he got to his feet.

Flood Moon looked up at her lover, knuckling the sleep from her eyes. "Small Bear—what is wrong?"

"There is something out there."

I came in low, tackling him from behind, snarling like a rabid wolf. Small Bear's rifle discharged as he hit the ground. Flood Moon screamed out her lover's name, driving the knife she'd kept hidden in her blanket into my right side. I yowled in pain and grabbed at the intruding blade, giving Small Bear the chance to roll free and get back on his feet. Unsheathing his own knife, he made to drive it into my heart. Growling, I knocked the weapon from his hands and pounced on him as a coyote would a prairie dog, my teeth sinking deep into his soft, hairless throat.

I don't want people reading this to think the fight was one-sided. Small Bear was a strong, swift brave, and he did not surrender easily to death. Still, I tore at his struggling body with my talons, gleefully ripping his bowels free of his stomach. Small Bear's liver, glistening brown-red in the campfire, lay on the prairie grass. Without pausing to think, I snapped the tender morsel up and devoured it on the spot.

Wiping my muzzle on my forearm, I turned my yellow gaze to Flood Moon, who stood transfixed, staring in horror at the ruined remains of her lover. Smiling, I plucked her knife from my side as if it were no more bothersome to me than a thorn.

"Wife," I said, holding up the dripping blade. "Is this how you greet your husband?"

She gave a sob of fear and turned to flee, but I was too fast for her. I grabbed her by her braids, wrapping them around my forepaws so her face would be within biting distance. Her eyes were huge with fear, and the smell of her terror radiated like heat from the sun. Grinning, I licked her face with my tongue, laughing when she shuddered and began to cry.

I took her there, beside the cooling body of her lover. She screamed and whimpered and pleaded with me repeatedly as I raped her—for that was what I did, I don't deny it—but all it did was increase my determination to punish her even further. By the time my lust had run its course, Flood Moon bled from dozens of deep bites and scratches on her breasts, belly, buttocks and thighs. Sated at last, I pulled myself from her quivering, sobbing body and collapsed beside her in a deep slumber.

I awoke to find Flood Moon astride me, ready to plunge her knife into my chest. I'll never forget looking up into the face of the woman who, until that day, I had loved with all my life and heart, her face rendered almost unrecognizable by the bruises I'd given her. The hatred that burned in her eyes was all-consuming. She screamed in triumph as the knife sank up to the hilt in my chest.

Nancy A. Collins

172

My first reaction was a primal one—without thinking, I swiped at her as she struggled to pull the blade free for a second strike, my talons sinking into the soft flesh of her jugular. Flood Moon clutched her throat, a rattling gasp coming from her lips. I had sliced open her windpipe.

Struggling to get to my feet, I tugged at the knife wedged in my ribs. I was fully expecting to die, but to my surprise, after an initial spurt of blood, my wound sealed itself. The same could not be said for Flood Moon, who lay writhing on the ground at my feet, blood spurting between her fingers.

I felt as if I had woken from a bad dream only to find myself trapped within a nightmare. My head no longer ached, and I was empty of the anger that had driven me so relentlessly to such a horrible end. I looked around me as if in a daze. When I saw the mutilated body of Small Bear, I cried out in horror. Even as I closed my eyes to the murder I had committed, my memory replayed for me how I had brutally violated the only woman I had ever loved. When I opened them again, it was to see that Flood Moon, in her last moments, had crawled next to Small Bear to die.

I buried them there, side by side, on the lone prairie. I wept as I dug their common grave with the knife Flood Moon had planted in my heart, mourning as much for myself as for my victims, for I knew I could not return to my tribe after what I had done.

I grew physically ill at the thought of how Eight Clouds Rising, Medicine Dog, Quanah, Peta Nocona and the others would react once they learned of my crimes. Flood Moon and Small Bear had wounded my pride, but the punishment I had meted out to them was beyond all decent measure. And, to make matters worse, I had compounded my sin by breaking the Comanche taboo against cannibalism.

I was ashamed and frightened by what I had done. I had lost control of my baser nature and allowed it to revel in the pain of others. I felt sick to my soul. I decided I needed to know more about my strange powers and the beast inside me, least I lose control again and harm someone else dear to me. There was only one way I could learn more about myself. I decided it was finally time for me to go into the white man's world.

Chapter Three

My decision to abandon the way of the Comanche for the white man's society was not an easy one. Even though, technically, I was one of their number, I had no reason to love or trust whites.

First of all, it was whites who killed my natural family. I'd know that before I learned to walk, since Eight Clouds made a point of telling me, early on, the story of how I came to be his son. Secondly, throughout my years as a member of the Wasp Riders, I had ample occasion to see how treacherous whites could be. They had broken numerous treaties and waged war against the Comanche in a cowardly fashion for years. And third, it was the whites who were responsible for the epidemics of cholera, diphtheria, influenza, measles, smallpox and syphilis that spread through the tribe like brushfire, claiming brave, elder, squaw and papoose alike.

The whites seemed stricken with a craziness the Comanche—and all other Indians—were at a loss to comprehend. Their buffalo hunters killed more than they could possibly eat in a lifetime. Their farmers wrapped the land in barbed wire and claimed the dirt below and the sky above as their property. Still, for madmen, they were privy to immense power. The iron horses and the buffalo guns that could kill from a mile away were truly impressive. So, was it not possible they might have knowledge as to how I might better control my wolf-self?

I knew better than to ride up to the nearest settlement and expect to be welcomed with open arms. What with my long dark hair and sun-browned skin, I looked more Indian than white. I was likely to catch a bullet between the eyes before I had a chance to dismount. Besides, my English was pretty bad—in fact, nonexistent. No, if I was going to introduce myself to white society, it was going to have to be through an intermediary of some kind.

A week or more after I had voluntarily banished myself, I came upon a black man traveling alone across the prairie, driving a wagon pulled by oxen. When he saw my pony approaching, he reined his oxen to a halt and pulled out a rifle. He rested it across his knees, watching me cautiously.

As I drew nearer, I recognized him as the man called Buffalo-Face, who traded on occasion with the Wasp Riders, swapping rifles, ammunition and liquor for ponies.

"Good day, Buffalo-Face," I said, speaking in the mixture of Spanish and Comanche dialect that was reserved for dealing with traders.

He squinted at me and spat a stream of tobacco juice out of the side of his mouth. He was a big, powerfully built man with skin that gleamed like polished stone. A mass of dark, nappy wool hung to his shoulders, which was the reason the Comanche had given him his name.

"You Comanche, ain't ya?"

"I am Walking Wolf of the Penateka."

Buffalo-Face's shoulders relaxed . "Walking Wolf? You're Eight Clouds's boy, am I right? What you doin' way the hell out here, son? You out scoutin' buffalo?"

"I'm looking for whites."

"You on the warpath?"

"I want to go into the white man's world and learn how it works."

Buffalo-Face spat another streamer of tobacco juice, narrowly missing the rump of his lead ox. "Why the hell would you want to do something like that?"

"Because I am white, too."

Buffalo-Face squinted harder, leaning forward a bit. "Damned if it ain't so! You *are* white under all that dirt and paint! Imagine that."

"Will you take me to the whites, Buffalo-Face?"

Buffalo-Face frowned and rubbed his chin for a spell, occasionally giving me a look from under his knitted brow. After a minute he shrugged.

"Son, you're a fool to ask me, and I'm an even bigger fool for sayin' yes. Hitch your pony to the back of the cart there and ride up front with me. I could stand the company. It gets pretty lonesome out here with no one but Goodness and Mercy here to talk to," he said, gesturing to the yoked oxen.

Although the idea of riding on anything besides a pony was alien to me, I did as he asked and joined him on the wagon seat. The oxen did not move nearly as quickly as horses, but they plodded along without protest or halting.

During the course of our first day together, Buffalo-Face told me things about himself. I learned that he had been born a slave in some place called Alabama, that his mother had been raped at the age of twelve by the white overseer of the plantation she served on, and that he had killed a man—the same overseer who'd fathered him—in order to escape when he was sixteen. I also learned that he had left behind a wife and two, possibly three, children, in a place called Philadelphia.

Buffalo-Face shook his head and spat a streamer of tobacco juice, drowning a bluebottle fly perched on Goodness' left rump. "I'll be damned if I can figger out why you want to get yourself turned white. Sure, they're your own kind, but you're as much a stranger to their ways as any full-blooded Injun. Hell, I spent the first sixteen years of my life doin' my best to put distance 'tween me and white folk. I thought once I was free, things would be different for me.

"Well, things may have been better for me up north, but they weren't no different. I was still a nigger far as they was concerned. I could never get my wife to understand that bein' free of the plantation weren't enough for me. I didn't escape Alabama so's I could turn myself into a white nigger and spend the rest of my life tryin' to be like them.

"Six years ago I come out west. I'm still a nigger to folks out here, but at least I can spit without hittin' one of 'em." He demonstrated. "I can be my own boss and do as I please. If white folks could look inside my head and see how much I hate 'em, I'd be hanging from the nearest cottonwood faster'n a jackrabbit. So instead of shootin' whites and burnin' their homes to the ground, I get my satisfaction by peddlin' guns to the Comanches. Way I sees it, they got as much reason as me to be fond of the whites."

———◆———

That night we set up camp. Buffalo-Face served up black beans, dry bread and hot coffee. I'd never had coffee before, and I promptly spat it out. Buffalo-Face laughed as I grimaced and wiped my mouth with handfuls of grass.

"Give yourself a week, son, and you'll be suckin' it up like it was mother's milk!"

I liked Buffalo-Face. Outside of a Mexican boy stolen from a *ranchero* during one of our winter encampments, he was the only non-Comanche I had ever spent any time with. I wondered if I ought to tell him that I was a skinwalker, but I remembered Medicine Dog's warning concerning who I showed my true skin to. Buffalo-Face wasn't a white, but he wasn't an Indian, either. I fell asleep, pondering the question of whether I should tell him more about myself.

When I awoke, the coffee pot was on the fire but Buffalo-Face was nowhere to be seen. I found him down by the creek, stripped to his waist, washing his face and upper body. His muscular back was covered from shoulder to waist by scars that ran from rib to rib. The wounds were very old, some of them five or six deep in places. I watched him for a few more seconds, then returned to the camp.

When Buffalo-Face came back, he had replaced his shirt and was shrugging into his braces. He bent to pour coffee into a dented tin cup. "You sure you want to go ahead with this plan of yours? You seen the stripes on my back when I was washing at the creek. *That's* what white folk had to offer me."

"Medicine Dog told me that whites are crazy. Is this true?"

Buffalo-Face nodded and swallowed his coffee, grimacing—whether from the bitterness of the brew or his memories was hard to say. "That they are. But not fall-down, foam-at-the-mouth crazy. Whites are singular creatures. They ain't part of nothing but themselves, not even other whites. Mebbe that's what makes 'em act so snake-bit.

"Let me give you a bit of free advice, son. Whatever you do, always watch your back. Whites may hate niggers, Injuns, kikes and chinks—but that don't mean they love their own kind. If they can find a way to get what they want and leave you bleedin' and nekkid in the snow, they will. Whites ain't out for no one but themselves. Bear that in mind whenever you're dealing with 'em—don't matter if they're a man of the cloth, an old spinster lady or a young'un in knee pants. Whatever you do, don't trust 'em any farther than you can throw 'em."

I spent most of the next four weeks learning to speak English—at least talk it good enough to get myself understood. Buffalo-Face was astonished at how quickly I picked up the lingo. I didn't realize it at the time, but I have a natural aptitude for learning languages. At last count, I've become fluent in thirty-seven, including Swahili, Cantonese, Mongolian and Aborigine.

On the second week on the trail together, we were drinking hot coffee and studying the stars overhead when Buffalo-Face looks at me and says, "Well, if you're so goddamned set on bein' part of the white man's world, you've got to have you a white man's name. Walkin' Wolf might be a mighty fine name for a Comanche, but it ain't no kind of name for a white man."

Buffalo-Face worked his chaw real thoughtful for a second. "You wouldn't happen to know your real name, would you? No? In that case, we'll have to come up with a name on our own. Wouldn't be the first time a man's named himself out here...."

"Let's see now... William's a good name. But you're too young for a serious first name like that. How about Will? Naw... You look more like a Billy to me. Billy. Yeah, that sounds good! But Billy what? Smith and Jones are popular, but not exactly what you'd call distinctive. You want yourself a handle that folks'll remember... " Buffalo-Face's bloodshot eye wandered about our camp, his gaze finally settling on the cookfire. He grinned suddenly, displaying tobacco-stained teeth. "That's it! Skillet! Billy Skillet! How that sound to you, Walkin' Wol—I mean, Billy?"

I gave it a thought, rolling the name around on my tongue for effect. Billy Skillet. Damned if it didn't feel good in my mouth.

"I like it."

Buffalo-Face let out with a laugh like a wild ass in heat. "Then that's who you are, by damn! Billy Skillet! And don't let no one tell you otherwise!"

So that's now I got my white name. Here I was, barely fifteen years old, and I already had me three—possibly four—names. That's as many, or more, than a Comanche brave gets in a whole lifetime!

I'll always remember that night—how the stars glinted in the sky, how the air smelled of ox dung and coffee grounds, the sound of tobacco juice sizzling in the campfire. I was enjoying the best of both worlds there—Indian and white—without knowing it. I knew there was no way it was going to last forever, but I had no idea how long it'd be before I would know such peace again.

At the end of four weeks, we'd finally come within passing distance of a white settlement big enough to think it was a town. Buffalo-Face took me up on a rise that overlooked the slap-dash collection of wood houses and dirt streets.

"That there's Vermilion, Texas. White folks live there. Few Meskins, too, but mostly whites. You'll excuse me if I don't walk you down to the city limits. I don't do no tradin' with white folk in Texas—except for Spaniards. They're pure out-and-out businessmen, them Spaniards. Don't give a rat's ass what color a man's skin is, long as his coins are silver or gold. Don't care if you're selling liquor and guns to Injuns, either. Man's business is a man's business."

Buffalo-Face turned to look at me, shaking his head sadly. "You've been good company on the trail, boy. I'm sorry to see you go. I just hope you don't turn mean-crazy once you get yourself civilized. I reckon there are kindly white folks out there, somewheres. Lord knows, I never run across one. But, then again, I ain't never seen an elephant either. Mebbe your luck will be better'n mine on that count. Just remember what I told you, and you'll stand a halfway decent chance dealin' with 'em."

I threw my arms around his wide, scarred shoulders and hugged him as I would my own father. "Thank you for giving me my new name, Buffalo-Face."

"Shoot, t'weren't nothing, son," he said smiling. Suddenly his smile disappeared and he wagged a tobacco-stained finger in my face. "But whatever you do, don't tell 'em you've been keepin' company with a black man who sells guns to Injuns! All that'll do is put you on the wrong foot from the get-go!"

With that, he returned to his oxcart laden with contraband. The last I saw of him, he was spitting tobacco juice and snapping his whip over Goodness and Mercy, cursing a blue streak. We never met again, although I heard, years later, that he had run afoul of white settlers in Oklahoma in '61, who—upon learning he sold guns and ammunition to the Comanche and Apache—lynched him from the nearest cottonwood tree.

CHAPTER FOUR

The first thing that struck me about the town of Vermilion, Texas was its smell. To say that it reeked would be kind. Not that living the Indian life made me all pure and natural. Indian camps were hardly known for their sanitary conditions. What with dozens of horses and people living, eating, breathing and crapping side by side, things tended to get mighty ripe. However, the Indians were nomads, and when their surroundings got too fragrant, so to speak, they'd up and find themselves a new campsite. Whites, on the other hand, had a tendency to stay put in their own stink.

Vermilion was no more than a collection of ramshackle one-story clapboard buildings and adobe huts occupied by forty-seven souls—give or take a couple of Mexicans. There was a combination saloon and bawdy house, a feed and seed store, a general store and a blacksmith who also stood in as the local undertaker. All of these businesses lined a broad unpaved street that, thanks to the rainy season, was composed of equal parts mud and shit, both human and horse. This foul mixture, when churned into the proper consistency by passing traffic, was capable of sucking a boot clean off a man's foot and swallowing it whole, never to be seen again. Because of this, wooden boardwalks fronted both sides of the street, with haphazardly placed planks connecting the two.

In retrospect, Vermilion was a wretched little one-horse town, clinging to the edge of the Texas frontier like a tick on a dog's ear. But as far as I was concerned, it might as well have been the mysterious Philadelphia Buffalo-Face had spoken of.

The moment I rode into town, I was aware of all eyes being on me. Everyone stopped what they were doing to stare after me, watching me the same way a cougar does a wolf that's wandered into its territory. What with my pony and my braids and breechclout, I must have looked like a full-blooded Comanche brave.

I dismounted in front of the saloon and tied my pony to the hitching post. The moment I turned around, I found myself looking at a big tin star. The star was pinned on the chest of a burly, red-faced man with a drooping yellow mustache and a shock of blonde hair, atop of which rested a derby hat of fashionable make. A Colt six-shooter jutted from the holster strapped to the big man's hip.

"What you think you're doin' here, Injun?" the big man growled, letting his hand drop onto the butt of his gun.

I smiled as Buffalo-Face had instructed me, averting my eyes and bobbing my head in ritual subservience. "My name is Billy Skillet. I have come here to be white."

The big man's brows knitted together and his eyes lost their hardness. "Come again?"

"I am white like you," I hurried to explain. "I was taken by Comanches when very young, but now I have come to my people to learn to be white."

He pushed back his derby and scratched his head, looking me up and down. "Well, I'll be dipped in shit and shot for stinkin'! You *are* white, ain't you!"

"Perhaps I can be of some assistance, Marshal..?"

My mouth went dry in terror at the sight of the tall, broad-shouldered man striding towards me. In place of eyes, he had two black circles, like the empty sockets of a skull.

"He has no eyes!" I cried out, pointing at the fearsome apparition bearing down on us.

The eyeless man laughed at my show of alarm and lifted the smoked glass spectacles he wore to allow me a glimpse of the eyes underneath.

"You needn't fear me, my son—I have two eyes, just as God intended."

The Marshal scowled at the eyeless man. "Oh, it's you, Near."

"*Reverend* Near," the older man corrected, adjusting the lapels of his dusty frock coat.

"What have you," grunted the Marshal. "What do you want, *Reverend*?"

"I couldn't help but overhear this poor lad's tale of woe," exclaimed Reverend Near, flashing me a sympathetic smile. "Back in Chicago, I read stories of how the heathen Indians kidnap the hapless offspring of Christian settlers and raise them as their own, but I never thought I would be so fortunate as to meet such a specimen! Marshal Harkin, it would be my utmost pleasure—nay, my sacred duty!—to take this wretched, confused youth and instruct him in the ways of Christian brotherhood and make him a useful and productive member of society!"

Harkin shrugged. "If you want to take on the boy, that's your business, Reverend. Just make sure he stays out of trouble, y'hear?"

⟫⟩◆⟨⟪

The Reverend Near's "church" was a shack placed on the farthest edge of town. The only thing that separated it from the other one-room shanties was a crude whitewashed cross nailed over the front door like a horse shoe.

The church was one large room, divided in half by a couple of blankets suspended from a clothesline. The front half housed a couple of long benches and a wooden lecturing podium made from soap boxes.

"Welcome home, my son!" exclaimed Reverend Near, flipping back the room divider with an expansive gesture, revealing a potbelly stove, a table, a chair, a stool and a narrow cot. Behind the stove, a built-in ladder led to a half-loft.

As I stood and looked around, not quite certain what to do or say next, the Reverend pulled a black bag out from under the cot and began rummaging through its contents, still talking the whole time.

"What's your name again, boy? I didn't quite hear it the first time."

"Billy. Billy Skillet."

"An excellent name for such a fine figure of a young man! But first things first—before I can begin instructing you, we must get rid of these heathen adornments," he said, gesturing to my breechcloth and riding chaps. "A proper Christian gentleman doesn't parade around dressed like a wild Apache!"

"Comanche."

Reverend Near looked up from his black bag, peering at me over the tops of his smoked spectacles like an owl getting ready to snatch a mouse. "Never correct me, boy! The Lord says honor thy father and mother. And, as of this moment, you are now my son. At least in the spiritual sense. Is that understood?"

"Yes, Reverend." Actually, I didn't understand, but it seemed like the right thing for me to say. After all, I was new to the white man's ways, and I was in no position to judge what was right or wrong.

"As long as you remember that, we should have no problems getting along," he said, his voice once again friendly as he pulled a large pair of scissors from the depths of his black bag. "Come here, Billy," he said, gesturing for me to draw closer.

I hesitated, my eyes fixed on the gleaming metal shears he held in his hand.

"You needn't fear me, my boy!" he laughed, showing too many teeth for my liking. "I intend you no harm!"

Still uncertain, I took a timid step forward. The Reverend, scowling impatiently, suddenly got to his feet and grabbed me by one of my braids.

"I said come here! Are you deaf, boy?" he thundered.

Before I could reply, he neatly severed my right braid, taking it off level with my ear lobe. I yelped in alarm, clutching the side of my head as if mortally wounded.

"You needn't carry on so," the Reverend clucked, waving the scissors in front of my nose. "The way you're behaving, you'd think I was skinning you alive! Now sit down and let me tend to that remaining pigtail of the devil...."

I shook my head violently, backing towards the blanket that divided the living quarters.

"Billy, you're making your father very angry with you!" growled the Reverend. He'd removed his spectacles and I could see that his pupils were dilated as he came closer. I also noticed that he gave off a strange smell—one I would later identify as a patent medicine whose main ingredients were alcohol, bloodroot and laudanum.

As I said before, the Reverend was a big man and, despite my status as a Comanche brave, I was still a youth of fourteen, and a rather slight one at that. While I had years of bareback riding and strenuous living on my side, the Reverend was a good six inches taller and outweighed me by at least fifty pounds.

Bellowing like a wounded bull buffalo, the Reverend grabbed me by my hair and threw me roughly to the ground, planting his booted foot on the back of my neck.

Why did I not shapeshift, you ask? While I could have easily killed him in my true skin, this was something I did not want. After all, it was my bloodlust that had driven me to seek the help of whites in the first place. What good would it do me to make myself a pariah amongst them so soon? So I kept my human shape and took the punishment the Reverend meted out.

"Honor thy father and mother!" he shrieked as he worked to remove his belt. "I'll have no sassin' me in this house, young man! No back talk! No misbehaving! You'll do as I say and like it!"

I winced as the belt came down across my bared buttocks, the buckle biting into my flesh, but I refused to cry out in pain. It came down again—and again—and again—until my ass streamed blood, but still I remained silent. His rage apparently spent, the Reverend let the belt drop from his numbed fingers and staggered over to his cot, where he sat for a moment, staring at me without seeming to see me.

"Sin no more," he mumbled, although I was uncertain whether this admonishment was actually directed at me. With that, he promptly closed his eyes and keeled over. He was snoring before his head touched the cot.

I slowly got to my feet, grimacing in pain. However, I knew my discomfort would be fleeting. I discovered I possessed miraculous recuperative powers years ago, when me and a fellow brave were trampled by a wounded buffalo during one of the hunts. The brave died within hours of massive internal injuries, drowning in his own blood, while I was up and about the next day. More important than my physical state, however, was the situation I now found myself in.

I had suffered a humiliating physical insult that, in Comanche society, would have called for the death of my attacker if I was to reclaim my dignity. On the other hand, the Reverend Near, as far as I could discern, was a holy man of sorts, not unlike Medicine Dog. Which meant that he had access to hidden knowledge and was thereby worthy of respect. And it is well known that shamans of great power are often quite mad, prone to fits of violent, irrational behavior. And those who wish to learn from a shaman must suffer ritual debasement to prove themselves worthy....

I searched the room until I found the pair of scissors Reverend Near had abandoned during his frenzy. I looked at them for a long time, then at the Reverend, snoring away fully clothed on his cot. Then, without any hesitation, I reached up and snipped off my remaining braid.

My time with the Reverend lasted three months, and every moment remains vividly etched in my memory. For the longest time, I had no idea whether my so-called "spiritual father" was a holy man or a raving lunatic. Since I had nothing to compare white society against except the Comanche way of life, I was at something of a disadvantage.

During our frequent "tutoring sessions," which consisted of the Reverend reading aloud certain passages from the Bible and a pamphlet called "What Every Good Boy Should Know," two things were stressed: that it was a dire and mortal sin to touch oneself below the waist, and it was an even worse sin to have someone else touch you there.

The Reverend also advised against strong drink, calling it "the devil's blood." However, this prohibition did not extend to his own favorite beverage, a patent medicine called Mug-Wump Specific, which he guzzled at an alarming rate. I have no idea what, if anything, the potion was supposed to cure. But I soon learned that the Reverend's erratic behavior and violent outbursts were tied to his drinking it. Whenever the Reverend hit the Mug-Wump Specific, he would wander from his usual topics and rail against "tempting devils that appear as fair women" or the unfairness of life in general.

Gradually I came to know more and more about my new "spiritual father." I learned that his first name was Deuteronomy and that up until six months previous, he'd been the pastor of a respectable church in one of the wealthier neighborhoods in Chicago. I was never able to discover how he ended up in a reeking shit-hole like Vermilion, but there was something about a young girl who had come to him to be taught her catechisms.

The Reverend claimed that the reason he was in Texas was to help bring the good news of the Lord and Savior, Jesus Christ, to the heathen Indians, and to provide spiritual guidance for the numerous cowboys, ranchers and settlers working their way west. However, his attitude toward Vermilion was hardly charitable.

He had a low opinion of the members of his parish, reviling them as harlots, sinners and ignorant barbarians. The reason for his acrimony stemmed from the town's steadfast refusal to acknowledge him as a pillar of its community.

I eventually came to know Vermilion's true opinion of the Reverend because he got into the habit of sending me on errands those days when he was feeling "poorly"—which was fairly regular. I would go alone to the general store to pick up his weekly supply of beans, bread, coffee, salt pork and

Mug-Wump Specific, which gave me the chance to view the town and its inhabitants without the Reverend being around.

On my first solo journey to the store, the Reverend lectured me at length on how important it was for me not to set eyes on the "palace of trollops," for fear of my mortal soul. Since the general store was two doors down from the saloon, it was hard for me to avoid seeing it, either coming or going.

As I was leaving the general store laden with groceries, I noticed Marshal Harkin seated in a bentwood rocker outside the saloon, rocking gently back and forth. Without missing a beat, he glanced over in my direction and beckoned me to come closer.

Although I was fearful the Reverend might be using the all-seeing eyes of God he was always talking about to keep track of my comings and goings, I was curious. Since my arrival in Vermilion, the Reverend had kept me sequestered from its other citizens, assuring me it was for my own good, as the town was—in his own words—a "hotbed for all manner of sin and un-natural vice." I was to speak to no one, and this included Marshal Harkin, who was not only Vermilion's resident lawman, but also its pimp.

"You're that white Indian boy the Reverend took in, ain't you?" he drawled, pushing back the brim of his derby.

"Yes, sir."

"He treatin' you good, boy?"

"Yes, sir."

"You look like a right enough young feller to me, Billy. Whenever you get your fill of hearin' about Jesus, you come see me. I'm looking for a boy to sweep up and empty the spittoons and slop jars. I'll pay you a dollar a week. Good hard cash. You think about it, hear?" He leaned forward and tucked a piece of candy into my pocket, winking broadly.

That was my first genuine introduction to Marshal Harkin, better known as "Gent" on account of his passion for fancy eastern headgear. During my brief time in Vermilion, I would come to know him better than I would the Reverend.

Gent was an open, straightforward cuss. He owned the Spread Eagle Saloon, where five rather tired-looking "dance hall girls" worked the cliente-le, taking them upstairs for two-dollar sex of the boots-on variety. He was fairly easygoing when it came to the cowboys who rode into town to let off steam during the roundup season. After all, they were his bread and butter. Gent was willing to overlook drunken cowpokes hurrahing the town—riding up and down the streets, firing six-shooters aimlessly into the air (and the occasional window)— but he was merciless when it came to saloon brawls. And more than one hapless cowboy found himself colder than clay after shorting one of Gent's girls.

On the whole, Gent saw the Reverend as a nuisance more than an up-standing member of the community. As far as he was concerned, the only reason anyone came to Texas was to get away from their past. The West was a place where a man could reinvent himself from the ground up without having to worry about phantoms from the old days coming back to haunt him. And it was clear to anyone with one eye that the Reverend was hiding out from a damn big spook.

But the real reason Gent distrusted the Reverend was because he occasionally made forays into the Spread Eagle, attempting to sway the working girls from their lives of debauchery and sin. He had yet to win any converts, but Gent still took a dim view of anyone trying to stir up trouble in the henhouse. He knew Vermilion was still too young and poor to succumb to respectability, but he realized that it was only a matter of time before its citizens went from being rough-riding pioneers to civilized townspeople, and he sure as hell didn't like the idea of Reverend Near getting a jump on making Vermilion a decent place to raise your kids up.

He needn't have worried. Assuming Vermilion had a future at all, the Reverend was hardly destined to be its midwife. Besides, he didn't fool the whores one bit. They knew a sinner when they saw one. But not even they realized how bad off the Reverend really was.

Which leads me to the little girl. I don't recollect her name—it's possible I never knew it in the first place. All I remember is that she was one of the children that belonged to an immigrant sodbuster who lived on a farm just outside of town. Every now and then the Reverend would ride out there on his mule and try to convert the half-dozen or so families scattered about the countryside, but with little success. Most of them barely spoke enough English to buy seed and sell their eggs and butter, much less understand the gospel according to Deuteronomy Near.

The little girl disappeared one evening around suppertime. Apparently a rather boisterous child by nature, she had talked out of turn at the dinner table, incurring the wrath of her parents. Her punishment was to stand on the front porch until the rest of the family had finished eating. When the mother got up to tell the little girl she could come back in, she was nowhere to be found.

At first they thought she was playing a trick on them, but when several hours passed and the little girl still hadn't returned, the father rode into town and reported her disappearance, as best he could, to Marshal Harkin. Gent rounded up a search party. I asked the Reverend if I could help search for the missing child, but he refused to grant me permission.

When the first day of searching did not turn up any sign of the missing girl, Gent became convinced that one of two things had happened—that either she had been kidnapped by wild Indians or carried off by wolves, possibly even a bear. When the farmer translated the Marshal's suspicions to his wife, the poor woman became hysterical.

They found the little girl on the second day. After searching the surrounding gullies and washes, it turned out she was in her very own front yard.

They found her in the well. She had a burlap bag over her head and she was missing her knickers. The Marshal arrested the hired hand, who was a touch feebleminded and got into trouble last season for fucking some of the livestock where the neighbors could see it. After a trial of sorts, they hung him. They never did find the little girl's knickers.

The Reverend, being the only man of the cloth in the county, officiated at the burial, even though the dirt farmers couldn't speak a lick of English and were probably Lutheran to boot. I was there to help officiate, although all I did was stand to one side of the Reverend and pretend to look sad. Since I didn't have anything else to do, I studied the grieving family.

The mother was a stout, round-faced woman who probably wasn't as old as she looked, her eyes red and swollen from crying. The father was tall and rawboned, his face unreadable as he tried to comfort his wife. His eyes remained fixed on his daughter's coffin, suspended over the open grave by a couple of planks. There were five other children, some older and some younger than the dead girl. One or two of them cried, but the others simply looked uncomfortable in their Sunday best, squirming and pulling at their starched collars.

After rambling on about innocence, sinners, lambs, Jesus and a better world beyond, the Reverend at last shut up. The grave diggers removed the planks, lowering the small coffin into the ground with looped ropes.

A week later, I found the little girl's missing knickers wadded up and stuffed behind one of the loft rafters. They were stiff with dried blood and semen. I didn't know what to do about what I'd found, but I knew what it meant. It also decided something for me.

The only reason I'd put up with the Reverend's madness in the first place was the belief that he might have the wisdom to teach me how to control the killing wildness inside me. But now I knew for certain that the Reverend lacked the ability to curb even his own bestial tendencies, much less mine. That night, while he was passed out, I packed what few belongings I could call my own and trudged over to the Spread Eagle. Gent was playing solitaire in the saloon, a bottle of rotgut at his elbow and a foul-smelling hand-rolled dangling from his lower lip.

"You get enough Jesus, son?"

"Yes, sir. I come to see you about that job."

Gent grunted as he lay down another card. "Figgered you'd be comin' round sooner or later. I pay a dollar a week, plus what you can roll off the drunks. All yours, Billy."

"Thank you, sir!"

"Now get to work! I got slop jars that need scrubbin'!"

⟫◈⟪

I must have scrubbed every slop jar in Vermilion that evening, and considering that most folks crapped in tin cans instead of porcelain chamber pots, that was probably a fair bet. After I finished with the slop jars, I had to clean and polish the spittoons, then sweep and mop the front saloon.

By the time midnight rolled around, I was so tired I couldn't raise my arms over my head to take my shirt off. The bartender showed me my room—little more than a storage closet next to the backdoor, but at least there was a mattress on the floor. I'd been sleeping on nothing but dirty straw in the Reverend's half-loft, so it looked fairly ritzy. I collapsed into a sleep so deep I didn't even dream.

The next thing I knew, there was a crashing sound coming from outside, and the sound of a familiar voice raised in anger.

"Where is he?"

My eyes flew open and I had to fight to keep my fur from rising to the surface in self-defense. A growl slipped from between my clenched teeth.

"Where is that thankless heathen bastard?!?"

"Hey! What the hell do you think you're doin'?" yelled the bartender. "Somebody go fetch Gent! The Reverend's gone loco!"

The storage room door was jerked open and Reverend Near's frame filled the threshold. The stink of Mug-Wump Specific and madness radiated from him like heat from a flat rock. I scrambled to my feet to avoid being kicked in the ribs.

"There you are, you ungrateful piece of shit," he hissed. "I go to sleep for a few hours, and what do you do—? You turn on me and embrace mine enemies!" He shook his head sadly, and for a moment it looked as if he was about to cry. "I thought I could save you, Billy. I really believed that God had a plan for you. But I was wrong—horribly wrong. You're just another sinner, given over to base fornication and intoxication!"

Sweat began to pour off my brow. Being so close to the Reverend's insane rage was making me twitch. If I didn't get out in the open soon, I would shapeshift involuntarily. I tried to move past the Reverend but he surged forward, grabbing me by the shirt, lifting my heels off the ground as he slammed me into the shelves lining the tiny room. His face was inches from my own, and one of the lenses in his smoked spectacles was cracked.

"Honor thy father!" he bellowed. "Honor thy father, you little shit!"

I lost control then—but only for a second. It was enough. For the first time in months I let my bone and skin shift and twist, let the fur bristle and fangs sprout. And the Reverend Near suddenly found himself nose-to-muzzle with a snarling wolf.

He screamed in terror and let me drop. My butt coming into rough contact with the floor was shock enough to bring me back to my senses. I quickly reverted to my human self. The Reverend staggered backward, clutching his heart, his skin suddenly the color of tallow.

"Demon!" he gasped. "Foul demon of Hell!"

"What in tarnation is goin' on here? Jesus on the cross, Reverend—didn't I tell you to keep outta my saloon?" It was Gent, looking bloodshot and none too happy to be ousted from bed at such an ungodly hour as seven in the morning.

Before the Reverend could respond, Gent clamped a big, calloused hand on his collar and literally yanked him free of the storage room. The bartender and a couple of the girls peeped in to see if I was alive then hurried after Gent, who was frog-marching the Reverend towards the front door.

"You're harboring a fiend from the very Pit itself!" The Reverend warned, waving an arm in my direction. "A murdering beast that serves Satan as its master most high!"

"What the hell are you goin' on about now?"

"The boy! The boy is a minion of the Devil! I have seen him turn into a wild beast before my very eyes!"

"Go sleep it off, Reverend," Gent growled, delivering a swift kick to the raving minister's pants that propelled him through the saloon's swinging doors. Reverend Near fell into the thick muck that comprised Vermilion's main street, floundering and flailing like a drowning man. A couple of the whores had come out to see what the to-do was about and were having themselves a good laugh at the Reverend's expense.

"Trollops! Harlots! You shall not escape the Lord's judgment!" sputtered the Reverend, wiping the mire from his smoked glasses with as much dignity as he could bring to bear. Even though I knew the man to be a killer and a lunatic, I couldn't help but feel sorry for him.

"Come along, boy," Gent grumbled, leading me back into the dim interior of the Spread Eagle. "It's over."

I cast one last glance over my shoulder at the Reverend, struggling to extricate himself from the mud, and followed him inside.

※

Later that same day, Gent arrested me for the murder of the little immigrant girl. I was sweeping up the front saloon when he walked up and, without any warning, pulled out his six-shooter and pressed its barrel right between my eyes.

"Hate to do this to you, son, but your under arrest."

Turns out the Reverend went home, got himself cleaned off, and returned with the pair of knickers I'd found up in the loft. They'd disappeared soon after I first discovered them, so I assumed the Reverend had burned them in the potbelly stove. Turns out he just moved them to a better hiding place.

The Reverend turned over the missing knickers to the Marshal, complete with a story about how he'd found them in my belongings the day after the little girl's funeral. Obviously, I had been tainted by years amongst the Comanche—I was no more than a murdering savage, inflamed by the sight of white woman flesh to the most horrific acts of rapine.

Gent hadn't been too thrilled on this key bit of evidence suddenly making its appearance—after all, he'd already hung a man for the crime—but the Reverend wasn't about to let this go by. So off to the pokey I went, manacled hand and foot.

Vermilion's "jail" was a airless adobe hut divided into two rooms. The front room, theoretically, was Gent's office, although he preferred lounging outside the Spread Eagle to spending time in that sweat-box. The second room was a tiny closet of a cell, with a wooden plank set on sawhorses for a bed and a rusty coffee can for a slop jar. The one door was made out of iron with a trap at the bottom for meals to be pushed through, and there was a single narrow window set with bars. It stank of tobacco juice, vomit and old shit, since Gent rarely had occasion to use it for anything but a drunk tank, keeping rowdy cowboys in check until their trail bosses came to round them up.

As I sat on the rough plank, studying the heavy manacles that hung from my wrists and ankles, I realized my time as a citizen of Vermilion had reached its end. I knew what I had to do, and there was no joy in that knowledge. I had come to this place in hopes of learning how to tame the darkness in my heart, only to be forced farther from the light than before.

Shortly before dusk Gent pushed a dented tin plate of red beans, cornbread and a cup of cold coffee through the trap. He did not say anything, but I could feel him looking at me through the observation slit as I ate what was to be my last meal in Vermilion. I pushed the empty plate back through the slot and remained crouched by the door, listening to the clock-clock-clock of his boots as he walked away, locking the front door behind him. I waited until it was well and truly dark before shapeshifting.

The heavy manacles dropped from my transformed wrists with a shake of my hands. I stepped out of my leg shackles, my paws scuffing the floor in ritual dismissal. I could have made a symbolic show of force by literally snapping the chains that bound me, but I had neither the time nor interest in such foolishness. Although my kind are stronger than a dozen men, our natural state is deceptively slight, with long, narrow hands and crooked legs that would make us seem ill-equipped for running at high speeds and bringing down prey with nothing but our claws and fangs. One should never rely on appearances.

Once transformed, it was relatively simple for me to yank the bars out of the window and squeeze myself through to freedom, leaving behind only empty manacles and my discarded clothes. The night was dark and windy, with lightning dancing on the far horizon. My pelt prickled, and my nostrils twitched as I caught the scent of distant rain.

I slid through the shadows towards the edge of town, careful not to be seen during the brief stutters of lightning. I needn't have worried—most citizens were already sound asleep, and the few that were still awake were busy whoring, gambling and drinking themselves insensate at the Spread Eagle.

The front door was unlocked—as usual—and the Reverend was passed out, face down, at the kitchen table, an empty bottle of Mug-Wump Specific at his elbow. Next to the bottle of patent medicine was an open Bible and a

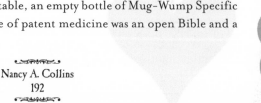

pair of drawers. Judging from the color of the stains, this pair was considerably older than the ones he'd taken off the little immigrant girl.

The Reverend made a slurred grunting noise when I tickled his left ear with the point of my claws, then screamed like a woman when I tore it from his head. He sat up with a violent spasm that nearly sent his chair toppling backward. Without his left ear to support them, his smoked spectacles dropped away, revealing eyes bulging in their sockets like hardboiled eggs. He grabbed the Bible with a trembling, bloodied hand and held it as if he meant to swat me across the muzzle with it.

"Child of evil! I command thee! Get back, Satan!"

I snarled and knocked the book from his hand, grabbing him by the throat as I pulled him out of his chair. As I slowly crushed his windpipe, the Reverend opened his mouth wide, gasping for air. He issued a muffled shout, his body bowing upward, as I shoved the pair of knickers down his throat. The Reverend thrashed under my grip for several seconds, and although he was a very strong man, there was never a chance of him breaking free. And he knew it.

I left him there for the others to find—his mouth filled with a dead girl's underpants. No doubt the whores down at the saloon wouldn't be surprised.

I crept from the Reverend's shack, pausing to warily eye the approaching storm. Weather on the plains has a tendency to be sudden and violent, quickly metamorphosing into the fierce devil-winds the Mexicans called *tornado*. And something told me that was exactly what was brewing out on the prairie.

I stood there for a second, studying the sorry cluster of buildings that comprised Vermilion. Pricking my ears forward, I could make out the Spread Eagle's piano in the distance, along with the occasional shriek of whore laughter. Maybe they knew there was a storm coming. Maybe not. Buffalo-Face had been right. Whites *were* crazy, although some seemed crazier than others. Wherever the knowledge I needed to understand and contain my beast-nature might be, it certainly did not lie in Vermilion, Texas. I turned my back on the town and headed into the surrounding night.

Less than an hour later, the storm caught up with me, pummeling me with hail the size of a child's fist. The wind was so fierce it knocked me down and kept me there, as if a giant hand were pressing me into the ground. I knew that if I remained in the open, I ran the risk of being sucked into the storm—I'd seen a buffalo shoot into the sky like a stone from a sling a few seasons back. There was so much dust and dirt kicked up by the storm, it was impossible to see more than a foot in front of me, but I had the impression that the air above me was alive and angry, seething with raw power. Using all my strength, I crawled on my belly until I came to a dry riverbed and rolled down the bank, pressing myself against the overhang for shelter. By this time, the rain was coming down with such force it stung like nettles and jagged fingers of lightning tore at the night sky.

There was a distant rumbling that seemed to be growing closer, and at first I thought it was thunder—until I realized I wasn't hearing it, but feeling it through my feet.

I looked up just in time to see a six-foot-high wall of churning water, mud and other detritus come rushing down the riverbed in my direction. Even given my superior strength and speed, there was nothing I could do. The flash flood hit me with the force of a full-throttle steam engine, pulling me under and dragging me along as it raced towards nowhere. I surfaced once, long enough to glimpse a sliver of moon peeking through the heavy clouds, then the branch from an uprooted tree crashed into the side of my head and everything went dark.

CHAPTER FIVE

"You dead, son?"

I peeled one eye open—which was fairly difficult, seeing how it was caked with dried mud—and looked up at a clear blue sky. I opened my mouth to speak but coughed up a lung full of dirty water instead.

"I reckon you ain't dead, then."

A pair of hands grabbed me under the armpits, levering me into a sitting position. Staring down at my mud-caked belly and genitals, I saw I was wearing my human body. A bottle was pressed to my cracked lips.

"Here, boy. Take a swig of this—good for what ails you."

I took a swallow. The liquid tasted like a cross between turpentine and gin, and burned my throat. Coughing violently, I pushed the bottle away and vomited a mixture of river water and stomach acid.

"See? What'd I tell you?"

Wiping the grime and mud from my eyes, I finally got a good look at my benefactor. He was a short white man with muscular, slightly bowed legs and long, wavy brown hair that hung down past his shoulders. He was dressed in a stained and frayed linen suit that had once been white. A stovepipe hat perched atop his head. He peered down at me through thick spectacles that made his eyes look grotesquely large. Even with my limited experience dealing with white society, I realized this man was not normal.

"W–who are you?"

The man in the once white suit smiled and extended his hand. "The name's Praetorius! Professor Praetorius! And who might you be, young sir?"

I took his hand and allowed him to pump my aching arm vigorously. "Billy Skillet."

I slowly got to my feet, looking around me. I stood on the bank of what was now a small river, surrounded by a tangle of driftwood, a dead cow made swollen and stiff from drowning, and other flotsam and jetsam left behind when the flood waters receded.

"I was scouting to see where the best place to ford the river might be," Praetorius explained, jerking a thumb toward the covered wagon waiting near the river bank a few dozen yards away. "That's when I found you. Weren't sure you was alive or not, seeing how you was completely coated in mud."

"W–where am I?"

"I reckon we're still in Texas. Yesterday I went through Vermilion, so you're twenty miles west of there...."

Massaging my bruised skull, I eased myself down onto an uprooted tree that was now lying on its side. "You said you were in Vermilion?"

"What's left of it. Twister didn't leave nothin' but a greasy piece. Killed every white in town—no one left alive but a couple of Meskins. Had to leave. It don't pay to play to a crowd that small and that poor."

"Play? Are you an actor?"

Praetorius smiled again and tugged on his lapels. "Why, my good man—I'm in business! I sell my very own Patented Hard Luck Miracle Elixir! Guaranteed to cure neuralgia, cholera, rheumatism, paralysis, hip disease, measles, female complaints, necrosis, chronic abscesses, mercurial eruptions, epilepsy, scarlet fever, cancer, consumption, asthma, scrofula, diphtheria, malaria and constipation! Good for both external and internal use!"

"Is it the same as Mug-Wump Specific?"

"Heavens no! My Patented Hard Luck Miracle Elixir is a thousand times more efficacious!"

I grunted and got to my feet again, doing my best not to wobble. I felt like a shirt that'd been beaten clean on a rock. Every muscle and joint ached, and my guts were full of filthy water. Praetorius grabbed my elbow and helped steady me. As I said, he was somewhat short and I found myself peering over his stovepipe hat.

Nancy A. Collins
196

"Dame Fortune lead me to find you, Billy!" he said, steering me toward the covered wagon. I was too weak to argue and allowed him to lead the way. "Obviously, the Fates decided that it was not yet time for you to die—they knew you had work to do! Important work! They saved you from drowning in that horrible flash flood in order for you to help me!"

"Help you?"

"That's right, my boy! I've been in dire need of assistance. A partner, if you will. I lost my last helpmate a week or so back—poor Jack's horse stepped in a gopher hole and threw him." Praetorius put on a sad face and shook his head. "Broke his neck clean through."

"Sorry to hear it."

Praetorius shrugged. "No use crying over spilt milk, I say. Especially now that Providence has been so kind as to deliver you to me! Here, you sit in the shade next to the wagon while I go find you some clothes. We can't have you walkin' about with your johnson hangin' out."

Praetorius disappeared into the back of the wagon, where I could hear him shifting things about. I noticed there was what looked to be a cage of some kind fixed to the side of the wagon, balancing out the barrels of fresh water and supplies strapped to the other side. The cage was roughly four feet by four feet, protected from both the rays of the sun and prying eyes by a carefully draped tarp. Curious, I reached out and flipped back the canvas.

I don't know what I was expecting to find in the cage. Perhaps a wild animal of some kind. But I was definitely not prepared for what I saw.

There was a little man—at least I think it was male—about the size of a five year old child in the cage. He wore a rag over his loins, and his twisted and stunted limbs were as filthy as any creature could possibly be without being all dirt. He had a large, long nose that connected with the top of his small skull without the interruption of a forehead, making it look as if his skull actually came to a point. This effect was magnified by his head being shaved except for a patch about two inches in diameter at the top, which was bound into a tiny knot with a piece of red yarn. The little man looked at me with permanently crossed eyes and smiled like an imbecile.

I took a couple of steps back from the cage and bumped into Praetorius. I had never seen anything like it before in my life. If a child was born with such deformities amongst the Comanche, it was immediately put to death. The Comanche way of life did not make allowances for those incapable of providing for themselves.

"What is it?" I asked, pointing at the little man in the cage.

"That's it," he smiled.

"That's what?"

"His name. Whatisit. He's my side attraction, in case no one's interested in a medicine show. I display him for a nickel a peek." He shoved an armload of old clothes at me. "Here, I found you some duds. Used t'belong to old Jack, rest his soul."

As I struggled into his late partner's clothing, I couldn't take my eyes away from the creature in the cage. "Is it human?"

Praetorius opened up one of the provision coffers and took out some bread and an apple and passed it through the bars to Whatisit, who chewed them with the complacency of livestock.

"Well, in the lecture I give the rubes, he's a man-monkey. 'A most singular animal, which though it has many of the features and characteristics of both human and brute, is not, apparently, either, but in appearance, a mixture of both—the connecting link between human and brute creation.'"

"Is that true?"

"Hell no! But you can't tell people, 'Now I've got this idiot here; take a good look at 'im.' That's bad for business."

"He's not dangerous is he?"

"Poor Whatisit don't have the brainpower to be mean," chuckled Praetorius, reaching between the bars to give the pinhead a scratch behind the ears. "Ain't that so, old fellow?"

Whatisit giggled and, as if in answer, hurled a handful of shit at me, dirtying the front of my new shirt and splattering my chin.

"I thought you said he was harmless!" I snapped, brushing the idiot dung from my face and chest.

"No. I said he wasn't *dangerous*. There's a difference. 'Sides, tossin' turds is his only vice. I can't deprive a man of his solitary pleasure, can I?"

And on that auspicious note, I began my tenure as a full partner in Professor Praetorius' Hard Luck Elixir Traveling Show.

⟫◆⟪

As I said, the Professor was as crazy in his own way as the Reverend, but I liked him a lot more. Where the Reverend had been brooding and pensive, obsessed with sin and guilt and divine retribution, the Professor was interested in one thing and one thing only—making a dollar. He knew he was a charlatan and did not pretend to be respectable—at least with me. Another big difference between him and the Reverend was that while he pushed his

patented cure-all on everyone from babies at the teat to old men with beards tucked in their belts, he himself never once put lips to it.

The Professor's way of making a living was unique, to say the least. Traveling from one pissant settlement to the next, peddling cure-alls to illiterate sodbusters and syphilitic townies, hardly guaranteed a steady or stable income, but it *was* exciting. And, in its own way, it reminded me of my boyhood, wandering from place to place. Every now and again, we'd catch distant glimpses of Comanche hunting parties in pursuit of buffalo and antelope, but they never offered to come near us. I'd watch from the wagon, part of me aching as I wondered if my adopted father, Eight Clouds, or my old childhood friend, Quanah, was riding past.

But back to the medicine show. People didn't get much in the way of outside entertainment back then, so even the lamest of diversions was apt to draw a crowd and generate some interest. The Professor did business this way: We would camp well outside the city limits of his intended venue. He'd ride in and pay the sheriff a visit and offer him a dollar or three for permission to stage a show. If the sheriff wasn't agreeable, we'd set up shop just outside the town's dividing line and do it anyways. Then he'd hand a stray kid two bits to paste up handbills advertising Professor Praetorius' Hard Luck Elixir Traveling Show's imminent arrival, and give it a day or two for the news to percolate amongst the locals via word of mouth. Then we'd ride into town.

Most of the Professor's wagon was taken up by a portable wooden stage he'd had made special back in Philadelphia that was designed so it only took fifteen minutes to set up (a half-hour if it was raining), so the Professor could address the crowd from a platform almost as high as their heads without leaving the safety of the wagon. There were holes drilled in the stage so you could fix poles with banners stretched in between them that advertised the Hard Luck Elixir and Whatisit. One such banner read: *Prof. Praetorius' Hard Luck Elixir—Strong Medicine For The Weak! $1-Free To All Veterans Of The Revolutionary War.* (Seeing how this was the late 1850s, the Professor rarely had occasion to part with a free bottle of his precious snake oil.)

The show would begin with me coming out onto the stage dressed in a bright blue frock coat with a double row of brass buttons and shoulder epaulets, a pair of shiny Wellington boots, and a brushed beaver high hat with a bedraggled peacock feather tucked in its brim. (That last touch of theatricality virtually begged to be shot off my head—and was so, on more than one occasion.) I would then take up a drum and begin beating away on it, drawing a crowd as I did. Once the crowd was of a decent size, I would stop drumming and announce, as loudly as I could, "Ladies and Gentlemen! It is my honor to present to you the one! The only! The esteemed Professor Praetorius!"

The Professor, who'd been waiting inside the wagon behind a blanket curtain, would step out, accompanied by a drum roll. The Professor had a special white linen suit he kept stowed in a trunk and only wore for shows. He kept it clean by boiling it in so much starch it could damn near stand up on its own. At every show, he'd present himself to the audience as an immaculate tower of medical knowledge, his elbows and knees crackling like dead leaves with every movement. (Of course, the damned suit chafed like a bear. After each show, when the crowds had left and we were on our way to our next destination, the Professor would be busy smearing salve on his neck, johnson and other tender parts that had been rubbed raw during his presentation.)

Watching the Professor work a crowd was a real education. He definitely knew how to talk a man into reaching into his pocket and handing over hard-won money for what amounted to rotgut whiskey mixed with horse liniment. I credit most of his success to his way with words. Only the Professor could get away with calling a simple glass of water "a chalice of Adam's ale." And for those unwilling to part with a dollar for a bottle of Hard Luck Elixir, there was always a nickel's worth of amazement in the form of Whatisit.

In order to lure the townies into surrendering their change, Praetorius puffed up Whatisit's pedigree from pinheaded imbecile to captured apeman. To hear the Professor tell it, you were a cast-iron fool is you missed this chance of a lifetime to gaze upon such a unique specimen from Borneo, or Sumatra, or Tierra del Fuego or wherever the hell the Professor decided Whatisit was from that day. He made coughing up five red cents to stare at a caged freak sound not only educational, but morally uplifting to boot.

In order to show Whatisit, the Professor rigged up a special canvas enclosure to one side of the stage large enough to allow up to twenty people to pass through at a time. Those foolish enough to crowd too close usually ended up splattered with pinhead shit, to the amusement of their fellows. It was my job to be sure that the line kept moving and that no one did anything to Whatisit, like poke him with sticks or give him broken glass to play with.

After the Professor had finished his pitch and wrested what money he could out of the crowd, we'd pack up and get moving to the next stop as fast as possible. The Professor's official motto was "Always leave the customers happy," though the practical translation was closer to "Always leave them before they find out what they've really bought."

Although Whatisit and I had gotten off on the wrong foot, I soon grew fond of the pinhead. As far as the Professor could tell, Whatisit was probably in his late twenties, which was fairly old for a pinhead. By and large, he was easy to control and wasn't hard to feed. The only time he got out of hand was when he had to be washed, but that wasn't often. Every now and again, I'd take him out of his cage and put him on a leash so he could exercise, but he didn't seem to like being outside his box. He'd scuttle about on his hands and knees like a dog and make a high-pitched whining noise, occasionally clinging to my pants leg and walking semi-upright.

The Professor told me Whatisit's lack of enthusiasm for the outdoors was on account of his natural parents keeping him in what amounted to a crate ever since he was a baby, showing him at fairs and carnivals from the back of a wagon. They sold Whatisit to the Professor in '49 in order to clear a debt. Whatisit's parents weren't too broke up over parting with their only son since they had a younger daughter with a parasitic twin that could clog. (The daughter, not the parasitic twin.)

I traveled with the Professor for close to two years, tending the mules, mending the banners, walking and washing Whatisit, decanting the foul-tasting Hard Luck Elixir into bottles and pasting labels on them. The elixir itself varied from brewing to brewing, depending on what the Professor could lay his hands on at the time. Often it was little more than watered-down rotgut, but I recall a couple of times when oil of turpentine, green vitriol and sulphate of iron were tossed in to the mix—not to mention the occasional rattlesnake to give it extra "bite."

During the time we were together, we traveled throughout most of Texas and into Oklahoma, putting on shows wherever there were enough folks with coins in their pockets to make an audience. As I stood on the stage before an endless parade of poverty-stricken farmers, illiterate ranchers and pig-ignorant townies—each of them watching me, listening to my every word, memorizing every gesture and nuance so they could repeat it, verbatim, to their kin stuck back on the homestead—I came to see myself through their eyes. I was no longer a skinny teenaged boy dressed in outlandish clothes that did not belong to him, but the herald of miracles, transformed by the glamour found in even the tattiest of traveling shows. It was the same magic that could turn a conman into the wisest of sages and a congenital idiot into a missing link from an nameless exotic land.

With all this folderol about cure-alls and tribes of monkey-men, no one knew—not even the Professor—that locked within me was a genuine miracle. I kept my condition to myself during my time with the traveling show, occasionally slipping away in the dead of night to hunt rabbits or howl at the moon. Once I shapeshifted in front of Whatisit's cage without checking to see if he was asleep first. Whatisit frowned at me and sniffed the air, looking more confused than usual. When I reached between the bars to scratch behind his ears, he whimpered and drew away. After that I made a point of waiting until I was several hundred yards away from the camp before changing.

As I said earlier, Professor Praetorius was careful to keep a step ahead of irate customers. We'd done our share of time in jail, here and there, none of it coming to more than a day or two at the most. But jail was actually the least of our concerns, since most towns we visited didn't even have proper law. What the Professor was worried about was angry customers who would show up with a bucket of tar and a sack of feathers. And when our time finally came, being tarred and feathered would have seemed like a pretty fair shake.

——◄►◆◄►——

I don't recommend getting lynched.

Even for folks such as myself, who are notoriously difficult to kill, being hung is hardly a picnic. While a werewolf can't die of a broken neck, it hurts like hell. Besides, if the person doing the lynching doesn't know what he's doing, instead of ending up with a snapped neck you'll get your head yanked off. And that'll kill *anything*, human or not. But I'm getting ahead of myself.

We were camped in the Oklahoma territory, near the Red River. We spent a lot of time crossing the Red River in and out of Texas and Oklahoma. It tended to put off dissatisfied customers intent on reclaiming their money. Two days before we'd sold twenty bottles of Hard Luck Elixir in Turkey Creek, Texas, and the Professor had considered it prudent to cross back into Oklahoma. Just in case, mind you.

We were feeling pretty good about that little bit of salesmanship. So good, in fact, we'd elected to give ourselves a break and rest an extra day. We'd found a nice little campsite, sheltered by a copse of trees, with plenty of game nearby. It was spring and the wild flowers were in full bloom, carpeting the banks of the river for as far as the eye could see. It had been such a fine day, I'd taken Whatisit for a little walk, which he actually seemed to enjoy.

It was getting dark, and the Professor and I were eating supper by the campfire. I reached out to pour myself some coffee, when there was this sound like the devil hacking into a spittoon; the coffee pot leapt four feet into the air.

"Put yore hands in the air and keep 'em that way!" thundered a voice from somewhere in the trees.

The Professor and I did as we were told. A half-dozen men emerged from the surrounding twilight, each of them pointing a rifle in our direction. I recognized most of them as being members of the audience in Turkey Creek.

"What's the meaning of this?" The Professor demanded, doing his best to keep a waver out of his voice.

A tall, grizzled man in buckskin pants and shirt stepped forward and pointed his rifle square at the Professor's head. I knew right then these unhappy customers weren't going to be satisfied with just getting their money back.

"I'll tell you what the meaning of this is about, Mister Perfesser!" he snarled. "It's about how that elixir of yores poisoned my little gal!"

"That is unfortunate—but did you follow the directions on the label? I definitely draw a distinction between adult and child dosages—"

The grizzled man's face turned red as he cocked his rifle. "Shut up! I don't wanna hear no more of yore fancy talkin'! You done enough talkin' already!"

A second man, this one with watery eyes, stepped forward. He carried a burlap sack . "Jed's girl ain't the only one you hurt, either! My Doris paid good money to see that freak of yores—we weren't home a hour when she went into labor! And look what she delivered me!" He took the sack and dumped its contents onto the ground in front of the Professor. "You did this!" he sobbed, pointing at the stillborn pinhead. "This is yore doin'!"

The Professor's eyes narrowed at the sight of the tiny pinhead corpse. He licked his lips. "How much—how much do you want for it? With a little pure alcohol and formaldehyde—"

"You goddamn murderin' bastard!" shrieked the dead pinhead's father, catching the Professor square in the chest with his boot. "I'm gonna kick you yeller!"

The one called Jed grabbed him by the elbow and pulled him away. "Hold on, Ezra! Everyone here wants a piece of that sumbitch. And there's only one way we're gonna get satisfaction, and that's lynchin' 'em good and proper." Jed turned to look at me. "You pick yore friend up and stand were's we can see you. And don't try no funny business, y'hear?"

I nodded my understanding and went to help the Professor off the ground. He was bleeding from the nose and mouth and his spectacles were busted, causing him to squint so hard that his eyes were slits. He shook his head and patted my hand.

"I'm sorry yore gonna die, Billy," he sighed. "I kinda always knew this would be how I'd leave this world. Goes with the territory. But you—you're a young man. Got your whole life ahead of you. Or did."

"Don't go talkin' like that, Professor. We can get outta this."

"My luck's played out, son. It's what I get for leavin' Jack to suffer the slings and arrows of outrageous fortune last time."

"Jack? Your old partner? I thought he died of a broken neck when his horse threw him."

"The broken neck part was true enough. But it was more on account of his horse being rode out from under him. I left Jack to hang in Burning Water, Texas, damn my soul. I make it a policy never to visit the same town twice, but it turns out some of Burning Water's citizens had moved there after losing a family member or two elsewhere. They recognized me when I rode into town to distribute fliers and followed me back to camp. They got the drop on Jack and I left him, curse me for the coward that I am!"

Before I had a chance to respond to what the Professor had confessed to me, there was a horrible shrieking noise from the direction of Whatisit's cage. One of the sodbusters had forced the lock and was trying to drag the terrified pinhead out. Judging from the shit dripping from his attacker's angry face, Whatisit had already exhausted his only mode of defense.

The sight of the tiny, frail Whatisit—frightened out of what little wits he possessed—shrieking and writhing helplessly in the grip of a rawboned cracker was enough to make me forget myself. "Leave him be!" I snarled, letting my teeth grow and hackle rise.

If any of the gathered farmers noticed the start of my transformation, I'll never know, because at the very moment I took my first step toward the struggling Whatisit, Jed reversed his rifle and brought its butt down square on my head.

I woke up to find my hands tied behind my back, a noose around my neck and a mule between my legs. They'd unharnessed the team that pulled our wagon. The Professor had his own mule, in deference to his position, while Whatisit and I were forced to share the other.

The one called Jed squinted up at me then at Whatisit, shook his head and spat. He stepped back a couple of yards, cocking his rifle in preparation for firing.

"Any last words?" Jed asked the Professor.

"My one regret is that when I die, so dies my medical knowledge! Not since Hippocrates has there been such wisdom! What a loss to the ages—"

"To hell with you!" Jed bellowed, and fired the rifle.

The mules left in a right hurry.

At least Whatisit and the Professor died quick. Their necks snapped like dry twigs. So did mine, for that matter, but I didn't die. Not that I felt good, mind you. Getting lynched, like I said earlier, is not my idea of entertainment. The first thing my body did was fill my pants, fore and aft, with shit and sperm.

Now, I've known folks who got their jollies from choking themselves, claiming orgasms on the brink of death are the ultimate in sex. I'd rather stick my dick into something living, personally. So there I was, jigging in midair, my eyes agog, my tongue stuck out, my lungs on fire and my pants full of stuff I'd have rather kept inside me for a while longer. The pain was so intense that I couldn't concentrate long enough to shapeshift. (Not that it would have helped me any. If I'd succeeded in shifting right then, my so-called executioners would have filled me so full of holes it wouldn't have mattered that they didn't have silver bullets.)

As I struggled against the rope, it suddenly dawned on me that I better put my physical discomfort aside and play opossum before one of the lynching party started feeling sorry for me and elected to put me out of my misery with a bullet in the brainpan. The moment I went limp, the lynching party issued a collective sigh and readied itself to leave. But before they left, they took the time to set the Professor's wagon ablaze—after they'd looted it and found the strongbox, of course.

As I slowly twisted in the midnight breeze, flanked on either side by a con man and a freak, I wondered just exactly where life was leading me and what was I expected to learn from this, my most recent experience. And, more importantly, I also wondered exactly how in hell was I going to get down.

CHAPTER SIX

There are a lot of things I've learned about being a werewolf over the years. And since I wasn't raised by my own kind, it's been something of a hard-knocks education.

Most folks assume the only thing that can kill a werewolf is a silver bullet. That's true enough—up to a point. Silver *is* lethal to my kind, whether in the form of a bullet, blade or bludgeon. But that's not the only thing that'll put us down. Like most living (or undead) things, being decapitated tends to slow us down. So does being burned alive. But outside of that, we're damn near indestructible. For instance, I discovered werewolves can grow back fingers, eyes and other body parts the hard way. Which doesn't mean things don't hurt, mind you.

So there I was, dangling like some strange fruit from the limb of a cottonwood tree, my hands bound behind me and my neck snapped. Normally, most folks would be somewhat dead under such conditions. Not me. Unfortunately, a snapped neck—while not fatal—was hardly a cold in the nose. It was going to take time for me to recover, and exactly how long I had no way of knowing.

As I was hanging there, I was extremely aware that the Professor and Whatisit didn't smell so good. Not that either of them had been particularly aromatic to begin with. So it wasn't long before we attracted visitors.

Carrion crows, to be exact.

One of the bastards landed on my head, dug its talons into my scalp for a better grip, then leaned forward so it was looking at me upside down. It peered at me with one shiny black eye, then the other, trying to decide whether I was dead. Before I could muster a moan to scare the damn thing off, it flapped its wings and plunged its beak into my right eye.

There are no words that can convey what it felt like to have an eye skewered and yanked out of its socket. There were several excruciating minutes as the carrion crow worked to sever my optic nerve, yanking and pecking at it until it snapped. When the eye finally came free of its socket, the bird cawed out in victory, gobbling down its prize. Lucky for me, *vargr* meat is not very appetizing to beasts of the natural world, so it did not attempt to reach further into my skull and peck at my brains.

I spent the rest of the day twisting in the hot, dry Oklahoma wind and being tormented by every breed of fly known to man and beast which—unlike the crows and other scavengers—were not so particular in regard to taste. They were buzzing and biting and swarming about me in the hundreds. I could feel the little sons of bitches walking over my face, laying eggs in the corners of my eyes and in my nostrils. The idea of thousands of maggots chewing away on my face from within didn't improve my mood. By the time the sun went down, I was one sorry, fly-bit son of a bitch, believe you me.

As the sun faded from the sky, I heard what sounded like a horse. I couldn't see who or what it was since I was dangling in the wrong direction. Next thing I know, there is a black stallion with a rider dressed in clothes the color of midnight just a few feet from where I was hanging. The horse made a weird whickering noise and took a nervous sidestep as its rider drew his gun and aimed it at me.

"Open your eyes, wolf-son," snarled the dark rider. Wherever he was from, it sure as hell wasn't Texas, judging from the thickness of his accent. "You can't fool me. I know you're not dead."

I lifted the lid of my remaining eye and glared at the stranger. "I can only open one. Damn bird ate the other one."

"They'll do that," grunted the dark rider. He fired his pistol point-blank, severing my noose just above my right ear.

I hit the ground and broke my shin, but compared to what I'd gone through that day, I didn't notice it. The dark rider climbed down from his horse and knelt beside me, using his knife to free my bound hands then rid me of my hemp necktie.

"You look like several miles of unpleasant road, as they so colorfully phrase it in this land," he laughed.

I squinted up at my savior with my left eye, more confused than grateful. "Who the hell are you?"

"My name is Saltykov, late of her serene highness, the Czarina Catherine II of Russia. But you can call me the Sundown Kid."

"Why?"

"Because I am a gunfighter, my friend! And all gunfighters have such colorful names! I find it most refreshing!"

I stared at the Sundown Kid for a long second. He was dressed like many of the cowboys I had seen—albeit far more expensively. His black shirt looked to be made from silk instead of flannel, and he wore what looked like gold-plated spurs on his boots. He was young in the face, but not in the eyes or around the mouth. He was lean without being skinny, his skin so pale it seemed to glow in the moonlight.

"You're not human, are you," I said. "What are you then?"

He laughed for a second, then realized I wasn't joking. "You really don't know, do you? I shouldn't be surprised, I suppose. The *vargr* are notoriously lax when it comes to the education of their by-blows."

"*Vargr*?" That was the first time I'd heard the word. The sound of it made my ears prick, even in human form.

"Yes. That's the name for what you are. Just as *enkidu* is the name for what I am. Although some prefer the more vulgar human slang of 'werewolf' and 'vampire.'"

I got to my feet, so excited by the immensity of my good luck I was close to both tears and laughter. The Sundown Kid clapped me on the shoulder and smiled, displaying pearly white fangs. "You better clean that eye out—you don't want a skull full of maggots, my friend." He gestured at my exposed socket with his knife.

"Thank you for cutting me down! I owe you a great debt!"

"And I fully intend to have you make good on it. I am in great need of an *aide de camp*, you see. While I have devised an ingenious mode of protection for myself during the day, I still require the help of someone capable of functioning in open sunlight. My last servant came to a tragic end in New Orleans, and I have yet to find anyone to replace him. Until now."

"It would be my honor, Mr. Sundown Kid."

"Please—there is no need to be so formal. Call me Sundown."

<hr/>

In the two years since I left the Comanche to seek answers amongst the whites, I had come across many different kinds of men: lawmen, bad men, madmen and conmen. And now, with my introduction to the Sundown Kid, walking dead men.

When Sundown told me he was a vampire, I had no idea what the hell he was talking about. As it was, I only had the vaguest notion of what a werewolf might be. I didn't want to let on just how ignorant I really was, so I kept my lip buttoned the first few days, although I was close to busting from curiosity. After all the time I had spent looking for someone who knew who and what I was, I was too tongue-tied to ask any questions!

Despite my initial ignorance, it didn't take me long to figure out that Sundown was a creature of dark and ancient power. He moved with the grace and strength of a wild animal, and when he spoke, his words had the ring of one who is used to being obeyed without question.

While he could pass for human at a distance, up close it was obvious Sundown was far from your average shootist. His flesh was chill, like that of a corpse, and his ears came to a slight point. His wine red eyes had cat-slit pupils.

Direct sunlight was something of a bother for Sundown, as it was for most of his kind. But he had devised a unique method of keeping himself safe from the deadly ravages of the sun: He kept folded in one of his saddlebags what amounted to a cross between a shroud and a sleeping bag made of sturdy but pliable leather. Every morning, just before dawn, he would crawl into his portable coffin, fastening it shut from the inside with a series of buckles, and go to sleep.

The trouble was that while he was sealed inside, he couldn't travel and—worse yet—was vulnerable to discovery. That's where I came in. I rigged up a pony drag and hitched it to Sundown's horse so it could haul its master during the day. Sundown was greatly pleased by my ingenuity. To show his appreciation for my abilities as a manservant, he allowed me to ride his stallion, Erebus, during the day.

<hr/>

It's hard for modern folks to realize how big and empty this land was, even as late as the turn of the century. The eastern seaboard, like the European cities its denizens had fled, was overcrowded and densely populated. But in the days just prior to the Civil War, civilization ended with St. Louis, and from Kansas City on, a man could travel for days—even weeks—without laying eyes on another human being—red, white or otherwise. It's easy to understand how folks came to see the West as a blank slate just waiting to be filled up with their dreams, expectations and hopes.

And the Sundown Kid, like the hundreds of thousands of immigrant settlers who would stream across the prairies and badlands in the years to come, was looking to reinvent himself. During our travels together, Sundown and I had numerous bull sessions. Sundown was a gregarious fellow and liked to talk about himself and the things he'd done and seen in the century since he fell prey to a vampire's kiss in Carpathia.

Essentially, Sundown was a romantic. He had the wanderlust and wearied of Europe during his hundred years of night-born immortality. He wanted to go somewhere new, somewhere fresh. Somewhere the locals didn't hang garlands of garlic and wolfsbane over their doors at night.

He had become friends with the American sailor John Paul Jones, who had come to Catherine the Great's court to serve as *Kontradmiral* during the war against the Turks. He was taken by the bold, straightforward seaman's manner and developed a fascination with Jones's native country.

I have yet to meet anyone who was more in love with the idea of America than Sundown. Granted, he spent most of his time draining the lifeblood of pioneers, settlers, Indians and cowboys, but his appreciation was heartfelt.

"While in Russia I became convinced that such a brash, newborn land would produce the freshest and most potent of nectars, free of the taint of inbreeding. I was correct! Even the sickliest rum-soaked derelict possesses the headiness of a fine claret!" he enthused.

I learned a lot from Sundown during our time together. He was an amiable and patient teacher, forgiving of my ignorance. He taught me most of what I know about the world that exists at the corner of humanity's eye, the societies that dwell in mankind's shadow, the races known as the Pretenders. And although he was not of my ilk, he knew enough about the *vargr* and their ways to answer most of my questions.

It was from him that I learned the name of my people and their history, albeit tainted by the disdain that the *enkidu* hold for those Pretenders who must reproduce through the messy business of physical sex.

I learned that what I was, in truth, was a species of being known as a metamorph, a creature who could take the shape of man or beast at will. I also learned that there are many different kinds of metamorph scattered all over the globe. There were the *kitsune* of Asia, the *naga* of India, the *birskir* of the Arctic Circle, the *anube* of the Nile, the *bast* of Africa, the *silkie* and *undine* of the north and south seas... and the *vargr* of Europe.

The *vargr*, my particular clan, are wolves. And, according to Sundown, they were the most successful (meaning aggressive) breed of metamorph on earth. Europe had proven a fertile home for their packs, and many had come into power in the world of man as popes and kings and warlords, albeit in human guise.

In fact, the *vargr* had proven so successful in getting what they wanted that they had grown bored with their original territory and begun traveling with their unwitting human cattle to the New World, often coming into conflict with the breeds of metamorphs and other Pretender races already established there. The *vargr*, like the Europeans they had tied themselves so closely to, were champion exploiters and imperialists.

"That is where I believe you originate from, my young friend," Sundance explained. "No doubt your sire was a *vargr* who came to this country in search of fresh pastures, intent on breeding his own pack. And, from what little you've told me, he was unfortunate enough to place his den too close to those familiar with the ways of the werewolf. Still, I must admire his courage in coming to this new world!

"While our peoples have warred with one another over dwindling territory and supplies in the Old Country, the *enkidu* have always held a grudging respect for the *vargr*. The *vargr* were the first of the Pretending kind to show interest in foreign soil, making them pioneers. And, in this strange and open country, I do not see any reason for such Old World animosities to continue. We are Pretenders together, wolf-son, surrounded by humans."

All of this information was heady stuff for a kid my age. Bear in mind, although I was almost seventeen years old (which is fairly young, even in human years) by *vargr* standards I was little more than a pup, still wet behind the ears with feet I had yet to grow into. For the first time in my life, I began to think of myself as something besides a man. True, I had been aware of my difference, my *otherness*, from an early age. But I was raised human and taught to act human and respect the customs erected by humans. Still, there were some taboos I could not bring myself to knowingly break, the strongest of which was the deliberate taking of human life and the eating of human flesh.

About a week after Sundown and I first teamed up, we came across a small hunting party of Apache braves. There were four of them, huddled around a small campfire. Three slept wrapped in blankets while a fourth stood lookout. We watched them for a few minutes from atop a nearby rise, then Sundown climbed off his horse and began heading toward the camp.

"Where the hell do you think you're going?" I whispered.

"I'm going to go down and pay my respects."

"Are you mad? The Apaches don't like anyone who isn't Apache—and they *especially* hate whites!" My warning was to no avail. By the time I'd finished my sentence Sundown was gone, swallowed up by the night.

Seconds later, the Apache serving as lookout staggered backward, clutching his throat with one hand. As he stumbled, he succeeded in firing his gun once, but it was too late. Sundown flitted amongst the hapless Indians like the shadow of a bat, killing before they even had a chance to realize they were in danger.

I hurried down the side of the hill, still too stunned to do more than gape at the carnage in front of me. The smell of fresh blood was heavy in the night air, causing the dead Apaches' ponies to whinny nervously and paw the ground with their hooves. Sundown stood in the middle of the camp, his pale face dripping crimson. Now that the hard part was done, he was taking his time, going from body to body, draining the dead and dying warriors of their blood before it had a chance to coagulate.

"I saved you one," he said, gesturing to a butchered brave he had yet to drink from. "I know *vargr* like their kills fresh and juicy!"

I stared at the dead Apache. My stomach growled and I began to salivate. Suddenly my mind was filled with the images of how I snatched poor Small Bear's liver from his bleeding carcass, and how I tore open Flood Moon's lovely soft throat with my bare hands. I turned my eyes away from the freshly slain brave in self-disgust.

"Go ahead! What are you waiting for—?" asked Sundown as he knelt beside his second victim. "They don't get any better with age, my friend!"

"I'm not hungry." It was a lie. My stomach was growling like a sore bear, but I could not bring myself to knowingly partake of human flesh.

Sundown shrugged his indifference and resumed his feeding. "More for me, then."

———◆———

It was only a few days later that we came across the Comanche. It was daylight and I was riding Erebus, leading one of the ponies we'd taken from the Apache camp. I saw them framed against the horizon. Although they were too far away for me to make out their clan, I knew they were following the buffalo, gradually making their way towards the Brazos River.

I reined Erebus to a halt and watched the cloud of dust stirred up by the hooves of the hundreds of ponies herded by the young boys of the tribe. So many horses together was a sign that this was a wealthy clan, one that had won many ponies through successful raids against the whites, Spanish and other Indian tribes.

A handful of braves broke off from the main group and headed my way, whooping and waving their lances and shields, but I did not move. As they approached, I recognized their clan markings as those of the Penateka, my old tribe.

The braves were young and fierce, eager to show their contempt for whites. They rode their ponies around me in a tight circle, giving vent to war cries that would have chilled the blood of a true white man. I sat quietly on my mount, watching them impassively. After a minute or two of shrieking and waving rifles and axes at me, they fell back. A young warrior rode forward. Although he could have been no older than myself, his hair was already plaited with the eagle feather of a sub-chief.

At the sight of the grim-faced Comanche, I suddenly grinned and lifted my hand in ritual greeting and called out in their tongue, "Good day, Quanah!"

The sub-chief seemed taken aback and blinked, frowning uncertainly. His eyes narrowed as he studied my face, only to widen in recognition a moment later.

"Walking Wolf! My brother!"

Laughing loudly, we climbed down off our mounts and embraced one another in front of the perplexed young braves. After a few moments of pounding each other's backs, Quanah turned to his fellows and pointed at me.

"This is my brother, Walking Wolf! The one I had thought lost to me!"

The braves muttered amongst themselves, and I could tell by the looks that passed between them that stories of my being the living hand of Coyote were still being circulated around the campfires.

"How have you been, Quanah? Is you father, Peta Nocona, well?"

At the mention of his father's name, Quanah's face darkened. "My father is dead. The season after you disappeared, rangers came and stole my mother and baby sister from the camp. Peta Nocona tried to stop them, but it was no good. He died in the Antelope Hills from the wounds the rangers gave him as he fought to save his wife."

"That's a shame, Quanah. Peta Nocona was a good chief. What of Eight Clouds Rising? Is he well?"

Again Quanah shook his head. "He died of the white man's pox last season, along with Little Dove and many others in the tribe."

Now it was my turn to look sad. Eight Clouds might not have made me, but in all the ways that counted, he had been my father.

One of the braves called out to Quanah, pointing in the direction of the main body of the tribe. A young boy riding a spotted pony pulling a drag was coming our way. Quanah smiled and turned back to me.

"It looks like Medicine Dog has seen your return, Walking Wolf."

"Medicine Dog? He's still alive?"

"The Great Spirit will not allow him to die, at least that is what he claims" Quanah said with a shrug.

The pony drew up beside me, and I could see the withered form of my old teacher huddled on the litter, wrapped in blankets like a grandmother. He turned his ancient face toward me and spoke.

"Greetings, Walking Wolf. You have been a long time gone."

As I stepped forward to reply, I could tell that the old shaman's remaining eye has joined its twin in darkness. "Greetings, Medicine Dog. It is good to see you."

"It is good to see you too, Walking Wolf. Although I see you with the eyes of my heart, not with the shriveled things in my head."

"How are you, Medicine Dog? Do you still council the tribe?"

The old man shrugged. "In some things I am consulted. The older ones still come to me for advice. More and more, the younger ones turn to Coyote Shit in such matters."

"Coyote Shit?" I couldn't believe my ears. I'd known Coyote Shit from when we were boys—he was always coming up with harebrained schemes that ended up landing those foolish enough to go along with him in trouble.

Perhaps the years had changed him, but I doubted he had half the vision with two good eyes that Medicine Dog had with none.

"You sound surprised, my son," Medicine Dog said, a sly smile on his lips. "Do you doubt Coyote Shit's ability?"

"The Penateka is making a mistake."

"Perhaps. You shall be able to judge for yourself in a moment or two. Coyote Shit is coming."

I glanced up and sure enough, there he was, riding toward the little band gathered around my horse. He looked pissed. Someone must have told him that old Medicine Dog had gone out to join Quanah. I'll give him one thing—he knew how to make a show of it; he hopped off his horse without waiting for it to come to a full stop and pointed his coupstick at me and thundered, "The white devil brings evil medicine!"

Quanah—who always had a low tolerance for Coyote Shit's antics when we were boys—rolled his eyes. "This is not a white devil, this is my brother, Walking Wolf."

Coyote Shit's face darkened as the other braves laughed. "That may be so, but I say he carries bad medicine! If you doubt my word, ask the old man."

Quanah looked to Medicine Dog, shrouded in his blankets. "Does he speak truly?"

Medicine Dog nodded. "Coyote Shit does not lie. Walking Wolf carries death with him."

Coyote Shit pointed to Sundown's leather sleeping shroud, lashed to the pony drag hitched to Erebus. "The evil lies in here!"

Quanah looked at me inquisitively. It was now up to me to explain myself. I decided to come clean.

"I carry with me a white man who is dead during the day and walks at night. He drinks the blood of the living—both animal and man. He hunts them as you hunt the buffalo, in order that he might survive. He is very old and very wise, in his way. I wish to learn from him—but to do so, I must serve him in this fashion."

Quanah eyed the leather bag, obviously trying to decide whether or not he should do something about its contents. "This living dead man—does he drink the blood of the Comanche?"

"He claims to prefer the blood of settlers."

Quanah mulled this over for a second. "Then I guess it is none of our business. If this dead man only drinks the blood of our enemies, we have nothing to fear."

I glimpsed Coyote Shit, out of the corner of my eye, hunkering down and poking at the leather shroud with his coupstick, as if trying to raise hornets from a nest.

"Stay away!" I snapped, allowing my *vargr* face to surface for a heart-beat. Coyote Shit yelped in alarm and scuttled backward on his hands and heels. I could tell, first by the look on his face, then by the smell, that he had soiled himself. This amused the assembled braves, who had a good laugh at Coyote Shit's expense.

His face burning with shame, the young medicine man strode back to his mount, doing his best to maintain some semblance of dignity amidst the laughs and catcalls. If I hadn't known him to be a pompous fool with delusions of grandeur, I might have felt sorry for him.

"I must go, Quanah. I have far to go. And I do not want to be close to where the Wasp Riders will make camp when it grows dark."

Quanah grunted and nodded. "Perhaps you will return to us some other day."

"Perhaps."

With that, my old friend hopped back on his pony and lead his band of braves back in the direction of the tribe. Only Medicine Dog remained.

"So—what do you think of Coyote Shit, now that he is grown?" he asked.

"The man's a fool!"

Medicine Dog shrugged. "Perhaps he is a holy fool. All I know is that the tribe would rather heed his words than mine." Medicine Dog pulled a leather pouch out of the tangle of blankets and shook it. I recognized the dry rattle of thunderstones—the fossilized bones of the great beasts that once wandered the plains in the time before the white man even dreamed of this land. Medicine Dog was looking into the future. "Coyote Shit sees but little. He is a small man who would walk in big shoes. What vision he has is dim, and he is too proud to allow his sight to grow. And in the end, his medicine will be false. He will lead the Comanche into the killing coral. Not within my lifetime. But soon."

"And what about me? What do the thunderstones say about me?"

Medicine Dog stopped shaking the bag and shrugged. He frowned, and his withered eyes seemed to grow moist. "They say you still have much to learn. Much to see. Much to suffer. And they say you will not see me again. Goodbye, Walking Wolf."

"Goodbye, grandfather."

The boy astride the pony clucked his tongue and it started away, hurrying to rejoin the others. I watched the old blind man sitting stiffly on the drag, facing backward, clinging to it as he was pulled across the plains, until he was swallowed by the dust on the horizon.

He was right. I never saw him again.

At least alive.

Chapter Seven

I met the devil at Pilate's Basin in 1861.

I don't mean the kind of devil you see wearing red long johns and horns with a pointy tail and a pitchfork. No, this devil was more real than that. More personal. He was my very own private demon.

I'd been traveling with Sundown for close to a year by the time we made it to the high plains of what is now Colorado and Kansas. The high plains is an arid stretch of nowhere that would make God Himself cuss Creation. A fine, crystalline snow swirled endlessly in the high wind, making it a lot like being rubbed down with a piece of sandpaper. I was so freeze-dried, I couldn't speak without making my lips bleed.

The sky was perpetually overcast, and sometimes the only way I could tell whether it was day or night was by Sundown climbing in and out of his shroud. It was late fall, heading into winter, and the days were growing shorter and the nights longer, so Sundown was spending more and more time out of his traveling shroud. Not that this did us much good—you could go weeks out there without seeing another soul, human or otherwise. As it was, we'd already sacrificed my horse to feed the both of us.

Pretender or not, I knew that if we didn't find some real shelter soon, Sundown and I stood a good chance of dying like any other poor bastard who gets himself lost in the trackless wastes.

That's when we came across Pilate's Basin.

It wasn't a town—not the way most folks picture one, leastwise. It was a cluster of adobe buildings—no more than large huts, really—huddled against the wind. The warm, yellow glow of lantern light seeped out from the main building's shutters, along with a thin spume of smoke.

With cold-numbed knuckles, I knocked on the door, not sure what to expect from whoever might live inside. There was the sound of a bolt being thrown back. The door opened.

"Come on in, stranger! And be quick about it! I don't want the wind puttin' out my fire!"

I hurried inside, and the door was quickly slammed behind me. The inside of the adobe was small and warm, but surprisingly neat. As I turned to thank my host, I caught a glimpse of what looked to be a shrine of some sort next to a narrow cot. A woman's lace shawl covered a crudely built table on which were set a couple of tallow candles placed in saucers, illuminating a faded and dog-eared rotogravure of a dark-haired, dark-eyed woman dressed in the black lace mantilla of a Mexican *señorita*.

Standing next to it was a man who was either thirty or eighty—it was hard to tell by his face, which had been severely weathered by the winds and harsh climate of the plains. Had he been without teeth, he would have resembled one of the dried-apple dolls children played with. Although his face looked prematurely aged, my host was powerfully built, with wide shoulder and big, callused hands.

"The name's McCarthy. Who might you be, stranger?" he said.

"Skillet. Billy Skillet."

This seemed to amuse him. "Is that a fact? Well, Billy Skillet, why don't you go put up your poor horse before it freezes, eh? The stable's around back. When you're done, you can join me by the fire for a chat."

"Sounds mighty good to me."

I lead Erebus around the back of the adobe and put him inside the stable, quickly hiding Sundown's shroud under a mound of hay. I then unhitched the pony drag and unsaddled the horse. As I worked, McCarthy's own horses watched me nervously. Like most animals, they knew an unnatural thing when they smelled it.

By the time I made it back to the main hut, McCarthy was already seated in front of the open hearth, sipping coffee from a tin cup. "Brewed you some mud," he said, pointing to a second dented cup sitting on the table. It was black as goddamn and had a bite like a rattlesnake.

"That's good coffee!" I said through my teeth.

"Set yourself down and warm your stumps, Billy," he said, gesturing for me to sit on a stool placed next to the hearth.

I did so and, without much in the way of prompting or preliminaries, McCarthy set about telling me the story of how he came to be stuck in the "devil's bunghole," as he put it.

"My parents came to this country from Scotland. They started out in Baltimore—that's where I was born. My father worked as a clerk in a bank, tending other folks' money every day of his life, bless him.

"Me, I never had much love for banks, or working jobs that killed a man from the inside out. I was the adventurous type. So I hired on with the U.S. Navy. I was a good enough sailor—until the day my captain accused me of insubordination. I didn't take to having the cat on my back, that's certain. So I jumped ship—deserted, if you will—and ended up in Mexico. I met a lovely young woman there—" his eyes flickered over to the shrine beside the door—"and I fell in love with her. And she with me. Her family did not approve, however, since I was nothing but a lowly gringo. What could I possibly offer her?

"They were right and I knew it. I guess I could have put the pressure on Carmelita—that was her name—and had her insist on having me as her husband, but I was proud. I wanted to prove to both her and her family that I was sincere, that I was something besides an opportunistic Yanqui. So I agreed to work for her family, who had considerable land both in Mexico and America.

"Her family used my willingness to serve them to send me to the farthest reaches of their holdings, to oversee their herds on the high plains and operate a trading outpost. It was their way of washing their hands of me without resorting to killing me themselves. That's why I call this place Pilate's Basin.

"I've been out here close to ten years. During that time, I've turned my place of exile into an unofficial traveler's rest for those who come my way. All I ask in way of payment is news of the outside world."

"What about the girl—Carmelita?" I asked, warming my hands as I spoke.

McCarthy smiled sadly and sighed. "She was very young. Younger than me by a few years, at least. After a couple of months, perhaps a year, she forgot about me. She ended up marrying some fellow her family approved of. I didn't know about it until I'd been out here, oh, six or seven years. By that time, she'd had a couple of young'uns and was fat as mud—or so I was told."

"If she went and married someone else, why are you still stuck out here?"

McCarthy shrugged. "I've gotten used to it, I reckon. Even though it can be mighty lonesome out on the high plains, least I'm my own boss out here. There ain't anybody to beat me or order me around. After all this time, I probably wouldn't know how to deal with a town full of people, all running around and getting into each other's business."

I found myself liking McCarthy, who had willingly exiled himself for the love of a fickle young girl. It was a shame he was going to die.

McCarthy got up to prod the fire with a poker as a particularly strong gust of wind slammed against the hut, rattling the shutters. He glanced in the direction of the door, as if expecting it to open. "It'll be dark soon. I hope that fellow didn't get lost out there."

"Fellow? What fellow?" I said, my scalp tightening. For a second I imagined McCarthy knew about Sundown and our plans to ambush him.

"Another traveler, such as yourself, that's all. He showed up a couple of days ago, just as the storm was getting ready to hit. He goes by the name of Jones. But don't they all? He headed out a few hours ago to look for some game. Hope he can find his way back."

As if on cue, there was the sound of heavy boots on the front porch. The front door swung open, letting in a chill blast of air. I turned around to get a look at McCarthy's house guest, and that's when I set eyes on my private demon for the first time.

He was huge, covered with hair, and had two heads—one of which was horned. Then I realized I was staring at a man dressed in a full-length buffalo-skin coat with a dead antelope tossed over one shoulder. He stepped inside the house and slammed the door shut behind him, shrugging the antelope onto the floor as if it were a woman's stole.

McCarthy bent over the carcass, shaking his head in awe. "I didn't believe you when you said you'd bring back venison! But, by damn, you done it!"

Jones removed his heavy buffalo-skin coat and tossed it in the corner. Underneath the coat he wore a shirt made from what looked to be timber wolf or coyote skin. This he did not offer to remove.

"Hunting is in my blood." His voice was deep, like that of a pipe organ, with a slight Slavic accent. As he turned to face me, I was struck by his bristling beard the color of McCarthy's coffee, which seemed to start at his cheekbones, and eyebrows so thick and bushy they literally covered his brow ridge from temple to temple.

Jones fixed me with piercing eyes the color of a coming storm and scowled. "I saw a strange horse in the manger. Who are you?"

Before I could answer, McCarthy piped in. "This here's Billy Skillet. He showed up just an hour or two back. Got himself lost in the storm...."

"Have we met before?" he asked, staring at me even harder.

"I don't think so."

Jones grunted and brushed past me to stand in front of the fire.

As he warmed his hands and stomped his feet to restore circulation, I found myself staring at his wolf-fur jacket. There was something... familiar about it. Something I couldn't place. Maybe I *had* met this hairy-faced giant before. Perhaps he was one of Professor Praetorius' erstwhile customers.

"That's a fine shirt you got there, mister. How many wolves did you have to kill for it?"

"Just one."

"Must have been a damn big wolf!" McCarthy snorted.

"It was. Big as a man."

I cleared my throat. "Excuse me, sir. I don't believe I caught your name?"

"They call me Jones." The giant didn't even dignify me by glancing in my direction.

"Jones? Is that all?"

There was a pause, as if he were deciding on whether or not to reply, then he slowly turned his head and fixed me with those gray eyes and said, "Witchfinder. Witchfinder Jones."

"Unusual handle. How you come by it?"

The big man returned his gaze to the fire. "I hunt things."

"What kind of things?"

"I hunt *things*. Vampires. Witches. Warlocks. Ghosts. Werewolves."

"That's plum silly! There ain't no such things! Ain't that right, McCarthy?" I laughed nervously, glancing over at the older man for support.

However, McCarthy was shaking his head. "I wouldn't say that, Billy. I seen a lot of things that couldn't be explained, both here and when I was at sea. Snakes with wings, women with the tails of fish, serpents that chased down and ate killer whales..."

I was starting to feel dizzy. There was a scent rising from Jones's jacket as the frost clinging to it melted away. I found myself needing to sit down. I looked over at McCarthy to see if he'd noticed, but he was busy hacking off one of the antelope's haunches with a cleaver in order to prepare the night's meal. The smell of the animal's blood made my stomach knot with hunger. It'd been a couple of days since I'd finished the last of my old horse.

With a deep, guttural sound, almost a growl, Jones lowered himself onto a chair next to the fire. Without looking at me, he fished a hand-carved briarwood pipe and a drawstring pouch out off his wolf-skin shirt. For some reason, I could not take my eyes from the leather sack that held his tobacco.

"That's—um—a mighty unusual tobacco pouch you got there."

Jones smiled then—it was an ugly sight, believe me. "This is the only one of its kind. It is a trophy. Just like my shirt." He leaned forward and held the pouch out to me. As if in a daze, I reached out and took it. Some faint memory squirmed in the back of my brain like a blind grub. A memory of warmth, the smell of flesh, the taste of milk...

"I took the pelt for my shirt off a werewolf seventeen years ago, just as I took his mate's left tit for a tobacco pouch. I keep the whore's vulva in a box in my saddlebag. Salted, of course."

I stared at my ma's breast, trying to summon further memories beyond those of a blind, suckling pup—but none came. I looked up at the man responsible for the slaughter of my family, meeting and holding his gaze. Although I realized he knew what—if not who—I was, I refused to let him rattle me.

"What you say is all very well and good," I remarked, handing back what remained of my ma's breast to her murderer. "But how am I to know you're not just flat-out crazy? For all I know, you took that off some poor Indian gal. And as for the shirt—well, a wolf skin is a wolf skin."

Jones shrugged his indifference. "It doesn't matter if you believe me or not. I know what I know. I do what I do." He produced a buck knife, its blade shining in the light from the fire. It was silver. "I use my knife and I use my silver bullets. Nothing unnatural can survive a wound dealt by silver. There are plenty who believe me—and pay me to rid them of these monsters."

"Is that what you're doing out in the middle of nowhere? Hunting monsters?"

Jones resheathed the knife and turned back to the fire. "I was hired to kill a vampire."

I felt my stomach hitch itself even tighter. "Vampire?"

"One I have been tracking since New Orleans. There was a young girl the creature—outraged—in the city of Boston. Her family is of some stature, and they hired me to track the fiend down and bring back his head. I first found him in New Orleans, in a fancy Basin Street whorehouse. I would have claimed my bounty then, except for the interference of his servant. The bastard shot me in the shoulder. It wasn't much of a wound, really, but it was enough to make me lose my prey. I dealt with the manservant, though. I put the silver bullet I had reserved for his master right between his eyes."

Jones was describing was the demise of my predecessor. The knowledge made the sweat rise on my brow and upper lip.

"It took me a couple of days to recover from my wound, but by then the fiend had fled the city. He had a head start, but not enough of one that I could not track him. I have since seen evidence of his passing: Indian raiding parties slaughtered to the man as they tended their campfires, isolated farmhouses where the family members were drained white at the dinner table, hotels where—after the stranger checked in for the night—half the residents were found dead in their beds the next morning.

"Somewhere along the line, the monster found someone else to serve him. Someone to hide and transport his body during the daylight hours. Someone else to help him do his dirty work. Or should I say, some *thing*?"

He was staring at me, the storm clouds in his eyes looking as if they were about to break. I could tell by his body language he was getting ready to lunge at me. I knew I should try to get up, move away from him, prepare my own counterattack, but my dizziness had grown worse. Sweat poured down my back and my head ached horribly.

Witchfinder Jones leaned even closer, until his hairy face was inches from my own. His wide nostrils flared like those of an animal scenting blood. "I can *smell* an unnatural thing from a mile away, boy."

Before I had a chance to respond, there was the sound of something heavy striking meat and Jones's eyes rolled up in their sockets. He pitched sideways out of his chair, narrowly missing landing in the open fire. I stared for a moment at the big man sprawled on the floor, a halo of blood forming about his skull, then turned to look up at McCarthy, who stood over the body, a hammer clutched in one hand.

McCarthy's eyes gleamed strangely in the light from the fire. They reminded me, in a way, of Sundown's eyes when he got the hunger on him.

"Had to wait him out. Wait until he wasn't paying so much attention to me and what I was doing." McCarthy rubbed at his mouth with his sleeve. "Tried slippin' the stuff in his coffee the first night, like I did with you, but he was too big. Too tough. It didn't take."

"Wh-what did you do—?" I tried to get up from where I was sitting, but my legs gave out and I found myself on the floor. McCarthy squatted next to me, peering down into my face.

"I don't like using force. Usually I just dose their coffee, then they go to sleep and don't feel nothing—not even when I brain 'em with the hammer. But this one—and you, for that matter—just ain't respondin' properly. I hate it when that happens. I don't like using violence. I'm a peaceable man, by nature."

I tried to change then, to slip from my human form into my faster, stronger *vargr* skin, but I couldn't focus. The room was swimming, and everything seemed to be pulsing with a rhythm all its own. I watched, helpless, as McCarthy raised his hammer on high.

There was a rush of cold air and something black struck McCarthy head-on, knocking him backwards. I heard the exile scream as my savior tore into his throat. I didn't feel so sorry for McCarthy anymore.

The next thing I knew, Sundown—his mouth wet with fresh blood—was helping me to my feet. "You all right, Billy?"

"He—he must have drugged me...." was all I could mumble.

"He put enough laudanum in your drink to kill a normal human three times over. I woke shortly after you placed me in the stable. I decided to check the other buildings, in case there were more humans about. There are. But they are all dead. There must be over a dozen corpses stashed in the outbuildings, all in various stages of decay. I'd say the oldest was five years old." Sundown shook his head in disgust. "Humans! And they accuse us of being monsters! But at least the madman did us the favor of riding us of that wretched bounty hunter!"

A groaning sound came from the direction of Jones's body. Sundown and I stared, openmouthed, as Witchfinder Jones sat up. His hair and beard was sodden with blood, and part of his brain bulged outward through the crack in his head. His left eye was so full of blood that it leaked from the corners like crimson tears. His right eye was as clear as before—only angrier.

"I got you now, you stinking whore-son!" the bounty hunter bellowed, pulling out a revolver.

"Run, Billy!" Sundown yelled, propelling me towards the open door. "Run!"

I stumbled forward, my limbs still numb from whatever drug McCarthy had slipped me. I turned to see what was happening, only to slam into Sundown just as Jones released his initial volley.

The first shot went wild of its target. The second did not. Sundown opened his mouth and vented an ultrasonic shriek of pain. I caught my friend as he pitched forward and dragged him out of the hut. Jones struggled to get to his feet, his boots slipping in a pool of his own blood.

I didn't look at Sundown or ask him if he was okay. I was too scared to do anything but run with him to the stable, where—reverting to my boyhood—I hopped on Erebus bareback and simply fled, clinging to the horse's neck with my right arm while I cradled Sundown to my breast with my left. As we charged past the front of McCarthy's hut, I glimpsed Witchfinder Jones slumped in the doorway, taking aim at me. I dug my heels deep into Erebus' flanks just as a silver bullet whizzed past my ear. I heard Jones bellow something into the storm that might have been a name, but it was quickly snatched up by the wind and made meaningless.

<hr>

It was close to a half-hour later before I was willing to slow my pace enough to check on Sundown's condition. I had him pressed between me and the horse's neck to keep him from falling off.

"Sundown? Sundown—? Are you all right?"

No answer.

"Saltykov?" I said, hoping he wasn't in such a bad way that he would not respond to his true name.

No answer.

I touched my friend's shoulder gingerly, hoping to rouse him enough to at least groan. To my horror, I felt the bone and flesh inside his shirt crumble at my touch.

I howled as the wind caught the dust and tossed it skyward—dust that had, until a few minutes ago, been my friend. I howled for my father, whose pelt now covered his killer's back. I howled for my mother, whose breast now served to carry her murderer's tobacco. I howled for my friend, now reduced to nothing but flakes of decayed skin and powdered bone. But most of all, I howled for myself, lost in the wilderness.

CHAPTER EIGHT

After the death of the Sundown Kid at the hands of Witchfinder Jones, I went a little crazy for a while. After fleeing the carnage at Pilate's Basin, I wandered the high plains for several days in a feverish delirium. At times I thought Medicine Dog rode beside me, his blind eyes undaunted by the snow. Other times I fancied I saw Sundown standing on the horizon, waving me on. Other times I imagined I could hear Whatisit's moronic laughter echoing from the darkness.

On the third day out, poor, faithful Erebus literally dropped dead underneath me, spilling me back into reality. There was little I could do but eat the horse, which strengthened me enough to press on. I wandered the plains in my true skin, preying on antelope, the occasional buffalo calf, and other four-legged creatures that crossed my path.

At the end of each day, I would find an outcropping of rock or dig out an abandoned prairie dog burrow in order to shelter myself from the unceasing winds of the plains. I listened to the true wolves howling from the distant hilltops like lost souls mourning their expulsion from Hell. Sometimes I would take up the howl, only to hear confusion and mistrust in their reply. Even without seeing or scenting me, my wild cousins knew an unnatural thing when they heard it.

I wandered westward without planning it that way. I was leagues beyond my old tribe's hunting boundaries, moving towards lands undreamed of when I was a boy tending Eight Clouds' horses.

I have no way of knowing precisely how long I spent in the wilderness—at least two, perhaps three seasons, of that I'm certain. I steered clear of both whites and Indians during that time. Since leaving the Comanche, I had found little joy in the white man's world. And while I had known a certain friendship with the likes of Praetorius and Sundown, I knew their types to be few and far between. Buffalo-Face and Medicine Dog were right—whites were bad-crazy. Not all of them were as demented as Reverend Near, McCarthy or Witchfinder Jones, but it wasn't from a lack of trying. I had come to the decision that it was best not to trust whites on general principles and give them as wide a berth as possible.

As for the Indians... well, I guess I didn't want to get close to anyone for fear of losing them. It seemed to me I was cursed. Everyone I had ever loved or befriended in my short life—for I was still shy of my twentieth year—had ended up dead. Some by my own hand.

My natural parents, who I never even got a chance to know, had been brutally taken from me when I was no more than a mewling pup. Then there was poor Flood Moon and Small Bear, whose deaths shame me to this day. After them came Praetorius and poor Whatisit, left to feed the crows along some godforsaken riverbed. And now Sundown was gone, slain by the same murdering bastard that robbed me of my mother and father.

But there's only so long anyone—human or *vargr*—can spend alone before anger gives way to loneliness, which then sours into madness. I thought of McCarthy, isolated from the company of his own kind until his mind turned in on itself like a fox in a snare. I began to fear that I would lose control of myself and slip back into the red-eyed savagery that had cost me the woman I loved. I decided it was time for me to leave the wilderness and seek out others. Even if they weren't my own kind.

⫸—◆—⫷

I smelled the wagon train before I saw it.

Its scent came to me on the wind, causing me to prick up more than my ears. The wind smelled of female. Several of them. There was also the distant odor of smoke and something fainter, yet disturbingly familiar, that I could not place. Intrigued, I set out in search of what could produce such interesting smells.

Nancy A. Collins

228

Three miles later, I crested a small butte and found myself looking down on a wagon train. It wasn't a big one, as such things went. There were four covered wagons, yoked to oxen, and a couple of horses and mules. One of the wagons had a busted wheel, and the train was halted in order to fix it. From my vantage, I could see a man dressed in the apron of a wheelwright laboring beside the disabled wagon. He was large and fleshy, his head and face completely devoid of hair. I could almost see the sweat trickling down his smooth pate and dripping from his thin eyebrows.

But what truly caught my interest were the women—there had to be at least a dozen of them, all young and healthy. Some tended the cookfire, others were mending clothes, others simply stood around in groups and laughed amongst themselves, combing out their hair. Except for one or two, they were all obviously pregnant.

The sight of so many women made my groin ache. I did not know whether to be excited or disgusted. I had been with only one woman in my life, and that was Flood Moon. Part of me—the part I had come to think of as my *vargr* self—wanted to go down and do to the women what it had done to Flood Moon. The temptation to succumb to my wild self's desires was strong— but then I forced myself to remember Flood Moon's screams and how she had looked at me with hate in her eyes, and my ardor lessened. Still, I found myself scanning the encampment for signs of males beside the wheelwright.

A second man, as equally chunky and bald as the first, emerged from the back of one of the covered wagons. He had a rifle in one hand, a knife stuck in his belt. None of the women paid him any attention. A third man, younger and not as heavy as the others, but equally hairless, rode up on one of the mules and dismounted beside the second man. The two bald men bent their heads over what looked like a map, looking up now and again to point in various directions.

My attention was drawn back to the females, and one in particular. She was younger than the others and one of the few not visibly pregnant. Her hair was long and unbound, hanging almost to her waist, and she had a habit of tossing her golden mane over her right shoulder, like it was a veil of spun gold. Perhaps it was her youth, or perhaps it was that I had gone so long without a woman, but in any case I fell in love with her in two heart-beats.

I was so bedazzled by this vision of loveliness that I did not realize I was being watched until my attacker was almost on me. Just before he struck, I got a strong whiff of the scent that had troubled me earlier. The familiar smell I could not place. I spun around, but it was too late. Something landed against the side of my head; all sound and vision fled. But not before I was finally able to recognize the strangely familiar odor.

It was the scent of my own kind.

⟐

The cold rag placed on my brow brought me back to my senses. As I started awake, the first thing my aching eyes happened on was an angel smiling down at me. My vision cleared, and the angel turned into the beautiful young girl with the long blonde hair I had glimpsed tending the cookfire.

I was trussed hand and foot, and was on the floor of one of the covered wagons. I was also in my human form, and stark naked to boot. I blushed despite myself. The girl giggled and drew her hand back from my brow.

"The intruder is awake, milord," she called.

"Excellent, Lisette," replied a male voice. "Leave us. I wish to question him alone."

As the girl vacated the wagon, the man who had spoken climbed in past her. Considering we were in the middle of wide-open nowhere, he was dressed rather extravagantly, sporting a single-breasted frock coat, dress trousers, an Inverness cape and a beaver hat. With his long hair curled and brushed upward and parted in the middle, and his bushy mustache, he looked more like a dude on his way to the opera than a settler headed west.

The dude pulled a thinly rolled cigar the color of mud from inside his breast pocket and eyed me intently.

"What pack do you run with, cub?"

"Pack?"

The dude bit off the end of his cigar as fast and as clean as a guillotine, displaying strong white teeth. "Don't play stupid, cub. It won't work with me. Who is your Master of Hounds?"

"I don't know what the hell you're talking about, mister—"

He moved so fast I didn't see it coming. My head rocked back from the force of the blow to my jaw. As he moved to strike me again, I bared my teeth at the dude and growled, staying his hand.

"My, aren't we the brave and loyal dog," he commented dryly. "Well, don't show your fangs at *me*, little wolf—unless you mean business." With that, he thrust his face into mine. Before my eyes, the dude's face flexed and twisted upon itself, as if something inside his head were trying to break free. His whiskers and muttonchops spread across his cheeks and chin as his nose grew longer and broader, transforming into a snout.

Nancy A. Collins

230

I cried out then, not in alarm as one might suppose, but in surprise and delight. For I was finally face to face with that which I'd been seeking for the last five years—one of my own kind.

"You're like me!"

The dude dropped his wolf-face, resuming his human guise like a man adjusts his johnson on a hot day. "Of course I am, you wretched lout! What did you expect?"

"I—I wouldn't know, sir. I was raised by humans from an early age."

The dude fell silent, narrowing his eyes and fixing me with a strange look. He leaned forward, sniffing the air like a bloodhound trying to pick up a scent.

"You smell vaguely familiar. Perhaps your sire was known to me. Do you know his name?"

"No, sir. I was just a baby when my folks were killed."

The dude's eyes narrowed even further. "Killed? By humans?"

"Yes sir. By a bounty hunter who calls himself Witchfinder Jones."

At the mention of Jones's name, the dude looked somewhat anxious. "Is that so? Would this Witchfinder be a large man? Very hairy?"

"Yes sir. That's him!"

"I knew him in the Old Country, under another name. But it seems his occupation is still the same." The dude rubbed his chin and stared off into space for a moment, then turned his gaze back on me. "You remind me of someone I once knew. His name was Howler. He came to this country almost two decades ago to start a new life for himself. He dreamt of founding his own pack, free of the squabbles and power plays that plague the Old Country. No one has heard from him since. Perhaps he was your sire."

"What about my mama? Did you know her, too?"

"She was a human female, what else is there to know?" he shrugged dismissively. "If you are, indeed, what you say you are—a loner—I need not fear you. Come, let me show you some hospitality." The dude produced a knife from his breast pocket and freed me from my bonds.

"I am called Poilu, my young friend. And you are called—?"

I hesitated, uncertain which of my names was more suitable for the occasion. Since Poilu, despite his ability to shapeshift, was white, I decided to go with my white name. "Billy. Billy Skillet."

"How American. Here, allow me to have one of my wives find you some decent clothes. It wouldn't do to have you parading naked in front of the ladies."

Five minutes later, I was dressed in a pair of linen trousers, a white dress shirt with too much starch in it, a loose-fitting sack coat and a pair of short Wellington boots. I hadn't been so finely tricked-out since my days as a drummer for Professor Praetorius. It had been so long since I had worn clothes that I had to fight the urge to revert to my true skin and tear the garments to shreds.

"You look quite respectable, for an American," Poilu said, smiling slightly. "Come, allow me to introduce you to the rest of my entourage."

As I stepped from the back of the covered wagon, the first thing I noticed was that the afternoon had given way to early evening. The second thing I noticed was that the wagon train's company was seated around the central campfire, their faces turned towards us in silent anticipation.

A big, meaty man, bald and devoid of whiskers, got to his feet and approached Poilu, his eyes averted and head down. Although he no longer wore a leather apron, I recognized him as the wheelwright. When he spoke, his voice was surprisingly high-pitched for a man so large.

"Milord, the wagon has been repaired, as you commanded. The train will be ready to move come the dawn."

"Excellent," Poilu smiled, displaying his magnificent teeth to full effect. "Billy, this is Henri, my major domo and master eunuch."

"Beg pardon?"

"Come now, my young friend. When one has a harem, one *must* have eunuchs."

I looked from Henri to the other two men—both of them hairless as well. There was no anger or resentment in their great, cowlike eyes. Instead, they regarded Poilu with the reverence others hold for religious leaders or lovers.

"And here are my wives—" Poilu gestured to the eleven women clustered around the campfire. "Are they not beautiful?" Indeed, all of the assembled women were strikingly handsome. And, except for the blonde who had ministered to my wounds, every one of them looked to have a bun in the oven. They sat there, hands laced atop their swollen bellies like ancient fertility goddesses, imperturbable, impassive and immutable.

"Evening, ladies."

"You needn't waste words on them, lad. I've had them all muted—except for little Lisette, the one who you spoke to earlier."

"Muted?"

"Yes—I had their tongues surgically removed. I find it keeps the bickering in the seraglio to a minimum. Besides, none of them spoke English to begin with. Except for Lisette. Her mother was British, her father Belgian. I allowed her to keep her tongue in order to have a human liaison capable of communicating with the peasants of this rough country."

"They're called settlers here, not peasants."

Poilu shrugged. "I can call a horse an equine and it still runs on four legs and produces manure. I must say, although you are of *vargr* blood, you do seem to have been infected with this country's mass delusion concerning democracy."

"I'm not used to thinking of myself as *vargr*. I don't know what the rules are, or how I'm expected to behave. You're the first one I've ever seen. Alive, at least."

Poilu fished another cigar from his tobacco case and bit the end off, spitting it into the fire. "There's no need to feel ashamed, Billy. Most *vargr* come into their power ignorant of what it really means. You see, *vargr* males outnumber females five to one. Unless a male joins a pack with a sexually active female, there's little chance of him breeding true. And, once in the pack, you have to wait until the bitch queen is in season, and then you must fight all the other males for the privilege to rut. So, necessity decrees finding breeding material elsewhere.

"Some take human females as life mates, others propagate themselves through acts of rape, casting their seed upon the wind, as it where, while a few breed with true wolves. In any case, most *vargr* born are of mixed parentage. Those sired by rape are the most plentiful. They are raised by humans, in the very bosom of human society, ignorant of their birthright. Many of these mixed-bloods are incapable of shapeshifting, although they possess the instincts and hunger of a *vargr*. These are the *esau*. Most of them are mad as march hares. The *esau* can be very dangerous indeed, and not just to humans."

Poilu reached inside his coat and produced a golden locket, flipping it open to reveal a cameo portrait of a woman, her hair piled atop her head in elaborate coils. "When I spoke of your sire earlier—and, the more I look at you, the more I believe that Howler was, indeed, your sire—I did not tell you the whole truth. Howler was my half-brother. We shared paternity, not maternity. I was sired within the pack, he outside it. He often spoke to me of his dreams of coming to this country and starting afresh. He wanted to be the Alpha Prime. The Master of Hounds of his own pack." With a twist of his wrist, he snapped the locket shut. "Poor Howler. He always had such small dreams. As for myself—I am unwilling to settle for such a modest future."

"I don't understand—"

"Come, lad! Why do you think I would travel to this godforsaken country? For freedom? Liberty? No, I have come to build an empire! *My* empire!" Poilu gestured grandly at the land beyond the campfire's glow. "Howler was right—Europe is old and overcrowded. Asia even more so. If an ambitious *vargr* is to find his destiny, it will be here, in this great emptiness!

"There is nothing here to keep me from populating this vast expanse with my seed! Your father was satisfied to start with a single female—and look where it got him: an orphaned son ignorant of his birthright! But I have eleven wives, and soon I will have eleven sons—possibly even a daughter! And, in time, I shall breed with my daughters and granddaughters, and my sons will breed with their sisters, nieces and daughters, and within two centuries all *vargr* that roam this land shall be of my breed. Or should I say our breed, nephew?"

Poilu did not wait for me to respond before barreling on. "You know the ways of this land, do you not? You are familiar with the human savages?"

"I was raised by the Comanche, if that answers your question."

Poilu clapped his hands, grinning broadly. "Excellent! Most excellent, indeed! I am in need of an experienced guide. While Henri and his compeers are loyal servants, they are far from expert when it comes to scouting. We have already lost one of the eunuchs to bad water. You will stay on and serve as our guide to the territory of Utah." It sounded more like a command than a request. It probably was.

"Utah? Why the hell do you want to go there?"

"Because of the humans who call themselves Mormons. They practice polygamy as a rule, so a man with eleven wives would not call undue attention to himself in such a community."

"I reckon not."

"You will be our scout." Like I said, Poilu didn't ask people, he told them. Since I didn't see any reason not to go along with his plan—after all, I'd spent years in search of those such as myself—I decided to go along for the ride.

Besides, the whole time Poilu was going on about breeding a new race and sowing America's wilderness with his seed, Lisette had been giving me the eye.

I bedded down under one of the wagons, curling up on an old horse blanket I'd gotten from one of the eunuchs. I was tired and had a full belly and, truth to tell, it had been a busy day for me. I fell asleep almost immediately.

I woke up later to the sound of hissing geese.

No. Not geese. Tongueless women.

While having their tongues removed might have reduced their bickering, as far as Poilu was concerned, it was evident his wives had devised a way of getting around their speech impediment. They sat around the dying campfire, hissing and gesticulating wildly. There was something ominous about the sight of so many heavily pregnant women discoursing amongst themselves in a private language. One of the eunuchs sat just outside their circle, a rifle cradled in his arms, but it was uncertain whether he was protecting the women from potential harm or guarding against escape. Finally the women tired of their strange conversation and returned to the wagons, followed by the gun-toting eunuch. I shrugged and went back to sleep, but my dreams were not easy.

Over the next few days, as I rode before the wagon train, scouting the territory that lay ahead, I reflected on my circumstances. After years of searching for those of my own kind, I had finally stumbled across not only a fellow shapeshifter, but a blood relation at that. Yet, there was a hollowness inside me. I always thought I would have been happier. Instead, all I felt was uneasiness.

Most of this I attributed to Poilu. I was glad my job allowed me to spend so much time away from his company. Despite our shared ancestry, I felt no kinship toward him. There was something disturbing about being around him, as if I were being smiled at by an enemy unwilling to show his true face. Yet, I was so ignorant of *vargr* custom and lore, I assumed my discomfort was born from a fear of seeming foolish in the eyes of my elder.

Whenever I returned to the wagon train, Poilu would debrief me and then, if I was lucky, talk about the Old Country. This soon became something of a ritual between us, complete with coffee served us by one of his tongueless wives. Poilu would treat himself to some cognac from a case he'd brought with him from Europe, along with his usual cigar. Realizing how little I knew of *vargr* etiquette and custom, he did his best to continue my ignorance, dispensing tiny dollops of information here and there to ensure my continued willingness to serve him as a scout.

Most of his stories began with him recounting something that had happened to him during his tenure as the Master of Hounds, the title given the consort to the Bitch Queen. To hear him tell the tale, he had been a powerful and much-admired figure. Then his beloved queen was killed, the victim of internecine warfare with a rival pack envious of her influence in the court of Napoleon III. Upon the death of the Bitch Queen, the center of the pack could not hold and they were forced to disband. Rather than swear fealty to those responsible for his beloved's murder, Poilu decided to leave the Old World in favor of the New.

Despite these chats, I did not find my uncle to my liking. Poilu was imperious and haughty, as cocksure as a Comanche brave who has never tasted defeat. And I was soon made well aware of how jealous he was of his traveling harem. While I was in camp, the eunuchs never let their eyes wander from me for a moment. On more than one occasion, I toyed with the idea of riding off and leaving the werewolf lord to whatever fate might await him, but the hope of learning more about myself—and the promise of a smile or kind word from the lovely Lisette—always reigned my horse back to camp.

Lisette.

Beautiful Lisette.

I can still see her face, smiling back at me through the years that separate us. She was so lovely—her skin smooth as a rose petal, her lips full and ripe as a peach. She smelled of cinnamon and cloves and woman. Her hair fell from her shoulders like a golden curtain, swaying in the breeze like a thing alive. She was beauty made flesh.

I knew it was foolish of me to fall in love with one of Poilu's wives. The older *vargr* made no effort to hide the fact that they were his property. Still, I was young and full of the juices all young males seem to overflow with. I found Lisette extremely attractive, and it was plain to see that she favored me as well. As I slept alone under the open skies, I found myself pondering whether Poilu would miss one measly wife. After all, we were kin. What harm could it do? One night, after everyone had retired, I was awakened by the sound of someone approaching my bedroll. I sat up, shifting into my true skin without conscious thought. To my surprise, I saw it was Lisette, dressed in a long white undergarment.

"What are you doing out here?" I whispered, sliding back into my human guise.

"I wanted to talk to you."

"Is that wise?" I glanced around warily, wondering where Poilu's prize castrati might be hiding.

"You needn't worry about the eunuchs. I put something in their coffee. They'll sleep for a hour or two."

"What about Poilu?"

She giggled and rolled her eyes. "I can handle him."

"I'm afraid I don't share your confidence. Please go back to the wagon, Lisette."

She smiled at me then, her child-bride innocence dissolving. "Why? Are you afraid of me, Billy?"

"I'm more afraid of what might happen if you stay."

She drew nearer, her hips swaying seductively with each step. She slowly opened the front of her undergarment, exposing the milky flesh underneath. I knew I should jump up and drag her back to her wagon, kicking and screaming if need be, but my body refused to listen to reason.

"I like you, Billy," she whispered as she knelt beside me. Her lips were so close to my face they grazed my ear. "You're young and handsome. You're not old like him. You like me, too. I can see it in the way you look at me."

"S-sure I like you, Lisette. B-but—"

"You're scared of him."

"It's just that—"

"You needn't be scared of him, Billy. He's not as powerful as he makes himself out to be. If he really was, he'd still be in Europe. He was once the Master of Hounds, that much is true. But he was deposed by a younger rival. That's why he came here—so he wouldn't have to see the Bitch Queen with someone else."

"Who is this Bitch Queen, anyway?"

"Why, his mother, of course."

While I was digesting what she'd told me, Lisette took my hand and placed it atop one of her firm young breasts. My brain began to sputter like bacon in the pan, short-circuiting any attempts at rational thought.

"I want you, Billy. I want you for my mate. Take me, Billy—take me now."

I've always been an agreeable sort, so it didn't take much in the way of pleading to get me going. Within seconds we were rolling on the ground, all fear and common sense lost in a wash of hormones. I pushed Lisette's cotton shift up over her hips, exposing the moist hair between her legs, all the while fumbling with my buttons. When I finally managed to free my johnson I discovered, to my dismay and embarrassment, the traitorous piece of meat was as limp as fresh wash.

"I–I'm dreadful sorry, Lisette," I blushed. "I don't know what's wrong. This has never happened to me before...." That part was true, since this was only the second time I'd ever been in such a position with a woman.

Lisette grabbed me by my hair and pulled me down on top of her. She writhed against me like a hungry cat, her eyelids fluttering as if she were in the grip of a fever.

"While you're human you can't get hard. *Vargr* can only get it up when they're in their wild skins," she breathed into my ear.

She wanted me to change. She needed me to change. And the only way I could ever delve the sweet mystery between her legs was if I did change.

But I just couldn't bring myself to do it. Every time I closed my eyes to focus my attention on shifting from human to wolf, all I could see was Flood Moon's blood-smeared face, screaming in horror as I ravaged her.

I pulled away from Lisette, gasping like a man who had just narrowly escaped the pull of a whirlpool. My face was flushed and my eyes swam, but I was still wearing the skin of a man.

"I'm sorry, Lisette. I can't."

"What do you mean you can't? I told you how to do it," she pouted.

"I just can't. That's all there is to it," I muttered, turning away from her so she would not see the look of disgust and fear in my eyes.

Lisette's displeasure darkened her face, twisting her beautiful features into something far from pretty. "Poilu might be a wheezing old dog, but at least he knows what to do with a woman when he's got her under him!" she snapped.

If she was expecting me to respond to this goad, I'll never know. For there was a sudden, sharp report and her head, from the nose on up, disappeared in a spray of blood, hair and bone. I was too stunned to do more that twitch when Lisette's brains splattered against my face and chest.

She sat there for a moment after the top of her head disappeared, her hands still fluttering in her lap like wounded birds. Then her body slumped to the ground as if it had suddenly become sleepy. I looked in the direction of the shot and saw Poilu standing by his private wagon. He looked tired and older than I'd ever seen him before. Even though the night was cool, he was dressed in a flannel night shirt, not his wolf skin. Beside him was one of the pet eunuchs, a smoking rifle gripped in its pudgy hands.

"The little minx fancied she could poison me with her pathetic little herbal mixtures," Poilu snarled, his words somewhat slurred. "Thought she could cuckold me like I was no more than a miller or a barber-surgeon! Wretched little creature!" He stepped forward, whatever drug Lisette had put his evening cognac slipping away as his skin became darker and hairier. "And as for you," he growled, lowering his head as his nose pushed and twisted its way into a snout, "you thankless little bastard, I'll deal with you like the dog you are!"

I shifted as the older werewolf came at me, leaping to meet his charge halfway. We struck headlong and began tearing at one another with all the fury of true wolves.

He may have been old, but Poilu was far from weak and inexperienced when it came to hand-to-hand combat. But, then, I was far from a piker in that field myself. Still, I'd never fought one of my own kind before, and I was unprepared for how strong my opponent was.

All my life, I had been accustomed to creatures that were weaker than me—and that included grown buffalo, mind you. But Poilu was powerful and knew where to bite and where to claw to do the most damage. While I had youth and vigor on my side, he definitely had years—if not centuries—of experience is dealing with rival *vargr*. Fur, blood, spittle and shit flew in every direction as we rolled about on the ground. It wasn't until I felt a sudden heat across my shoulders and back, followed closely by intense pain, that I realized we had rolled into the campfire and set my pelt ablaze.

I howled in agony and snapped fiercely at Poilu, taking a couple of his fingers off as neatly as he would have bitten the ends off his cigars, but the old werewolf refused to let go.

"You were going to cuckold me, you worthless piece of shit!" he growled through bared teeth. "You were going to steal my Lisette from me and set up your own pack! Let's see how many cubs she'll bear you now, interloper!"

Poilu forced my head back, exposing the soft meat of my jugular, and for a moment it looked like I was truly done for. Although I had endured what would have been certain death for a normal human time and time again, I knew that a killing bite from one of my own would prove genuinely fatal. Just as Poilu lowered his head, there was a horrible, high-pitched scream from the direction of the wagons. Poilu, distracted, turned to see what was going on, and I used that moment to break free of his hold and put some room between us. I fully expected Poilu to press his attack, but to my surprise he seemed to have completely forgotten me.

The screaming continued. It was high and womanish—and for a second I thought it was one of Poilu's wives. I looked in the direction of the sound and saw Henri, Poilu's chief eunuch, standing as if transfixed, his chubby hands clutching his chest. There was blood coming out of his mouth. There was also an arrow sticking out between his red-stained fingers.

Suddenly the sky was full of burning arrows. They lofted upward then, like falling stars, plummeted to earth. Some of them thudded harmlessly to the ground. Most of them, however, landed in the canvas rigging of the covered wagons, setting them ablaze in seconds. Poilu's remaining wives poured from the burning wagons, their tongueless voices filling the night with mute screams.

Poilu stood on crooked legs and shook his fists at the night, bellowing at his unseen attackers like a vengeful Old Testament patriarch. "Who *dares*?!? Who dares attack Poilu!?!"

His only answer was a single rifle shot, which caught him in the chest and hurled him backward a good ten feet. To my surprise, he stayed down, twitching like a dropped fawn.

I'd like to point out that I was hurt pretty good myself. I'd suffered some serious burns and sustained substantial internal injuries. I could feel myself bleeding inside, and some ribs had snapped off and punctured my left lung. Poilu had also done a far amount of cosmetic damage as well, tearing off my right ear and biting through my nose so it bled like a sieve. Still, despite all that had happened, I crawled to where he lay dying.

"Poilu?"

He was still alive, but just barely. Blood was pumping out of his shattered ribcage and running out the corner of his mouth. He looked stunned and more than a little shocked, like a child thrown from a beloved pony.

"Silver," Poilu whispered, his words made bubbly by the blood filling his lungs. "They've got silver bullets." And then he died.

I didn't need to hear any more to know who was behind the attack on the camp. I knew all too well. It was my very own private devil, come to make sure I didn't get lost on my way to Hell.

Somehow—I'm not exactly sure myself, since I was rapidly becoming delirious from my injuries—I managed to drag myself away from the camp and escape into the night before Poilu's attackers swept down from their hiding place in the surrounding hills. I got as far as a rise overlooking the massacre before my strength deserted me entirely. Broken, burned and bleeding from more than a dozen deep wounds, I looked on helplessly as more than twenty whites—most of them sporting heavy beards—rounded up Poilu's harem. It slowly dawned on me that these were the Mormons Poilu had hoped to blend in with and, eventually, prey upon.

The eunuchs were killed as they tried to protect their fallen master's wives. I'll give them one thing—they might not have had testicles, but those poor bastards certainly had guts. The women, unfortunately, did not fare as well as their keepers. Makeshift torture racks were made from the wheels of the unburnt wagons, and each wife was, in turn, stripped naked and lashed in place, her arms and legs spread wide.

It was then Witchfinder Jones stepped out of the crowd of gathered men. Even from such a distance, I had no trouble in identifying him, for he still wore my father's pelt as a shirt. I watched as he methodically gutted each of the pregnant females, yanking their unborn children out of their bellies and crushing them underneath his boot heel.

A great sadness filled me and I began to chant prayers to the Great God Coyote in the Comanche tongue. Somewhere along the fifth or sixth wife I blacked out, my eyes swimming with visions of half-formed things crushed to jelly and the screams of tongueless women ringing in my ears.

CHAPTER NINE

I don't know how long I was out. All I know is that when I came to, I was lying on a pony drag. I struggled to sit up, but the pain that filled my body made me stop. I fell back and moaned.

"You are awake, skinwalker?"

The voice made me open my eyes again, for it belonged to a woman and spoke in the tongue of the Shoshone, a cousin tribe of the Comanche.

The horse came to a halt, and I heard the rider dismount and walk back to where I lay on the drag. Standing before me was a woman dressed in a long buckskin skirt and tunic, the front decorated with elaborate beadwork that marked her as a medicine squaw. She was neither beautiful nor ugly, although I guessed her age to be no more than sixteen or seventeen. On her head was a cap made from the skull and pelt of a badger, its paws tied under her chin.

"Y-you are Shoshone?" I asked, my voice sounding so weak it frightened me to hear it.

She shook her head, causing the badger's empty paws to sway. "My mother was Shoshone, taken in a raid. My father is Lakota Sioux. Hunkpapa. I am called Digging Woman."

"Digging Woman—how did you come to find me?"

She smiled, and it was then I glimpsed the beauty and power held within her. "I saw you in a vision, Walking Wolf. I had traveled into the wilderness in quest of visions. The Great Coyote came to me and showed me where to find you."

I should have been surprised she knew my Indian name. But having learned at Medicine Dog's knee, I knew better. I had prayed to Coyote and he had heard my prayer, sending this woman to my aid.

I tried to sit up again, but the pain was still too great. Digging Woman's eyes flashed alarm and she pushed me back with a gentle shove.

"Do not try to move, skinwalker. Your wounds are grave. Give them time to heal."

As I scrutinized what little I could see of myself, I could tell she wasn't exaggerating. The backs of my hands and my forearms were covered with scar tissue—no doubt from the fire. I tried to touch my left ear—only to find a raw nub. My regenerative abilities were no doubt taxed to their limit. It would be some time before my body could rebuild itself properly.

"I owe you my life, Digging Woman."

She shrugged and pulled a handful of dried herbs from a pouch secured to her waist and handed me a drinking skin. "It is a long ride to my people's camp. Chew these and wash it down with water. It will help dull the pain."

I did as she said. Although I have a high pain threshold, something told me I'd be stepping over it quite a bit in the next few days. As with most unpleasantness, I was right.

⇒•◇•⇐

Digging Woman was a remarkable person. If I did not have reason enough to consider her so from the start, I quickly came to respect my savior during the two days she dragged me through strange and doubtless hostile territory.

The Sioux were much like the Comanche, seeing how they were both nomadic tribes that wandered the Great Plains and relied heavily on the buffalo for their day-to-day existence.

Both tribes were noted for their ferocity in battle and skill as horsemen. Both were proud warrior societies. The big difference between the two, however, lay in their attitude toward religion.

Comanche, like I said earlier, were rather pragmatic people. They observed the taboos and rituals imposed by their gods but did not put much stock in supernatural things. While medicine men were respected, they were not treated with the respect one gave war chiefs. The Sioux, on the other hand, were great believers in visions—and not just those given to shamans and elders. The Sioux went in for rituals and dances and saw signs and portents in many things.

Digging Woman was a wise woman, schooled in the knowledge of roots, herbs, grasses and the phases of the moon. There was no such thing amongst the Comanche, unless you counted the Grandmothers who attended the women when it was their time to give birth. And, to judge by her dress and manner, Digging Woman had attained a great deal of stature within the tribe at an early age. Although the Sioux could be as dismissive of their women folk as the Comanche, the strength and truth of Digging Woman's visions and her skill as a healer had won her great respect from the various Lakota tribes.

She explained to me that she was born of a family famous for its medicine. Many great and powerful shamans had been born of her clan. In fact, her uncle was none other than Tatanka Yotanka, better known as Sitting Bull, the most revered of the Hunkpapa medicine men. The night before we reached her tribe's camp, she informed me she would send a dream to her uncle, to tell him of their arrival. Later that evening, I saw what looked to be an owl rise from where she was sleeping, its muffled wings beating silently as it flew in the direction of her people. A coincidence? If I was 100 percent white, and human to boot, perhaps I could believe that. But I have walked the thin line between the real and the unreal all my life, both as a Comanche brave and a shapeshifting werebeast, and I know better than to dismiss such things out of hand.

In any case, the very next day as we entered the Hunkpapa camp, Sitting Bull strode from his tipi and warmly greeted his niece without anyone telling him we had arrived. I was able to understand most of what he said, as I'd spent the past couple of days learning as much of the Lakota tongue as possible. Once again my gift for languages had come in handy, allowing me to become fluent in a matter of weeks instead of months.

"Digging Woman! Little daughter! I saw you in a dream last night! It is good to know my vision was true."

"It is good to see you as well, uncle."

"In my dream, you said you were bringing back powerful medicine to help us in our war against the whites. Is this true?"

Digging Woman hopped off her horse and gestured to me, wrapped in blankets and curled up on the pony drag like an ailing grandmother.

"Judge for yourself, uncle."

Nancy A. Collins
244

Sitting Bull frowned and moved to lift the blanket from my face. Groggy from the herbs used in blunting the pain that stitched its way through my body like lightning, I felt my nose elongate, becoming a snout. I flashed my fangs in warning lest he touch me. Sitting Bull's eyes widened, and he stepped back from the pony drag, clearly shaken.

"Coyote!"

"Not Coyote. But one beloved of him. He calls himself Walking Wolf."

Sitting Bull nodded his head as he digested what she was telling him. "You have indeed done well, Digging Woman. Our medicine will be made strong against the whites! I will see to it that the skinwalker is welcome here."

That was my first meeting with Sitting Bull, and it would prove to be far from the last. True to his word, Sitting Bull had one of his subordinates surrender his tipi, in which I would spend the next month recovering from the grievous injuries dealt me by Poilu.

During most of that time, Digging Woman tended to me personally, but Sitting Bull was often a visitor to my tent as well. There was much on the chief's mind, and he often talked with me when he was troubled. The Sitting Bull I knew was still a young man, but he lacked the bloodthirsty brashness that marked so many of his fellow war chiefs. He was a thoughtful man, in his way. He reminded me of Medicine Dog, and I guess that was one reason I came to trust and respect him so quickly. When I looked into his eyes, I could tell he was a man who could see true.

Word soon got out that Sitting Bull was playing host to a skinwalker, and many of the rival Sioux chiefs came to pay him homage. I distinctly remember the day Red Cloud, chief of the Oglala Sioux, rode into camp. Red Cloud was feared far and wide, by whites and Indians alike. Before the whites found their way onto the Great Plains, Red Cloud's name struck fear into the Utes, Crows and Pawnees. A ruthless warrior, he was known as a man of pronounced cruelty, even by Indian standards. One story told how he pulled a drowning Ute out of the river by his hair, only to scalp the poor bastard once he got him to shore.

When he arrived at Sitting Bull's camp, his party rode in whooping and shrieking so that everyone would know they were fierce and mighty warriors. Red Cloud was, by this time, an older man—older than Sitting Bull by a decade or more. He dismounted, and Sitting Bull greeted him cordially. Red Cloud was a proud figure of a man, although he now limped from an imperfectly healed wound he'd received from a Pawnee arrow a few years back.

I was sitting in front of my tipi, wrapped in a buffalo robe and smoking my pipe. I had been amongst the Sioux the better part of a month and was close to being completely healed. My left ear had yet to grow back completely—I wasn't exactly sure why it was being so stubborn, perhaps because my attacker had been a *vargr*—but the burn tissue had all but disappeared, except for a thick patch on my right shoulder the size of an eagle dollar. I watched as Sitting Bull and Red Cloud strode in my direction. I could tell by the look in his eyes that Red Cloud was dismayed to see I wore the skin of a white.

"You told me you had a skinwalker, Sitting Bull," he protested. "How can this be a skinwalker when he is white?"

Sitting Bull simply smiled and said, "He is white on the outside, but hairy on the inside."

I lay aside my pipe and stood up, shrugging off my buffalo robe, and looked Red Cloud square in the face. It was a hard thing to do, for he indeed had the eyes of a born killer. And, without speaking a word, I shifted into my true skin. Red Cloud's face showed no trace of fear or surprise, but I could see something change deep within those merciless eyes.

He nodded, more to himself than to show approval of me. "With such powerful medicine, we cannot lose against our enemies."

He was wrong, of course. Horribly wrong. But at the time it seemed like the truth.

<hr>

I spent thirteen years living as a member of Sitting Bull's tribe. They were good years, although far from idyllic. The U.S. government considered the Sioux hostile since they didn't hold with the whites trying to build roads across their hunting grounds. Conflict was a constant part of Sioux life—as was death. But I had been raised amongst the Comanche, and the idea of being constantly at odds with those around you was far from unusual. Peace was good, but war was the way of things. This the Sioux and Comanche understood.

During those days amongst the Hunkpapa, I came to be regarded as a living good luck piece. Braves who wanted success on the warpath came to me so I could bless their shields and arrows. War chiefs who needed help in keeping control of their braves came to me for support. Women heavy of child came to me, so I could breathe into their nostrils and impart the blessing of Coyote on their unborn.

In time, I came to know all the great chiefs and warriors of the Sioux, not to mention the Cheyenne. They all came to my tipi, bringing gifts of ponies, food, buffalo robes and fine beadwork. Their names read like a Who's Who of the American Indian: Rain-in-the-Face, Gall, Scarlet Point, Lean Bear, Black Kettle, Little Robe, Blue Horse, Dull Knife, Pawnee Killer, Little Thunder, Spotted Tail, Crazy Horse. All of them brave men. All of them now dead.

Soon I became quite wealthy, as the plains tribes judged such things, and I could take whatever woman I pleased to wife. So I picked Digging Woman. She might not have been a great beauty, but she was strong-minded, loyal and fearless.

And what about my fear of shapeshifting during intimate moments, you ask? Was ours a marriage in name only? Certainly not. During my recovery, Digging Woman spent many nights underneath the buffalo robes with me, chasing the illness from my bones by pressing her body against mine. When my fever finally broke, my body celebrated its escape from death and I soon found myself atop Digging Woman, but she was not frightened by my bestial appearance. For the first time in my twenty years of life, I found myself actually making love to a woman.

As Sitting Bull's nephew-in-law, my status in the tribe became even greater. The only thing that would bring even stronger good luck to the Hunkpapa would be if a child were born of the union between skinwalker and Sioux. And in 1865, I was presented with a son. No man could have been prouder or happier than I was on the day my firstborn was presented to me, wrapped in the skin of a rabbit, squalling lustily and waving his tiny hands as if he would pull the clouds from the sky. His skin was covered with a light down, like that of a pup, and he yipped just like one when he was hungry. We named him Small Wolf.

As I held my son, I no longer wondered who or what I was. It did not matter if I was white or *vargr*, or even Sioux as opposed to Comanche. As of that moment, I was 100 percent Indian. And I knew that from that day forward I would always be Walking Wolf, no matter what I might call myself in the years to come.

The seasons passed. Became years. The whites eventually resolved their fight against themselves down south and began refocusing their time and energies on winning the Indian territories. The government insisted on building a road to Bozeman along the Powder River, but Red Cloud would have none of it. He had threatened to fight all whites who tried to use the

Bozeman Trail, and constantly harassed the soldiers sent there to build the three guardian forts needed to secure the road.

Then, in December of 1866, just as the gray clouds hovering over the Bighorn Valley warned of coming snows, Red Cloud and High-Back-Bone of the Miniconjous conferred on how best to destroy the whites stationed at Fort Phil Kearney, along the banks of Little Piney Creek.

They came to me for my blessing, and I gave it to them, although I secretly feared their efforts would prove futile.

Red Cloud and High-Back-Bone marshaled their men and sent a small decoy party out to attack a wood train hauling timber to the post. A second decoy party, lead by Crazy Horse, rode boldly toward the front of the fort. Naturally, the commanding officer sent out his soldiers—eighty of them, to be exact, lead by a Captain William J. Fetterman. Crazy Horse's men fell back and Fetterman followed, over the high ridge to the north and down the other side, where close to two thousand Sioux and Cheyenne braves burst from hiding places along the slope. The startled, overconfident soldiers found themselves engulfed by a sea of arrows. None survived.

In what the whites would call the Fetterman Massacre, the Plains Indians had succeeded in landing a solid blow against the whites. With Colonel Carrington and his remaining soldiers trapped inside their fort by the fierce winter weather, and the troops at Forts Reno and C.F. Smith equally incapacitated, Red Cloud and his companions had proven themselves to be more than ignorant savages, nipping at the heels of their betters.

To my private amazement, the government agreed to abandon the Bozeman Trail, confine military operations to defense of the existing Platte Road, and set aside eighty thousand square miles of the Missouri and Yellowstone river basins for exclusive occupancy by the Indians.

Now full of confidence, Red Cloud's war party attacked some woodcutters near Fort Kearny during the summer of '67. The woodcutters, and the soldiers protecting them, barricaded themselves behind wagon boxes. As the soldiers were armed with the new breech-loading rifles, the war party was eventually driven off. However, the outcome at the Wagon Box Fight did not leave the Sioux feeling defeated. After all, they had denied the Bozeman Trail to all emigrant travel, trapped the soldiers in their forts, forced army supply trains to fight their way through, and had stolen enormous numbers of horses from the bluecoats.

When the government sent messengers into the hostile camps with an invitation of peace talks in Laramie, Red Cloud dismissed them out of hand.

He was too busy preparing for the fall buffalo hunt to waste his time on such foolishness. As far as Red Cloud was concerned, he had won his war. But he had no way of knowing that the whites had agreed to surrender the Bozeman Trail only because the Union Pacific Railroad was opening better routes to the Montana mines farther west.

The summer of 1868 was another good season for Red Cloud—he told the government's runners that he would not attend the Peace Commission's talks until Forts Phil Kearney and C.F. Smith were abandoned. And, at the end of July, he saw his demands carried out, as the soldiers marched out of Fort C.F. Smith, the northernmost post along the Bighorn River. Flushed with victory, he rode down from the mountains and set fire to the abandoned encampment. A few days later he was able to do the same to the much-hated Fort Kearny, after its garrison left.

However, he still refused to attend the peace talks at Laramie. When I asked him about it, he said he would think about it after he had put in the winter's meat for the tribe. But by the time he finally got around to signing the Medicine Lodge Treaty, as it was called, it had become a worthless piece of paper. The workings of white government were beyond Red Cloud, and he had no way of knowing that a new president had been elected—a president who had seen to it that the Peace Commission was permanently adjourned and had publicly announced that the settlers headed westward were to be protected even if it meant the extermination of every Indian tribe. Like I said, there was no way he or any of the other chiefs who had put their names on the peace treaty could have known that.

But they would soon find out.

⟫=⟩◆⟨=⟪

Black Kettle was a Cheyenne chief, much respected by his fellows, although he had lost control over some of his younger warriors in the last few years. Black Kettle was old and tired of fighting. He wanted peace with the whites and had been instrumental in talking many of the chiefs into signing the Medicine Lodge Treaty.

Angered when the bluecoats refused them the rifles promised in the treaty, some of Black Kettle's more hotheaded young braves went on a raid into Kansas, killing settlers and stealing their horses. Their war party left a trail across the snowy prairies that pointed to Black Kettle's winter camp as starkly as a finger. On November 27, 1868, just as dawn broke, the blare of a military band woke the unsuspecting Cheyenne and brought them, sleepy-eyed, from their tipis. A bluecoat with golden hair ordered his men to open fire with their carbines. Black Kettle grabbed his wife and jumped onto a pony tethered outside his lodge and galloped for safety across the Washita River. A bullet struck Black Kettle in the back, while another struck his wife. They fell, dead, into the icy water of the Washita.

The Indian Wars had begun.

———⟫◇⟪———

Over the next few years, the white government's Peace Policy proved itself to be just words on paper. The tide of settlers heading ever westward kept increasing. There was no end of the white man and his covered wagons. The Sioux were not the only tribe to find their treaties violated—the Kiowa, Arapaho, Cheyenne, Comanche and Apache all ended up lied to. Horses, blankets, guns and ammunition that had been promised them by the white man's treaties in exchange for allowing trails to be built across their lands never materialized.

Equally disturbing was the effect the Union Pacific Railroad was having on the great buffalo herd that was the source of all life and social structure amongst the tribes that roamed the Great Plains. The railroad had, effectively, divided the buffalo into two herds, the northern and southern. At first the buffalo refused to acknowledge the iron horses that cut through their ancestral grazing ground, often blocking the tracks. Soon the railroad hired hunters, equipped with long rifles that could shoot as far as a mile away, to make sure the way was kept clear.

The whites slaughtered the great buffalo in numbers undreamed of by even the mightiest Indian hunter. And, in what seemed to be genuine perversity on their part, the white hunters usually left the carcasses to rot where they fell, taking only a tongue or a hump in order to collect their bounty.

There was a madness on the land, and its name was Extinction.

———⟫◇⟪———

In the spring of 1870, Red Cloud did what none had ever thought he would do. He rode to Fort Fetterman, Wyoming, named after the bluecoat he had helped kill four years before, and told the commandant that he wanted to go to Washington and talk to the Great Father about the Fort Laramie Treaty and the possibility of going to a reservation. It is hard to say whether Red Cloud's desire for peace came from a need to protect his people from certain extermination or if he had simply grown weary of the warpath. I do not know for sure, and I was there. In any case, Red Cloud never took up arms against the whites for the rest of his life.

Still, he was far from a whipped dog. He had many complaints against the government, and he voiced them quite eloquently. The cold-blooded killer had, over the years, developed into a skilled statesman.

Red Cloud intended to trade and draw his treaty rations and annuities at or near Fort Laramie, although the government was equally determined to get the Sioux off the Platte and onto the reservation. Red Cloud gave in little by little, walking a narrow line between the white government and his own people. Any concessions not widely supported by the Sioux weakened his leadership—which rested, largely, on his ability to manipulate the whites. Finally, in 1873, a compromise was reached. An agency would be created in northwestern Nebraska, just outside the boundary of the Great Sioux Reservation. The government built the Red Cloud Agency for the Oglalas and the Spotted Tail Agency for the Brules, their ancestral enemies.

Although the whites saw this as a victory, it soon began to turn sour. Violence still proved a problem, contracting frauds plagued the agencies from the very beginning, and the Sioux did not respond well to the Indian Bureau's high-handed attempts to "civilize" them by educating their children in the white man's ways while stripping them of their language and culture.

Many of the Indians resented—or simply did not comprehend—the whites' desire to keep them away from the settlements and travel routes. Indians off the reservation did not automatically mean hostility. They might be out hunting, or visiting friends and family in neighboring tribes, or just wandering around the country, seeing the sights. However, the whites felt greatly threatened by the Indians' refusal to stay in one spot. The peace was as illusory as the treaties the Indians had signed. Although Red Cloud stood fast, remaining on the reservation, hundreds of Oglala braves flocked to Sitting Bull and Crazy Horse.

The army, under the command of General Sherman, was determined to break the will of the free-roaming Indian tribes. They set forth to find the enemy in their winter camps, killing or driving them from their lodges, destroying their ponies, food and shelter, and chasing them mercilessly across the frozen land until they died or surrendered. And if women and children were hurt and killed along the way—so be it. And as the open land and the wild game that had once seemed inexhaustible began to disappear, the reservations began to be seen as the only alternative to complete obliteration.

Although Sitting Bull still held immense respect for Red Cloud, he considered him deluded. Reservation life was confining; the clothing and rations were often scanty and invariably of poor quality. The whiskey peddlers and other opportunists that were drawn to the agency were decidedly bad influences on the more impressionable young braves. As Sitting Bull once said at one of the tribal talks, "You are fools to make yourselves slaves to a piece of fat bacon, some hardtack, and a little sugar and coffee."

As it was, many of the Sioux traveled back and forth between the agencies and the nontreaty camps, enjoying the old hunting life during the spring and returning for the hardtack and coffee during the winter. The Indian Bureau saw these "unfriendlies" as dangerous, as they were ungovernable and sometimes raided along the Platte and the Montana settlements at the head of the Missouri and Yellowstone rivers. Still, as much as the whites complained about the Sioux disregarding the treaty, they were busy breaking it in even bigger ways.

In 1873, surveyors laid out a route for the Northern Pacific Railroad along the northern margins of the unceded territory. And in 1874, "Yellow Hair" Custer, the hated murderer of Black Kettle, led his soldiers into the Black Hills, part of the Great Sioux Reservation itself, and found gold. Naturally, miners swarmed into the territory and the government did nothing to stop them, except to make a lame attempt at offering to buy the land from the Sioux for a paltry sum.

It was at this time I had a vision.

I was asleep, but in my dream my eyes were open and I could see someone standing at the entrance of my tipi, watching me. When I looked harder, I saw the person watching me was none other than Medicine Dog. I was very glad to see my old teacher, but at the same time there was a strange feeling inside me.

"It is good to see you, Medicine Dog," I said, getting to my feet. "But are you not dead?"

Medicine Dog nodded and smiled. "Almost ten years, as the white man reckons time. Much has happened since I last saw you," he commented, pointing at Digging Woman and Small Wolf, still sound asleep on either side of me. As I drew closer to him, I realized that not only had he regained his vision, he now had both eyes.

"Why have you chosen this time to visit me, old friend?"

"I would give you a vision, Walking Wolf." Medicine Dog motioned for me to follow him as he held open the flap of my tipi. "One you would do well to heed." Without another word, the old medicine man slipped out of the tent. Uncertain of what to do, I followed him—and stepped out of Montana into the choking dust and heat of the Texas Panhandle.

I was more disoriented than frightened by the chaos around me. I had walked into the middle of a Comanche war camp, the braves painted for battle and preparing to meet their enemy. As I looked around, I recognized several faces, including those of Quanah Parker and Coyote Shit. Everything seemed extremely real. I could smell the sweat of the braves, hear their war songs, even count the hairs on the tails of their pony—but no one seemed to be able to see either Medicine Dog or myself. Coyote Shit, who wore the buffalo headdress and sacred amulets of a medicine man, was busy evoking the blessings of the Great Spirit, but if he sensed our presence, he gave no sign.

As I looked about, I noticed that many of the assembled warriors were wearing strange-looking shirts decorated with eagle feathers and painted with symbols of power. As they listened to Coyote Shit's prophesy of victory, they became more and more agitated.

Medicine Dog did not try to hide his disgust as he listened to the man who had replaced him as the tribe's shaman. "The years have not served Coyote Shit well in wisdom. His vision is false. His medicine untrue. He has convinced these warriors that the only way for the Comanche to become a great nation again is to kill all the whites they can. He has provided them with "medicine shirts" that he claims will turn aside the whites' bullets." Medicine Dog spat, producing a sizable gob for a dead man. "They are doomed."

Before I could say anything, Medicine Dog grabbed my hand. I felt myself shooting through the air like an arrow released from a bow. When he let go, I was standing on a distant hilltop overlooking the battlefield. I recognized the place as Adobe Walls, one of the oldest settlements in that part of the country. Below us, Quanah's warriors attempted to attack twenty-eight buffalo hunters barricaded in the ancient fort. The buffalo hunters were armed with rifles that could shoot a mile and bring down buffalo as easily as rabbits.

The first wave of Comanche rode in headlong, arms thrown wide, screeching their war cries, exposing themselves to enemy fire without fear. After all, they had their medicine shirts to protect them. Most of them were blown clear out of their saddles.

I shook my head and looked away from the slaughter below, only to find myself standing beside Coyote Shit. He was desperately singing prayers and working medicine, no doubt hoping to effect some change in his tribe's favor. A brave rode up from the battlefield, bearing a message from Quanah. Where was the magic promised them? Before Coyote Shit had a chance to respond, a stray bullet—fired by a rifle seven-eighths of a mile away—crashed into the hapless brave, splashing his blood all over the frightened medicine man. Not to mention myself.

Medicine Dog and I stood over Coyote Shit as he shivered and hugged himself, his eyes wide with fear. I expected Medicine Dog to gloat over his rival's downfall, but he looked sad, almost pitying.

"What will become of him?" I asked.

"Quanah will not kill him, if that's what you're thinking. He will forgive Coyote Shit what he has done. But he will not forget, either. Coyote Shit's power with the Comanche is at its end. He will go to the reservation with the others next year, and spend the rest of his days as an object of ridicule. He will live to be old. Much older than those who believed in his medicine shirts, at any rate."

"And Quanah?"

"He shall become old, as well. And fat. And corrupt. The reservation will make all of the great chiefs rot before their deaths."

"Why are you showing me these things, Medicine Dog?"

"So that you will see the folly that came to the friends of your youth, so that you might warn your adopted family of the trouble that is to come."

"But I don't understand—"

"Understand later. It is enough for now that you remember." With that, Medicine Dog touched my hand one more time, and I felt my body turn into lightning and shoot across the sky, back to the land of the Sioux.

When I opened my eyes again, I was back in my own tipi, my wife pressed against my side. As I puzzled out what my dream meant, I lifted a hand to wipe the sleep from my eyes. The back of my hand was caked with the blood of a dead Comanche brave.

In the winter of 1875, runners appeared at the winter camps of all the nontreaty chiefs. They bore a grim message from the Great Father in Washington: They were to come to the agencies at once or be considered hostiles against whom the army was prepared to make war. Of course, Sitting Bull and the others chose to ignore the summons. As Sitting Bull was fond of saying, using the white man's parlance, "God made me an Indian, not an agency Indian."

During the late winter months of '76, Digging Woman took Small Wolf with her to visit her sister, who was in a village on the Powder River. I was loath to let them go, but Digging Woman had not seen her sister in a long time, and the aunt was a particular favorite of our son. On March 17th of that year, General Crook led an attack on the village. It was a short but vicious skirmish and did more than its share of damage against my family. While Digging Woman managed to escape unharmed, her sister was shot while attempting to flee. Eight-year-old Small Wolf, standing over his fallen aunt with nothing but a toy spear for protection, was shot through the head by one of the bluecoats. There was little pleasure to be taken from the knowledge that Crook had bungled the follow-up to the attack and was forced to retreat in the face of winter.

When the news reached me of my son's death, I was inconsolable. After all I had endured to live the life of a normal man, one who could look forward to his son growing up and taking his place beside me, it was nearly enough to shatter my spirit. Our son—our only child—was dead at the hands of the whites. I screamed and howled like a thing gone mad and ran into the snow-covered hills on all fours, baying at the frigid moon until my lungs bled. Digging Woman was equally distraught. She cut off her braids and burned them as a token of her grief, ritually cutting her breasts until they were wet with blood. Sitting Bull assured us both that there would soon come a time for vengeance against the bluecoats. And that it would be sweet indeed.

———⋙⟡⋘———

By June 1876, the number of Indians fleeing the reservations for the nontreaty camps had reached epidemic proportions. There were twelve hundred lodges represented, and easily two thousand warriors gathered in one place. Our camp along the Greasy Grass River extended for three miles. Never had there been such a gathering of tribes in the history of the Plains Indians. Hunkpapa, Oglala, Brule, Miniconjou, Sans Arc, Blackfoot, Northern Cheyenne—they were all there. Several powerful and influential chiefs made camp with Sitting Bull, among them Black Moon, Hump, Dirty Moccasins and Crazy Horse. None of these men were looking for a fight, but neither would they avoid one, should it come looking for them.

Earlier that season we had staged the annual Sun Dance on the banks of the Rosebud, where Sitting Bull had received a vision of great strength and clarity. He claimed to have seen many dead soldiers fall into our camp as if they were dolls dropped by fleeing children. Everyone liked this vision and no one doubted its truth, for Sitting Bull was known to be a true seer. And, besides, he had the luck of Coyote at his right hand—how could his medicine not be strong?

Then news came that bluecoats were marching down the Rosebud. Crazy Horse took a large war party and rode off to do battle. They fought the bluecoats for six hours, after which Crazy Horse called off the fight and the soldiers retreated. While this fight had been good, Sitting Bull knew it was not the battle he'd seen in his vision.

Meanwhile, General Terry was approaching from the east, Colonel Gibbon from the west. They joined on the Yellowstone at the mouth of the Rosebud, and Terry sent out a strike force of six hundred cavalry under the command of Custer. The same Yellow Hair Custer who had violated the sanctity of the Black Hills, the most holy of Sioux places. Custer followed the Indian trail up the Rosebud, across the Wolf Mountains and down to the Greasy Grass, which the whites called Little Bighorn.

I did not take part in the Battle of Little Big Horn. Neither did Sitting Bull, for that matter. Shortly before Custer's regiment arrived on the scene, we retired to the nearby mountains to work our medicine. We were so wrapped up in our prayers and rituals that we did not hear the clash of sabers or the crack of gunfire until the battle was well underway.

I remember looking down at the blue-clad figures scurrying about in the dust. The smell of their fear rose to greet me on the wind. Most times, fear smells rank and animal, like sex. But the fear that day smelled sickly sweet, like dead roses, for the soldiers knew they were going to die. As I watched my adopted people slay those responsible, in part, for the death of my son, I knew I should feel elation or victory. Instead, there was a taste of ashes in my mouth.

I turned to Sitting Bull and said, "The whites will not let this go. They will hunt us down like wild animals."

Sitting Bull shrugged. Although he could not read or write, he was far from a fool. He knew that bringing down a white war chief was a dangerous thing to do. "Better to be hunted down like wolves than to live like dogs."

After the battle was over and the gun smoke had cleared, we left the mountains and headed into the valley to count the dead and aid the wounded. Over the years, all sorts of wild tales have come out of Custer's Last Stand. The one that gets repeated the most is that Crazy Horse took Custer's scalp for his lodgepole. That's pure crap. The other story is that Sitting Bull cut open Custer's ribcage and ate his heart. That's an out-and-out lie. I was there and I can testify that Custer's body was not mutilated in any way. We butt-fucked the bastard, but that's a different thing entirely.

What should have been the Plains Indians' greatest triumph ended up being their undoing. Custer's massacre shocked and outraged the whites and shook the Peace Policy to the point of collapse. It also brought a flood of bluecoats into Indian country, and rationalized the forcing of agency chiefs into selling the Black Hills to the United States.

Within a few days of their victory at Greasy Grass, the various bands broke up and went on their way. Some even headed back to the reservation. Despite being faced with a common enemy, it was still difficult to get the different tribes to band together. Little Bighorn was an exception, not the norm. Tribal rivalries and intertribal animosities remained as strong as ever. Although tribes would occasionally band together against the whites, it would never last for long. The individual character of tribal society kept those capable of bringing together diverse opinions and philosophies from gaining any power. Although Sitting Bull was greatly respected, he could not hold a three-mile-wide camp together. Then again, the Indians did not see war as the clashing of armies but as the maneuvering of war parties. And that is where they were doomed to fail.

Man for man, there wasn't an Indian brave who couldn't lick his weight in bluecoats. But braves, no matter how skilled in the ways of war, were not soldiers. And faced with the discipline and organization of the U.S. Army, there was no way they could compete. Hell, they hadn't even invented the damn wheel yet.

Five months after Custer's Last Stand, eleven hundred cavalry under the command of Colonel MacKenzie fell on the villages belonging to Dull Knife and Little Wolf. Forty Cheyenne were killed, and the rest were forced to watch the soldiers burn their tipis, their clothing and winter food supply. The temperature plunged to thirty below that night and eleven babies froze to death at their mothers' breasts. Those who managed to escape made their way to Crazy Horse's encampment on the Tongue River, but the soldiers followed them there as well.

On May 6th, 1877, not even a year after the death of Custer, Crazy Horse led his Oglalas to the Red Cloud Agency and threw his weapons on the ground in token surrender. Four months later he was dead, stabbed by a soldier's bayonet during a skirmish with guards.

Sitting Bull, on the other hand, refused to surrender. Rather than go to the reservation, he led his people northward to Canada. The army watched the boundary line like a hawk the whole time, making sure Sitting Bull didn't ride into Montana to hunt buffalo.

While the Hunkpapas got along with the redcoats, there simply was not enough game available to feed them. After four increasingly lean years in Canada, Sitting Bull finally surrendered to the United States government at Fort Buford, Montana. However, Digging Woman and I were not in the group that rode onto the reservation that summer day in 1881.

I figured that if the whites had trouble with Indians like Sitting Bull and Crazy Horse, then they certainly would make life difficult for one such as myself. So I took my wife and disappeared into the wilderness, preferring the life of a renegade to that of a reservation squaw man.

Chapter Ten

After Sitting Bull surrendered and went on the reservation, I took my wife and built myself a camp on Paintrock Creek, up in the Big Horn Mountains. While the white government was adamant about keeping Indians on the reservation, they tended to turn a blind eye to settlers who'd set up housekeeping with squaws. And, to the casual observer, that's all I was.

Digging Woman suffered more than I did from being separated from her tribe. The Sioux, like the Comanche, were a social bunch, given to getting up and visiting one another whenever the mood struck them. It didn't sit well that she should be kept from seeing her various sisters, aunts and other kinfolk.

When, miracle of miracles, she came up pregnant again, her hankering to visit her folks became so strong there was nothing I could do but let her go. A lone squaw traveling back and forth wouldn't have raised suspicions, but I was still fearful she would be caught and forced to stay on the reservation for good. But my fears proved to be unfounded. Digging Woman managed to sneak in and out of the Pine Ridge Agency, where Sitting Bull's people had been placed, without anyone being the wiser. In fact, she became so adept at it over the years, I stopped worrying about her trips altogether.

However, the stories she brought back concerning the quality of life on the reservation were troublesome enough. The reservations might have seemed ideal for the whites, but they were proving extremely unhealthy for the Indians corralled upon them. Where once crime had been rare within the tribes, and most disputes were settled by giving ponies to the aggrieved parties, now the white agents dealt harsh punishments to even the most trivial offender. There were few pleasures allowed them, as the native dances had been banned by the authorities and the missionaries were busy stamping out many of the ancient customs that had held the tribes together for centuries.

A communal, nomadic people by nature, they were suddenly expected to appreciate and respect the value of individual land and free enterprise. And, to top it all off, they were expected to dry farm in flinty badlands soil that wouldn't have raised a prayer.

Their rations consisted mostly of cheap green coffee beans, coarse brown sugar and wormy flour. Half-wild longhorns were occasionally turned loose to be hunted on horseback by braves desperate to reclaim a fraction of the pride given them by the buffalo hunts of old. Those chiefs and elders who had not been bribed into embracing the white man's ways with gifts of sewing machines, oil lamps and iron bedsteads spent much of their time dreaming of the old days, when the buffalo were dark upon the land and the white man was a minor inconvenience.

Bereft of leadership and stripped of their traditions, the younger members of the tribe began to succumb to the apathy that had consumed many of their elders. The Sioux and Cheyenne women began sleeping with soldiers for food. The young men, desperate for adventure but denied the traditional warpath, began enlisting as Army scouts or Indian Police, even if it meant being pitted against their own people. More and more Indians were taking up "citizen's dress," wearing the shabby cast-offs provided by the missionaries instead of the traditional breechcloth and blanket.

The proud Sioux who had brought the mighty Custer low had been cruelly broken by the whites. While I grieved for my friends, I could see no way of freeing them from the fate destiny had delivered.

In 1884, I was given a second child—another son. Like his brother before him, he was born with a pelt of light fur that fell away within a week of his arrival, leaving him hairless everywhere except his legs, for some reason. So we called him Wolf Legs. He was a good-natured child, bright and inquisitive and with the brave heart of a true warrior. He was my pride and joy,

and when I held him in my arms the day of his birth, the love I felt for him was almost enough to make me forget the loss of my firstborn son. Almost.

I was a happy man in those days. When I look back on that time, I see it through an autumnal haze, as if the nine years I spent along Paintrock Creek was one long Indian Summer. I was living free, away from the misery of the reservations. I had a sod lodge, divided into two areas—one for eating, the other for sleeping. Although my camp was far from the agencies, many of the southwestern tribes sought me out over the years. Most came seeking visions from the fabled Walking Wolf, Hand of Coyote, or cures from his shaman wife. Some of them could still afford ponies, blankets, pemmican and beadwork in exchange for my services, as in the old days, but most were too poor to give me anything besides their respect.

Even though the fortunes of the tribes had dwindled, the number of braves seeking help did not slack off. Somehow these young men always managed to find their way to my camp, most of them rail-thin and racked with fever by the time they arrived. Many died on my doorstep. I have no way of knowing the number who died along the route.

Eighteen eighty-nine was a very bad year for the Sioux. During that summer, the beef herds issued to the Indians were decimated by anthrax, and a terrible drought and grasshopper plague destroyed what few crops they had. And, to top it all off, nine million acres of their best cattle range was stolen from them by way of a convoluted government boondoggle. About this time, the pilgrims to my camp began to speak of a phenomenon amongst the reservation Indians that made my ears twitch. There was talk of a strange new religious movement sweeping the tribes. Something called the Ghost Dance.

I questioned a Sioux warrior named Young Mule about it. Although he had made his way into our camp as close to death as any man could be and still draw breath, when he spoke of the dance his eyes took on the fiery gleam of a fanatic.

"The Ghost Dance was dreamed by Wovoka of the Paiute. In the dream, he saw a time soon coming where the whites will be swept from the land. The earth will be reborn and those family and friends the whites have sent to the Spirit World will be returned whole. The buffalo will return in their numbers and we will be free to hunt and follow the herds as in the days of the Grandmother Land."

"That's a very fine vision, Young Mule. How does this Wovoka plan to make it true?"

"We are to dance the Ghost Dance. If enough of us dance long enough, and if we please the Great Spirit, then the believers shall be suspended in midair as a flood of new soil engulfs the earth, swallowing the whites whole. Wovoka has promised this shall come in three years' time. Wovoka has also promised that he will take away the whites' secret of making gunpowder when the time comes, and any gunpowder the whites might still possess will be unusable."

I tried to listen as politely and noncommittally as possible, but I didn't like the sound of it at all. For one thing, for a religion designed to rid the Indians of whites, it sure smacked of the white man's belief. It especially reminded me of the Mormons, who I had held in contempt since the night they attacked Poilu's camp and helped slaughter his wives. It did not make me feel any better to know the Ghost Dance had spread throughout the territories and had been embraced by many tribes, including the Utes, Mohave, Shoshone, Cheyenne and Kiowas.

Deeply disturbed by what Young Mule had told me, I decided it was time to venture onto the reservation and speak to Sitting Bull face to face and see where this nonsense was going. So I saddled up a pony and kissed my wife and son, and rode out in the direction of Sitting Bull's camp, forty miles southwest of Fort Yates.

When I arrived, I got to see firsthand the depredations of reservation life upon the Sioux. The abject poverty of the tribe shocked me. While they had lived free, they possessed none of the things that whites consider "wealth"—they had no gold, or precious gems or houses full of furniture— but they had possessed the wealth of their world: buffalo robes to keep them warm in the winter, meat to keep their families fed, ponies to ride, beads to work into their ceremonial costumes. Now they were stripped of even the most meager pleasures of their former lives, reduced to beggars panhandling crumbs and castoffs from their jailers. Still, there were those who clung to their pride, refusing to bow completely to the dictates of the white man.

One such man was Sitting Bull.

As I rode into Sitting Bull's camp, dozens of eyes watched me. Since I was wearing the buckskins of a mountain man, most did not recognize me as Walking Wolf, assuming I was just another agency employee sent by McLaughlin, the head of Pine Ridge's Indian Bureau, to keep an eye on the troublesome old chief. As word of my arrival spread, Sitting Bull left his cabin to see who the intruder might be.

Although I had not laid eyes on the Hunkpapa medicine man in eight years, there was no mistaking him. He was bowlegged, like most Indians,

from his years on horseback and now walked with a pronounced limp, from an old wound he received on the warpath, years ago. His thinning hair was carefully oiled and plaited, and his massive jaw and piercing eyes made him look like a great bird of prey. In defiance of the agency, he wore the traditional fringed shirt, leggings and moccasins of smoke-tanned buckskins, a trade-cloth blanket draped around his waist. As he drew closer, his thin lips pulled back into a warm smile, showing fewer teeth than I remembered.

"I dreamt last night that a wolf walked into my camp and smoked the peace pipe with me before the fire. Now here you are, old friend! Welcome to my camp, Walking Wolf!"

At the mention of my name, the Indians who had been looking daggers at me began to talk excitedly amongst themselves. I got off my horse and hugged the old man.

"You look as young as the day we worked our war medicine on Yellow Hair Custer," he laughed. It wasn't really a joke. I had stopped aging—at least noticeably—somewhere around my thirtieth birthday. As it was, at forty-three Digging Woman looked old enough to be my aunt instead of my wife. "Come, sit with me before the fire and smoke tobacco. There is much we must speak of, Hand of Coyote."

Sitting Bull's "lodge" was an exceptionally humble two-room cabin he shared with his three wives, his son Crowfoot, and one of his nephews—a deaf-mute boy named John. It smelled of grease and smoke and sweat. As we sat before the small cookfire, Sitting Bull pulled out a small bag of government-issue tobacco and placed it in his ceremonial pipe.

"Why have you come to see me, old friend?" he asked quietly, lifting an ember to the pipe's bowl.

"I would ask you about the Ghost Dance."

Sitting Bull grunted and handed the lit pipe to me. "Kicking Bear brought the Ghost Dance back with him after visiting his cousin, Spoonhunter, in Wyoming."

"Kicking Bear? You mean old Big Foot's nephew? He was always something of a hothead, if I remember correctly. Hardly the kind to turn prophet."

Sitting Bull nodded, as if I were saying things he himself believed but dared not speak aloud. "This Ghost Dance is a strange thing. I have seen it performed. There is power in the dance—that, I cannot deny. But I am not certain the visions it gives are true.

"While I do not trust it, I do not forbid it. Kicking Bear's voice is powerful. Almost as powerful as mine. His disciple, Short Bull, is as dedicated as he is—and even more headstrong. If this Ghost Dance makes my people happy and gives them something to believe in—even if it is a thing that will never be, then where is the harm?"

"What of the whites? How do they feel about the Ghost Dance?"

"It worries them. To know that my people dance for their destruction—it makes the whites sweat, even though they do not believe it will come to pass."

"What about McLaughlin?"

At the mention of the Pine Ridge Agency's chief bureaucrat, Sitting Bull spat in disgust, making the meager fire sizzle. "McLaughlin would have my scalp, if his chiefs in Washington would permit it. He would have all Sioux sing from the missionaries' books and chop off our braids. He knows I am against that and he fears me."

"Perhaps he's jealous of you. I'm sure he'll never have the chance to perform before the Queen of England."

Sitting Bull smiled and straightened up a little bit. "Yes. The Great Mother. Those were good days, when I rode with Bill Cody. Not as good as when we killed Custer, but better than now."

There was a knock on the door, and one of Sitting Bull's wives answered it. Short Bull entered and approached Sitting Bull. "Greetings, father," he said. Sitting Bull was not Short Bull's father, but all Sioux used the honorific when addressing their chiefs and respected elders. "I bring word from Kicking Bear. He would hold the Ghost Dance tomorrow in honor of Walking Wolf's arrival in our camp."

Sitting Bull lifted an eyebrow and looked at me. "Would you be interested in witnessing the dance, Walking Wolf?"

"Of course. But why tomorrow night? Why not hold it tonight?"

Short Bull looked somewhat surprised that I was unschooled in the ritual of the dance. Having grown up Comanche, I still harbored a mistrust of the Sioux's obsession with mystic rigmarole.

"The leaders and dancers must fast for a full day before entering the sweat lodges for purification."

"Oh. Of course."

"Tomorrow then," Sitting Bull agreed, ending the audience. After Short Bull was gone, the old medicine man shook his head. "They will try and use you to give credence to the Ghost Dance."

"I know. But I still want to see it for myself."

⇒◇⇐

Just before dusk the next day, I went with a hundred others from Sitting Bull's camp to a site a few miles away where sweat lodges had been built. The men and women crawled into separate lodges. I had not undergone the sweating ceremony in several years, and I had forgotten how the heat opened the pores and allowed the toxins trapped inside the skin to pour out. It was like purging yourself of everything holding you to the material plane. At the end of the ceremony, the dancers would crawl from the lodges, after which they were painted red by medicine men and their bodies were rubbed down with handfuls of sweet grass.

As I watched the others dress themselves in their finest regalia, a young Sioux medicine man called Black Elk handed me a carefully folded bundle.

"You honor us with your presence, Walking Wolf. It would give me great pleasure if you wore this shirt I made."

"Thank you, Black Elk." I held up the garment and studied it. It was a shirt of unbleached muslin, cut like the old-time ceremonial war shirts, with fringe on the sleeves and seams. It was marked with strange symbols and had eagle feathers tied to it here and there. I felt there was something horribly familiar about the shirt as I put it on, but I could not pinpoint the source of my disquiet.

The dancers, male and female, young and old, seated themselves in a huge circle around a dead tree with colored streamers tied to its branches. Kicking Bear, the official leader of the dance, sat at the base of the tree. At his command, a young girl came forward and was handed an elk-horn bow and four arrows made with bone heads. As we watched, the maiden dipped the arrows in a bowl of steer's blood and shot them into the air, sending one to each of the four points of the compass. Then the bow was tied to the branches of the tree, and the maiden took up the sacred redstone pipe and held it to the west.

The dancers began to chant, their voices joining in a plaintive drone as Kicking Bear passed around a vessel of sacred meat. The dancers got to their feet as one and joined hands, shuffling slowly. I had been raised Comanche, where the sexes were strictly segregated during any public observance, and the sight of men and women dancing together was indeed shocking.

The dancers continued chanting and dancing, their eyes shut as they worked to conjure forth the image of a world free of whites. A world where the buffalo ran unhindered. A world where all those slain by the white man came back from the Spirit World, whole and untouched. During the next few hours, the weaker members of the dance collapsed one by one. Exhausted but exhilarated, their eyes burning with renewed hope, they spoke of having glimpsed dead loved-ones and friends.

"I saw Walks Backward, who died at Black Kettle's camp."

"I saw Blue Drum, who died at Dull Knife's camp."

"I saw Queen-of-Flowers, who was raped and shot by settlers."

And so on and so on.

After the fourth hour, many of the dancers had collapsed and were recovering on the sidelines, watching the heartiest and most fanatical of their number continue the dance. Suddenly, Black Elk broke away and snatched up a rifle and, to my surprise, leveled it right at my chest.

"The Great Spirit has given to me a vision!" he crowed. "A vision of power! All who dance the ghost dance—all who wear the ghost shirts—shall be made invulnerable! The white man's bullets will turn from us and be no more than the stinging of insects!" And with that, he shot me.

The bullet kicked me onto my back, but even as I fell I remembered why Black Elk's shirt had seemed so familiar. Over the years, I had all but forgotten my dream of Coyote Shit and his "bulletproof" medicine shirts, but now that it was too late, it was coming back to me. I could hear Medicine Dog's voice echoing in my head:

So that you will see the folly that came to the friends of your youth, so that you might warn your adopted family of the trouble that is to come.

But it was too late. The damage had been done.

The assembled ghost dancers were gasping and pointing at me in amazement. Blood stained my ghost shirt a bright crimson as I got to my feet. I knew that whatever dark path the Sioux would find themselves on in the future, there was no way I could hope to steer them from it.

I glowered at Black Elk and Kicking Bear but said nothing. Both men no doubt had heard Sitting Bull's stories of my apparent immortality. I had known from the outset they would try to make it look as though I supported the Ghost Dance, but I had not guessed at their ambition. I had been outside the tribe too long. I'd forgotten how ruthless medicine men could be when in search of power.

I staggered away from the dance site, brusquely shoving away those who wanted to touch the blood stain spreading across my chest. Although I was in pain and greatly angered, I did not allow myself to shapeshift in front of them. It was bad enough that Kicking Bear and his disciples had used me to validate their Ghost Shirts, but I refused to allow them to say Coyote had made himself manifest to bless the Ghost Dance.

I left for home that very same night. As far as I was concerned, the Ghost Dance was nothing more that a con job being run by unscrupulous petty chiefs, willing to manipulate their people's desire to return to a simpler time. If ever there was proof that the white man's madness had finally rubbed off on the Indians, this was it.

———————

I spent the next several months doing my best to ignore the growing phenomena of the Ghost Dance. It was especially aggravating to discover that many of my old friends—men and women whose opinions I had once valued—had embraced the movement. I guess I should count myself lucky that Digging Woman was not taken in by it.

If 1889 had been a bad year for the Indians, 1890 was certainly heaping insult atop injury. With the "savages" penned up on reservations and the countryside supposedly made safe to settlers, immigrants literally steamed into South Dakota, most of them Scandinavians and Germans who went by the description of "honyockers," a good number of them bringing scarlet fever and the grippe with them.

During the spring, the Indian office ordered a new cut in the beef issue, which was already scanty to begin with. And, if the tide of active Indian resentment against the whites wasn't high enough already, Congress adjourned for the summer without passing Sioux appropriations or making sure that emergency funding was available, though they somehow found the time to pass a law prohibiting the killing of wild game on the reservations.

The bureaucrats stationed at the agencies might have not been the most honest or intelligent of men, but with so much anger, resentment and bitterness building up on the reservation, it didn't take a genius to figure out that something was bound to blow. The most visible sign of discontent was the Ghost Dancers. The heads of the Pine Ridge, Rosebud and Lame Deer Agencies put their heads together and decided it was about time they tried to defuse the situation.

In late August, one of the senior bureaucrats at the Pine Ridge Agency rode out to No Water's camp to confront him about the Ghost Dance. No Water refused to hear the agent out, and when he attempted to have the old chief arrested, he suddenly found himself faced with three hundred armed Ghost Dancers. Needless to say, his report to Washington did not sit well with his superiors.

A couple of weeks later, Young Mule—the very same Sioux who had struggled to make his way to my camp the year before—and his companion,

Head Swift, killed a settler. Two days later, they rode into the Lame Deer Agency and attacked the troops stationed there. It was a foolhardy gesture, of course, as there were at least seventy men to their two. Both died wearing their Ghost Shirts.

In October, McLaughlin tried to order Sitting Bull to come to the agency for questioning concerning the Ghost Dance. Although the true leader of the cult amongst the Sioux was Kicking Bear, the whites insisted on believing Sitting Bull was behind it all, simply because the old medicine man refused to denounce it. Needless to say, Sitting Bull ignored McLaughlin's orders.

In early November, the Brules—under the direction of Kicking Bear's disciple, Short Bull—deserted their homes and followed their leader to Pass Creek, which marked the boundary between the Rosebud and Pine Ridge Agencies. Although this upset the whites a great deal—no doubt they had visions of marauding Indians in their heads—you have to bear in mind that up until this point, the Ghost Dancers still intended to hold out until they were joined in this world by their ghost relatives. As far as they were concerned, there would be no need to fight the whites. But the agents in charge of running the reservation were hardly in touch with the Indian way of thinking.

The government, already nervous over the reports of the mysterious "Indian cult," ordered all whites and mixed-blood agency employees in the reservation's outlying camps to abandon their schools, farms and missions and come into the agency for protection. It also instructed all the Indians considered "friendlies" to gather at White Clay Creek.

A few days after Short Bull's exodus, two hundred Ghost Dancers swarmed the Pine Ridge Agency, virtually taking over all the offices and buildings, hurling files and requisitions into the street and trampling them underfoot.

Five days later, the Sioux found themselves shorted yet again on their beef rations. A Ghost Dancer began haranguing the crowd, soon inciting them to nearly riot. All that kept violence from breaking out was the intervention of Jack Red Cloud, old Chief Red Cloud's son. Two days after that, soldiers sent from Fort Robinson in response to McLaughlin's telegraphed plea for assistance marched into Pine Ridge. It just so happened to be the Seventh Cavalry—Custer's old unit.

The sight of their old enemy's former regiment sparked a panic amongst the assembled Indians, friendlies and hostiles alike. Convinced they were being set up for Custer's death, they piled their pony drags with tipis and winter clothes and moved west of Pass Creek, to join the Ghost Dancers already there. Short Bull and Kicking Bear then decided their numbers had swollen so much that they needed a new camp, one where they could feel secure against possible attack by the bluecoats. They picked the Stronghold, a two-hundred-foot butte known to the whites as Cuny's Table. It would be impossible for anyone to sneak up on them there without being seen.

However, while on their way to the Stronghold, many of Short Bull's Brules—who tended to be somewhat high-spirited even in the old days—got their blood up and attacked a settlement of squaw men and mixed-bloods at the mouth of Porcupine Creek. Ranches and homes were wrecked, horses stolen, harnesses and wagons chopped to pieces, cattle driven off and, to top it all off, they burned the government beef ranch to the ground.

Of course, I had no way of knowing this at the time. I had a few visitors who made a point to keep me current as to the state of the tribe, most of them mixed-bloods who were allowed to travel freely between the agencies. But where I kept my camp was a good three or four days' ride from the Pine Ridge and Rosebud Agencies, so by the time I heard what was happening on the reservation, it was usually old news. But sometimes I had visitors who came to me in dreams.

⸺⸻◆⸻⸺

Just after Thanksgiving I woke from a particularly troublesome dream to find Sitting Bull seated, cross-legged, beside my cabin's hearth. He was smoking his pipe and looking fairly calm and composed. At first I imagined that my wife's uncle had somehow succeeded in smuggling himself out of Pine Ridge and had come to us for sanctuary. Then I realized that the medicine man was as insubstantial as the smoke rising from his pipe. Only then did I know that I was dreaming.

"Uncle! Why do you come dreamwalking?"

Sitting Bull looked at me with surprise in his eyes. "This is a dream?" Heaving a weary sigh, he turned into smoke and disappeared up the chimney.

I found the dream confusing, and thinking it was probably not an authentic visitation, dismissed it out of hand. But then the next day, Digging Woman said, "I had a strange dream last night. I dreamt that my uncle came to visit us, then turned into smoke and went up the chimney. What do you think it means, husband?"

I lied and told her it probably meant nothing—that it was a silly dream, nothing more.

A week later I awoke once more, this time to find an Indian I did not know sitting in front of the fire in the same place Sitting Bull had occupied.

"Who are you?" I asked warily.

The strange Indian turned to look at me and smiled. Although his face was younger than I had ever seen it, his hair as dark as a raven's wing, I recognized my old mentor, Medicine Dog. "Do you not know me, Walking Wolf?"

"Grandfather!" I gasped. "You are younger than I ever knew you in life!"

The dead medicine man nodded. "It is the way of the Spirit World. The dead grow younger here, walking back through time, from elder to brave to boy. In time I will be so young I will not be born—then it will be my time to return to the land of the living, dressed in the flesh of a new life."

"Does this happen to all the dead—or just Comanche?"

"There are many spirits here, gathered in great herds like the buffalo. Many are from places strange to me when I was alive. It is most interesting. Eight Clouds Rising, your adopted father, is now no older than the son that sleeps by your side. He will be reborn as a temple dancer in someplace called Siam. Yellow Hair Custer is here, too. He is to be reborn as a sled dog in a place called Alaska."

"But why are you in my dreams, grandfather?"

"I am here to warn you."

"Of what?"

"I am not certain."

"Grandfather—does this have anything to do with the Ghost Dance?"

"In its way. The ritual you call the Ghost Dance is not what its disciples think it is. No dance, no matter how sacred, can ever hope to pull the dead back into the world of the living. We shall return, but only in the way I described to you. This dance, however, is more than capable of pulling the living into the land of the dead."

"Grandfather—what are you telling me?"

"The Ghost Dance has set a series of events in motion. Blood—rivers of blood—will be spilled in the next few days. But perhaps it can be averted if one thing is kept from happening."

"What is this thing?"

"The murder of Sitting Bull by his own people."

"Then it will never come to pass. No Sioux in their right mind would dare to raise a hand against Sitting Bull!"

Medicine Dog shook his head sadly. "The one called McLaughlin is awaiting word from his chiefs so he may have Sitting Bull arrested. Once he has approval, he will call his Indian Police to him and order them to Sitting Bull's camp."

"But what do you expect me to do—?"

Medicine Dog held up a hand for silence. He seemed to waver before my eyes like the reflection in a troubled pool. "I came to warn you—I spoke of the danger to your friends, but I have not finished. There is a darkness coming your way, Walking Wolf. A darkness familiar to you, yet still a stranger. Be wary, Walking Wolf, for the darkness would eat your soul."

"Grandfather, what is this darkness you speak of—?"

"My time here is over. I can say no more. Farewell, Walking Wolf." Medicine Dog's body was now as thin as a cloud on a hot summer's day. With a wave of his hands, he disappeared into himself.

⇒●⇐

I'm not proud of the fact I lied to Digging Woman the day I left. I told her I needed to go off on a vision quest. That I needed to be alone in the wilderness for a few days in order to commune with the Great Spirit. I knew if I told her I was on my way to prevent the murder of her uncle, she would have insisted on coming with me, and I feared that she and Wolf Legs would either be hurt or taken from me. It was not an irrational fear. I knew that if McLaughlin was desperate enough to go after Sitting Bull, anything might happen.

Still, ours was a special marriage, and it pained me to be deceitful—even when I had her best interests at heart. I do not know if she completely believed me—she had her own inner sight and visions, not all of which I was privy to. She was not happy with my leaving, considering the first of the punishing winter storms would soon strike the camp. I remember looking back at her and Wolf Legs standing in front of our cabin, watching me head into the mountains. They looked so small—almost like dolls. I lifted a hand in farewell and, after a moment, Digging Woman and Wolf Legs waved in return. For a moment I was overwhelmed with a surge of love for my wife and son that was so strong, so profound, it knocked the wind out of me. I came close to turning my pony around and heading back to camp right then, but for some reason I didn't.

I told myself I'd make it up to my wife and son when I got back.

It gets cold in the Dakotas early and hangs on like a pup to the teat. By the time I saddled up and headed for Sitting Bull's camp, most folks, Indian and white alike, had already settled in for the season, barricading themselves against the heavy snow storms and brutal sub-zero temperatures. But the winter of 1890 was far from normal, especially for the Sioux.

Still, I was astonished, on my second day out, to run across a band of Indians traversing the hostile winterscape. There were close to a hundred of them, shivering and starving as they trudged through the snow. I could tell with a glance that most of them had the fever.

The band's leader was none other than Big Foot, an elderly chief once respected for his wisdom but whose people had fallen on exceptionally hard times. Big Foot, wrapped in a trade-cloth blanket that was no replacement for the buffalo robes of old, seemed glad to see me. Although it was close to zero, he was sweating and his eyes burned.

"Greetings, Big Foot. Why are you away from your winter camp?"

"Have you not heard? Custer's old regiment has been brought in to punish the Sioux once and for all. They would wipe us out so we cannot perform the Ghost Dance one last time!"

"You're headed for the Stronghold?"

"My nephew, Kicking Bear, is there. He has promised not to start the last dance until I have joined him."

I looked at the rail-thin, fever-stricken men, women and children that comprised the band of pilgrims. Most clutched spears and stone axes, while fewer than a handful carried firearms. Even a blind man could see they were far from the warpath. "Big Foot, if you continue on your way, many of your number will perish."

"It does not matter. Come the dance, all shall be returned from the Spirit World."

I knew there was no point in arguing the point with the old man, so I rode on, leaving them to whatever fate they had dealt themselves.

It was December 15th when I made Sitting Bull's camp, the dim winter sun climbing toward noon. The sound of female voices raised in mourning struck me between the ribs as surely as an arrow. I had come too late.

A couple of crude huts still smoldered, and in front of Sitting Bull's lodge lay the bodies of several men, placed side by side, shoulder to shoulder. The women of the camp huddled nearby, rocking back and forth and weeping. Some of the women had cut off their braids and tossed them, like empty snake skins, at the feet of their slaughtered menfolk, while others rent their garments and slashed their bared breasts with knives and sharp rocks.

As I lowered myself from my horse, I realized I knew all of the dead men. I recognized Catch-the-Bear, Brave Thunder, Black Bird and Spotted Horn, all warriors I had fought alongside and hunted with during my years with the Sioux. One brave's face had been so savagely kicked in there was no way of identifying him—it wasn't until later that I discovered that it was Crowfoot, Sitting Bull's eldest son. But, to my relief, I did not see the medicine man's corpse on the ground.

I spotted an old Indian I had been friendly with in the days before Greasy Grass hovering at the edge of the mourning, his face so grief-stricken it seemed at first to lack all expression.

"Strikes-the-Kettle, my old friend, what has happened here? Where is Sitting Bull?"

Strikes-the-Kettle shook his head, passing a hand before his face as if to block some horrible image from his mind's eye. "Sitting Bull is dead."

"Dead? How?"

"Yesterday Shave Head of the Metal Breasts came to the camp to speak with Sitting Bull. Sitting Bull allowed him to share his lodge for the night. Then, just before dawn, Shave Head opened the door to the lodge for his friend Bullhead and the others. They had been hiding across the river the whole time, drinking whisky to make them brave. They had bluecoats with them. They had come to arrest Sitting Bull.

"Bullhead grabbed Sitting Bull and dragged him outside. But they were so noisy, everyone was awake and coming out of their lodges, angry that the Metal Breasts would try and do this thing to our chief. Catch-the-Bear pointed his rifle at Bullhead and told him to let go of Sitting Bull. Bullhead just laughed, so Catch-the-Bear shot him in the leg. Bullhead shot Sitting Bull in the left side as he fell down. Then Red Tomahawk shot Sitting Bull in the back. So I shot Shave Head and then shot Bullhead twice.

"In all the confusion Sitting Bull's horse—the one he was given by Cody—broke loose, sat back on its haunches and raised one hoof in salute. The Metal Breasts became scared then, thinking Sitting Bull's spirit was in the horse. That was when the bluecoats took charge, firing into the crowd, killing Catch-the-Bear, Black Bird and the others.

"Bullhead was bad hurt—dying—but he ordered the troopers to shoot Crowfoot in revenge. Red Tomahawk kicked Crowfoot's face in, then started hitting Sitting Bull's head with a neck yoke. The bluecoats and the Metal Breasts went crazy then, ransacking the camp and burning the lodges of those who dared stand against them.

"When they were finished, they loaded Sitting Bull's body onto a wagon, along with the bodies of the Metal Breasts. They said they were taking Sitting Bull back to the agency for burial."

"What of the *wotawe*, Sitting Bull's war medicine?" I asked, fearful that one of the drunken Indian police or troopers might have taken my old friend's most sacred personal possession as a trophy.

"It is safe," Strikes-the-Kettle assured me. "John, Sitting Bull's deaf-mute son, smuggled it out of the camp. That much we have been able to save."

"Strikes-the-Kettle, did they say *what* they were arresting Sitting Bull for?"

The old warrior shook his head, tears running down his seamed face. "Does it matter?"

⟫•◆•⟪

By rights, I should have turned my horse around and headed back home. I had failed in my mission—reaching my destination almost six hours too late. But, instead, I rode in the direction of the Pine Ridge Agency—a collection of trading posts, schools and office buildings clustered behind garrison walls.

The troopers guarding the entrance to the agency looked at me funny, but because I appeared white, they let me in. The first thing I saw was Sitting Bull's corpse, propped up in a crudely fashioned pine box in front of the blacksmith's. There was quite a crowd gathered there, composed mostly of the settlers who'd been called into the agency for protection against the "savages," and I had to shoulder my way to the front to get a look at my old friend's remains.

Sitting Bull's head had been reduced to a pulp, the jaw twisted so that it was positioned under his left ear. I counted at least seven bullet holes in his body. A sign was hung around his neck which read: *Sitting Bull: Killer of Custer & Enemy To All Americans.*

Tears of rage burned the back of my throat. I had to turn away to keep from losing control of myself. It would have been so easy—and so sweet—to simply cast aside my human skin and fall upon the killers of my friend. But

I knew there was nothing to be gained from such an action—unless it was my death. I had yet to die from a gunshot wound, but I wasn't sure if having an entire garrison shooting into my hide might not prove fatal.

One of the armed guards standing watch over Sitting Bull's pitiful remains was a member of the Indian Police—those who Strikes-the-Kettle had called "Metal Breasts." To my surprise, I recognized him as High Eagle, a Sioux warrior who had once followed Sitting Bull in the days before the surrender. The older Indian recognized me as well and shifted about uneasily, trying not to meet my eyes. I would not let him get away so easily.

"So, High Eagle," I said in the tongue of the Lakota. "Are you proud of the thing you have done today?"

High Eagle stiffened at my words and met my gaze. What I saw in his eyes as he spoke was sad and horribly aware. "We have killed our chief. What is there to be proud of?"

I did not bother to look at Sitting Bull's body again. I got on my horse and rode back out of the agency. What else was there for me to do but go home? I had no way of knowing that once word of Sitting Bull's assassination reached the Ghost Dancers, Kicking Bear would saddle up for war. Nor could I have known that in ten days' time Big Foot's band of starving, pneumonia-ridden pilgrims would meet their final, futile end on the banks of the Wounded Knee Creek. In any case, it would not have changed what I found when I got back to my own camp, several days later. At least, I like to tell myself that.

Chapter Eleven

It was colder than a politician's heart that winter. I'm not just talking about the amount of snowfall—which was sizable—but the harshness of the weather. As I rode across the Wyoming grasslands, where the buffalo had once roamed as thick as fleas on a hound's ear only a handful of years ago, an ice storm came whipping down out of the mountains. The ice froze to me almost immediately, and I was forced to shift into my true skin to keep from freezing to the saddle. As it was, my pony wasn't faring well. I was forced to find shelter and wait out the ice storm, huddled against my mount for warmth.

That night my dreams were full of Sitting Bull's ruined face and the sound of women wailing. But amidst my troubled slumbers, I thought I could hear a familiar voice calling my name. The voice was distant and feeble, as if the person was trying to yell over the howling of the winter storm. I struggled to identify the voice. And then, with a surge of fear, I realized who it was that was calling my name. It was Digging Woman.

I started awake, terror racing inside my gut like a live mouse. Something was wrong. Something was horribly, horribly wrong. My horse was close to dead, but I somehow got it to its feet and forced it on its way. Not much later it died, collapsing into the snow without so much as a whinny.

Although sore and frozen, I kept plowing on through the bitter cold, possessed by a desperate need to reach my wife and child that transcended all rational thought.

I finally reached camp on Christmas Day. The snows had relented, and the pale winter sun shone down on the place I had called home for almost to a decade. Even from a distance I could tell there was nothing left alive.

The humble two-room cabin my wife and I had first made, then raised, our son in was nothing but charcoal and snow-flecked soot. Although the barn was left standing, the corral was full of dead horses, all shot through the head.

I found what was left of my wife and child not far from the ruins of the house. I did not see them at first because they were covered with snow. I tried to cradle Digging Woman's body in my arms, but she was frozen to the ground.

Digging Woman was missing her eyes, tongue, nose, breasts and scalp. Wolf Legs was relatively untouched, except that he'd been skinned from knees to ankles. As if their mutilations were not humiliation enough, their attacker had pissed in their wounds.

I dug through the charred remains of my home until I located a kettle and took the axe from the barn and chopped a hole in the creek so I could draw water. I then built a fire, boiled the water and poured it over the bodies of my wife and child, although it still required my inhuman strength to pull them free of the cold, hard ground they had died on. It was impossible to move their limbs into anything resembling repose.

The Sioux—like most Indians—believed that physical indignity done to a dead body would be carried by that person into the Spirit World. The only way to right such a disgrace was cremation. I could not bear the idea of my poor Digging Woman and Wolf Legs going into the afterlife bearing such grievous injuries, but finding the fuel to build a suitable fire was impossible. The best I could do was to stash them in the hayloft of the barn, where the animals would not be able to get to them until after the thaw.

As I tended to my dead family, my face made rigid by a sheet of frozen tears, I did not have to ask myself who could have done such a cruel and heartless thing. I knew who was responsible for the death of my wife and child, even though I had no evidence to prove it. I'd known the identity of the culprit from the moment I woke with my wife's dying screams ringing in my inner ear. Their slayer was the one who had, forty-six years earlier, slaughtered my parents and left me an orphan, the same butcher who, twenty-nine years ago, killed my best friend. The destroyer of all I had ever loved and held dear to me wore the face of a man, but was a demon in disguise. A demon sent from the very bowels of Hell to make my life miserable. And the demon's name was Witchfinder Jones.

※

It wasn't hard for me to figure out where my quarry was headed. Even though he must have known I'd follow him, he made no effort to hide his tracks. He was moving high into the Bighorns, where the snows would be even heavier and the cold even more extreme. No one in their right mind would have dared set out under those conditions, into such hostile terrain, with close to no food, no horse and no gun. But I wasn't in my right mind— I was crazy. Crazy with grief. Crazy with hate. Crazy with guilt. All I could think of was how my wife and child must have suffered under that bastard's knife, and how I would find peace only after I'd torn the life from his body the same way he'd tortured my wife—slow, mean and evil.

I cut strips of meat from the horses he'd butchered, knowing in advance I was not apt to find much in the way of game so late in the season. I did not know if I could starve to death, but I was unwilling to weaken myself. I wanted my strength when the time came for me to send Witchfinder Jones back to Hell.

He had at least a two-day head start, and he was on horseback, but I did not let this discourage me. I had stalked Apache as a barefoot boy, tracked renegade Pawnee as a Sioux brave. I was not about to let a blizzard keep me from finding the man responsible for the murder of my family.

I struggled along the snow-choked mountain passes for more than three days, trying my best to ignore the frigid winds that bit into my flesh like a whipsaw. During that time, my mind closed inward and began feeding on itself. I could see Witchfinder Jones, unchanged from our last meeting, grinning maliciously as he gouged Digging Woman's eyes from her head with his silver buck knife. But part of me knew that couldn't be right. It had been almost thirty years since I'd last run across Jones. And, assuming he'd been a young man when he disposed of my parents, he'd have to be well into his sixties by now. Granted, Jones had been an impressive physical specimen, considering he'd lived through having his skull cracked open like a walnut, but he was only human, after all. But, surely, my dreaded personal demon was an old man by now.

I did not know what I had done to attract this human monster's ill will, but he had been the bane of my existence from its very beginning. He was the bloody-handed architect who had set my feet on the strange and twisting path I had walked since the day Eight Clouds Rising found a squalling baby hidden inside a frontier smokehouse. By killing my natural parents, Jones robbed me of self-knowledge and my heritage as a *vargr*, and now, by slaughtering my family, he had squashed what chances I had of being a loving husband and doting father. Without my family to give me purpose and to make me whole, he had reduced me to the level of a beast. If he wanted to turn me into an animal, I would be happy to oblige. Stripped of mercy, hope and love, I stalked my prey through the mountain wilderness with no thought in mind save to taste my enemy's blood.

I spotted the cabin on the fourth day out. I knew I was getting close when I found Jones's horse—frozen stiffer than a missionary's dick—the day before.

I knew the cabin to be the property of a mountain man who went by the name Clubfoot Charley. I'd traded with him a few times over the years and found him a decent sort, if given to the eccentricity common to whites living alone in the wilderness. There was a thin plume of smoke rising from the chimney, and I hoped Charley had chosen to ride the winter out in one of his cabins on the lower slope instead of staying put to mind his traps. There was no point in sneaking up on the cabin. I was expected.

I opened the door without knocking. The heat from the potbelly stove struck me like a invisible hand, making my frostbitten ears feel as if I were wearing red-hot coals for earmuffs. The smell of cooking stew wafted from a bubbling pot atop the stove. Seated at a crude table next to the stove were two men. Both were big and burly and sported beards, but there was no mistaking Witchfinder Jones.

Although I knew he had to be well into his sixties, there was only the lightest hint of silver in his heavy beard and long, matted hair. A large, puckered scar ran along his left brow. It looked as if someone had roughly shoved the split halves of his skull together and saddle-stitched them shut. His left eye was white as an egg, the pupil gone cloudy, but outside of that he was little changed from the first time I saw him, twenty-nine years ago. He was even dressed the same, down to the wolf-skin shirt that had once been my father.

"Howdy, Billy," Jones said. "Long time, no see. You'll have to pardon by dinner companion," he gestured with his spoon. Clubfoot Charley was stripped naked to the waist, his head thrown back, mouth and eyes wide open. If that didn't tell me he was dead, the gaping hole in his chest sure did. Most of his right breast had been carved away, revealing the ribs beneath. "He wasn't one for the social graces, even when alive. Besides, you've got me at a disadvantage, brother," Jones smiled, spooning a mouthful of stew into his maw. "I'm in the middle of dinner."

Despite all the hours I'd spent fantasizing about what I'd do to my enemy once I caught up with him, I found myself at something of a loss. I had expected to find Charley dead, but I certainly hadn't reckoned on Jones eating him.

"You look confused, Billy," Jones chuckled. "Close the door and pull up a seat, brother."

"I no longer call myself Billy. And I'm not your brother, murderer."

"Oh, but you *are*, Billy. We're as much kin as Cain and Abel. Or haven't you figured that out yet?"

Jones seemed intent on distracting me, toying with me. But I was determined to have none of it. "I've come to kill you, you murdererin' filth, for what you done to my family!"

Witchfinder smiled a slow, nasty smile that made me want to rip it off his face. "Which family would that be, Billy? The squaw and her half-breed cub, or the werewolf settler and his human bitch?"

"You know me, then?"

"Aye, I knew you from the moment I laid eyes on you in McCarthy's cabin, all those years ago. Just as you knew your sire's pelt and your dame's teat. Blood knows blood, brother. There's no denying it."

"Stop callin' me brother! I ain't your brother!" I snarled, bringing my fist down hard on the table. Coarse grayish silver hair sprouted across the backs of my hands and up my arms as my teeth grew longer. "You killed my brother over forty years ago!"

"That boy wasn't your brother," Jones said, his voice completely serious. "He was a servant Howler brought over from the Old Country. In a year or two he would have undergone the induction ceremony and been ritually castrated, like all human males must be if they are to serve the pack. Remember Poilu's brace of eunuchs?

"I guess you want to know why I've done all this—why I skinned your sire, why I torched your home and killed you wife and child. It was on account of what your sire did to my mother—and to me." Jones leaned back in his chair and stroked his shirt like he would a pet, fixing me with his good eye. "How old do you think I am?"

"I don't know—sixty-five, perhaps. Although you don't look no older than forty."

"I'll be eighty-seven come next July."

"That's bullshit!"

Jones smiled again, and this time when he spoke, he allowed the accent I had first heard in his voice, years ago, to come to the fore. "It started in a country called Rumania. My mother was a beautiful young woman of gypsy blood. Her people had long known, feared, and, in some cases, served the wolf lords and bitch queens of the *vargr*. When a handsome and influential *vargr* noble decided to take her as a brood mare, she chose to look upon it as an honor, not a disgrace. "For the first few years, our family was happy enough. My sire kept us in high style, in an isolated chateau, with servants to wait on us hand and foot. I did not see him much, as he spent most of his time at the Bitch Queen's floating courts in Paris and Vienna. But, during the brief periods when he was at home, he was a proud, if somewhat aloof, figure I worshipped from afar. Then, on my twelfth birthday, my sire took me to Paris, where I was presented to the Bitch Queen.

"She was indeed a *grand dame*, dressed in lace and expensive silks, her hair fixed with ribbons and smelling of perfume. She looked the same age as my mother, even though I knew she was older than the kingdoms of Europe. I was so intimidated by her high manner that I could do no more than tremble. As my sire pushed me forward, her eyes widened. She sniffed the air about me like a hound scenting a blooded animal. The smile on her face faded and grew cold.

"She turned to my sire and said, 'You have not bred true, Howler. The whelp is *esau*.'

"I'll never forget the look my sire gave me that day. The pride and hope that had been in his eyes a moment before was suddenly gone, replaced by a loathing that stung as surely as if he'd swatted me with a bundle of nettles. It was as if I had done something so terrible, so disgusting, that it had curdled what love he ever had for me. And I had no idea what it was that I had done to earn my sire's hatred.

"I had been judged *esau*. Although sired by a *vargr*, the human blood in me was too strong. While I might possess the instincts, the needs and the hunger of a true-born *vargr*, I would never shapeshift. Because of that, I could never be one of the pack. No matter what I did, I would never be accepted as *vargr*. And, as such, I was useless to my sire. I was imperfect—a genetic freak—a mongrel of the worst sort.

"My sire no longer had any use for me or my mother, who had yet to produce any more live issue, although she'd endured several painful pregnancies and miscarriages over the years. My sire turned us out of the chateau that had been my home since my earliest memory with nothing more than the clothes on our backs.

"My mother, no longer young and made unattractive by her failed pregnancies, tried to go back to her people. They would have nothing to do with her, as she had willingly consorted with an unholy thing. They were especially hostile to me, since I bore the Mark of Beast." Jones gestured to his thick eyebrows and hairy palms.

"My mother was never a strong woman, and the years spent pampered did not prepare her for such cruelty. Cast aside by my sire and shunned by her own people, it was not long before my mother lost her mind completely.

"She began to believe that she was, indeed, the devil's mistress and began threatening the local villagers, demanding tribute in the form of food or money, or she would put the Evil Eye on them. It worked at first. But, in her madness, she eventually went too far with her demands. The townspeople stopped being frightened and began to get angry. A year after my sire turned us out, she was accused of being a witch and hanged at the crossroads of a village in Transylvania. I would have died with her as well, but I somehow managed to escape the mob. "It was then I decided to vent my rage on the unnatural world. To become a witchfinder-for-hire, if you will. Vampires, werewolves and ghouls held no horror for one such as me.

"I might be incapable of shapeshifting, but I am a *vargr* born." He rapped his chest with a clenched fist. "I was raised savoring the taste of human flesh. I was taught to see humans as cattle to be herded and culled. And then, after all that, my sire cast me aside—hurled me in with the cattle and ignored my pleas for help and guidance!

"The blood of the wolf lords runs strong in my veins. I do not age like mortal men—or even other *esau*. And I have suffered wounds that would have killed a normal human three times over." Jones leaned forward, his single eye gleaming in the dim light of the cabin like a polished stone. "And I swore that one day I would make my sire pay for the cruelty he had shown my mother. And I made good on that oath the spring of 1844, when I tracked him and his latest brood mare to the wilds of Texas. It wasn't hard. He'd been preying on a few of the Spanish ranchers in the area. They were more than ready to believe it was the work of *lobo hombre*, especially if it happened to be a gringo.

"Howler thought he could come to this country and lose himself, escape his past. I made the bastard pay. Pay with his hide. Pay with his woman. He would have paid with his son, but I somehow managed to overlook you that day. But, in a way, I have taken as much pleasure in tormenting you, younger brother, as I did in skinning our sire alive."

"Why? What harm have I ever done you that would justify what you did to my wife and child?"

The sardonic smile disappeared from Jones's face. "What have you done? You have friends. You have family. You have people who love you and admire you. Me, I've never had a friend in my life. I'm too much of an outsider—normal humans can tell I'm trouble just by looking at me. And as for women—I can't get it up unless I hurt 'em, or worse. The way I see it, if I can't have what you got—I'll make sure you can't have it, either."

As I listened to this failed monster drone on and on about the unfairness of his life, the rage I'd harbored for so many years stirred deep in my gut, twisting like a knife.

"Is that *it*?" I hissed. "Is that the sole reason you slaughtered my family like you would a buffalo cow and her calf? Because you're jealous of me?"

"You're seeing this all wrong, brother. Things like us, we aren't meant to be husbands and fathers. Besides, I did you a favor. That whelp of yours was *esau*. He must have been, sporting all that hair. He wouldn't have amounted to much." Jones picked up the empty tin plate in front of Clubfoot Charley and went to the stove, ladling brown, savory stew onto it. I was salivating despite myself. Jones set the plate down on the table and pushed it in my direction.

"Here, to show you I don't mean you any ill will, I'll share my grub with you. You must be hungry after all this time...."

I was starving. And I don't mean it figuratively. The initial adrenalin rush from confronting Witchfinder Jones had blunted my hunger, but now the smell of the stew was making my gut rumble and my mouth fill with water. Without even thinking, I reached out and drew the plate toward me. There was something peculiar amongst the lumps of meat, carrots, potatoes and onions.

It was an eye.

My wife's eye.

"What's the matter, Billy?" Jones leered at me from his side of the table. "She was good enough for you live—ain't she good enough for you dead?"

Walking Wolf
283

With a single roar of anger, I overturned the table. My roar grew longer, higher. It became a howl as the knot of hatred and rage and guilt inside me unraveled, wrapping my body in the painful joy of the change. Witchfinder Jones was on his feet, his revolver free of its holster. Even though I knew it was loaded with silver bullets, I did not care. It did not matter to me if I died in that lonely, snowbound mountain cabin. What did I have to live for, anyway? My wife and child were dead. My friends were dead. All I had known as a boy had been swept away in a cloud of gun smoke, dust and lies. I had nothing to lose. And all I wanted in the world at that precise moment was to tear my half-brother to shreds with my bare hands.

The first shot went wild. The second one went through my right side, just above the hip. The pain was immense, but such things no longer mattered to me. When I struck Witchfinder, it was like running into a solid wall of muscle and bone. I had never experienced anything like it before, and I'd brought down grown buffalo in my time.

He seemed surprised that I was still on my feet, so I used his confusion to my advantage, digging my talons into his wrist, forcing him to let go of the gun. Swearing in a language I did not know, he grabbed for the knife sheath on his belt. I leapt back just in time to see the silver blade cut an arc through the air where my throat had been only a second earlier.

"I don't know why those silver bullets didn't drop you, and I don't care! I'm going to take real pleasure in gutting you, brother," he snarled through bloodied lips. "I think I'll turn you into a pair of boots. Maybe a nice fur hat."

"Go ahead and kill me," I replied. "I don't care if I die. But I'm going to drag you to hell by the scruff of the neck like the sorry half-breed cur you are!"

Witchfinder's face crumpled inward, as if I'd somehow dealt him a painful blow. He bellowed like an angered bull and charged me, knocking me backward into the potbelly stove. The stove tipped backwards, disconnecting from the flue and scattering red-hot embers in every direction. Clubfoot Charley's cabin was small and cluttered. Within moments, the cabin was ablaze.

Witchfinder came at me with the knife again, roaring wordlessly. His face was distorted by a bloodlust that was beyond anything I had ever seen in a human. He was in the grip of a fearsome animal rage that knew no mercy, gave no quarter. And that suited me just fine.

We circled one another in the middle of the burning cabin, growling like wild beasts, looking for the first sign of weakness in order to attack. Jones made the first move, lunging at me with his knife. I surged forward to meet him, grabbing his hand and twisting it one hundred and eighty degrees while driving the talons of my other hand into his face.

Jones screamed as his forearm shattered like a green branch. He dropped to his knees, his face a mess of blood and lacerations. His dead eye lay against his cheek like a limp dick. I twisted his arm again, turning it almost completely around in its socket.

"You're real good at killin' when you've got yourself up a posse of Mexicans or Mormons or whoever the hell you can talk into hirin' you, ain't you? And you're real good at killin' from a distance—or butcherin' helpless women and children. But when it comes to fightin' one on one with a full-blooded *vargr*, you ain't nothin' but a sorry sack of shit! Our father was right to shun you—you're nothing but a mad dog!"

Witchfinder looked up at me with his remaining eye and spat a bloody wad of saliva that struck me square on the chest. "I'm just like you, Billy—except I wear the same skin all the time!"

Just then Jones went for his fallen knife with his good hand, but he was too slow. I snatched it up and plunged it up to the hilt in his empty eye socket, twisting it a full turn. Although this would have killed a normal human right on the spot, Jones's *vargr* heritage gave him the strength to lurch to his feet, clawing at the hilt jutting out of his head. He knocked me down as he blundered blindly around the burning cabin, screaming at the top of his lungs.

As I moved to tackle him and tear out his throat, there was a loud sound and the roof collapsed, burying me under burning rafters and a ton of snow.

<hr />

I'm uncertain as to how long I remained buried under the remains of Clubfoot Charley's cabin. While I was unconscious I was visited by a number of friends and family, all of them dead. First there was Sitting Bull, who looked in far better shape than when I last saw him. He was traveling in the company of Medicine Dog. I really wasn't surprised they'd hit it off in the Spirit World.

"Medicine Dog told me of how you tried to help me," my friend said. "Perhaps you could have changed things. Perhaps not. I appreciate your effort, though."

"Am I dead, uncle?"

"No. Not for good, anyway."

Someone touched Sitting Bull on the shoulder and he moved aside, allowing them to come forward. It was Digging Woman. Beside her stood our children, Small Wolf and Wolf Legs, holding hands. Although Small Wolf was the elder of the two, he looked to be half his younger brother's age.

"I bring you a gift, my husband," she smiled, lifting her right hand. Six glittering silver bullets fell onto the snow. "While you confronted my killer, I used my spirit to exchange his bullets with those of common lead."

I struggled to speak, but every breath I took made my ribcage feel as if it were trapped in a vise. "Digging Woman—I'm sorry—I'm sorry I wasn't there to protect you—to save you—I failed you—"

"That is true. But I still love you, Walking Wolf." She reached out to smooth my pelt, as she had often done as we lay curled together under our buffalo robes. Her hand had no weight and passed through me, making my skin tingle the way a leg does when it falls asleep. "I must go, my husband."

"Don't go—stay—stay with me—don't leave me alone—"

Digging Woman smiled and suddenly she was as young as when we first met. "I will love you forever, Walking Wolf. In this life—and all that follow."

"Digging Woman—no—" I raised my hand in a feeble attempt to grab her ghost and make her stay, but it was no use. She was gone. In her place were two shadowy, indistinct figures that moved just outside my field of vision. One stood upright while the other seemed almost to move on all fours. They seemed uncertain—hesitant—then one that stood upright stepped forward, kneeling beside me. It was a woman, her hair the color of gold, her scent warm and familiar. I lifted my head and tried to get a better look, but her features remained fuzzy and indistinct.

"Mama?"

The second figure made a snuffling noise and my mother reluctantly pulled away, following my father into the dim haze of the afterlife.

When I woke up, it was to the sound of something digging at the snow covering me. I was pinned under a charred rafter, my pelt was scorched, I had more broken ribs than whole ones, and there was a bullet in my hip. But outside of those injuries, I was relatively unscathed. Opening my eyes, I found myself muzzle to muzzle with a lone timber wolf. When I groaned and moved, it danced away, watching we warily from a safe distance as I climbed out of my frozen tomb. The timber wolf, recognizing me as being an unnatural thing, quickly quit the scene.

After extricating myself, I started digging out the ruins of the cabin. I did not find Witchfinder Jones's body, nor did I find the shirt made of our father's pelt. However, I did manage to locate the tobacco pouch that had once been my mother's left teat. I also found six silver bullets laid side by side in the snow.

Epilogue

I took what was left of my ma and, come the spring thaw, I cremated it along with Digging Woman and Wolf Legs. I spent the rest of that winter in my true skin, fending for myself as best I could, shunning all company, human or otherwise. During that long, cold, lonesome season I traveled so deep into grief and madness I came out the other side. The world I once knew no longer existed. Hell, it'd begun to disappear long before Sitting Bull's murder. In many ways, I had still been innocent—if not in deed, then at least in spirit. But after Digging Woman's death, I was a changed man. Or werewolf, if you will.

Once I saw to it my loved ones got a proper sendoff into the Spirit World, I left that part of the country for good. With my friends and family dead, there was no reason for me to hang around, so I struck out west. I eventually made my way to California and settled in the San Fernando Valley. Truth to tell, I own a good chunk of it, under various names and holding companies. No one would ever guess my wealth by looking at me or my house. I live modestly—some would even say austerely. I've discovered that it pays to keep a low profile when one does not appear to age. But, then, the area's penchant for plastic surgery has provided me with camouflage for the last few decades.

I stand still as the years race past, like a rock in the middle of a swift-running stream. I have seen fortunes made and lost—dynasties rise and fall.

I've watched the white man's magic expand beyond all known boundaries. Electricity. Antibiotics. Moon flights. Genetic engineering. Atomic energy. Indoor plumbing. I still don't trust them, of course. They're all still crazy. Maybe even crazier than before.

As for other *vargr*... I have made it a point to avoid them. They suffer from the same madness that afflicts the whites. Not surprising, considering they are from the same world.

As for Witchfinder Jones, I do not doubt that my elder brother survived the battle in Clubfoot Charley's cabin. If he'd crawled away to die, I would have found him. Although it's hard to imagine anyone taking such a wound and surviving, my brother is a uniquely tough individual. As much as I still hate his guts, I can't deny him that.

I suspect he managed to hole up somewhere after the fight and nurse himself back to health. But what would have been left of him after having his frontal lobes chopped into mincemeat? Is he able to remember who he is or—more importantly—*what* he is? Is he still an infernal engine of retribution, hunting down the monsters he so envies? Or is he drooling in his beard on a street corner somewhere, destined to an eternity of selling pencils?

Or is he finally at peace with himself, settled down with a family of his own?

It's been one hundred and five years since we last met. I have yet to catch a sign of him, although I have had ample opportunity to witness the atrocities of others of his misbegotten clan. Hitler, Manson, Dahmer, Rifkin... This century has been rife with the bloody misdeeds of the *esau*. And even though I have not seen or heard of him in over a century, I still keep an ear cocked for the sound of his tread on my porch. Creatures such as my brother do not give up the hunt lightly. Nor do they forgive.

Maybe its time I went out looking for him. Sitting down and writing out all the things that happened to me as a boy has made me nostalgic for the open spaces I once knew. It's been a long time since I wandered the countryside as I did as a youth. Digging Woman's newest incarnation is only six years old. It'll be another fifteen or twenty years before I can properly reintroduce myself to my wife. (We've been married twice since her death in 1890.) I've got the time, the opportunity and the money to wander if I like. Yes, the more I think about it, the more I like it. It is time for Walking Wolf to stride the plains again.

What will I do if I find my long-lost brother, you ask?

Will I forgive him his trespasses and embrace him as my only living kin? Or will I show him the same mercy he gave my wife and child? And there *is* the matter of our father's pelt to be resolved. So, what will I do?

I ask you, dear reader—am I my brother's keeper?

The Tortuga Hill Gang's Last Ride

Maybe you heard of me. I used to be famous, in a roundabout fashion. But that was a long time ago, and the missus don't like me talking 'bout the old days, so's most folks hereabouts don't know I was ever anything but a dry goods merchant who come West for his health.

I used to be known as Coyote Pete, and I rode with the Tortuga Hill Gang from '87 to '91. My Christian name was Pete McGonagall, but that don't have much of a ring to it, outlaw-wise. Hard to believe that was fifty years ago.

I can tell you're disappointed. Bet you was expecting me to up and say I was Butch Cassidy or Jesse James, weren't you? Well, I knew them boys. Knew 'em a sight better than those fancy-ass city slickers that wrote dime novels, that's for damn sure. I should know 'bout them fool books, since there was a few 'bout the Tortuga Hill Gang. There was even one 'bout me in particular: *Coyote Pete: Six Gun Devil,* as I recollect. The missus made me throw out the copy I had long time back. It was nothing but silly-ass lies and made-up stories. Weren't no truth in it at all. There 'specially weren't no truth in *The Tortuga Hill Gang's Last Ride,* which was supposed to tell about what happened to us and why we disappeared all of a sudden. If you want to know the real truth, I'll tell it to you. And it's a damn sight stranger than anything you'd find in any dime novel, believe you me.

The Tortuga Hill Gang's Last Ride

You might not have heard, but the Tortuga Hill Gang was fairly well known in those days. There was me, Black Hat Johnson, the Chandler brothers—Caleb and Davey—and Horseflesh Donnigan. Black Hat was the bossman, seeing how he could bite the head off a rattler with his bare teeth. Not a nice feller, if you get my drift. The Chandler brothers was twins, as identical as peas in a pod; they was fond of romancing the same dance hall girl without letting on there was two of 'em until they got her alone where it was dark. Horseflesh was an Irishman, and he had an Irishman's way with horses. He could sweet-talk a prize stallion out of a corral as pretty as you please.

Me, my specialty was shooting.

We rustled cattle, knocked over a few banks, held up a couple of stages—you know, the usual business. We'd raised enough of a stink for the authorities to put bounties on our heads, but that weren't unusual back then. Most outlaws went out of their way to earn themselves a bounty.

Anyways, we used to hole up 'round Tortuga Hill, near the Rio Grande, when things got too hot. It was kind of an open secret, as you could tell by our handle, but no lawman or bounty hunter was ever fool enough to follow us there. I reckon that's why we was so surprised when Little Red showed up, literally, on our door step.

Me, Black Hat and Horseflesh was playing cards in the cabin when we hear what sounds like someone on the porch. Now, we know the Chandler brothers are out keepin' guard, supposedly watching the mouth of the canyon to make sure we don't get any unwanted visitors.

Black Hat stands up real slow and quiet, motioning for me and Horseflesh to do the same. I take my rifle and sneak over to the widow, careful not to disturb the gunnysack curtain, while Horseflesh eases out the back way with his pistol. Black Hat moves behind the door. I don't know what we was expecting; maybe the cavalry to come busting in, six-guns a-blazing like they do in the moving picture shows nowadays. But we sure as hell weren't expecting whoever it was creeping 'bout on our front porch to knock.

Black Hat looks at me funny and I shrug, but neither of us puts down our weapons. Then I hear Horseflesh yelling from around the corner of the house, "Git yer hands up where's I can see 'em!" Then I hear him swear. Black Hat opens the door and goes outside, 'cause whenever Horseflesh started swearing, that meant the danger was over.

Standing on the porch was one of the biggest galoots I'd ever laid eyes on. He must have been six-eight, if he stood an inch. Black Hat was far from puny hisself, but he looked like a 98-pound weakling standing next to this feller! His chest looked like it had barrel staves for ribs, and since his hands were locked behind his head, I could see his upper arm was as big around as a girl's thigh. He was dressed in a set of peculiar buckskin drawers and a homespun shirt that was big enough to fit both the Chandler brothers. He had a head full of copper red hair that stuck out like porcupine quills and two of the biggest, bluest eyes I've ever seen.

The stranger looked down at Black Hat and smiled real friendlylike, as if he was happy to see him. That's when I pegged the feller for simple. Nobody but nobody in his right mind would have been happy to see Black Hat.

"You're Black Hat Johnson, ain't you?"

"Yeah, what of it? You looking for me?"

The redheaded giant nodded, his smile growing wider. "I run away from home."

Black Hat blinked. "You what?"

"I run off from home so's I could join up with your gang!"

We all exchanged looks, and I saw Horseflesh roll his eyes.

"How'd you come to find out about us?" Black Hat growled.

The giant's grin grew wider and he dropped his hands, reaching into the waistband of his pants, oblivious to the fact that we were ready to ventilate him seven ways to Sunday. He pulled a rolled-up dime novel out from under his shirt. It looked tiny in his hands, like one of them children's bibles. It had been read so many times the pages were falling out. On the front it was printed *The Tortuga Hill Gang Rides Again*. He held it out to Black Hat with this worshipful look on his face. Black Hat glanced at the cover, trying not to let on he couldn't read, then back at the giant.

"You read this, huh?"

"Yes, sir, Mr. Black Hat."

Horseflesh sniggered and Black Hat shot him a look. "What makes you think we're looking for someone? We're not in the market for a hired hand."

"I can help! Really I can! I can help you hold up stages and rob banks and all kinds of things!"

I could tell that Black Hat was getting a kick out of having this huge, strapping oaf fawning all over him. That's how Black Hat turned. He was a great one for tormenting things weaker than him.

"Well, I don't know...." Black Hat scratched his beard and tried to look thoughtful. "If you want to ride with us, then I'll have to put you to some kind of test." He snapped his fingers and smiled real nastylike, as if an idea had just come to him. "I know! Why don't you try and take Coyote Pete's gun away from him? You got to stand twenty feet from one another, and Pete'll be trying to shoot you! That sound fair?"

"Now wait a minute, Johnson—" I began.

"I weren't talking to you, Pete! I was talking to our friend here—what you'd say your name was, son?"

"I'm named same as my daddy. My folks call me Little Red."

I knew better than to talk back to Black Hat, less I wanted to get myself a new bellybutton. Still, I didn't cotton to shooting some poor simpleton in cold blood just so's Johnson could have himself a good laugh.

We moved out into the sunlight, away from the cabin. Horseflesh was looking kind of queer, watching Little Red the same way a chicken watches a fox on the other side of the fence. Black Hat was grinning to beat the band, ready to have him some fun.

"On the count of three! One—two—three!"

I shouldered my rifle, hoping I wouldn't have to shoot the fool. Maybe I could get away with putting the stock in his teeth. That would be hurtful enough to satisfy Johnson's sense of humor without killin' the dummy. But it never got that far. It was as if someone slung an invisible lariat 'round the rifle's muzzle and jerked it out of my hands. I heard Horseflesh gasp and Black Hat swear a blue streak. The next thing I know, my rifle was suspended in midair, between me and Little Red. The giant laughed and clapped his hands, like a little kid pleased with hisself, and the rifle started to spin like a bottle on its side.

"Jesus, Mary and Joseph!" Horseflesh crossed hisself and looked like he swallowed his chaw.

Black Hat don't say a thing; he just stood there, his eyes all bugged out, watching my rifle spin like a crazy compass needle. Finally he gets enough presence of mind to tell Little Red "whoa." When the rifle fell in the dirt, I could see the barrel had been tied into a bowknot. It was my favorite shooting iron, but I couldn't bring myself to get riled up about it.

Black Hat looked at what was left of my rifle, then at Little Red. "Son, you're in."

Little Red was real pleased with hisself. "You really mean it? I'm really a member of the Tortuga Hill Gang?"

"Well and true. Here, why don't you let Pete show you where to bunk?"

I lead Little Red to the ramshackle barn where we kept the horses and me and Horseflesh bunked in the loft.

"I'm sorry 'bout your gun, Mr. Coyote Pete."

I looked up into his sky blue eyes and I could tell he honestly did feel sorry. I wasn't sure how I felt about this big, strange man, but I didn't fear him—least not the way I was scared of Black Hat. Little Red easily made three of me and could have broke me cross his knee like so much kindling, but I could tell he lacked the viciousness that made Johnson a dangerous man to cross.

"That's okay. You can call me Pete. Most folks do."

"Okay, Mr. Coyo— Pete."

While I was showing him where he could stow his belongings, I took the opportunity to get a real good look at Little Red. Up close, he looked even stranger than I'd realized. At first, all you saw when you looked at him was his size. But once you got used to that, you noticed the little, weirder things, like how his ears was pointed, and that he didn't wear shoes because his toe nails seemed to curve like a bird's, and how his back was kind of hunched. I also noticed that the horses nickered and whinnied when he walked into the barn, only settling down after he'd whispered something under his breath.

Little Red said he was tired and wanted to get some rest, so I left him to bed down in a pile of clean straw and hurried back to the cabin. The Chandler Brothers were there, and I could hear Black Hat chewing them new assholes for letting Little Red slip by.

Caleb and Davey was both blushing to their roots, and I could tell what Johnson said had stuck in their craw. If I didn't step in, I knew they'd lose their tempers and call Black Hat out. We didn't need that kind of infighting right then.

"We're telling you, Johnson, we didn't let anyone by us! If there was someone in the canyon, we'd have known about it and settled it!" Caleb snapped. Being the elder of the two, he always talked first.

"Well he sure as shit got in somehow! You can't tell me you didn't see him—the bastard's big as a house!"

The muscles in Davey's jaws twitched. "You calling us liars?"

I held up my hands for silence. "It don't matter *how* he got here! The fact of the matter is he's here. Now what are we gonna do with him?"

"I say we burn him at the stake." Horseflesh had his worry beads out and was fingering them like crazy.

"What? And pass up an opportunity as golden as this?"

"Are you daft, man? He's not natural! I could tell it the minute he stood in daylight! He's one of the *Sidhe*, I'm telling you!"

"I thought leprechauns was little green men that sat on pots of gold," chided Black Hat.

"Go ahead and laugh! But there's no denying that *whatever* he is, he ain't right!"

"I don't care *what* he is," Johnson sneered in reply. "He could be a shaved go-rilla for all I care! The thing is, we can use him! You saw what he did with Pete's rifle! Imagine what he could do with a safe!"

"You're flirting with damnation, Percy Lafayette Johnson!"

I held my breath as Horseflesh spoke Black Hat's Christian name. Sure enough, Johnson spun 'round and put his boot between the Irishman's eyes.

"You'll be counting your teeth instead of them beads, next time you mouth off! Little Red's in, and that's that!"

As you might guess, Black Hat wasn't big on the democratic process.

Our first job after Little Red joined up was a stage outside El Paso. We rode out to meet it—all of us, that is, except Little Red. He ran alongside, his tongue hanging out like a dog's, sweat lathering on him just like a horse. When we got to the spot we'd picked for the ambush, Black Hat whispered something to Little Red, who grinned and nodded.

We heard the stage before we saw it, the rattle of harness, hooves and wagon wheels growing louder with every second. I pulled my bandanna up over my nose, more to keep from getting a mouthful of dust than to protect my identity. As the stage came into sight, and I could make out the Wells Fargo man riding shotgun, cradling his piece in his arms like a baby.

Suddenly, the shotgun leapt from the guard's grip, just like someone had yanked it out of his hand. He stared at it, open mouthed, for a second as it hovered over his head. I saw him reach over and grab the driver's shoulder. The poor bastard probably thought he was dreaming. Then the shotgun spun around and let him have it with both barrels. The guard's face disappeared like it'd never been there, and he flipped backward off the stage onto the road.

The driver, having seen the guard murdered by his own shotgun, decided he better get the hell out of Dodge, so to speak. He started laying into the horses with his whip, and I thought we'd lose them for sure. But I hadn't counted on Little Red. He broke away from his place beside Black Hat and started running after the stage. And damn if he didn't pace them without breaking a sweat! The stagecoach driver tried hitting him with his whip, but Little Red didn't pay him no never-mind. Instead, he got even with the lead horse and, I swear, whispered something in its ear. The horse made this weird screaming sound and turned, sending the stage into a roll. I saw the look of shock on the driver's face just before he was crushed.

That's when we rode up, nice as you please, without firing a shot. There weren't nobody but a destitute corset salesman inside the coach. Black Hat being Black Hat, he shot the feller in the leg for not being more prosperous. But the payroll in the lockbox made up for the slim pickings in the passenger compartment.

The Chandler brothers moved to shoot the lock off the strongbox, but Black Hat waved them aside. He looked at Little Red.

"Reckon you can handle that, boy?"

"Sure, Mr. Black Hat!"

"Go to it, then," he said, folding his hands over the horn of his saddle.

Little Red frowned at the strongbox for a couple of seconds, then it shot straight up and hovered about ten feet in the air.

Black Hat nodded his approval. "Well now, let's git while the gittin's good!"

We rode back to our hideout, the strongbox bobbing along behind us like a toy balloon.

Despite our success, Little Red didn't sit well with the others in the gang. The Chandler brothers didn't like the idea of being made redundant by a simpleminded freak, while Horseflesh disapproved of him on general principles. Me, I didn't have nothing against Little Red, and I was the only one willing to bunk with him. Horseflesh moved into the cabin with Black Hat and the Chandler Brothers, even though the reason he was in the barn in the first place was on account of Black Hat's farting in his sleep and the Chandler brothers' snoring.

Sometimes I'd get to asking Little Red about his folks. He didn't say much about them, except they was from "the Old Country," and that his pappy could sing up a storm, or something 'long those lines.

Anyways, we did a couple more jobs with Little Red. One was this assay office we knocked over where Little Red lifted the safe out from behind the desk. It must have been pretty tough, even for him, 'cause just before we got back to Tortuga Hill, the damn thing began to wobble something fierce then fell smack-dab on Horseflesh's right foot— crushed the sucker to a bloody pulp. Little Red got all upset and started to blubber like a baby and kept apologizing to "Mr. Horseflesh."

The thing was, although Horseflesh had done everything but spit in his face, Little Red was fond of the damn horse thief!

Horseflesh tried to nurse his foot with a couple bottles of Old Panther and a tin full of opium tablets, but he ended up with gangrene. Black Hat offered to chop it off, but Horseflesh was pretty much out of his mind by then, raving about leprechauns and boogey men, and how if his foot was chopped off it had to be baptized and buried proper so it'd be there to meet him in Heaven.

Little Red, like I said, was all torn up over what happened, and spent most of his time sitting next to Horseflesh's sickbed, trying to get him to take some soup. Horseflesh would drift in and out of his fever, babbling about monsters and such like, and occasionally he'd come to his senses and find Little Red hovering over him, and he'd start shaking and praying in Irish gibberish all over again, his eyes rolling in their sockets like greased ball bearings.

One time I come in and see Little Red rocking back in forth on his haunches, singing some strange song. Even though I'd never heard it before, I could tell it was some kind of lullaby. I sneaked a peek at Horseflesh's face over Little Red's shoulder, and damned if he didn't look as sweet and peaceful as a baby at its mama's teat! Then Little Red turns to look at me, and I see he's got tears in his eyes.

"He was hurting so bad, Pete. Hurting so awful bad. I couldn't let him hurt anymore. So I sung him to sleep. Did I do right?"

I didn't get what he was talking about, so I just patted him on the head. "Sure, you did the right thing, Little Red. Sure you did."

Horseflesh didn't wake up after that and died two days later, peaceful-like. Little Red dug him a grave without using his hands, and I made a marker out of a plank from the buckboard. It said:

Here lies Horseflesh Donnigan
A right fine Horse Thief who
Died of Having a Safe Dropt on
his Foot, although it weren't
Little Red's Fault

This seemed to cheer Little Red a tad when I read it at the funeral. Then, after we put Horseflesh in the ground, Black Hat walked up to Little Red and handed him Horseflesh's worry beads.

"Here, kid. I know he would have wanted you to have 'em."

I glanced down to make sure Horseflesh weren't making like a whirling dervish, but he was keeping put.

Little Red was too choked up to say anything; he took the worry beads and hung them round his neck, letting them drop inside his shirt. I could tell by the way he was grinning, Black Hat figgered he was playing one hell of a joke on ol' Horseflesh, not that the Irishman was in any condition to appreciate it.

I didn't see no humor in it, though I guess it didn't make no difference in the end, seeing how Little Red couldn't tell the difference between a kindness done him and being made fun of. But *I* could, and it didn't set well with me.

I never was scared of Little Red like Horseflesh was, or jealous of him like the Chandler brothers, so I guess it was only natural that I should feel sorry for him. And it wasn't long before my feeling sorry for him extended to feeling ashamed whenever Black Hat fooled with him. What made it galling was that the idiot worshipped the very ground that bastard walked on! I reckon Little Red wasn't really seeing the flesh-and-blood Black Hat but the steely-eyed, rock-jawed, raven-haired outlaw hero of the dime novels.

The main reason I stayed with the son of a bitch was the firm conviction that he'd shoot me like a dog should I try and strike out on my own.

We did another job not long after Horseflesh died. It wasn't until then that I realized Black Hat knew a sight more about Little Red's "gifts" than he'd first let on. We rode into town late, keeping to the back streets, and snuck up on the bank from behind.

"We don't get it, Black Hat," whispered Caleb. "How can you expect to rob a bank when it's closed up tighter than a Baptist preacher's wife?"

"You know what you boys' trouble is? Y'all don't know how to adapt to circumstances! Why spend your time cracking open an oyster, when you can get it to give up the pearl on its own?"

Since the Chandler brothers had never known nothing but catfish and crawdaddies, they didn't see what Black Hat was getting at, but I did.

"You planning on using Little Red again?"

"Hell, yes! You don't think I brought him along for the company, did you?" He waved Little Red over to him. He pointed at the rear of the bank. "That there's the bank. You reckon you can walk through them walls for me, son?"

"Yes sir, Mr. Black Hat!"

"Well, don't just stand there lollygagging, boy! Get on in there and rustle us up some money!"

"Did I hear you right? Did you just tell him to walk through a wall?"

Black Hat shot me this real disgusted look. "Shut up and you'll see."

Little Red stood nose-to-brick with the wall, breathing quick and shallow, like a man readying himself for a jump in a cold pond. Then he rounded his shoulders, straightened his hump and stepped forward—right through the wall!

I sat there gawking for a second then turned on Black Hat. "How come you knew he could do that?"

Black Hat shrugged. "I might not have cared what Horseflesh said about Little Red being one of them *Sidhe* critters, but that don't mean I didn't ask him questions 'bout them. Horseflesh said them *Sidhe* could fly, talk to animals, walk through walls and pull all kinds of hoodoo. I figure if that's so, there's no reason for us not putting the idjit's talent to proper use."

Caleb and Davey exchanged uneasy glances. "Maybe Horseflesh was right, after all! Maybe we got no business messin' with things that can walk through walls!"

"You jackanapes got no vision, y'all know that? No vision! Here you got a chance of making more money than God; in a couple months time y'all could be swannin' 'round Chicago with a pretty society gal on each arm and a diamond the size of a pigeon egg for a stickpin, drinking champagne out of slippers, and you want to pass it up on account of being scared! You make me sick!"

I had to admit there was something to what Black Hat said. We'd fallen in a honey pot, all right. Letting Little Red handle all the fuss of outlawing definitely had its attraction. I wasn't as young as when I'd first started out, and the prospect of getting a decent night's sleep without worrying 'bout being shot in my bed was starting to have the same allure as holding up a stage did when I was a raw kid. But I couldn't help thinking: Where there's honey, there's bees.

The haul Little Red made from the bank job was the biggest we ever made. And don't you know the sheriff spent a good while scratching his head, trying to figure how all that money up and disappeared in the middle of the night without no one forcing the doors or even messing with the safe. It still makes me chuckle, just thinking about it.

Seeing that we had all this money burning a hole in our pockets, Black Hat reckoned it was time we went to town. So we saddled up—excepting Little Red, of course—and headed for Limbo.

Now, don't go looking on any maps trying to find Limbo, 'cause it ain't there no more. And even when it was there, it weren't on any map. Limbo, you see, straddled the line between Mexico and Texas, and was famous for being a wide-open town where desperadoes could get themselves a hot bath, a clean shave and a decent bed, not to mention drunk and laid. And whenever the Rangers or the Federales would come riding up, folks just upped and went to the "safe" side of town, depending on the circumstances.

Limbo weren't exactly what you'd call a metropolis—there was a handful of saloons and couple of whorehouses, a general store, plus some adobe hunts scattered here and there—but it was as close as to a safe haven as we were likely to find in that neck of the woods.

So we rode into Limbo and right off I can tell Little Red's calling attention to hisself. I'd been around the halfwit so long I'd forgot just how different he was. And it was obvious this was the first time Little Red had ever seen so many people in one place in his life.

"How come everyone's staring at me, Pete?"

Before I could come up with an answer, Black Hat butted in. "Why, can't you tell? It's on account of you not having proper outlaw duds!"

Little Red looked down at his homemade buckskin pants and wool shirt. I'd never seen him take off his clothes, not even to bathe. But that was hardly 'cause for comment back then. When I was preparing Horseflesh for burial, I'd discovered his long johns wouldn't—or couldn't—come off.

"I don't reckon they'd have any duds that'd fit you right off," Black Hat said. "But I figger we can at least get you a proper hat. That ways folks will know you're a for-real outlaw."

I told Little Red I'd see him later at the saloon and headed off to get a bath and a shave. It was a couple of hours later, and I was sitting in the saloon on the Yanqui side of town, drinking rotgut whiskey, when Little Red busts in, all excited about his new hat.

"Pete! Pete! See my new hat? Black Hat hisself picked it for me!"

It showed. Little Red's hat was at least two sizes too small and sat in the very middle of his head, making him look more like a moron than before. He kept fiddling with the strap that held it in place, cinching it right up under his chin.

"It—it's real nice, Little Red," I said, blushing for him. "It, uh, makes you look like a real outlaw."

I could see a couple of guys sniggering and pointing at Little Red behind his back. If I couldn't lay into Black Hat for making fun of Little Red, then I was going to by-damn make someone bleed for it. It must have showed in my eyes, 'cause when I made to get up they stopped their snickering and went back to drinking.

Next thing I know, Black Hat and the Chandler brothers come in and join us at the table, grinning like dogs choking on a chicken bone.

"There you are, Little Red!" Black Hat claps him on his humpback real hard—something I noticed Little Red was peculiar about. He didn't like having his back touched, and the one occasion where I'd accidentally done so was the only time he ever came close to getting mad at me. I could tell he hadn't liked Johnson doing that, but had said nothing about it on account of Black Hat being his hero. "Me and the boys got a big surprise for you! Don't we, boys? We was talking it over, and we decided that since you've been doing a man's job, it's about time you started enjoying a man's benefits."

Little Red sat there and grinned at them like an idiot. It was obvious he didn't have a clue as to what they was getting at.

"Is there something you want me to do, Mr. Black Hat?"

The Chandlers snorted and elbowed each other. I rolled my eyes.

"You could say that, son. I want you to go upstairs to the third door on the left, and get in bed and wait until Miss Lupita comes in, then I want you to do everything she tells you to."

Little Red seemed perplexed by these orders—they didn't seem to have anything to do with being an outlaw—but he did what he was told. I waited until he was upstairs before laying into Black Hat.

"Lupita? You fixed him up with Lupita? The biggest crack this side of the Grand Canyon? That clapped-out whore is so old her crabs got dentures!"

"What's it matter? It's the only piece of tail he's likely to get." In his own twisted way, Black Hat thought he was extending Little Red a kindness. "Come on—let's spy on them through the transom! Should be worth a laugh or two!"

I was too disgusted to spit. I felt the need to get clear of Black Hat Johnson and breathe clean air—even if Limbo's streets were full of nightsoil and dead dogs.

Fifteen minutes later the Chandler Brothers came and got me out of a cantina on the Mexican side of Limbo. I could tell something bad had happened 'cause Davey spoke first.

"There you are! Thank God! Come on—we gotta git!"

"Hell, we only just got here—"

"Black Hat sent us to get you—we gotta leave *now!*"

"What's happened? Where's Little Red?"

"*He's* the reason we got to leave! Now will you come on?"

I followed them to where Black Hat was waiting with Little Red and the horses. I could tell that whatever had happened had been very bad indeed. Black Hat looked like he'd swallowed lye soap, while Little Red was blubbering his eyes out.

"What's going on? What's wrong with Little Red?"

Black Hat just shook his head and mounted his horse. It wasn't until we were a mile or so from Limbo before I could get anything out of him.

Although he might have been a few bricks shy in the noggin, it seems Little Red worked just fine from the waist down. When he'd put it to Lupita, she started hollering and carrying on and yelling in Spanish about how it was too big and he was killing her. Since Black Hat and them couldn't see too well since it was dark, they thought she was just putting on a show. Then she started screaming real funny. That's when they realized it was for real.

Black Hat and them busted in and made Little Red get off her, but it was too late. "She was nothing but blood down there, Pete. And there was bite marks—bad ones—all over her neck and shoulders. But the horrible part is... I saw his thing."

"Beg pardon?"

"You know, Little Red's pecker." He shook his head in wonder, and it was one of the few times I ever saw Black Hat go pale. "It was all red and sticky from the blood, and I'll be switched if it wasn't as long and big around as my arm! But the worst part was it had these... barbs sticking out, like a harpoon or something!"

I knew Black Hat well enough to know blood didn't put him off, and I remembered a few times when he'd been rough with his women, so I couldn't figure his squeamishness. Then I realized what was upsetting him was the fact one of his "jokes" had backfired on him, banishing us from Limbo.

Limbo might not have been what anyone would call an "upstanding community," but it did have it's own standards of decency. Limbo tolerated bank robbers, murderers and even horse thieves; but if there was one thing it couldn't abide, it was a pervert.

We decided to stop after a couple of hours and make camp for the night. Little Red was still crying and sniffling about "hurting the nice lady," and I could see it was starting to get on Black Hat's nerves. So I pulled a bottle of squeeze out of my saddlebag and shoved it at Little Red.

"Here, drink this. It'll make you feel better."

I wasn't terrible sure if liquor and Little Red would mix that well, but it seemed to cheer him up after a spell. He sat cross-legged near the fire, rocking back and forth, hugging the empty bottle to his chest. He still had that damn stupid hat on. I wondered if he'd bothered to take it off when he humped Lupita. Then I thought about what Black Hat told me about Little Red's thing, and I couldn't help but shiver. I could tell by the way Black Hat and the Chandler brothers kept sneaking looks at him that they was thinking about it too. We'd gotten so accustomed to seeing Little Red as a big, lumbering simpleton, we'd forgotten he wasn't human.

I sat down next to Little Red and watched him watch the fire. Maybe it was just the light, but it looked as if his eyes were the color of blood.

"Little Red? Do you mind me asking you a question?"

"You want to ask me something?" Little Red was more used to being told than asked.

"What're your folks like? I mean, what do they *do*?"

Little Red smiled slow and sweet, just like a little kid. "My pappy's a Singer." The way he said it I couldn't be sure if it was a last name or an occupation. "He can sing up a storm, my pappy can. I can sing too! You want to hear?"

"Yeah. Sure."

Little Red tossed back his head and opened his mouth and this weird, fluting sound came out. It wasn't exactly a song, since there weren't no words to it, leastwise none I recognized as such, but it wasn't *not* a song, neither. It sounded like music, the way a coyote baying at the moon or an owl calling to its mate can sound like music. Little Red seemed to be enjoying himself, and as he continued singing, it became more and more complicated, and for a minute it sounded as if someone else was singing along with him. As I sat listening, I noticed a stiff wind had come up all of a sudden. Then the song took a turn, becoming almost painful to the ear, like a pair of cats screeching while they fight. The wind gusted stronger, and I heard the horses nicker in fear.

Before I could get to my feet, the storm was on us full force, blowing hot ash from the campfire into my face. I tried to take a couple of steps against the wind but fell down. Then I realized the earth was shaking. I'd heard tell of quakes, but this was the first one I'd been in. I hugged the ground while it humped and rolled under my belly like a five-dollar whore. Then something shot up out of the dirt a few inches from my nose. At first I thought it was some kind of walking stick. Then I realized I was staring at a snake standing on its tail, stiff as petrified wood.

The wind had died down and I scuttled backward on my heels and palms, desperate to put some room between me and the rattler. I looked around and saw two more snakes bust through the soil like venomous cornstalks. One of the Chandler brothers was trying to keep the horses from bolting, while Black Hat shot at the snakes. I grabbed Little Red by the shoulder and shook him as hard as I could. After a second he opened his eyes and the song stopped. The rattlers collapsed to the ground, each and every one of their skulls pulped from being driven through dirt and solid rock with incredible force.

I could tell Black Hat was shook up after that night. I guess it finally dawned on him that Little Red had far more power than even he reckoned, and it was starting to spook him. That's not to say it changed his plans. Black Hat Johnson was nothing if not obstinate. He had decided that Little Red was his ticket to fame and riches, and he'd be damned if anything got in his way.

In the end, it was that exact same bullheadedness that got him killed.

We was back at Tortuga Hill when it happened. The events with the whore and the earthquake were a couple of days gone, giving Black Hat the time to recover enough to be back to having Little Red do for him like a slave.

I was out seeing to the horses when I got the feeling I was being watched. I turned around and saw a huge shadow blocking the door to the barn. The horses started making noises like a cougar was loose in the yard, and I knew that Little Red's folks had come for him at last.

Little Red's pappy stood eight feet high, his shoulders as wide as a man is long. He was dressed in a long, loose-fitting coat that hung almost to his knees. He wore buckskin leggings, similar to Little Red's, and I realized then that the leather they were made from hadn't come from no cow or antelope, or anything else four-legged. His feet were gnarly and wrinkled like those of a lizard, with toenails as sharp and curved as an eagle's talons.

His hair was the same color as his son's, only longer and braided like an Injun's. When he talked, it sounded like rocks being rubbed together.

"I've come for my boy."

I pointed in the direction of the cabin. I was already calculating how long it'd take me to saddle up my horse and ride for the border.

Little Red was coming back from gathering firewood when he saw his pappy walking toward him. He dropped his burden, his jaw falling open like the flap on a union suit. It was hard to tell if he was happy to see his old man or not.

As Big Red towered over his son, placing the two in proper perspective, I realized that what I'd mistaken for simplemindedness was, in fact, a child's innocence. He wagged a huge, talon-tipped finger at the boy.

"Your Ma's been worried sick over you!"

"But, Pa—!"

"Don't go giving me any buts, boy! You're coming back home, y'hear? And I don't want to hear no more nonsense about outlaws and dime novels, is that understood?"

"I can't go home! I'm an outlaw now!"

"Outlaw my pinions! You're my son and you're going to do what I say! We didn't come all the way here from the Old Country for you to go gallivanting off playing Cowboys and Indians!"

Big Red knitted his bushy, upswept brows and squinted at the necklace hanging round Little Red's neck.

"What's that you're wearing—?" His nostrils flared when he recognized Horseflesh's worry beads. "Take that off! Take that off right this minute!" Big Red snatched at the rosary, breaking the string and sending worry beads in every direction.

Little Red stomped his foot, pushing his lower lip out in a pout. "No! I won't go! You can't make me!"

"Boy, until you're fledged, there's nothing I *can't* make you do! You're not so big I can't tan your shanks right here, in front of your big bad outlaw friends!" Big Red grabbed Little Red by one pointed ear, twisting it until the boy squealed like a pig.

"Mr. Black Hat! Mr. Black Hat! Help!"

Black Hat dashed out of the cabin, gun in hand. "What he hell is—? Jesus on Calvary!"

Big Red let go of his son's ear and turned to face Black Hat. "This here's family business. Stay out of it, human."

"How in Hell did you get past Caleb and Davey? They sure as shit couldn't have missed a sumbitch your size!"

Big Red smiled, revealing a row of razor-sharp, crimson-stained teeth. "Ah, yes! The twins. *Very* tasty."

That did it. I ran into the barn and threw a saddle on Old Paint. I wasn't planning on hanging round to see how things was going to come out between Johnson and Little Red's pappy. I paused one last time before heading out, and I'll carry what I saw with me to my grave.

I reckon Black Hat, faced with having his ticket to the good life snatched away, went a little loco in the end. That's the only reason I figure why he would something as foolish as trying to shoot Big Red.

I heard the gunfire and saw the bullet strike Big Red square in the chest. Big Red flinched like he'd been bit by a horsefly, then pushed Little Red behind him, out of harm's way. Then I saw his hump flex and the black coat split down the middle as his wings unfurled and beat the air with powerful, angry strokes.

There was a noise like cats being boiled and dogs being skinned and babies being burned alive, and I felt my scalp grow tight, just like it does before a bad thunderstorm, and I dug my heels into Old Paint and got the hell out of there. Just before I left, the clouds over Tortuga Hill turned black as a bruise, and a twister's tail fell from the sky like a whip cracking across a slave's back.

I rode hell-bent for leather and didn't look back after that, trying to get the sound of Big Red's singing out of my head.

I never saw Black Hat Johnson again, and no one ever found out what happened to him. He'd never been famous like Billy the Kid or Jesse James, but there was enough interest in him to fuel some rumors after he and the rest of the Tortuga Hill Gang up and disappeared. Some fancied he'd gone south and was raising hell with the senoritas and the Federales. Others thought he'd gone north to give the Mounties a few gray hairs. One story even had him facing down the devil in Hell and spitting in his eye, which was closer to the truth than any of them. But that was a long time gone, and no one remembers Black Hat Johnson anymore, much less the Tortuga Hill Gang.

As to me, I took my escape as a sign that my outlawing days was over. I still had a fair amount of money left to get some proper city duds and a train ticket to Chicago. Once there, I bought myself a partnership in a dry-goods store, married my partner's daughter, started going to church regular, and raised me a passel of young'uns.

When the time came to hand the business over to my oldest boy, I had the need in my bones to go back West, so we bought ourselves this little spread out here in Tucson. Sure has changed since I was here last. Then again, a lot of things have changed.

Now that I'm old, I can't help but think about Little Red and his pappy and wonder exactly where it was they came from. I seen in that there Lon Chaney picture them Frenchies got churches with winged critters that look something like Little Red's folks carved all over 'em. So maybe they was immigrants, just like my grandparents was from Scotland, coming to this country in hopes of starting fresh.

Every time there's a lightning storm out on the desert, I can't help but wonder if that ain't one of Little Red's folks out there, singing their terrible, wordless songs. Anyways, that's my story of how the Tortuga Hill Gang come to its end. And I'm sticking to it.

No doubt Little Red's still out there somewhere, high atop one of the windswept mesas and buttes that dot the countryside, a young monster perched on his knee, telling tall tales about the time he was a real-live Wild West outlaw.

8 ♣

The Tortuga Hill Gang's Last Ride

Calaverada

When they first rode up on the town, it looked as if the streets were full of hanged men.

As they drew closer, what they'd at first mistaken for bleached bones turned out to be papier-mâché mannequins painted to resemble skeletons grinning an idiot's welcome to all comers.

"What in hell is this shit?" growled Big Luther.

"Dia de los Muertes," Alvarez replied, gesturing to the locals in the town square who were busy buying and selling fruits, flowers, and gaily-colored masks. "Day of the Dead," he added, when it became clear the others did not understand.

"Sounds Meskin to me," Clell replied, eyeing the macabre decorations.

"Not surprisin', seein' how we're fifty miles into Mexico," Hop replied.

Big Luther turned in his saddle to fix Hop with a baleful glare before continuing to address Alvarez. "Where's this cantina the Wolf Pack is so damned fond of?"

"Over there," Alvarez said, pointing to a squat adobe structure. A few rough-hewn tables and chairs were scattered along the dusty shade of its porch, along with a yellow dog with ribs like barrel staves sprawled on its side.

On the wall of the cantina that faced the square was plastered a broadsheet depicting a skeleton, sombrero crowning its skull and serape draped over one bony shoulder, eagerly chugging a jug of tequila.

"Again with the damn bones," Big Luther grunted. "What is it with you Meskins, Alvarez?"

"It is as I said, my friend; it is the Day of the Dead."

Big Luther looked thoughtful. "Big fiesta, huh?" He glanced at the cantina, then back at the marketplace. "You think Dixie Jim and them are likely to show up for it?"

"*Si*. It is a big party, with singing and fireworks—like you Yanquis have for Fourth of July."

"It ain't likely Dixie Jim's one to celebrate the Fourth of July," Clell snorted. "What with him bein' a Vicksburg boy and all."

"How long this bare-bones carnival of y'alls go on?"

"Couple of days. Tonight is *la Noche de Duelo*—the Night of Mourning. Tomorrow begins the big celebration in the square."

"Well, this seems as good a place to wait for them as any. Let's go get us a drink."

They had come to this nameless little town to kill the bandits called the Wolf Pack, led by a former Confederate soldier known as Dixie Jim. The desperados had managed to become enough of a nuisance that the Golden Rule Mining Company had seen fit to hire bounty hunters. And in Big Luther Tatum and Clell Yoakum, the owners had found the kind of men necessary for such bloody business.

Alvarez, however, was harder to figure out. Hop assumed he was riding with them because he knew the area and needed the money. Besides, the Mexican was the one who knew someone who knew someone who had heard that Dixie Jim was sweet on some *mamacita* in this flyspeck of a village.

The cantina owner was tending a small table decorated by a faded tintype of an older woman, bouquets of marigolds, sweetbreads, and fruit. "Tequila or whisky, *señor*?" he asked, lighting the votive candles that framed the picture.

"Tequila," Big Luther replied, tossing a silver coin onto the bar and holding up two fingers.

The cantina owner nodded and went behind the bar, from which he produced a stone crock and handed it to Big Luther, who ambled back out onto the porch, where Cell and the others were waiting. The cantina owner followed with a pair of smudged shot glasses, which he placed in front of the hulking American.

"I figger we got until nightfall before they show," Big Luther grunted, slopping the golden liquor into the shot glasses.

Hop knew better than to ask for a glass. Big Luther had made it clear from the start that while he was willing to ride with Hop and Alvarez, and even split the bounty, he drew the line at drinking with them. As Hop ambled over to the marketplace, Alvarez fell silently in step alongside him.

On a blanket spread over the cobblestones, a gnarled old man displayed papier-mâché masks, fashioned to resemble leering devils and snarling animals. Hop wandered over to another vendor selling circular breads that smelled of cinnamon and anise, as well as a selection of elaborately decorated skulls made from sugar paste.

As he paused to study the macabre treats, a crocodile made of children, each outfitted in a skull mask, twined its way through the crowd, laughing and singing merrily, toy wands tipped by brightly painted eggshells held in their hands. As Hop watched, one of the children smashed his wand against the head of a playmate, resulting in a shower of confetti.

"It begins already," Alvarez said, smiling and nodding at the youngsters. "There will be much *calaverada* the next few days."

"Beg pardon?"

"*Calaverada*. It is what you call…" Alvarez trailed off, wrinkling his brow as he tried to find a proper translation. "High spirits. That is the word. This is the one time of the year when the dead are given back their former lives, and are welcomed back by their friend and family. That is why they are selling *pan de los muertos* and marigolds… so the living may build *ofrendas*—altars—and make gifts of food, drink and flowers to the dead."

Hop scratched his head. "Do the spooks or whatnot, do they actually eat the food folks set out for them?"

Alvarez laughed and shook his head. "No, they can only consume the spirits of the *ofrendas*. It is up to the living to dispose of the physical food and drink."

Hop nodded. "I reckon I better get started then." He withdrew a handful of coins from his pocket. "I got a hell of a lot of dead to remember."

Alvarez glanced at Hop uneasily. "Is it true then?" He spoke very fast, as if rushing out the words were the only way they could be said.

"Is what true?"

"That you have killed many men?"

"Yep."

"How many?"

"As many as you have teeth in your head. How many teeth you got, Alvarez?"

"Eighteen."

"That sounds about right."

<hr />

Big Luther didn't have much use for Mexicans, save for tequila and tamales. Then again, Big Luther didn't have much use for anyone—the one exception being Clell. If it had been up to him, it would just be the two of them riding after the Wolf Pack, as they had gotten used to watching each other's back. But the president of the Golden Rule had insisted that they take a few men from the camp with them.

Big Luther had been against it at first, but when he saw there was no budging the old man, he agreed, but only if he got to choose those he rode with. He'd recognized Hopper from his wanted poster, and was surprised to find the man listed on the camp's rolls—even more so to find him smoking opium with the coolies. He didn't seem anything like the gunfighter Big Luther had read about, but he knew you didn't get a reputation like Hopper's without just cause.

When twilight approached, the vendors removed their blankets and hurried home. As Big Luther and Clell watched, the villagers left their houses carrying lighted candles and bundles of food and flowers and made their way to the cemetery at the edge of town.

"Damn fool Meskins," Big Luther muttered between mouthfuls of tamale. "Don't they know they'll be in the grave soon enough?"

Clell shrugged and helped himself to another shot of tequila. That was another thing Big Luther liked about Clell: He didn't talk much.

"Luther!"

Big Luther looked up to see Alvarez and Hop high-tailing it across the square toward the cantina. "What is it?" he asked, wiping tamale sauce from his mouth with his sleeve.

"They're here!"

Big Luther exchanged a look with Clell before returning his attention to the others. "Is that so? So where are they, then?"

"The bawdy house on the other side of the village," Hop said. "We saw them ride up not five minutes ago. Ain't that right, Alvarez?"

"Si," the Mexican replied, nodding his head for emphasis. "The girls came out to greet them—I heard one of them call the leader Jim."

"That'd be the Wolf Pack, all right," Big Luther grunted.

"What now?" Clell asked.

Big Luther fished a pocket watch out of his vest and studied its face. "We wait a little longer. Give 'em time to get comfortable, drink some mescal and some pulque, maybe get themselves a little cunny. Give 'em time to get drunk and careless. Then we hit 'em fast and hard."

Clell pointed at the sack Hop was carrying. "What you got there?"

Hop untied the sack and emptied its contents for the others to see. Several sugar skulls and couple of braided loaves of bread rolled out onto the table top.

Big Luther stared at the candied skulls for a moment, and then glanced back up at Hop. "I don't like sweets," he said flatly.

"They ain't for you," Hop replied, sweeping the *calaveras* and *pan de la muertos* back into the bag.

———————⟫◆⟪———————

They couldn't have gotten better conditions for an ambush if they'd set it up that way. Nearly everyone in the village was out at the cemetery, weaving garlands to adorn the graves of their dead, leaving the town practically deserted. The only living souls left were the outlaws whooping it up at the brothel on the edge of town... and the men sent to kill them.

Hop and the others were hiding in the shadows near a small copse, listening to their prey's raucous shouting and the laughter of women. Though they could not see inside, there was no doubt that the man who spoke with the heavy Southern drawl and lustily sang "Dixie" was none other than the Wolf Pack's leader.

Bored, Hop fished one of the candied skulls out of the sack and bit into it. His mouth was instantly filled with sugar and saliva, and for some reason his mind flashed to the story of Samson and the carcass full of honey. He grimaced and hurled the grisly confection aside, then turned his eyes toward the cemetery. Dozens of candles flickered like fireflies in the cool autumn evening. The wind was redolent of marigold and copal incense. He could hear the strains of a mariachi band moving from grave to grave, singing the favorite sounds of the deceased.

When Big Luther gave the sign, they went in through the front door easy as you please, since no one had bothered to bar it, and caught the Wolf Pack with their pants literally around their ankles.

Except for the distinct image of a swearing man dressed in a tattered Confederate jacket standing in the door of one of the rooms—Navy Colts blazing—and the sound of a woman screaming, Hop didn't remember a whole lot about the attack.

When he came back to himself, he was staring down at a bandit sprawled half-in, half-out of a bed, his bare chest punctured by bullets, an unfired pistol clutched in his dead hand. Then Hop noticed the naked female body lying facedown on the blood-soaked straw mattress.

Big Luther stood in the doorway behind him, looking like he'd been dipped in a slaughtered pig. In one hand he held a machete, in the other he gripped Dixie Jim's head by its blood-soaked hair. "What are you waitin' for, Hop? It's a thousand in gold per head!"

Hop licked his lips, fighting to keep the sick down. His mouth still tasted of sugar skull. "The woman—what about the woman?" he croaked.

"Meskin whore heads ain't worth a plug nickel," Big Luther snorted as he stalked out of the bedroom. "Leave 'er be."

Hop nodded dumbly and reached for the machete sheathed at his side. It took three good chops to completely sever the outlaw's head from his shoulders. He stuffed it into his saddlebag without looking at it.

There had been a time, not that long ago, when such bloody business would have not cost Hop a moment's sleep. Now all he could do was tell himself that once it was all over and done with he would finally have enough money to smoke out the dead faces that lived behind his eyelids.

As he left the bloodied bedroom, Hop was surprised to see the other bounty hunters still standing in the main room. He was even more surprised to see Alvarez shouting at Big Luther.

"Do you *realize* what you've done?"

"They was in the way," Big Luther replied.

"Shooting up a bunch of gringo outlaws is one thing, but killing the only whores in town—and before a big fiesta! They'll have the Federales on us!"

"That don't matter once we're back over the border."

"*Crazy gringo!*" Alvarez spat on the floor, narrowly missing Big Luther's boot.

Big Luther, however, did not miss Alvarez's head. The machete buried itself in the Mexican's skull, directly between the eyes.

"Damn Meskin," Big Luther growled. "He shoulda knowed better than to do that."

Hop had to agree.

They rode off through the hills and into the desert to throw off pursuit, saddlebags stained and bulging with their grisly trophies. Now that the deed was done, all that stood in their way was sand and rock. Big Luther and Clell became more relaxed—or as relaxed as Hop could remember ever seeing them.

Neither man seemed terribly concerned about the possibility of pursuit from the Mexican authorities. Nor, for that matter, was Hop. But he kept looking over his shoulder anyway.

It was well after midnight when they finally pitched camp. The sky above was clear, cold and full of stars, like jewels poured from a burglar's bag. Hop made a fire from deadwood and brush while Big Luther and Clell unsaddled the horses.

"You reckon them Meskin police are gonna head out after us?" Clell asked casually as he put the coffee on the fire.

Big Luther shrugged his wide shoulders. "If I can get shed of Texas Rangers on my tail, I ain't gonna worry myself about a bunch of beaners."

"I'll tell you one thing," Clell said with a sigh. "I'll be happy to get back to white man's land."

"Ain't that the truth," grunted Big Luther. "All this skeleton nonsense just ain't right."

"Speakin' of things that ain't right," Clell said, looking about. "Where did Hop get himself off to?"

"Damn his eyes," Big Luther snarled, squinting into the darkness beyond the ring of light cast by the campfire. "He better not be off smokin' that heathen pipe of his." He gave voice to something between a groan and a growl as he got to his feet. "Hop! Where the hell are you?"

"I'm over here."

Hop's voice came from behind a collection of small rocks roughly fifty feet beyond the campfire. As Big Luther and Clell drew closer, they could see Hop hunkered down on his haunches, his attention focused on something at his feet.

"What are you doing behind them rocks, boy?" Clell sneered. "Having yourself a shit?"

Hop did not bother to answer the bounty hunter's taunt. Instead, he moved aside for they could see the *ofrenda* made from a loaf of *pan de la muertos*, a couple of sugar skulls, and the wanted poster of Dixie Jim held in place by a small flat stone. A tiny flickering flame from the candle stub taken from the cantina made the face of the dead man on the handbill look like it was winking at them.

Big Luther's eyes widened until they looked like they would pop right out of his head. "What in the name of hell do you think you're doing?"

Hop looked up at Big Luther with eyes the color of smoke. "Alvarez told me that tonight the dead walk among the living—and if you want to keep from being dragged to Hell, you gotta honor 'em."

"You're out of your cotton-pickin' skull!! Now pack that shit up and take your watch!"

Hop looked down at the makeshift altar, then back up at Big Luther, but did not offer to move. "What are you afraid of, Luther? You of all people should come to terms with the dead."

"What th'—? You threatening me, Hopper?"

Hop did not answer but instead turned his attention back to the *ofrenda* and began to hum "Dixie."

Big Luther stepped forward, throwing back his duster so the holster was clear. "Fill your hand, Hopper!"

Hop glanced up at the man towering over him and began to slowly rise, still humming "Dixie" under his breath.

"Fill your hand or I sweat I'll shoot you like a dog!"

Suddenly Hop feinted with his right hand. That's all Big Luther needed to open fire.

The Colt took off the top of Hop's head like it was a hat, sending brains, blood, and bone flying across the desert floor. The body hit the dirt like a sack of feed thrown off the back of a wagon.

Hop's right hand opened as he struck the ground and a sugar skull rolled out, grinning sweetly up at Big Luther and Clell.

Big Luther, his face gray and sweaty, stared down at the dead man sprawled at his feet. "Shit," he whispered, licking his lips with a dry tongue. "I could've swore he was drawin' down."

Clell nodded in agreement but said nothing.

"Crazy damn fool," Big Luther said, holstering his gun. "He shoulda knowed better than to do that. I reckon all that opium smoke clouded his mind. Either that, or he was lookin' to get himself killed. He was clean out of his skull, that much I know. Goin' on about dead walkin' and all that Meskin hogwash." The bounty hunter stepped forward and, with one kick of his boot, obliterated Hop's altar. He shrugged and turned back to face

Clell. "It's a shame about ol' Hop, but I guess it just means more for us, don't it?"

The two men exchanged looks for a moment, and then burst out laughing so hard they had to bend over double to keep from falling down in Hop's blood.

After a couple of minutes Clell finally was able to stem his laughter long enough to straightened back up and catch his breath. He tilted his head to one side and frowned.

"Do you hear that?"

"Hear what?" asked Big Luther, wiping a tear of merriment from his eye. Even as he spoke Big Luther caught the sound of horses headed their way.

Whoever it was, they were riding hard and fast from the direction of the village. There was another sound mixed in with the drumbeat of the approaching riders, something that that became more and more distinct the closer they came. Someone with a heavy Southern accent was singing at the top of his lungs. By the time Big Luther recognized the song the riders were upon them.

The bounty hunters turned to face the oncoming horsemen, guns in hand, choking on the screams rising from their guts, the sound of hooves and "Dixie" thundering in their ears.

⊰⊱◈⊰⊱

The Mexican authorities found the gringos sprawled like broken dolls among the cold ashes of their campfire. There was no doubt that these were the same men responsible for the massacre at the brothel. All three had been decapitated, though a quick search of each man's saddlebags revealed their missing heads. However, there was no evidence to point to who was responsible for slaughtering the trio.

All concerned agreed that it was odd that they never found the severed heads of Dixie Jim and the other four members of the Wolf Pack. Stranger still, they had found a sugar skull resting atop the chest of one of the slain bounty hunters.

It was missing a bite.

ABOUT THE AUTHOR

Nancy A. Collins is the author of several novels and numerous short stories, as well as having served a two-year stint as a writer for DC Comics' *Swamp Thing*. A recipient of the Horror Writers Association's Bram Stoker Award, The British Fantasy Society's Icarus Award, and the Deathrealm Award, as well as a nominee for the Eisner & World Fantasy Awards, her works include *Knuckles and Tales: A Southern Neo-Gothic Collection, Tempter,* **Sunglasses After Dark**, **In the Blood** and *Avenue X*. Her most current books include the short story collection **Dead Roses For A Blue Lady** and the novel **Darkest Heart**, both featuring her cult character, Sonja Blue, which has also been optioned for film and television development. Ms. Collins currently makes her home in Atlanta with her husband, underground artist/provocateur Joe Christ, and their two dogs, Scrapple and Trixie.